The Empire

George de Mare

THE EMPIRE

G. P. Putnam's Sons   New York

*To my three sons
with deepest love*

The great corporation, like an ancient king-dom, dominates directly or indirectly the lives of men today. This is the story of such a corporation "from the inside" and of some of those on whom it cast its shadow. The central events and all the people are imaginary and do not refer to any in life.

"Alas most noble . . . realm whom I have loved above all other realms and in thee I have gotten a great part of my worship and now I shall depart. . . ."

Le Morte d'Arthur: XX Chap. xvii
Sir Thomas Malory

Contents

Morning . . . 11

BOOK I   Carlyle   13

BOOK II   Somers   93

BOOK III   Harwood   171

BOOK IV   Kilgore   221

BOOK V   Brill   265

Evening . . . 309

Morning . . .

Somehow it did not seem that long.

That morning had been the culmination of the struggle.

He turned in the strange new office—the office that he was sitting in now on an evening of late September in the first flush of fall. The trappings were all there, the marks of a victory— and of a crushing defeat.

It was about time to leave—it was after five-thirty, and already the evening bustle had begun to subside in the misty autumn air. Far over the city, the lights were twinkling on. The big town was giving itself up and submerging into the haze as the day ebbed softly away.

As he sat there, he gazed out of the window and thought about it, about how it could have happened—to him, of all people, who had watched and fought it so long and relentlessly. Where had it snared him? How had it engulfed him? For there it was— all unforeseen, unprepared for, unexpected. It had caught him— taken him by surprise. But when? How?

He turned his gaze away from the violet haze outside the windows and looked across the large office, across toward the table and the low book shelves. He had been so alert. He had noticed it in others. How had he missed it in himself? It was as

11

if the years had somehow been a trap, a pit covered with leaves and he a hunter stalking the woods, searching, searching for something, and suddenly there he was—here he was: the ground had given way and he found himself in the pit; he was trapped unfairly and here he sat with all the years drifted away, and looked across the green rug of the new office and wondered what had brought him to this.

It was what had happened this morning that had drawn the whole situation to a head. Almost, he supposed, like crossing the autumnal equinox of existence, and what had been a normal progression of his career had abruptly become a crisis—the climax of the long, sometimes bitter, struggle.

He shifted in the comfortable leather swivel chair.

Now the words returned to him again—words spoken in different tones by varied voices: "Were the years, then, worth it?" they seemed to ask. "Had it all been worth the effort?" Soft voices, clipped voices, voices from the mists of the scarcely regarded past. "Were the years wasted, Martin? Did you win after all?"

12

BOOK I   Carlyle

1.

MARTIN BRILL emerged from the subway slowly and blinked in the bright autumn sunlight. It was ten in the morning. He stopped and looked at his reflection in a drugstore mirror. He was not too familiar with this part of town.

He looked down again at the scrap of paper in his hand. It read: *Mr. Carlyle. 10:30 a.m.*

The face he had looked at in the mirror—his own—was that of a young man in his late twenties, handsome in a pleasant way, with blond sun-streaked hair and tanned complexion. The expression that saved it from being commonplace was a combination of sincerity and faint strain—a concentration line between the otherwise smooth brows—that never left the face. It was the face of a smart, careful boy who was on the level. He was what was known as "a sincere type" before that phrase gained a disparaging connotation, and he was concerned about the scrap of paper in his hand.

For this was his second job. He had made a mess of the first.

It was a good year for a veteran to get a job. The war had reached its first crescendo—a new kind of war, a businessman's war, it was called. The words "production" and "know-how" were everywhere. It was thought the war would not be won by men but by great corporations outproducing those in other countries. Every big company was deep in war work, including the Company. Men were mobilized, training, fighting, and had already begun to die—mostly men in other countries. But this part of it was all over for him. The bombs that had smashed his

15

plane in Manila before it had taken off in combat had put him in the hospital for four months and out of the war for good. And the newspaper job afterwards had been little better.

He walked to the corner and looked up. No one could mistake that building. He stood for a moment hesitant, assaying the situation. It was what he had been afraid of—impressive, pompous, entrenched-looking and solid. This business was here to stay, the giant granite pillars seemed to imply. Well, he didn't like this, either, but he knew he would not last much longer on the paper, and he hated everything the paper stood for. So this was it. He crossed and walked toward the high, bronze-grilled entrance.

The lobby was like an enormous temple—vast marble pillars at least twenty feet high looming into the shadowy upward reaches of the ceiling. He walked across great stretches of floors, across an echoing expanse of marble toward long banks of elevators. He felt somehow intimidated and a little exasperated. How pretentious, he thought. A cathedral to the gods of enterprise, a votive offering to the fat material gods under whatever name they might masquerade—whether as the makers of chewing gum or of tractors, of automobiles or of toasters, the deliverers of electric power, the earth movers or the time and distance annihilators like this gross, bloated organization which had strung the land with wire and the sole business of which was the carrying of the human voice across the world.

He had forgotten which floor it was. Hastily he fumbled the scrap of paper from his pocket. The elevator operator, a girl in a smart green uniform, was patient and polite. "We don't stop on the ninth floor," she said. "This is an express. Take the elevators around the corner on your left."

That was the way the morning started.

Jeff Carlyle leaned forward at his desk and rubbed his temple where the slight headache persisted. If Stella had only not let him drink so much the evening before or if she hadn't had so much herself, the whole thing would never have started. But

16

he knew that wasn't true. It was the way it had always been—and perhaps always would be.

He was a man in his later forties, accomplished, cynical and in some odd way impressive. He had a small, well-trimmed gray mustache and his hair was just graying at the temples. The morning was like so many mornings of the last two years since the war work had started . . . things growing more hectic . . . the early feeling of depression preceding hostilities, the moments of heartsickness as disaster deepened . . . then all of the despair blown away to be succeeded by this vast chaotic euphoria, this bustling boomtime atmosphere, as the boys really lay into it. War had been good for business, all right, he thought tiredly. Say what one will. Even with that madman in the White House, things were certainly booming. And they were right in the middle of it. The old saying that the war would be won in the factories was now the rage. It was bunk, of course. War was never won anywhere. Battles were still won by men, not factories, though it was gradually growing into the war of machines, the "push-button war" they all talked about. Still, men had to die, and machines did the job better. . . .

The hell with it, he thought. Still, this is my war—the middle-aged man's war, the war of men in plants, and even I, old Jeff Carlyle, who's seen so many good times in the twenties and so many bad times in the thirties—the breadlines were not so long ago really, nor were the days when there was a party every night—even I, who have had all the good times I can stand, have to sit through this war and work. . . .

Yes, he'd had them all—the good times and the bad, and in some sense he had lived them to the full. More than most, he thought. But now . . . He looked up. His secretary stood at the door of the office.

"Mr. Brill is here for his appointment," she said. "Are you all right, Jeff?" she asked.

"Yes, sure, April. Hold him a moment and ask Dave Randall to step in. Also I'm expecting a report from Saunders on the instruction booklets this morning. Remind him, will you? Just

17

a report. I don't want a bum joke or his life story. Also, April . . ." He smiled thinly. "You look good in that dress. Wish I felt the way you look."

"Flatterer," she said. She went out.

He had thought it a hundred times. It was a thought without passion. If he knew a really bad girl who looked like April Tremaine, he'd have everything. Someday maybe he'd get over his weakness for bad girls. Then he'd be free. Oh, Stella . . . he thought again and put the thought aside quickly. No use going over that again.

Randall's glasses glinted in the morning light.

He was wondering what Carlyle thought of the "Bulletins for Servicemen" idea he had sent in. He had entitled it *Keeping Up with the Company,* and it was to go to the men in service to keep them in touch with what their friends in the Company were doing. Randall felt it would be a great morale builder. It would show the boys who had gone that the Company was in there pitching for them, that their jobs would still be waiting for them—well, some of them anyhow—when they got back, and that the Company was still their company and behind them one hundred per cent. After all, just because they had left for war didn't necessarily mean they had gone forever, and they were still Company men. The war would be over someday and then jobs would be harder to find and a good job a really valuable asset.

Not like today, he thought a trifle bitterly. Today every Tom, Dick and Harry could walk in off the street and get a job, and any incompetent, anyone who could just breathe, was being hired by good firms.

Randall had come up the hard way. He had been an engineer and started in at one of the Company's largest Works, in the menial jobs that the Company seemed to reserve for engineers. And eventually, since he had done a few technical papers for scientific societies, even though someone else's name had been

18

signed to them, he had ended up in what he privately considered the dump heap—Public Relations.

Basically, Randall did not believe in public relations, although he tried hard to do so. There was really no need for it, especially in a company like this—a company so well known, whose fundamental job was of such importance to our industrial society. "Our main business is not to talk about ourselves," he liked to say, "but to carry on the important jobs we have to do. We are not in the business of turning out press releases. . . ."

Things would be different, if he were in charge, he thought. Carlyle was a good man, but too lenient, too easy-going. If you've got to turn out booklets—and instruction bulletins that gave information on how to operate complex equipment were, he felt, the only essential booklets—then you ought to turn them out in quantity. Press releases, magazines or company papers— so many per person, per month or per quarterly—something measurable, so Management would see you were doing your job. That was the way to do it. He wondered whether Carlyle had shown his report to Old T. L. Mr. Lowry was a man who would appreciate that report. But sometimes Randall didn't think that Carlyle let T.L. realize what he, Randall, was doing or the kind of job that he was doing. Yes, Mr. Lowry would appreciate him. Carlyle, with all his brilliance, he felt obscurely, did not sufficiently understand him or his work.

The times were out of joint anyhow, Randall thought. Hiring people from anywhere, people without training or background. What was the System coming to? Well, back to work. . . . First, he'd get in Phil Harwood and Bob Kilgore and maybe Jim Carruthers, three of his men, and they'd have a little conference.

He looked up to see Mrs. Tremaine standing at the door of his office. April, they called her. Well, he was old-fashioned about that too. She was too pretty, too indecent looking. It wasn't businesslike. Maybe she was a good secretary but he wished she would say "Mr. Randall."

"Dave, would you step into the Boss's office a moment?" April said. "He has your new man waiting to see him."

19

"Thanks, April," Randall answered shortly. He rose heavily. He was a heavy-set man in his late forties, inclined to paunchiness, and with thinning gray-flecked hair. He owned a good house in the right part of New Jersey, a Buick, a wife and two daughters, and had been with the Company twenty years. He had seen a safe world made unsafe. He did not like the way the world was going.

"Dave," Carlyle began as Randall walked in, "I have this new man waiting for an interview. He's a veteran—wounded, not eligible for the draft—just our meat. We can use him, if he's any good, in Simmon's place syndicating to the Associated Companies. Will you be free to talk to him afterwards?"

"Yes, sir," Randall said. "Did you get a chance to read my memo, Jeff?"

Carlyle frowned. "Oh yes," he said. "I'll talk to you about that later, Dave." He paused. "Let me ask you something. Do you really think servicemen need to keep up with the Company? They have a lot of other things on their minds and the Company papers are sent to them anyhow. At any rate, let's talk about it later. I don't want to appear unsympathetic," he added quickly as he saw Randall's face. "It just seemed to me they'll be a little too busy just trying to stay alive . . . oh well . . ."

Then he turned to April. "Send Mr. Brill in."

The interview was almost over and he knew he would get the job and that he didn't want it. Well, it would be a stopgap anyhow until he found something better, some work he really wanted to do. He'd stick with this job for a couple of months or so, then he'd find himself a good one. That would give him time.

"You got it in Manila?" Carlyle was asking him again. Carlyle was being polite. He didn't really want to know.

"I didn't even reach the plane," he said slowly. "They got most of us as we were running."

He didn't say it was only he who had through some blind panic run toward the hangars when they had been repeatedly warned to take shelter. All that training—then the dull roar over the revetments and the hangars and there he was running like a crazy man toward the plane and the next thing he knew he was in a hospital bed and the nurse was saying something about he'd be all right.

He'd been lucky. He scarcely limped except when it was damp —they'd put his foot together fine, and the other stuff had missed all the vital parts.

"I never fired a shot in anger to win this war," he was saying with his slow smile.

The shrewd tired eyes settled on him quizzically.

"Don't be discouraged by what I've told you of the Company, Mr. Brill," he said. "It's a big company and there's a lot to it. You won't be able to set the place on fire, no matter how good you are. And it's slow and steady all the way. But there are compensations. And barring another recession, a certain amount of security for a bright fellow. Now what did you say you wanted in the way of a salary?"

And so, at least temporarily it seemed, another Company man was born.

2

IN THE FIRST WEEK of the job, his worst fears were realized. This was the type of company that stood for everything he found sinister and repellent.

It was part of a vast sprawling empire, spreading over the entire country, its major plants and distributing houses in most of the big cities of the land, its installers working out of a thousand towns putting in the equipment that made up the physical plant of the System. True, he sat in an ordinary outer office here on the ninth floor at headquarters amid a sea of desks with a lot of ordinary harmless people.

And true that in those plants and locations which he could not yet visualize, tens of thousands of ordinary harmless people were working in offices or on conveyor lines or assembly lines or at intricate machines. And true also that without this vast empire and these nameless, faceless people, the voices across the land would fall silent, distance would separate and the instantaneous communications by which the economy of the country was sustained would be no more.

All this could be true, as the Company's ads and its public relations tried to explain. But the fact remained that this was a giant monopoly—a monopoly by virtue of wealth and skill—against which no competitor could ever rise, the services of which were of such importance to the life of the nation that its needs were almost a public responsibility, and as long as its management, no matter how banal and uninspired it might be, committed no really heinous crimes, it could continue to rule a kingdom of a million people and twenty billion dollars in assets from coast to coast, and it could rule it wisely or it could bumble along hopelessly but its rule within its province would be absolute and no one would be the wiser.

"My name's Saunders." The loud booming voice could be heard over the whole office. Martin looked up in consternation.

A large moon-faced man in his middle thirties with expensive sloppy clothes was leaning over his desk. "Glad to have you aboard!" Saunders said. "I'm in production. I see you're one of Randall's new boys! How about lunch with the gang!"

Martin was tired. He smiled. This was just the sort of friendly sport he was prepared to hate. A real goon.

"Glad to," he said.

Lunch in the downtown business district of the city is at its best a terrifying experience. During wartime, with more people working, more bustle, more turmoil, food less plentiful and poorer, it was nothing less than a cataclysm. They ate at a place called Mike's—Saunders, Bob Kilgore, quiet, a pipe-smoking, thoughtful man with kind appraising gray eyes, Jim Somers, a

22

handsome, rather meticulous, reticent man in his late thirties, Phil Harwood, smooth, excessively polished, cool, contemptuous —a man they said would go far—and Sam Carruthers, a rather ineffectual older man in the advertising department whom they classed as a has-been.

"You're going to jump right into it, boy," Saunders boomed at him over the sauerbraten. "Carlyle's sending you to the War Exhibit next Thursday, I hear. So you can write it up for the Company papers. I'll be there with old Haggerty to help give a spiel. It's to show the world and the families of plant people that we're in there pitching. Of course, we can't say much about our war effort, most of it's secret, but we can show them examples of the older stuff Labs developed. . . ."

"So you're the new syndicate man with Randall?" Bob Kilgore said in his soft low voice. He had a serious face older than his years, yet there were humor lines about his eyes. "Well, we're all in this thing together," he added, "so don't despair."

"I suppose Sandy here has already welcomed you to the horrors of Randall's organization?" Sam Carruthers commented. "Has Randall given you the Word yet?"

"Not yet," he had answered. "I only saw him briefly. He said he'd talk to me this afternoon, if he gets time."

"You have something to look forward to then," Carruthers said. "He and Mr. Doyle and our boy Phil here are the boys to look out for. We're all one big happy family but some of us are happier than others."

"All right, Sunshine," Saunders said jovially, "let's not talk about our heartaches, let's talk about women!"

At three that afternoon, Mr. Randall was ready to see him.

"Your first assignment," Randall said, "will be to cover the System War Exhibit. This is our biggest exhibit and should indicate something of what we are doing." Randall leaned back and smiled. "From there on out, you'll be in the thick of things."

"You're a veteran, Martin," he went on pleasantly, "and you'll realize how important our Company's contributions are.

23

The Nazis showed us that men don't count any more in war—it's machines, equipment. So it's to companies like us that the nation must turn when the lights begin to go off one by one all over the earth. They laughed at us once and maligned us and belittled us in peace. Now they see what we mean. They need us now. We're coming into our own. And I must say you'll see every bit as much of an all-out effort on the assembly line as you saw . . . er . . . on the front lines. . . . Of course, I don't mean we've done more than you, Martin, or you boys. . . ."

Martin writhed.

"You don't have to tell me, sir," he said slowly. "The Government spent a lot of money on me, to train me, to get me ready. . . . It was all wasted. I never got to fire a round. I never got the plane up. . . ."

"Well, my boy," Randall said. He seemed to expand, to relax a little. "Well, my boy, you tried. That's all any of us can do. I think you'll make out all right here. I think you may some-day be a good System man, if you'll pardon the expression." He tried to make it sound humorous. "I've been here twenty years myself. It's not been all honey nor all jam. They push you around a little. But if you've got it, it pays off in the end."

Martin had touched his sun-bleached hair. This was a lonely and chaotic period of his life and he hated to have to listen to this prematurely middle-aged man bumbling bromides in his phony executive voice. Maybe Randall wasn't a bad fellow underneath it all, but there were so many layers of it on him now—year after incompetent year—and the inner insecurity that they all had. He didn't think he could stand much more of it. He still had those nightmares of running . . . running for the plane. . . . He shook himself.

". . . and you'll have plenty of chance to get acquainted with the way things are being done." Randall's throaty voice was reaching him as if from a great distance. "Carlyle is a great one for having one go to the sources, for having a man get out into the field, so to speak—'hit the road,' he calls it. You'll be

24

collecting material and syndicating it to the magazines of the other System companies and to our own fourteen plant and division papers—all kinds of material from new developments, new products, stories of the war effort, even to something on the lives and activities of the people as they work there, though I feel there has been perhaps too much of that sort of thing. We're here to do a job, not to pander to our own or anyone else's people, and the more we concentrate on the job and forget about the frills, the better we'll do. Most of those we're picking up for the plants are . . . well, second-rate, you might say. Some might even call them trash, incompetents, the leftovers. . . . Our good boys, of course, have gone to war. . . . And now we'll take anyone . . . anyone. . . ."

And later:

"You'll find I'm of the old school, Martin," Randall concluded in a low baritone. "Mr. Carlyle thinks perhaps I'm a little hard on people, that I subscribe a little too much to the old-line production man's philosophy: 'Get 'em young, treat 'em rough, tell 'em nothing!' Well, maybe I am. That's the way they used to operate and that's the way this Company grew. Not the namby-pamby philosophies we've got nowadays with unions and coddling of people and nice-Nelly stories. We've gotten soft. We need some of those old-fashioned virtues that all this government womb-to-tomb security has sapped from us. We don't know where we're going. We don't know what we're doing. And the common man's got too common. Still, sometimes I must admit, wasteful and extravagant as it all is, motley as are the crews we scrabble together, somehow we're turning it out . . . and that's what you'll be recording for us. . . ."

The interview was over. He had had a slight headache. And then the week was over.

3

CARLYLE HATED the thought of the coming weekend. Would it happen again? Would he have to go through it all again? He just didn't think he could take any more of it. It's all right when you're young and there's always tomorrow or another drink or another doll or the work seems important and you think you're doing well and getting on. You can forget it then once in a while. But when you're forty-eight—well, you've had it, you've had about all there is, and your taste for hard liquor and bad girls has about worn out. . . .

That's how it had all begun. He'd always had a weakness for bad girls and good times. There was some essential element about them—some weakness, some challenge to or hatred for life that satisfied a need in himself. A decent, clean, straightforward girl left him cold. She could be beautiful as the morning, virtuous as the suckling babe, kind, loving, understanding and attached to him. That was not what he wanted. He wanted something else. Some perversity in him demanded the immature, the sordid, the sad. So it had been easy and exciting in the old days. That had been the late twenties when he was young—the gay, the jazz-loud decade when every night was one continuous New Year's Eve and it was always three o'clock in the morning, day after day.

There had been a succession of the good times and the bad girls then, and he'd had the money and the security too. He, a Princeton boy with brains, had had it all—everything in front of him. He had had it and the Company had realized it and they'd had some bigtime boys working for them then.

Well, the party was over, not just that party—the scintillating decade and the solid million-dollar conversion picnic—but the succession of girls and drinks up all the years to now—to Stella and what was happening to him and this weekend, to this war

26

he'd never really be a part of and this scrabbly, chaotic, produc-
tion-mad antihuman world where even young, sloppy, evil Stella
was a miserable anachronism.

So that evening he stopped in at Sakele's before going home.
At the long bar on this late summer dusk, there was no one he
knew. Several businessmen and a couple of office girls with
their bosses or their office friends having those surreptitious
affairs so frequent and so natural in the commuter's crowded life
sat on stools or farther back in the leather booths.

He had had some gay old times here, he was thinking. He'd
had one or two too many and visited many a hotel with many
a moment-to-moment girl in his heyday—that is, when he wasn't
traveling or, as they said, on the road. This evening it all seemed
a little sad. All the husbands he'd helped girls betray, all the
loving men he'd contributed the horns to, and now someone was
doing it to him—and with the last of the girls, the last of the
bad girls he'd ever have or even want, with the last and only
girl he'd ever loved and—he admitted it to himself ruefully—he
ever would love.

Why did it have to be Stella of all the long succession of the
gay, the sad, the wonderful—that sloppy, evil, beautiful, pleasure-loving little slut? He could have had a hundred better. But
he didn't want them. He didn't want anyone. No one had it for
him except her. All he wanted in the world was her.

And he didn't exactly know what he could do about it. That
was what made it hopeless. What really could he do? He could
ignore it. The affair had been going on now for some time, for
more than a year. And she didn't try to hide it any more. There
wasn't anything, nothing in the world he could do to her, because she didn't care. She had somebody else now—that was all
there was to it.

He'd seen it happen before in the old days—the hopeless
hanging-on by one or another of two people when it was all over.
And he'd thought: Why do they do it? Why do they deceive
themselves? When you're through, you're through. When it's
over, it's over. There was no use raking it about. Couldn't people

27

retain some dignity? "A ten-day bender or a dose of Epsom salts should cure any heartache," he had liked to say. He had had a philosophy that went: "Take hold strongly, let go loosely." Well, now he knew. Talk is one thing. Philosophy is fine. A man's life is another. And he'd come to the end of this road. He'd got his now. Now he was facing the music himself.

He tried to see himself in the mirror over the bar. What he saw was a masked face, a controlled face, younger-looking than his years, yet a little tired, a little dissipated. He ordered another one. This was his third, but the stuff didn't help him any more. He could knock himself out with it and he'd had his hangovers the last few months. In fact, he felt that perhaps April and even Randall were beginning to notice. You couldn't keep anything secret in that big whispering gallery that was the office. You could drink secretly or commit some terrible obscure crime and your friends in the outside world would never know, would never hear of it. But they'd know it in the office. They'd know, and it would spread like wildfire, and there you'd be. Why you couldn't even die in peace there. The Benefit Committee would be on your neck in a minute. Your whole life was mapped out on those little raise-sheet cards: when you were born and where, who your parents were, what you did, where you were educated, what you looked like, what jobs you'd had. . . . Like a fitness report and what everyone you had ever worked for thought of you. But worse than that, the people who worked with you— they would know. . . .

He ordered another. Joe, the bartender, smiled at him. "Everything all right, Mr. Carlyle?" he asked jovially. Mr. Carlyle was one of the big ones, a V.I.P., and a gentleman to boot. Joe had seen a lot of 'em and he reserved his comments for the best.

Carlyle answered mechanically. He'd said "Righto!" to how many hundred bartenders in his time? It had been a long bar-filled street he had strolled down. Yes, it was all a big whispering gallery, and there would be no getting away from it. Not that he hadn't been tagged once or twice before by the disgraceful girls he had loved down the years. He guessed that that was

28

what had put the quietus on his career. Of course, the job he had wasn't a bad one, one of the best, in fact—manager of a department with sixty-odd men in it. But there were better and he could have gone further—that he knew. Perhaps it had been that second wife of his, and then there was the episode of that little slut named Queenie who had barged in one morning. People don't forget those things. Well, you can't have everything. That's the way he had been, and he'd made his choice. The Company came to know these trivia somehow. And suddenly, there you are: you've had it. Nobody says anything. No steps are taken. No one's really against you. There's no talk or anything special like that. It's just that one day you realize you're pegged. They know you. They know what you are and where you've been. And you know you're there to stay. You're not going anyplace any more. The division-head jobs that come up—somehow your name won't be among those considered. You'll not be on the list of the white-haired boys any more. You'll never be a V.P. You never know exactly how they find out, but somehow the Company eventually knows.

So it will be in every little detail of your life. Somehow they'd know about Stella pretty soon—not that he'd care any more. But it was queer. He himself was on the receiving end also. He knew more than he could account for about almost any of the men in the division right now. Maybe he didn't know everything but sooner or later it drifted to him: what was happening to Jim Somers, for instance. And that Kilgore's sister was not well and that there was some trouble between the gorgeous April and her overseas husband and that Saunders had found a new hat-check girl. And that MacClaren's daughter was in trouble, and even that the little girl who worked for Towers and whose name escaped him was having a torrid time with some married man in the accounting group. And the new man —he'd soon know all about him too. What was his name— Brill? A nice fellow, a nice-looking chap, sincere, on the level. Well, you couldn't escape it, that's all there was to it. But oh God, the weekend again—that weekend and Stella. . . .

29

He hoped somehow she'd be home this time, and just smile at him. He looked at his watch. It said eight o'clock. He was hungry and tired and perhaps a little drunk. No, no matter how much of it he took, the stuff didn't do him any good any more. Well, he'd better be going. He might as well face it.

He grimaced mechanically as one of the men said hello to him. In the group stood Cecil Brent, assistant to the president. Well, that was one more item they could chalk up on old Jeff Carlyle, one more infinitesimal pointer. "Used to be a good man," they'd say. "You never know. Too bad Too bad. Getting to be something of a sot. Well, that's what a bad woman will do for you. . . ." How often he had smiled at that phrase—so absurd, so forlorn. Not if you were a man, he'd always thought. Not if you were a man. Nobody does anything to a man. He only does it to himself. Well . . .

In the street, there was still a lot of light and bustle considering the hour. Wartime meant overtime. Many of them were still working—many of his own gang too. They were good boys. They were doing the best they could—old 4–F's, superannuated cheerleaders, and tired heads of families who ought to be home with the wife and kiddies in Larchmont, rattling the paper in the Little Woman's face.

The Little Woman—he laughed and someone looked around at him. "The Little Woman!" he said aloud. What an absurd phrase. They should see his Little Woman sometime. There was a Little Woman for you! But then, they wouldn't understand. Stella wasn't really a mean kid. She was just a type. He'd seen a lot of 'em—dynamite. But it was out of the ordinary fellow's ken. The moment-to-moment girls, the original "I don't care" girls, only worse, because they weren't pretending—they really didn't care. They were it!

He stumbled a little, then walked to the corner and stood looking for a cab. He wondered again just who it was she was seeing. The evening was cool and beautiful, one of those summer twilights that came earlier now and compensated for all the dog days that had broiled them for so long.

As he stood there, he looked up at the Building, gleaming in the velvet evening air. Lights were on in many of the windows. The granite outer pillars and the heavy lines appeared to melt together into the upward thrust of the great stone structure with its row on row of massive windows. It seemed to him then for a moment that there was an essence both sinister and foreboding in that vast pile. They'll never lick us with something like this to fight against, he thought irrationally—this vast monolith of mediocrity, this tremendous monument to the power of the many.

He whistled and a cab screeched to a stop.

"If you're goin' uptown, mister," the cab driver growled. "I ain't goin' to Brooklyn again."

Carlyle got in slowly. "I'm going uptown," he said.

At that moment Brill walked thoughtfully out of the shadows between the pillars guarding the entrance to the Building.

The week at the office had ended.

4

CARLYLE LOOKED at Stella from his relaxed position on the white sofa. Please God, he said to himself, don't let me say it. The words spilled out anyhow.

"Where are you going, Stella?"

The girl's full red lips pursed at him as if she were speaking a line. She turned from fixing her lovely hair—jet black and lustrous. The face was the face of a dissipated Madonna— beautiful and sensual. She had on her low-cut, black cocktail gown, which emphasized her superb figure.

"Out," she said.

"That's a fine answer," he replied in an attempt at something of his old gaiety. "I can take you out just as well as the next fellow."

"Can you?" she asked. She raised a delicately plucked eyebrow. "I'm not so sure."

"Stella," he continued heavily, "come on, I'll take you out. We'll go to them all—the way we used to. I'll take you to Jack's and the Mombo. We'll have fun."

She didn't answer for a moment, touching her bosom and ears with perfume. The scent filled the room.

"You're no fun any more," she answered softly. "Let's not go all over it again. I'm late."

"My God, Stella, you're not a kid!" he said. "D'you have to have fun all the time? Can't you think of anyone but yourself?"

"Yes," she replied. "You know me, Jeff. You knew me when. You've had all the words and music. Yes, I have to have fun *all* the time."

He wanted to yell at her, to ask her who the man was, but he knew he couldn't. He was helpless. That would tear it. Perhaps he could get up and hit her, smash that half-smile off that beautiful and evil face. But it would be no use. She would just laugh and pick herself up and leave and never come back again. Ten years meant nothing to her, nor the good times nor the bad. She was thirty-two—in the full flower of her beauty. He was forty-eight. He could never again touch her. He didn't have it for her any more—didn't know how or why or even exactly when, but he hadn't had it for her for a long time.

But she still had it for him—for him and for them all, he thought bitterly. When he spoke again, his voice was humble. She was putting on her little Paris jacket.

"Stella," he asked softly, "will you stay with me later tonight?"

She paused, considering, one eyebrow slightly arched.

"We'll see, Jeff," she said. "Good night, Gay Man. Don't wait up for me. You need your sleep."

He rose with some vague half-thought of kissing her as he was wont to in the old days, but she had walked out into the living room. He heard the click of her high heels in the foyer, then the door slam. Stella always slammed doors.

He walked slowly to the easy chair on his side of the bedroom and threw himself down. His throat was so tight he could scarcely swallow. How had he ever gotten to this, he wondered again. By what road had he ever reached this degradation and sadness?

All the years he had been the Gay Man. All the years he had known what he was doing. It wasn't Stella's fault, really— that was what made it so hopeless. She was the way she was. You got what you paid for, and when you didn't have the price, you just didn't have it any more. There had been so many of them—some as beautiful, a few gayer, most of them as fun-loving, evil and sordid—like himself. You couldn't get around that. That was what he had wanted—passion without love. And he had found it. And now everything else had evaporated, every-thing—even that—and there was left only this terrible ache for it, this terrible jealousy and longing. Why now, though, of all the heartless sluts he had had, should he have to end in bondage to this last, this most sordid, this most beautiful?

For in the old days, it had been he, not she, who had called the tune. He was the Gay Man. He never gave her a moment's thought except when he needed her for a good time or to show off to friends. It had been she at his beck and call, she who had cried when he wanted her to cry and laughed when he wanted her to laugh. And when he had told her they were going to be married because he needed a wife as he went up in the Company, it was she who dressed the part, and with one or two small exceptions had managed to masquerade as an ordinary wife —a great deal better-looking than most, but also a great deal more expensive. For she had been dynamite. There was no getting around it. He had explained to her, when they were married, that fidelity was not important to him but discretion was, and she had said she didn't care since he was the only one who held her passion. She must let him have the others if he wanted them, he had told her, and she had agreed to this readily enough.

Then suddenly one morning—he could not recall exactly the day—it was all over. He tried to ignore it. But though he could not remember the precise period now after all this time, he could

33

recall almost exactly how it had been. He had slept late, he remembered, after an expense-account dinner with some minor executives, and he had had a slight hangover.

She had entered the bedroom. "Bring me a Bromo, Stella," he said. Ordinarily, she would have gone immediately to mix it and smiled at him with some soft words of sympathy or a humorous reference to the night before. Now she stood a moment, hesitant. It wasn't anything she said or did. It was the hesitation, seeming to say more clearly than words: Should I bother? And the silence. Then she had turned and walked out to fetch it.

It had been like that always after that morning—was it two, three years ago? How could he place it exactly? It did not really matter anyhow. And the situation had been growing worse steadily—the indifference, the coldness, the lack of spark, and then gradually the stepping out more and more in the evenings, not with just one or another man but with many of them, two and three times during the week, the parties, at first with vague subterfuges, then without even the suggestion of an explanation —just fun-loving and insatiable and warm for everyone but him.

At first he had been too proud to notice. After all, he had been the master and she the concubine. He didn't even ask her for love any more, though once or twice he had wanted her so badly he had forced her, half asleep, to submit. She submitted agreeably but without enthusiasm. And suddenly one evening not so long ago, he knew he was licked. There was finally, he realized, not just men, but, all at once, one man. How he knew, he could not tell, but he was sure of it. She had found someone else. It wasn't just fun now. It was one man, and the telephone calls had died away. The parties were over. In her closed and vacant heart, someone had finally taken over. And now middle age had ambushed him unfairly.

He rose and walked into the living room—their messy, expensively furnished, modern living room where so many wild parties had ended in burnt cigarette ends, broken glasses, drowning consciousness and despair at six in the morning. His and hers —a life of shambles and loose ends and no tomorrows. Well,

34

tomorrow—the tomorrow of middle age and longing and reality
—had arrived for him. It would never come for her, he knew.
Perhaps a headache now and then, but she had years of her
beauty and badness ahead of her. How she had become what
she was he had never quite known. He had not been interested
then. She had been only twenty-two and strikingly beautiful
when they took up together after his second divorce. She was
well on her way to being a lost girl then—without care, without
a motive except to have a good time. Now she was thirty-two—
more beautiful if anything, though more dissipated, but as unconsciously enchanting as the arts of passion could render her
—and the ten years with him had completed her education in
heartlessness. He could not say exactly that he had made her
that way; he had added a certain quality to her life. But he
could not say, either, that he had not put the finishing touches on
the taste for evil, the indifference, the hardness and the utter
degradation.

Well, now he was reaping it all—all of it—in full measure.
Again the thought: "What has happened to me? What have the
years done to me? How did it ever get this way? And now what
will become of me? The years have caught up. I've lost the
capacity not to care. I've lost the only protection a man like me
has—indifference, the hard heart. The harlot finally has me.
She standeth in the street corners . . . he quoted to himself
softly. She waiteth . . . He turned quickly. He looked at himself in the hall mirror for a moment. He couldn't sit there all
evening, waiting, wondering, as he had so many evenings now
during the last months. He couldn't drink the evenings away and
pretend he hadn't noticed. He couldn't ignore those telltale
touches any more, the lateness, the obviousness, the lipstick
askew, the gown a little rumpled, the garter broken. . . . He
knew her so well. They had done it all so often together. Who did
she think she was deceiving? But of course, that was the trouble.
She didn't care. They had experienced it so often together in
cars, in doorways, in strange apartments, in cloak rooms, down
the sliding years when it had been illegal and he had had another

35

wife. And everything that could happen he knew, knew only too well. Now despite himself, the telltale touches burned him, gnawed at him . . . the slip with the cigarette hole in it . . . the lost compact. How far he had sunk, how terrible it had all been—the sickness, the aching sickness, the deep sickness.

Well, he could not remain here now. He had to stay away from this place until she was back again, home, safe from those alien arms for a while, home again with him, and his for the moment, even though it were a travesty and a sham and he was sick with that terrible sickness.

His face in the mirror was detached, cool, a little pale perhaps, but the suffering, the longing, did not show. The small gray mustache, the coolness, the faint cynical good looks were all there. The hell with it, he thought. He was not going to drink tonight again. He was not going to kill himself, bleeding for it. He'd take a walk and try to think of business, of what they had to do, of important matters, not of this trivial nightmare, this miasma. After all, in this town you can find something, and if there's nothing here, there's always a way to get out. The Company would arrange a transfer. They'd take care of him again. They always had. They'd given him a lot really, since he had come there twenty-six years ago, a smart boy from Princeton, out to set the world on fire. Yes, they'd done a lot for him and most of it had been fun—it was the life. And those expense accounts were all right. He'd seen a great deal at the Company's expense. He'd learned a great deal and had a lot of fun. He'd met a great many people and the Company had given him a lot of power and prestige.

It wasn't their fault that he'd had a taste for the low places of life, the gutter. They had tried. They had treated him right. They'd never let him down. When he needed that transfer from Chicago because of that Chalmers kid, Old Man Schaefer had gotten it for him. And it never reflected on him either. He had come up to headquarters—a white-haired boy still. They had even asked him what he wanted. He could have used the engineering degree to get into the guts of the Company, but he had wanted the frills. And they had given him the frills. Yes, they'd treated him well. They've treated a great many men a great deal worse than they've treated me, he thought tiredly.

And suddenly, he felt a deep affection for the Company. It was only an impersonal, cold conglomeration of hundreds of thousands of unsentimental, commonplace people, machines and buildings, tracks and towers, lights and voices, but somehow it was a solid thing, and it was there to stay. He and his trials and difficulties, the others and their little concerns, were fleeting breaths, but the Company, which would see thousands like them come and go, rise and fall, would endure, would remain there forever, substantial, unchanging, powerful, enjoying a species of immortality, not as humans but as humanity itself, a monument to the creative force and endurance of collective men, no matter how mediocre, how banal—and to the power of human need.

Often he had cynically surveyed the less pleasant aspects of the corporate world, the Company's vast, almost incomprehensible stupidity, its hardening rituals so devoid of meaning, so senseless, so divorced from the realities of life, its inexorable yet capricious demands and oddly ruthless selections of men and means. But basically, somehow, with all its waste and scramble and chaos, it did the job: it kept the voices singing over the wires and across the earth.

Its great shadow was the shadow of thousands of commonplace people, some so incompetent that nowhere else could they have survived, a very few talented and even brilliant, but the great generality of them as common as grass and as mediocre and uninspired. The jobs had been broken down and broken down to simpler and simpler operations—operations that anyone off the street could perform—and the machines themselves had become more and more complex, some almost self-regulating, others having "learned" to tend other machines, until the thousands of human hands were scarcely skilled enough to push buttons or throw switches or set a jig, and on assembly lines stretching mile on impressive mile, girls with ten minutes' train-

37

ing were putting together by the thousands electronic complexes, "brains" and switches that the most skilled craftsmen could not duplicate by themselves in a year.

It was a strange phenomenon. Ordinary people through their collective efforts, through the corporate organization, accomplishing colossal ends. So that in the last analysis it was not courage, not bravery, not love, not heart and soul, that could save the world from its grim tyrannies, from the stain that was upon them all, but the iron foundries and the great Corporation. He smiled a little ruefully to himself. Of course, that was not true, but there was just enough of truth in it to make it appalling and sinister. And now his affection for the Company returned once more. Whatever its shortcomings—and they were many—it had been good to him. It had bestowed on him power and prestige, money, travel and good times, and an expense account to serve the very tastes that had trapped him in the end.

He found himself walking toward the river in the cool August night. It was late, yet the lights in hundreds of buildings were still on. There had been a practice air raid drill earlier in the evening, and the white-helmeted wardens—young girls, middle-aged businessmen, fat women so ridiculous in their unaccustomed gear and blue and white Civil Defense armbands—were just going home from their duties. Soon he left the midtown section behind and crossed under the elevated on Third Avenue and walked east into the wilderness of shuttered shops, mysterious warehouses and lofts.

This had been his town, all right. But then, any town with lots of people and lots of lights was his: Chicago, San Francisco, New Orleans—he'd seen them all on expense account, lived for a while in one or another of them as he traveled on Company business. He'd carried a month of sleep on each eyelid. He'd lived high and done well for the Company too—given of himself to it, exhausted his little talents and odd-job abilities in its service and enjoyed the whole of it all the way up. Now those years of travel and work for the Company were among the freshest remembrances of his burnt-out, misspent existence—memories unsullied by that degradation to which he had now fallen, the degradation of his love for Stella. Where was she now? The thoughts began to seep in, in the cool night, and the throbbing began again. Who was she with? What was she doing? To whom was she giving the fullness of her passion? With whom was she sharing that terrible, secret bag of tricks that was her love? It kept hurting. He could not stop it or control it. It kept throbbing.

He stopped—a quiet, impressive, well-dressed man with a small gray mustache, on a mean and lonely big-town street between the rumble of the night's last El and subterranean murmur of the morning's first Express. He had never in his life been so alone.

He looked at his watch. It was almost three in the morning. She would surely be home and in bed by now. He had walked all night. Now perhaps at last, she would be his own; in sleep at least he could watch over her, and she would, even if only for the moment as if it might be forever, belong to him. And then his thoughts moved on again over the same old paths. At least in the end, if he made no false moves, no steps that would drive her away, he would always have her after a fashion; she would be his in the tag-ends like this— all he had left of her anyhow.

He turned and increased his pace back, his footfalls loud in the sleeping city. When he reached the street on which his apartment house stood, the chill had penetrated him a little. The doorman was not on, and the lobby seemed strange. A sleepy elevator man took him up. He let himself in quietly. The apartment was still in shadow, only the one light burning in the bedroom, as he had left it. She had not returned.

He stood stock-still, his heart sinking. The terrible depression was creeping over him again. Then it came to him—the sound of the key in the lock. Hastily, he went into the bedroom, removed his jacket and tie and put on a bathrobe. Obscurely, he did not want her to find him up. He opened the bed and sat down on it. By that time, the fumbling had ceased. She had finally mastered the lock. She was giggling a little. She must be very drunk, he thought.

39

Then she stood in the doorway. She was still dressed beautifully but slightly swaying, a rather silly half-smile on her lovely face. She was dragging her little jacket on the floor and then he saw that her dress had been ripped at the side. Her eyes were unfocused and her red lips slightly open.

"Oh, iss you," she said slowly.

"Stella," he said softly, "oh, Stella."

"Had a time," she said. "God, had a time," she said slowly, as if the very sensation were returning to her again. She stood before him, only half conscious, swaying slightly, the beautiful and distracting face deep in its sensuality.

He could scarcely breathe. He rose as if to approach her, as if to strike her. She drew away a little and staggered.

"Too tired," she said. "Go to bed. Had it," she said. "Had it. Go way. . . ." She turned and began to tear off her clothes with drunken abandon. She sat heavily on the bed. Her gown came away and then he noticed she had nothing but a slip on. She turned away from him.

"S'all righ', Tom," she said softly, then fell back on the bed in a deep sleep.

He undressed slowly, sitting on the bed away from her, and crept under the covers, leaving her where she lay. The hurt was so intense he could scarcely contain it. At last, painfully, he stretched out, trying to quiet the ache. Tom, he thought. He didn't even know anyone named Tom. It was someone he did not even know. If he could only find out who it was. But what good would it do? What good would anything do?

Then suddenly he felt the wetness on his cheeks, the first time in all the long years—the tears, the terrible tears, that he had despised and laughed at and believed would never fall—and he was weeping uncontrollably, soundlessly. He had reached the end of the long line, the last stop on that terrible road to the death of the heart.

5

IT WAS at the big show at the Eastern Works—the memory comes back to Martin now, and how long ago it seems—that he had visited a plant for the first time in his life. It was not a cheering experience. He had passed factories fleetingly, glimpsed them from train windows and had a vague concept of what they were like—places with machines where the objects of their civilization were fashioned—but the hot, early fall afternoon the three of them, he, Jim Somers and Saunders, were sent to the War Exhibit at one of the works was the first time he had actually entered one, and it had remained something of a shock.

The Works lay across a vast expanse of plain. From the spires of the big town, it seemed to be separated by marshes of swaying cattails. It appeared as a series of long, low buildings, and from a distance, as they were being driven toward it—the three of them, an officious research man and a morose engineer in the special Company car—the place looked to him like a penitentiary. At the gates armed guards stopped them. They climbed out slowly, showing their passes.

The impression was one of noise and confusion. Wide, high areas with fantastic convoluted iron machines at spaced intervals under high neon lights . . . the continuous clack clack and whir . . . the monotonous pounding, as parts were stamped out or others fed into the hungry, insatiable maws . . . the sounds of grinding, planing and milling . . . the clanging . . . the confusion. . . . Machines had always frightened him, and after two hours of the seemingly endless expanses of operating machines, conveyor lines, assembly lines and more machines, he was ready to call it a day.

They stood in the sun in the late afternoon, he and Jim Somers. Somers did not look well. He had had a hangover that morning and his hands were shaking. "So that's what a plant looks like," he said to Jim.

Jim's impassive face twitched slightly. "That's what a plant looks like," he said without expression. "The Company has lots of them. This is one of the big ones—a works—but not the biggest."

"You mean, I ain't seen nothin' yet," Martin had said, trying to smile. Saunders had joined them. His florid face was a bit drawn.

"You ain't seen nothin' yet!" he said.

Back in the office the next day, Martin had been grateful for the respite. Here the chaos was bad enough, and in the midst of war the big town had a sort of rakish and ragged gaiety, a sense of purpose and bustle amid the confusion that was distinctly exhilarating. Disasters abroad month after month had finally driven them to the realization that they were at the end of the line— this time, they were in it for good, no compromise, no easy way out. They would either do the job or they would learn to live, if they lived at all, to the measure of some other way of existence. That way might be better or it might be worse—the question was debatable—but at any rate it would be different, and on one point they were all agreed: they wanted their own kind of meat and their own kind of poison. They did not want it different. The events of the last few years had forced upon many of them a re-examination of their basic tenets and beliefs, and for many the conclusion had become obvious that this was not a very good civilization— no civilization whose center of gravity was Detroit, whose capital was New York with its outposts of London, Paris and Hollywood, could stand before a weary world with any complacency—but good or not with its tasteless machine-made products, its deification of mediocrity, it was only the best there was, and those alien cultures with their threats to bomb them all to death with their new bombs and to bore them all to death with their kindergarten dialectic had even less to offer.

*   *   *

In the third week, the war finally hit the office with its first taste of reality. Hal Tremaine, April's husband, was killed in action during the battle of the Coral Sea. The news came as a real shock. April was out for several days but returned, dry-eyed and composed. She seemed subdued and responded quietly to the awkward gestures of sympathy. Concealed forever now, Carlyle thought looking at her flushed beauty, was whatever rift there had been between her and her husband. In the office, they had only known him vaguely as an extremely handsome man with flashing white teeth. But it was the first time the war had swept close to them personally—the casualty figures finally clothed with the image of a single person, like the sight of a horrid accident with blood spilled in the gutter.

And April Tremaine, at twenty-eight, was a war widow.

Carlyle called her into his office the morning she returned.

"April," he said, "you know how I feel—how we all feel. Is there anything we can do? Would you like more time off?"

She looked at him warmly. He thought again what an attractive girl she was, physically—a doll, he thought, a real doll—and all that physical beauty wasted and asleep, perhaps never to be awakened, unless Hal Tremaine had awakened it, and somehow he doubted it. That was the trouble with good girls—they never knew, they never learned, they never found out . . . a real doll like this with that hair, that figure . . . never to know. . . . She'd find a good man again and marry and be a good wife and never in the world know what it was that he had had and all the bad girls he had known had had of life. And perhaps they were better off, but he didn't really think so.

She was shaking her head. "I'm all right, Jeff. You're about the only one I can be honest with. I had some trouble with Hal before he went and while he was away—I won't go into it—but there it was and we were not as close as we could have been. And now . . ." Suddenly her eyes filled with tears, and they began to brim off her long lashes onto her cheeks. "I'm sorry I'm so silly. . . . It's just I can't imagine Hal being . . . being

43

gone for good. Even . . . even if he hadn't come . . . come back to me, I . . . I can't stand the thought of his being . . . drowned. He was so good-looking, so filled with . . . with life. I . . . I know it's silly but I can't get over a feeling almost of guilt. . . . Can you understand that, Jeff?"

"Yes," he answered softly, "I can understand it, April. And it does you credit. I'd feel that way myself. You must realize there's no blame attached to you for anything about that other matter, whatever it was. It's only that everyone feels guilty when a young man dies, especially when he dies at war. The death of a man like Hal or any man at war makes us all feel guilty, puts a curse on us, and there's no getting around it. You of all people should be exempt, April. But the rest of us, miserable old middle-aged men, we know in our hearts it should have been us, not the young and the handsome, and the feeling of guilt is everywhere, you can't slough it off. . . ."

She shook her head. "I'm glad I talked to you, Jeff. I don't want any more time off. I'd rather work. It's better that way."

"All right, April," he said. He placed his hand over hers for a moment, and then she got up and went out.

He sat for a moment after she had left, thinking of her. A terrific girl, he thought again, a deep-water beauty. She could have married anybody; she could have possessed it all—wealth, social power. What man would not have been glad to have that body to display? And why was she here? It was simple. She was a good girl. She subscribed to the right brand of love. She had no ambition, no understanding of life's infinite possibilities.

With that exquisiteness, she could have skimmed the cream, but instead she would accept only the mediocre, the humdrum, the second-rate, because she didn't know and didn't want. That was the trouble: not to know and not to want. Was it Holmes who had said something like: "It was given us at the outset to know that life is a profound and beautiful thing . . ."? Well, she didn't know and kids like her didn't know—none of them there, he wagered. Not to know and not to want—that was their trouble, the trouble with them all.

44

He turned slowly. Even now . . . He looked moodily out of the window over the lower stoneworks of the buildings. It was late afternoon, almost evening, and the coming of the terrible time for him. For soon it would be quitting time, and he would have to go home . . . go home to Stella. He stopped the thought again. So Hal Tremaine was gone. . . .

It was not that they had not grown accustomed to death, he thought, to hearing of death, death far away in all manner of frightful forms: the death camps, the furnaces, the starvation, the tramp of boots at night and families disappearing from their homes. They'd had it breakfast, lunch and dinner, like living next to a slaughterhouse or walking down a dark street every night where you knew the dirty and the depraved were lying in wait for any little weakness, any moment of off-guard. Compared to these, the deaths of war seemed clean, and even to be doing something about it, no matter how small, how trivial or how irrelevant, was a welcome relief, even a profound stimulation.

So now the land was astir. There was only one fly in the ointment, where they were concerned, he thought a little ruefully. All over the land, people had buckled to, and the new concepts were seeping to the roots—not compromise or what will it cost any more, but a concept expressed perhaps a little too dramatically in the phrase *total war*. *Total war* was the phrase and it was beginning to be bandied about in the streets, at the plants and in the shops, in the offices and in homes now without men. *Total war*—it was a brand-new concept but it was clean-sounding and alive. It was bold and had both terror and stimulation in it.

The war was not just on the battlefields any more. It was over big cities as far as bombers could fly. It was over target factories. It was in towns where machine shops and mills were suddenly on a twenty-four hour a day schedule and men who had never seen the inside of a workroom had dragged in from the fields for the high wages and the urgent needs. It was beginning to show on farms where old men—men in their sixties and seventies—got up at four-thirty in the morning to do work hired men would have done if there had been any men to hire, or their sons or grandsons

45

would have done if they had not been off to war. It was in stores from which hoarding housewives, the ragged band of black-marketeers and the hungry armies of war were draining the goods. And finally, he thought tiredly, it was in the great corporations of the land where the facilities and the real burden of turning out the weapons of war lay. Yes, they were in it—in full measure. But when he said *they*, he did not mean himself and the others here—that was the fly in the ointment.

About the most useless group in these big corporations in time of war, he was thinking, was a public relations division. Informing the public of the Company's efforts and bestowing on the Company a personality in the eyes of the world appeared now hardly an essential expenditure of effort. Yet here was this tremendous flood of advertising and promotional material, not only from the new "war babies" but also from even old-line firms like theirs, designed to explain to the public how essential their work was and how greatly they were contributing to the total effort.

Yet, he thought, there must be something they could do that had bearing on the whole—something that would somehow have value when it was all sifted down and sorted out and that would amount to more than the frivolous bombast churned out now. There should be something they could do to make it possible to record or assess the Company's total effectiveness. If not that, at least would it not be possible to catch the flavor of a land at war, to record honestly its odd and rakish gaiety, its slapdash *élan*, its strange and chaotic drive? Yes, he thought, he must mull it over, consider, meditate. . . .

And suddenly he saw that the office was emptying. It was after five and time to go home. Once more his personal agony must begin.

In the streets, it was almost dark and there was that pronounced touch of chill. Everything, everything . . . winter, he thought. It would come to us all. It would get to us all in the end. To have to do this every night, every night . . . but the week-

46

ends were the worst. He didn't know how much longer he could survive those weekends. Well, it would have to be. It would somehow have to be.

As he walked along in the crisp-tasting coolness of the evening, he thought once more of that giant whispering gallery that was the office. Eventually, you'd hear it all. It would all wash out. Sooner or later it couldn't be hidden from the casual, searching eyes, the ceaseless whispering voiçes. It had not quite reached him—the trouble between April and her lost husband. And there were the others with their problems—sixty men for whom he was responsible, sixty men in his group, somehow, in some unconscious fashion depending on him, and how could he even depend on himself? And performing their routine, run-of-the-mill jobs—what they were paid to do—yet all of them, himself included, not going below the surface.

The lights of the town were sparkling in the clear cold air as far as he could see. He walked more slowly, wondering what he should do, where he could go to delay the inevitable, to soften somehow the now rising ache. He shut his eyes, wishing he were somewhere else, that he was his old self once again, as he had been five, ten years ago—free and different and uncaring. Well, there was no help for it. Another night, another day . . . and he'd have to get through them one by one somehow—those weekday evenings and those weekends, worst of all—yes, he'd have to meet them as they came, one following another . . . and Stella always there in his heart, eating at him, her beauty, her poisonous loveliness, eating him away. There was no way, no way at all, of getting around the evenings.

It seemed to Martin—and the sense of possessing those old talents was with him still—that as the pattern of the work grew clearer the routines were not so meaningless after all. The syndicate material he found he could organize and produce at least as well as, if not better than, his predecessors. The theme was, of course, the same—the one they were all playing: the slow music

47

of people working, of people producing great devices on which the success of the whole venture rested—a theme played in a hundred variations.

And he was beginning to like it, to see some sense in it and to enjoy appearing at the big Building each morning. His intensity was receiving an outlet and also that need to identify himself with a larger enterprise, a more serious intention. There was indeed beginning to grow in him that odd sense of high adventure, almost as if he were part of a bigger, more important cosmos. In a strange industrial world, he was a member of the new Knights of the Round Table. Or so, at moments of his resurgence, it appeared.

One morning in late autumn, he was summoned with the rest of them to Carlyle's office.

Randall, Phil Harwood, Jim Somers and Carruthers were already there when he walked in. Randall motioned him to a chair at the side of the office and he sat down.

Carlyle was his usual neat, handsome self but looked unusually pale and tired, and there were lines about his eyes Martin had not noticed before. Yet the faintly cynical brilliance of the personality still reached them. Martin looked vaguely, tensely about, as he always did, while they waited for the arrival of Miland. Carlyle's was one of the largest offices on that floor and contained all the trappings that befitted his rank. Martin had begun to notice how carefully every detail was arranged in these offices—and indeed in the ritual of the Company—to conform to the prescription of rank and preferment. A manager was entitled to an office with three windows, a silver decanter for his water, a certain number of office chairs, tables and bookcases.

The Company was not subtle about it except in the more refined gradations, and where, for instance, Carlyle could have the silver decanter, Randall, a supervisor immediately under him, must be content with a brown plastic decanter. Randall's office could have but two windows and one table, and the rug instead of being green was brown. Eventually, as you went up, the rug would become maroon. There were other distinctions that were subtler within the same rank, so that a Company favorite like Carlyle received telltale furniture privileges as in the case of an easy chair that most managers would not be permitted, and all down the line the signs and symbols were out for the discerning eye, the understanding and the knowing.

Carlyle leaned forward as everyone settled down.

"It's probably worried you, as it has me," he began, "that our work does not reach to the heart of the main effort. We are not, in short, contributing anything much to the Company's most important business now—the business of war. I'm not saying," Carlyle continued, giving them his thoughtful, somewhat quizzical stare, "that you are in any way shirking the jobs assigned. It's not you so much as myself about whom I'm concerned in this respect. Our trade may have significance in peacetime. In war, it's hard to believe the ordinary routines of public relations are enough." Carlyle paused. His voice was low. "So I'm going to try an experiment.

"What I propose is that three or four of you go out to the various plants, distributing houses and installation areas and wherever we're making or transporting stuff or doing any important war work, and stay there for a reasonable time to try to get into the life of the place, to report exactly what is being done, not just in cold facts, as we have been doing, but in terms of the people, the spirit and flavor of that little area of the world at war. . . ."

Carlyle paused and leaned back again. He seemed to them now even more tired. He was a hard man to know and to most of them somewhat remote.

"I'm going to start by sending four of you to different places, if you can make the arrangements in your personal lives. These places are the key production fronts of our effort. They are where the stuff is actually being made in volume, where the work is actually being done. But what we are trying in this experiment is more than just a report on the work, the production. What I

49

should like you to do who go out there is to capture the movement and life of the places and the people, catch the overtones as
well as the core. And I want the truth in the deeper sense, not a
residue you can sift here from production reports. Out of this, I
think perhaps all of us together can construct some kind of new
report on war, on the war as it is in plants and production lines,
and preserve some essence of the flavor and detail of this un-
precedented job. . . .

"Now you, Phil, will take the Works in New Jersey. . . ."

Carlyle's quiet voice droned on, assigning them. Martin had
been up late the night before, as he had so many other nights
during those last few months, trying to put together a project
that would improve his lot, that would make him different, better
—the return of old hopes, the hopes of his dream heritage. Why
could he not be different after all, be outstanding in some
manner? To be ordinary, to be mediocre—that was a curse worse
than a disease, the doom of having no great assignment from
Destiny.

And he knew another thing about himself. He would have to
find a way to struggle out of this all-embracing inertia. He had
caught glimpses of it already—the very bigness, the enormous
overriding weight of the surroundings with their slumbering and
overshadowing power upon the individual. He'd been there long
enough to see it by that time—to see the men and women marked
by it, carrying its secret brand within them. It was not that they
were dissatisfied or discontented in their work. It was that they
were *not* dissatisfied. They were content. Life had given them
less than they wanted, and they had accepted and were at peace.
And now they were somehow the creatures of a defeat. They had
become subjects of a vast and shadowy kingdom whose wealth
and power were enormous, and they scarcely realized . . .

Carlyle's quiet voice was being directed at him.

"And you, Martin, I should like to send to the big Works in
Chicago. I am selecting you for this assignment to the very heart
of the Empire because you will approach it with fresh eyes.

50

You've never seen it before. So perhaps you will see in it something the rest of us miss and be able to piece together notes on that world. . . ."

That was how he had hit the road.

The packing and getting ready had been easy. There was no one to leave behind, except that one . . . one person who had begun to haunt his thoughts at odd times. He was to leave on a Thursday morning, gathering his notes and papers at the office that Wednesday. The project, it was anticipated, would take perhaps five months, although they would be returning at intervals to report and rest before going out again. The Monday evening of the week he was leaving he had a leisurely dinner at Colby's and walked slowly back toward Fifty-fourth Street.

It was almost eight o'clock. There were several things he wanted to do. First, he had to check in at the air warden headquarters to which he had given some of his evenings during his stay in that section of town. The quarters were in a small hotel with a separate entrance halfway down the block. He had to tell them he would be away a few months. The rooms seemed rather bare and forlorn as he entered, and one dim bulb lit the main office and threw odd shadows into all the corners. Only one person, a block warden, Miss Jansen, was on duty. She wore her warden's armband, and her helmet lay nearby. She was a wizened, middle-aged lady with a persimmon-puckered mouth, a nice person, rather worried and overconscientious, who ran a little lending library and card shop in that area.

"So you won't be back for a while?" she asked worriedly.

"I'm not sure exactly when I'll be back, Miss Jansen," he replied, "but I'll be in here the moment I return to town. You can count on that. I hope they won't bomb us before I have the chance to get in on it," he added.

"Please, Mr. Brill," she said. "The Major—" he was the commander of their sector, a purple-faced army major—"the Major says time is running out. They've had reports. And there've been more rumors.

"The thing that really worries me, Mr. Brill," Miss Jansen continued tiredly, "is that we won't really be ready or know what to do or do it when the time comes."

"That worries us all, Miss Jansen," he replied slowly. "That worries us all."

"Well, I'll tell the Major or Mr. Callahan"—he was one of the deputy sector commanders, a lawyer with a loud booming voice who enjoyed organizing. "I'll tell them you stopped in and that you'll be in again in a few months when you get back. And good luck to you, Mr. Brill."

"Good luck to you," he said, rising slowly. "Good luck especially to you all."

It seemed unusually cold as he walked slowly back that evening toward his apartment house. The throb of the big town lay all around him. This would be one of the last evenings he would be seeing the city for a long long time—his town. Well, like everybody, he had come from somewhere else—his father's people were Southerners. But this city was in his blood, and if they bombed it, that to him would be a major crime—a crime against humanity, against civilization. Here he had found loneliness and also hunger and also dreams and also his life. . . . In all the little towns that were New York. You move from one neighborhood in the city into another and it was like moving from one town into another, from one village into another, rather, because each little neighborhood like the one he was walking in now was a small world in itself. Well, he would miss this town terribly during those months—that he knew.

And if the planes flew over and he returned to find this neighborhood rubble, he knew also that Miss Jansen would have acquitted herself well and so would the Major and so, even, would the loud-voiced Callahan. There they would be—all of them, cab drivers and lawyers and an elderly spinster who owned a card shop, climbing among the rubble, dirty, scarred and stupefied with exhaustion, picking among the ruins of the town they loved, and he hoped to God, if it ever came to that, he'd be there

52

with them too. Yes, their time was running out to the strains of an alien civilization.

Then he thought: there's another item on the list before I go. At the drugstore on the corner of Sixth, he turned in and went to the phone booth. He riffled through the pages of the directory. It was just a hunch. Her name was listed. In the booth, he put in the nickel and dialed. For no reason at all, his heart was pounding. The phone rang on the other end. One ring . . . two rings . . . three rings . . . The palms of his hands began to perspire. The phone rang and rang. Well, she wasn't in. So that was that. He had a sudden sense of let-down. He replaced the receiver slowly. He sat there a moment wondering idly where she might be. Then he rose and pushed out. It had been just an impulse. It had been so long since he'd thought about anybody or even cared about anybody except himself that he didn't know how to act. He smiled.

Out in the coolness again, he turned off the avenue. From somewhere in one of the apartment houses across the way rose the bleat of a French horn in a crescendo. He stood still a moment listening to it above the low throb of the city. It was being skillfully played. Then it seemed to fade away. Oh well, he thought again, it had been an impulse. It was just as well she hadn't been in.

In his rooms, the place appeared suddenly lonely. Even with the comfortable, messy, book-strewn air of the apartment, he could not seem to settle down. He thought he might put on a record but that would only aggravate this melancholy. He put down the *"Clair de Lune"* he had intended to play. That would have been the worst possible choice for this type of mood. What else? What else? He mulled over papers on his work table. Well, he couldn't concentrate tonight anyhow. He kneeled beside the long low bookcases where most of the old classics he loved lay rakishly on their sides or stood at angles. He'd have to straighten his books sometime, he thought, as he had thought so many times. Anyhow, they were well used, he comforted himself. He riffled through pages. . . . *Whenever he snatched a troubled sleep—*

53

the phrase leapt up at him—*it was at the peril of his life.* . . .
He looked to see what he had been reading. It was from Frazer's
The Golden Bough. He put the book back and picked another.
The words blurred at him: *While reason embraces a cold medi-*
ocrity, our passions hurry us with rapid violence over the space
which lies between the most opposite extremes. . . .

He read for a while the cool, smooth, detached phrases of
Gibbon like chilled cream to soothe the hotness of his inexplicable
melancholy. And then once more he began to think of the girl.
It was his last evening in town for five long months.

6

SOMETHING WAS HAPPENING to Jim Somers. Both Carlyle and
April noticed it. He would arrive in the morning, looking flushed,
his hands shaking. It was as if he had taken to drinking. Carlyle
was concerned. It was not that he cared what a man did in his
private life but he knew how they were here, and what would
happen if the voices began their whispering. Give a dog a bad
name and you might as well shoot him. There needed to be only
a few whispers: Jim drinks, you know, or did you see what's
happening to Somers, and it would spread and spread. . . .

It did not seem to Carlyle that Somers was in condition to
start on this new experiment, either, so he did not assign him.
It might be that Somers was having trouble at home or a personal
crisis, but sending him on a grueling assignment like the ones
to the plants was not the way to save him.

And April noticed it also.

April had always liked Jim Somers, as almost everyone did.
He was a gentleman, and granted that he was not really competent and appeared to have extremely limited ability, yet a man of
his personality was too rare to allow him to be sacrificed to the
hurly-burly and callousness of the offices that were their field of

operations. It seemed to April that he was not suited to the rough-and-tumble existence of their business world, and somebody was going to have to protect him, if he were to survive. He was a lamb among wolves, but it was important that someone like Jim should survive. He had no brains and no talent. He was even a little peculiar, but he was conscientious and loyal, good-looking, she thought, in a rugged, rather substantial sort of way, meticulous, clean as a whistle and single-minded. And he loved the Empire as few of them, perhaps none of them, did.

It was strange, April was thinking, how of them all, Jim who loved the Company most, with the most purity of devotion, was among the least venal, the least touched by it, the last who might be called an old Company hack. There was no question that Jim depended on the Company. The Company was his life—not just the work assigned him, but the whole aura and meaning of it. To the last sordid detail of the Empire's dealings, Jim was acqui-escent in the sense that he believed in it, believed that it was good and that in the end it was important and for the public weal.

April herself did not like to bother about such matters. She had come to work quite young, before she was married, while she was still trying to support her father. Whenever she thought of her father even now after all those years, the tears welled to her eyes. He had been a drifter, Lord knows, had always been a drifter, but she loved him. A foot-loose man who had once been a seaman, her father had taken only odd jobs. All his life, he had moved from one kind of off-beat work to another, never having more than a few cents in his pocket and spending that for drink, but he was always good-humored, kind and easygoing and a wonderful storyteller. She didn't know how any girl could have had a better, more interesting father, even if she had had to help him home many a night and put him to bed, and had had to support him as soon as she was old enough to work until he died from that terrible cough he developed the summer he spent in the quarries.

April had always enjoyed the company of men. She liked men and they liked her, but despite her sensuous beauty she was

55

asleep physically and she felt this obscurely. No one had ever really stirred her or released her, and she had these periods of yearning and crankiness that were becoming, she realized, more frequent. It worried and exasperated her. She had a pleasant disposition, though inclined to be somewhat hot-tempered. But she did not bear grudges, and she was bighearted and generous. Now she was worried about Jim Somers.

On that morning a few weeks after some of the men had left on the special assignment, it appeared to April that Jim was in really bad shape. He sat at his desk, his head bent, his eyes vacant, staring at the papers in his hands. Though dressed meticulously and carefully shaved, he had the bruised look of a man who has been up most of the night, and he seemed to be having trouble co-ordinating.

April rose from her desk and strolled toward him. When April walked, the men looked up. She had a swaying palm-treed walk and her arrogant beauty seemed to say: Look but don't touch. I am not for you.

She nodded to Saunders and Miland. Carruthers was talking to Miland and he essayed a heavy compliment. At Jim's desk, she paused.

"You didn't even say good morning to me, Jim Somers," she said. "I'm mad at you."

Somers looked up vacantly, then his eyes focused.

"Oh hello, April," he replied heavily.

"Jim," she murmured, "why don't you buy me a drink tonight and tell me your troubles."

Somers shook his head to clear it. "All right, April," he replied slowly, "I'd like to buy you a drink." His voice was courteous, but it was obvious he was making a supreme effort.

She walked slowly back.

It was funny, she was thinking about herself, but anybody who was hurt appealed to her. Why should she care about Jim Somers—nice as he was? Still it haunted her. Perhaps being with her and having a few drinks would relieve him for the moment of

56

whatever it was that was gnawing at him. His very helplessness and stupidity were a goad. She didn't want to be that way but that was the way she was. It was too bad that Hal had never reached her. She should never have married him in the first place, but she supposed she had been flattered by his good looks and his good family. The Tremaines had had quality. It was her complete loss of respect for Hal after she had supported him for two years that had killed it. And even if he had returned she would never have gone back to him. He had never awakened her either. There had been nothing there. It was not his fault really. She knew that now. He had always been a man's man, and the love he had had for her, as genuine as was possible with him, was not the sort of love a man should have for a beautiful body and a full-blooded woman. Even if she had cared much for him that way, he would never have been adequate—and that was that. That was the way it had been.

Now here she was, she was thinking, haring off after someone else who was tumbling into the darkness. What was the matter with her? And here again, Jim was not the sort of man who would interest her physically. It was the old toboggan slide, but no thrills. She shook herself. Why was she always thinking of that? It was getting to be ridiculous. She could live without that, even if she couldn't live without the company of men. It had been a long time and she supposed it would be an even longer time before she married again. Still . . .

The buzzer sounded. She picked up her pad and clicked slowly into Carlyle's office. He looked up as she entered, his smooth, cynical face controlled and quiet as usual, the gray mustache as neat and trim, but the eyes with the faint humor lines tired. He smiled at her briefly. "How are you, April?" he said.

"All right, sir," she answered and moved forward to her chair with the notebook.

When she had left, Carlyle leaned back and lit a cigarette. Randall would be in in a few minutes and he would have to go over one or two matters with him: Harwood's expense vouchers

57

—Harwood was not supposed to be on a picnic nor to be bribing his way through the Works—and something about Carruthers. But for the moment, he could sit back and relax.

Then Mr. Lowry wanted to see him at three-thirty so he'd have to go to the sixteenth floor where the lesser of the big brass resided. He rather hated the thought of having to sit there and talk to old Lowry for half an hour or so. The Old Man was so long-winded and ineffectual. Mr. Lowry had risen through merchandise and in his day may have been a crack merchandise man, but years of sitting in conferences and never having had to make a single clean-cut decision had completely sapped his power to render any decisions at all. And the burden of actually getting anything done had now largely fallen on Carlyle. Carlyle was the only person Mr. Lowry seemed to trust. He had the suspicion not uncommon in the higher brass that anyone and anything connected with public relations was *per se* unreliable, and he lived in the fear that something in the way of a news release or a piece of copy or a statement might somehow get published that would catapult the Company into chaos and bring down upon them all the wrath of the powers that be. The men under him appeared to him a particularly odd and suspect lot—all, that is, except Carlyle, whom he loved as if the younger man were his son. If the Company only had a few more men like Carlyle, it seemed to him, a man could rest easy of nights. But Mr. Lowry had the definite and distinct impression that somehow "they"—those people down on the ninth floor—were out to get him, and eventually in the end they would get him. He had been placed or found himself in a difficult, dangerous and uncomfortable spot to serve out his last two years in the Company. He would be retiring next year.

Carlyle was aware of this unreasoning fear Mr. Lowry entertained and had done his best to keep the Old Man on an even keel and still complete the most rudimentary of the public relations tasks. He was aware also that Mr. Lowry was at heart a kind and fatherly old man, but he found him nevertheless insufferably boring and he thought of the afternoon he would have to spend

58

up there with an infinite weariness. He also wondered what it was that was eating the old man at present.

But now he had a few minutes to himself, and abruptly, as it was beginning to do increasingly, that ache was with him again. He'd just have to do something about it. He couldn't bear returning home in the evenings any more, every single evening becoming more and more of a dread, more of a horror, like some ugly disease. Perhaps if he could go off by himself, he could somehow recover. Perhaps he might tell Stella he was taking a business trip and spend a few evenings—maybe a week—by himself at a hotel in town. There he could try to shake off this desolation, this entrapment, and find once more the oldtime feelings, return in spirit at least to the days when it was all fun and there was always a party and this terrible thing had not happened to him. He'd see how it was. He couldn't afford to be away from Stella too long or she would leave with her lover. He couldn't let her go but he had to see if there were anything left of his old self that he could save. Cut your losses and start fair on Monday, he thought. That was the way to do it. And he'd make the try.

Randall's thick-set figure loomed in the doorway. "Come in, Dave," Carlyle said. "Let's talk for a moment."

At twenty minutes after three, Carlyle rose and went out into the hall to the elevators. He took the elevator to the sixteenth floor. It was time for his appointment with the Old Man. He wondered again what it was the Old Man wanted. He ticked off in his mind the things that might have happened to set the Old Man on edge, but none of them seemed adequate, and he could think of nothing else that was disturbing him at the moment or that required his presence. It was odd because generally he could anticipate anything that would bring a summons from on high and every occurrence that could possibly set Mr. Lowry's nerves jangling.

The office he entered was large and richly furnished, principally in mahogany. Mr. Lowry, a wizened little figure of a man, kindly and well meaning, was bobbing and nodding his head about behind an enormous mahogany desk with a glass top. He had a cigarette in a holder in his left hand and was waving it around nervously. He was under the impression that smoking a cigarette through a holder was almost the same as not smoking. It strained out the nicotine, and the doctor had told him to cut down on his smoking. His desk was absolutely clear of papers, but a line of finicking little mementos—tiny statues of monkeys, little bulldogs and a paperweight figurine— was arranged neatly next to his inkstand and leather calendar.

"How are you, J.T.?" Carlyle asked gently. He could not help a twinge of affection for this preposterous little man, whose business it was to serve out his career in this alien and frightening field. It was his, Carlyle's, business to protect him all he could, but he wished when the Old Man was gone the Lord would have mercy and not send them another character like this.

"Come in, my boy, come in!" the Old Man cried nervously. "Glad to see you, Jeff. There are one or two things I'd like to ask you about and I have a bit of information for you I'm sure you will welcome."

Carlyle took the chair before Mr. Lowry's large desk, the one he generally sat in. Mr. Lowry was farsighted and if a person sat too near him, he could not see him clearly, and this made the Old Man nervous.

The Old Man sat back in his chair and began to wave his cigarette holder about expansively.

"You know, Jeff," he said in the tone he generally used before becoming boringly philosophical, "I sometimes wonder whether we realize what we're doing when we bandy about words and statements so freely. The power of the word, printed or spoken, is greatly underestimated by us who are . . . er . . . word practitioners. . . ." Mr. Lowry had never written a word in his life, which was a blessing, Carlyle thought. Even his letters were answered almost entirely by his very efficient, if dictatorial, secretary. But he liked to identify himself with all the material that issued from that mysterious group under him, and it was

60

almost as if he had produced with his own sweat and blood every word processed sluggishly from the department.

"I sometimes think," he went on, "that we are unaware of the great consequences that sometimes attend the working out of these statements and reports, and that perhaps we are not giving them sufficient thought."

Carlyle had heard this theme before. He shook his head.

"I think perhaps you're mistaken there, J.T.," he said softly. "Very few people pay attention to statements. There are millions of them every day and out of them all how little is there worth hearing. People know this, and they've ceased to care. People with little knowledge of our business think of printed matter as golden, each word as if chiseled in stone. But we know—we who work in these mills grinding it out—that the stuff is as common as grass and generally as unregarded. I wouldn't worry too much, J.T. If there were a little slip, no one will notice it."

"You really think so?" the Old Man asked anxiously. "I've been a trifle concerned about the statements Mizner's been giving the press about our war work. And I'm even more concerned about his taking out these newspaper people all the time and continually fraternizing with them. They may cause him, despite himself, to make statements that are unwarranted about the business or reveal information that we do not wish to have publicized."

"It's Mizner's business to take out newspaper people and to fraternize with them, J.T.," Carlyle replied. "You know that. As news manager, he must be acquainted with all the responsible members of the press, and he is. And an old hand like Mizner would never be betrayed into giving out any information that he did not wish to give. Mizner knows all the ropes. But more important for us and for the firm: he knows the right editors and he is trusted by the press. I don't think you need worry about Mizner. I am scarcely familiar with that end of the business myself, but Mizner's been in it a long time and I think he's doing a good job."

61

"I'm glad to hear you say that, Jeff," the Old Man answered. "I was just getting a little worried."

And now the Old Man started shifting around in his chair and a pleased expression flitted over his features. He was finally approaching the reason for his summons.

"Jeff," he said, "I have a piece of intelligence to give you that I must give you in the strictest confidence. I am telling you now not only because I wish to reserve that pleasure for myself, but also because it seems only fair that you should have some warning. It is not the Company's policy to tell anybody anything. You know that as well as I, and that's another reason I wish you not to permit any of this piece of news to slip out until such time as the Company makes the formal announcement. That will be some seven months from now. . . ."

Carlyle leaned back. He was curious but at the same time bored. It did not appear to him likely that any piece of news the Company was holding in reserve was of a particularly startling nature.

Mr. Lowry waved his cigarette. "As you know, I am retiring in eight months, and there has been for some time in the wind discussion of my successor. I can tell you, as Mr. Wygand informed me in confidence, that eight people were considered. Among them, as you may have suspected, was your name. The others—it doesn't matter. However, they were important men with high ranks. I am happy to inform you that a week ago you were the one who was chosen. The official announcement will be seven months from now—a month before my retirement. . . ."

Carlyle sat quietly in the silence that fell. He didn't believe it possible but they had managed to surprise him. He thought they'd had his number long before, that his career had reached its apogee. It seemed to him that where he was concerned, somehow they had had an infinite tolerance. He could scarcely believe it, but there it was. The Old Man was beaming at him. Carlyle roused himself.

"Why . . . why, Mr. Lowry," he said. "Why, I . . . I must

62

say I'm surprised. And of course honored. I . . . I'm afraid I didn't expect this. . . ."

"I can't tell you how delighted I am, Jeff," the Old Man said. "You'll be one of the youngest division heads in the Company —and one of the most trusted. You'll go far, Jeff. I've always said so and I say so now. You'll go far. You're the kind of man the Company can trust. They all feel that way—right up to the very top. Yes sir, right up to the top. Tomorrow, Mr. Wygand would like you to step up to his office. He has allowed me the privilege of telling you first, but when you hear it from him, it will be official, though of course nothing must be said about it until the Company is ready to make the announcement. . . . Well, that's what I wanted to see you about, Jeff— a piece of rare news, what?"

7

IN TIMES AFTER, Martin remembered he had liked to talk about those five months of fury and fatigue on that war production assignment. He would say casually they had been his baptism of fire and secretly he felt they had given him some quality that only those who had lived through the desperate tiredness of that home-front cataclysm could ever know or understand.

It was perhaps because he took the project seriously and did try to live to the depth of it that it became a soul-searing experience and hardened him as well as broadened his concepts of people and of the world.

The first of the minor trials arose in the transportation. The train was late and slow. Plane seats were only for the important, and everything was dirty and rundown. For this was the full cry and center of the war as it was waged at home. This was how it looked. He began to notice too the turmoil, the seething —not only the uniformed men in stations, bus terminals and airports, but the men with brief cases, the middle-aged men already showing the signs of fatigue and heart strain, the men who had to live out of suitcases.

Then there they were, moving slowly into Chicago, and it was a gray, dirty afternoon, the soot-streaked snow drifting tiredly down. The train was five hours late. At the station there appeared to be no cabs free. He felt himself drifting aimlessly in a world that had speeded up too fast. The big town was noisy and dirty and brawling, and at the same time worn-out looking and unkempt. No hotel rooms. No nothing. Sorry. They knew he'd wired ahead and they'd confirmed it, but well, sorry, it's the war. It's the war. It's the war. He lugged the suitcase along. Then he called the plant.

Mr. Cassidy was not in the office at the moment, they told him. Oh, it's Brill—well they had finally found him a hotel room for a couple of nights. Then he'd have to move on. But perhaps they'd be able to find him another by that time. And Mr. Cassidy would expect him in the morning. Would he take down the hotel address. Sorry they couldn't send a car for him, but everything tied up now, you know. It was the war.

So he unpacked in the gloomy, bare hotel room. This was to be the best hotel room he lived in during the whole five months of his strange, nightmarish sojourn in that roaring town.

As the cab approached the outskirts of the city, the towers of the Works loomed up ahead. "Yes," the cabby said, "that's it. Some place, eh?" The buildings were long and low like those of the other works but clearly much vaster and more sprawling. This was truly a city in itself. Its landmarks were the huge stacks of the powerhouse and the giant water tower. At the iron gates stood guardhouses, and as they approached, the armed guards were there waiting. He climbed out. He felt suddenly alone and lost in this tense and formidable city.

Cassidy was a short, stocky, grizzled man, graying and balding, with an ill-fitting upper plate. They called him Pop. He was an

64

old production man and had been made plant public relations manager because the management of the Works trusted him and felt he spoke their language. Oddly enough, he was a good plant public relations manager and an intelligent man. His intelligence was sufficiently buried under layers of gruffness and sufficiently disguised by Works shop language so that it did not offend his superiors. But he was aware of the implications of his job and under him the vast civic relations program—one involving a city in itself on the outskirts of a big, corrupt town on which more than two million dollars a year was spent by the Works in tribute, taxes and various official payments. The Works was a landmark in that community. It had existed there for half a century, and it was known far and wide even in that vast population center, and its needs were of concern to the local government.

Cassidy knew how to talk to these people and how to deal with newspapermen, civic organizations, charities and the thousand and one private groups whose interests impinged on that of the great Works he served. Though nominally reporting to the director of public relations back at headquarters, actually Cassidy, as in the case of all the plant public relations managers and commercial men, in effect operated under the rule of the Works manager, who in each plant was a little king in his own right.

Martin sat in Cassidy's large, airy office, from which the faint rumble of the great plant could always be heard, although the offices were in six or seven buildings across a wide, grassy area separated from the first groups of manufacturing locations. The snow had dwindled to a dirty drizzle and the skies were still overcast. He had a deep sense of dejection as he waited, and the moments seemed to pile up.

Abruptly there was a flurry and then Cassidy strode in, a short, impressive, bustling man with a chewed-up cigar in his mouth. Behind him strode two of his henchmen.

"Well, well, well, young man," Pop said pleasantly, "so you finally got here! About time. Sit down, sit down! Things are all screwed up as usual. Glad to have you with us—that is, in a

65

pig's eye! But we'll make out! We'll make out all right! Say
Cox," Pop addressed the tall, pale young man—one of the two
who were always at his beck and call. The other, a hearty,
bulbous-nosed man of indeterminate age, was named Ike Sillman.
He and Cox made up the retinue which the people of the plant
called "Pop's bodyguard." "Say, Cox," Pop said gruffly, "see if
you can't rig up some kind of lunch in the office in an hour or
so. I've got these press reports to go over, and Brill here will
want something too. We can talk while we're eating, if you don't
mind. Also, Ike, get up some more ads for men for the new
line in the special devices section. Make 'em good. Anyone
that can breathe—we'll use 'em, as long as they can get here.
They're crying for people down there again. . . .

"Now, my boy—" Pop turned to Martin and leaned back—
"let's see what we can do for you and see if we can't get squared
away here somehow. . . ."

Martin felt those quizzical, appraising eyes on him while
he was talking. What he was saying about the project, about
what he hoped to accomplish and would try to accomplish
seemed abruptly childish and immature under the older man's hard
gaze. It also sounded idealistic and unreal. Worst of all, it
sounded irrelevant to the work they were doing. But, by God,
that's what he'd come out there to do and he'd spell it out the
best he could. Cassidy listened to the end. Then he sat and looked
at Martin.

"Well, for the love of Jesus," he said at last in a low voice,
"what won't you boys back in the ivory tower think of next?
Martin, my boy," he began slowly, "far be it for me—an old,
hard-bitten, money-grubbing production man—to break into the
golden dreams of our heroic war effort you boys may have
visualized back there. But you're in for a shock when you get a
taste of the reality. If anybody but Carlyle had tried such a
project, I'd have said the hell with it, but somehow you can't
beat the big boss—that guy always knows what he's doing. Well,
it looks as if the first part of your job will be to tramp about a

66

thousand miles at all shifts at all hours under all kinds of conditions, and that's about the size of it.

"That part of it alone will take you about three or four weeks —just getting through the place and talking to some of the boys. As for going on a production line for a week or so—well, we'll see later. I suppose I can arrange it somehow. . . .

"But it's what you boys seem to think our war effort is like here that's going to shock you. Wait till you see the men we have on the lines now. They're not the noble workmen you boys may think of back in the dream factory in New York. These boys—a lot of 'em—are bums. They look like bums and they are bums. We need men . . . we need 'em so badly we've picked 'em up off the streets and out of the alleys—guys that have scarcely done a day's work in their lives before, wild-eyed drunks and others. We don't care any more. We just need men. . . . And then, worst of all, unless you like 'em—and I don't, never have—we've got women—thousands of 'em. They've teetered in out of the homes and even out of the whorehouses and gone to work. And I hate to say it, but they're better than men, most of the time—work better, stand up better, are more careful. But wait'll you see 'em. They outnumber the men three to one now. They're everywhere—and they're probably here to stay. The place is a shambles—and it's not just here—it's all over the country. Every plant is picking up these armies of ragged men, 4–F's, psychos and God knows what else, and bringing 'em on the lines, and they're all hiring women—women by the thousands —and these women—you mark my words—they're here to stay. The war has done it all. So your noble workman is a woman or a bum, and they're making money hand over fist.

"Oh hell, boy, I'm not saying they aren't doing the job. That's the damn part of it—they're doing the job and doing it faster and turning more out than has ever been turned out before. Our rejects are piling up; our safety rules have gone to hell; our turnover is terrible; and the waste, the inefficiency, by any of the old measures is beyond the imagination. The waste—my

67

God in heaven!—it's all over the land—waste, waste, waste. . . . The watchword nowadays is *Get it out*. The hell with the cost. Get it out—and that's what these bastards are doing—and doing it pretty good too. I don't know, boy, what you think you'll find—" Cassidy passed his hand tiredly over his rumpled face —"but there *is* a damn story, and if anything, it's the story of how a bunch of ragged, untrained riffraff and a lot of women turned out the greatest production of materials in the history of the world. . . . Damn it, I don't know exactly what the story is or how it came about. It's still a mystery to me. Of course, a lot of the story lies in what the production engineers have done. But I wouldn't have believed it a few years ago, if someone had told me this gang here could turn it out the way they're doing! I wouldn't have believed it—these bums, and young girls —kids, some of them—and middle-aged women right out of the kitchen— Good God! And not all of 'em all they should be. Let me tell you what happened to a friend of mine—Skip Harris— in the Eastern Works—he's a production foreman there . . . This boring you, boy?" Cassidy broke in.

"No, no, this is what I want," Martin said. "This is my story. . . ."

"All right, son. Well, Skip—he's a production foreman in the Works in Delaware, and there he was one day breaking down some blueprints over a warehouse grating when he happened to look through the grating into the warehouse below. Well, there she lay down there in the storage room, behind some bales, with a line of ten men waiting at the break, and flat on her back with the first one. At four dollars a throw—and Skip had a ringside seat at the whole proceedings. She managed four of 'em in fifteen minutes and then the break was over. Hell, Skip is all for enterprise, free or otherwise, as I am, but that was too much for him. And she was working on a screw machine too, pretty as you please, and damn appropriate, considering. Well, as Skip told me later, he had to give her time even though they needed her bad. And God knows how many more there were and are even still working that kind of shift. . . . Yes, boy, we have

68

'em too. . . . The camp followers of war have moved in on us, into the plants. And the drinkers and the riffraff. But they're turning it out. We've got 'em all—the bad wives, the fun-lovers, the tired and the sick . . . three shifts, twenty-four hours, seven days a week. . . . They're really turning it out. . . ."

Cassidy had not exaggerated when he said they would be tramping a thousand miles. By the end of the second week, Martin had blisters on his feet and was so tired from the noise and movement the days were beginning to merge into a mist of machines—planing machines, milling machines, punch presses, extrusion presses, conveyor lines, assembly lines—a continuous, roaring, pounding bedlam that seemed never to let up, never to cease.

And the hotel rooms. He would be able to stay only one or two days, then another cheaper, more run-down place for two or three days, until finally, after three weeks of this, he found a room in a fleabag in Cicero where they would let him stay a week at a time, from week to week. The hotel was in a sinister neighborhood, and across from his room a cerise neon sign advertising Tony's Bar flashed on and off all night long. A bowling alley nearby diagonally across the street was running full blast every evening, and he could hear the clash of the pins as the balls struck far into the swing shift.

And now the long night shifts began. . . .

Gradually he grew to recognize the people who worked around him as more than the nameless faces, gray with fatigue, that were everywhere. It was true: they were making money hand over fist on the lines, but the pace was beginning to tell—the tiredness, the running down, and that ragged crew Cassidy had spoken of was certainly with them. But they were turning it out, turning it out.

And at night, he'd stop at the all-night diners and have coffee with one or another of them. They talked . . . the special language of men growing tired and irritable and wanting something different, the constant grumbling and subterranean complaining.

Sometimes, walking toward the hotel at three in the morning along the dirty streets, he wondered whether this was to be the story of the way the war was fought after all, whether this was the truth of it all—dirty, tired men who hated every step of the way, who had lost their early spark, who had grown sick of trying to beat production schedules, of competing with other production lines, as they used to when the war was young, even of chalking wisecracks on the stuff as it went out, and talking it back and forth about how the war was progressing and what the stuff they were making would do for it . . . men who had lost their sense of humor and were suffering from overtime nerves. . . . "Christ, the war—a man gets sick of it! We've ate it and slept it and lived it twenty-four hours a day, and we're through with it. . . . It's for the birds . . . and those sonsabitches in Washington are lettin' the boys get killed—for what? They don't seem to know what the hell they're doin' anywhere, and oh hell . . . You just wait—I'm goin' fishin' one of these days soon—you just wait. . . ."

But they kept turning the stuff out.

And now Martin's own fatigue made him less responsive and more exasperated, less interested in what was going on. He'd lived it and Christ, he'd be glad to get back. The noise of the machines was always with him. . . . He couldn't get rid of it. It seemed to be a permanent part of his background—that low, constant roar of the Works like an underground accompaniment, a dreary music that no matter how fast he walked or where he went he could not escape. It seemed to keep time, a certain odd and ugly rhythm, haunting him. When he closed his eyes at night, there it would be—the thump-thump and whir—the machines and those low, growling, complaining voices—all become a part of his dirty pounding existence. The messy hotel room, the unmade bed—he was sick of it all. The lousy food . . . And he noticed in the line one woman—attractive, in her late thirties—always watching him. She was well built, even exciting, and he could feel her eyes on him as he passed—the famished look.

70

"You like a nice home-cooked meal?" she asked him one night as the shifts were changing. And that helped. He walked back from her boardinghouse in the small hours and it had been good —about the only good thing he'd had, even the sweaty body, the full lips, the hunger were good, the best he'd had there. But beyond it, nothing . . . nothing . . . If it would only end somehow and he could get back. He couldn't even see any more to finish the reports, the notes. He'd had it—there just wasn't any more and why in hell didn't they let him come back. . . .

It had been fine to know they liked what he'd sent them, they'd liked his stuff. But what did they think he was? A machine? When he'd taken the damn job, he hadn't contracted to work in a noisy, grinding plant and to talk to these damn, dirty, complaining men on the assembly lines, making twice as much as he was. He'd had enough. He was through. They could find themselves another boy. Well, it wouldn't be long now anyhow. As soon as this stinking stretch was finished, he'd be leaving and breaking away. He had known this wasn't for him from the start, even in the offices. It had begun as temporary, and by God it was going to remain temporary. And there wasn't going to be the likes of him sweating under the pressures of this ominous place. For the Company, as it looked from here, was terrifying —an empire of machinery, of noise, of power, of tired men and disheartened, grubbing assembly-line people—a complex of little kingdoms all over the land where little men—he'd never even seen the Works manager here—toiled in the depths of some roaring miasma of neon lights and machines. If this was it, they could have it. He'd had all he wanted, all he'd ever want.

And so he went home to bed.

It was true he had not been able to read his Tacitus or listen to good music or do any of the things he had hoped to have time to do when he first came out here. It had been too much. The vortex had engulfed him, and the squalor and the intensity of what was transpiring around him had made all these preoccupations that had been so much a part of his life seem irrelevant. And this also was another indication to him that he was not the

71

man he had thought himself to be. Another person with his background would not have been so completely swamped by his environment, would have been able to pick up Martial at six in the morning and forget the dreary routines of the day or listen to Sibelius and have the grimy hours washed away. This also worried him. He was such a failure, among other failures as human beings. And not even a special kind of failure like those who have undertaken great ventures and been defeated. He could not find anything to try, nothing but this dreary assignment and the long shapeless days and nights blurring one into another.

So as he ran down, his views of every phase of his living ran down with him. He was beginning to assume the coloration of his surroundings, to be influenced by the grimy routines, the coarse language, the continual complaining, and his own language was becoming coarse, his own values slipping slowly, slowly into the gutters of their weariness.

It was at this stage, at the lowest ebb of his existence after five months of weariness and a seemingly never-ending stretch of the plant's pounding, wasting noise and messy, gnawing routines, that the telephone call finally came.

8

STELLA WAS SITTING in her slip at the boudoir table, looking at herself in the mirror and combing her beautiful jet-black hair. She couldn't stop yawning. She had been up late the night before and was tired.

Carlyle riffled the bills in his hand.

On the bed lay her new sequin dress.

"Stella," Carlyle said slowly, "I hate to bring it up, but don't you have enough clothes at least for this month? Here's another sheaf of bills . . . , I'm beginning to get a little worried."

72

She looked around at him in surprise. She yawned again.

"What's the matter, Jeff? Are you broke?"

"Well, not exactly—" he hesitated—"but, honey, you're so extravagant. I . . . I . . . well, let's forget it."

She was irritated. "Good God, Jeff, you're not going to start fussing and getting stuffy about money after all these years, are you!" she said. "We've always been broke that way."

He threw the bills on the bed.

"No, of course not," he answered softly. "It's just that we've always lived like millionaires and—well, it's beginning to catch up with me. But actually, I guess it'll be all right," he continued. "They . . . they've given me a promotion at the office. That should help."

She yawned. "How much?" she asked.

"What do you mean how much?" he said.

"I mean what's your salary now?"

He sighed. "We didn't discuss salary, Stella. I suppose it'll be quite a substantial increase. But that's not for two more months. Anyhow, I . . . I'm sorry I brought up the bills. I don't know what's wrong with me. Everything's getting me down. . . ."

"I should think so," she replied indifferently. "I just saw a little fur piece I really must have, Jeff, and I hope you're not going to grumble about the price. . . ."

He turned away wearily.

"Stella," he said, "I have to make a trip for the Company. I'm going to New Orleans for a week or ten days."

He had searched his mind for the name of a city that possessed glamor, feeling obscurely that it might arouse her interest. If she wanted to go with him, that could be arranged. He would undertake such a trip after all.

She twisted her magnificent body about on the low boudoir seat.

"When are you going?" she asked, stretching. She was terribly sleepy.

73

"Next week," he said.

She searched among the litter on her boudoir table for her lipstick.

"Will . . . will . . ." he knew he should not say it. He tried to shut his lips on the words, but they came anyhow. "Will you try not to do anything foolish?" he said softly.

"I always do foolish things," she replied.

"You . . . you know what I mean, dear," he continued. "Please, Stella, won't you miss me just a little?" He tried to make it sound light. His voice betrayed him.

She turned to him suddenly full face—the beautiful chiseled features, the Madonna loveliness, the perfectly formed sensual lips a little parted.

"No, I won't miss you, Jeff," she said quietly. "You can come or go as you please. Let's face it now once for all. I've always been honest with you, and I don't want you starting all over on these things again. I won't miss you, Jeff, and I intend to do a lot of foolish things. Now let's not talk about it any more."

He turned and walked slowly over to the bed and sat down. He felt as if he had been struck in the pit of the stomach. His hands were trembling. All right, he thought, I asked for it.

He could hear the swish of her negligee as she rose. "Will you be here when I get back?" he asked.

"I don't know," she answered. "I may be here when you get back and I may not. I'll be here just as long as I want to be here and I'll leave here just as soon as I want to leave. I don't know when that will be but it will be when I want it to be. I can't make it any clearer than that, can I?"

"No," he answered softly, "you can't make it any clearer than that."

So now it had come at last. Now it was out in the open and there could be no subterfuges, no evasions, no escaping it. It was what he had most dreaded. It was the eventuality he had tried to avoid at all costs. But he had been helpless. There was nothing he could have done. He'd known that all along. When the chips were down, he could not pay. He was licked. This miserable, sordid love had stolen from him his resources and love of life, his manhood and his integrity. There was nothing left for him unless he could somehow salvage a small part of it. If he could not redeem even a little of the old-time sparkle, it was really all over with him. And this was something he could not face.

He rose slowly and walked into the living room and sat down in one of the low modern easy chairs. It did not matter now what he said or did. And he knew it. Stella had him. She had him right down to the end of the line, and she could get off whenever she wished. It didn't matter what he thought or how badly it hurt or how many nights he'd lain there and ached for her and for his lost self and for all this terrible, burning passion. It didn't matter about the years they had been together, about the times they had had, about the days when he had been the mogul and she the dancing girl. All that was gone, gone with the pleasures and the twenty thousand years of fun they'd crammed into their short time together. Yes, all of it was vanished and nothing he could say or do would ever bring it back. She had had no heart when he found her—and that was the way he had wanted her— and she had no heart now. What was the use of playing it and playing it again, when there could never be any more music for him?

And so she had finally called him and he had had to lay his cards on the table for all to see. They were plain to see, all right, and he had had nothing. But now that they were plain to see, now that it was all out in the clear, he had but one recourse. He would have to leave for the week. He would have to make the effort to recapture some essence from his existence. It was either-or. He could not bluff it any more. And he could not go on if he were not a man.

He could hear Stella dressing in the bedroom, the swish of her gown. Tired as she was, she was going out again.

*   *   *

75

Toward the end, at the office, it had been impossible to keep the news of Carlyle's impending appointment as director of public relations entirely a secret. No announcement had yet been made, nor was the official one contemplated until a month before Mr. Lowry's retirement. No one actually said anything. But somehow more and more Carlyle found himself the center of attention, the recipient of sudden friendly handshakes, a greeting in the lobby by one of the vice presidents whom he scarcely knew, veiled hints from equals who wanted to indicate that they had inside information, and a flurry of interest by men who ordinarily would not have had business to transact with him. And obviously in that great whispering gallery that was the general organization the word had gone around. No one had said anything, but it was plain that everyone knew.

He noticed now that his slightest remark had assumed importance, and his casual conversation had almost imperceptibly taken on the proportions of pronouncements. Worst of all, Mr. Lowry had insisted that he attend the luncheons at the Executives' Club and his name had been put up for membership. And finally he found himself deluged with outside invitations to lunches and dinners into which he was not inclined for any reasons whatsoever to permit himself to be dragged.

All of these signs of his approaching power annoyed Carlyle, although he was aware they were part of the trappings of the office he was to assume. His ambitions, however, did not lie in those directions and they never had. He had never even sought preferment in the career which he had chosen. The satisfactions he derived from his work lay on other levels and in different parts of that existence. It was obvious, as he found to his dismay, that he was fully sensitive to the responsibilities that went with the power that had come to him. Indeed, it irked him that he was so constituted that he could not shake off the sense of responsibility. It was quite possible for him to delegate power to others, and Carlyle was in no sense a detail man, but even after he had effected his assignments he felt a concern in the success with which those to whom he had given the assignments completed them, and he could not disassociate himself from the failures of subordinates.

All of these disadvantages in the preferments that his years with the Company had brought weighed on him. He had been happiest in the old days, he knew, when he had had few of these responsibilities, had indeed been only another of the Company's men on expense account and on an interesting job. Those had really been the days! Those had been the golden times! Now they were gone, gone for good. Yes, those aspects of life had been the parts he had lived for—the fun he had loved so deeply, the excitement he had craved, the beautiful girls—they had been what had made up life for him, and with all their wildness and irresponsibility they had given existence more zest and more meaning than it had had for him now for a long time.

Yes, he thought, I'm just a good-time man at heart really. I'm just the boy who would show them how to do it! It's strange they never knew me after all, or they would never have trusted me. They'd never have given me this power up the years. I never tried to hide it, but somehow they ignored it. A dozen times I knew I was through, and each time they overlooked it and brought me on. Why was it? What was there that the Company wanted of me to keep me so long so well?

Yes, he thought again, as he had thought of himself so often, he was the good-time man. He was the boy who was going to burn down the village, who was going to run the fire trucks through town. He was the fellow who was traveling from boyhood to scaffold and loving every minute of the way. It was to be nothing but the best and the world well lost. It was the red, red rose and no price too high. And the coffee in the morning to be black as hell, strong as death and sweet as love.

Oh well, he thought, he hadn't found everything. You can never have everything. But somehow they'd kept him. He didn't know why. He'd never understand why. And somehow all of them, even the Company, had finally got him. Somewhere along the road he'd gone astray. He'd lost the good times. He'd missed the red, red rose. He'd taken the wrong turn and it had vanished,

77

disappeared. He'd had the power and he'd had the honors, but there'd been a Stella, one of a long line of them—and not much different for all her beauty—but she'd been enough to do it.

Now, preferments were all right and so were honors and power but they were not what he had lived for. And to have others depend on him like this, depend on him for something so important, so precious as their livelihood, was a terrible burden. It was not as it should be. A man who'd played it for the laughs, who cared only for the big night out. They should have pulled the card on him long ago.

So now he would have to make that one last try to find it all again, to recover the sparkle, the zest, the red, red rose. The last throw for him on the tables of life . . .

The office was quiet for a moment. He buzzed April and asked her not to allow him to be disturbed. Then he leaned over and lifted the receiver. It was almost four-thirty and this was Thursday. This would be his fourth night on the town. The first three had been marvelous—a release such as he'd not experienced for a long, long time.

The first three nights he had spent alone. He'd taken the suite at the hotel and gone to a show. Then he'd sipped a drink at one of the night spots he used to frequent in years gone by. The big town at night was wonderful, wonderful. For three nights he had not even thought of Stella. It had been as if a crushing weight had been lifted from him, as if all the squeezing, iron sadness had suddenly been removed from his heart and lungs and brain and he could breathe again. It was almost as if he were his old self once more. And now he would try the old loves. He would see perhaps if any of the girls he had once known were still around and still available. He would see now whether that might quench the old ache for good and completely free him. That, if anything, should do it. For it isn't the one—it's the all of them that count. It isn't the single person, it's them! They were all the same, really, and one was just like another in the fundamentals, in anything that was important—the long silken limbs, the full lips, the soft arms. What did it matter whose they were, as long as they were there? That was the essential thing. When he'd been younger, he'd had so many he'd hardly even known some of their names. He'd finally come to call them all Sugar or Honey and they were good names for them. Yes, there'd been lots of Sugars and Honeys and they'd been, as they should be, in all the important aspects, essentially the same. It was not that he disdained them or derogated these beauties. On the contrary, they were it. That was the way a woman should be. They were the heart of the matter. They were, in a way, the very meaning of life. They were the thrills and the desire and the big time, and what else in the world was so important, so wonderful?

No, he didn't look down on them in any respect. He didn't feel they were the lesser of life's magnificences; he felt they were the greater, the more important, the flower of the long years existence had worked to create something beautiful. They were it, all right. They were the full and perfect expression of all life's splendors. He loved them. The old sex factory but beautiful, beautiful! To have made them into individual girls—individualized into their own limited, neurotic personalities, so banal, so commonplace—would have been criminal. Abstracted in her beauty, the sex machine with her gorgeous hair and lovely eyes was it, was everything; the girl herself, as she really was, with her narrow uncultivated mind, her petty money hunger, her spitefulness and meannness, was nothing, nothing. A man could not waste two seconds of his time on the girl herself as she was, but as the love goddess, how many magnificent hours, how many days and years could he not while away with all that loveliness?

So tonight he would try once more after all this time several of the girls he remembered from short years ago. Perhaps one of them would be free. Perhaps one of them would remember him and remember what he had been like after all these years. At any rate, here goes.

He dialed a number slowly. The phone on the other end rang several times and he had about decided there would be no answer and he had better hang up and try another, when the

79

receiver was picked up and he heard the soft Southern voice on the other end of the line.

"This is Jeff Carlyle, Jacqueline," he said. "Remember me?"

Over the line came the intake of breath and the surprise.

"Why Mr. Carlyle," the girl said. "Of course, I remember you—Atlantic City. Why Mr. Carlyle, how are you? Where have you been?"

She had a lovely soft voice. At least she hadn't lost that, he thought. She was a tall redhead, as he remembered her, with beautiful dead-white skin.

"Yes—Atlantic City," Carlyle said. "I still think you should have won, Jacqueline."

"Oh Mr. Carlyle, you say the nicest things!"

"What have you been doing, Jacqueline?" Carlyle asked. "Are you married?"

"I was for a while, Mr. Carlyle—" the voice flowed over the phone sweetly, though a trifle petulant—"but I'm not now. He was a louse. He lost his job!"

"I see," Carlyle said. "Well, Jackie, would you care to have dinner with me tonight and see the town? I'm over in a suite at this hotel, and I have a free evening just to spend with you."

"Oh Mr. Carlyle," she said softly, "that would be just lovely."

"All right," he concluded. "Suppose you meet me in Suite 1109C, say about seven? And Jackie, take a taxi over, will you? And if you find you're a little short, perhaps I can let you have something to tide you over."

"Oh thank you, Mr. Carlyle. I'll be seeing you."

Carlyle replaced the receiver. The first try. Strange that they should still remember him. Well, so much for the list and for them all. He hoped Jacqueline was as lovely as she had been when he knew her. He hoped she would be lovely and long-limbed and beautiful, as he remembered her, forever. And he hoped he'd want it, too, when he finally got it. That was the crux of the matter. He hoped he'd want her and all she stood for when he had her. That would be the question. That was what would tell when the time came.

80

At the moment, however, he was seized by a sense of well-being, of euphoria, a gladness he had not experienced for years. It would all go better from now on, he thought. It would all be different after this. The ancient succubus would be torn away, the old ache and sadness dissolved. He would be a free man after tonight. He would be his old self, and he could tell them all—all of those who had trapped him—Stella and her lover, the loneliness, the heartsickness, the grind and routines—he could shuffle them all off again and be once more out of bondage, carefree, without concern. The free man—that was what he wanted to be. The good-time man he had once been.

He looked at his watch. It said five o'clock.

He took his time dressing.

The radio was playing a soft and languorous melody. He put the Scotch highball on the low end table in the bedroom and leaning over toward the large mirror began to tie his tie. The sense of well-being that had been with him since the beginning of the week was heightened as he trimmed his gray mustache. Yes, at last he was beginning to feel like his old self.

The whole mood of his former evenings was returning. Here he was in this luxurious suite—dove gray with coral curtains, flame valances, ivory furniture, the huge mirrors and soft, deep pile rug—the throb of the big town, its diamond lights twinkling far below, a wonderful sight from the large windows, and he waiting for a beautiful girl. Yes, that had been the old-time evenings all right. It reminded him of other evenings in other hotel rooms on expense accounts in the old days. That had been the way he liked it. A hotel was home to him—he wanted the service, the luxury, everything, none of the petty and irritating details of life to annoy one. And waiting for someone beautiful.

There was the time he had taken that ballet dancer to a hotel in San Francisco—a cute little thing, so pretty and so graceful. But all she had talked about was cooking. She loved to cook. And right in the middle of everything, she had asked him if he didn't love bouillabaisse. And there was that soppy Southern girl—a magnificent creature really—he had taken out in New Orleans. They had spent the evening gambling outside the city in the Parish and he had won as he always did but po' little old she was always losing, always jus' fresh out of every littl' thing, and those delicious gin alexanders—a drink fit for the gods—hadn't helped her po' little ol' judgment either. So in the end it had cost him a pretty penny at the Beverly Club.

Then they'd meandered back to his suite and in the bedroom they'd gambled for love—she lipsticking numbers on the lovely old-fashioned fan above the big luxurious bed and marking an arrow on the ceiling (he'd stood on the bed and lifted her so that she could reach it), and when they'd switch on the fan he'd call out a number, and if it stopped at the arrow, one more piece of her clothing fell to the floor. It had been fun, even drunk as she was and with that irritating sweet magnolia drawl.

And then, of course, there had been Stella—a beautiful, a magnificent girl of twenty-two at that time—and their having to sneak off to that place in Philadelphia so that his current wife would not cause a scene. And had Stella loved it? He could say she had. Always willing enough then. And the sweet words, as abandoned then and as honest in the fullness of their passion as her hard coldness was now. Yes, she'd been a bad girl, even though he could not say he'd done anything to dissuade her. It had been she who pleaded with him the very first time. He would not have asked her in the normal course of their acquaintanceship. She had been the girl of one of his friends—engaged in fact—but all that had gone by the board when she first saw him.

Stella was a girl who had known what she wanted and made no bones about it. And he had been what she wanted, and she had told him so plainly, without pretense, without subterfuge. Almost the very words of her whisper returned, the little line she quoted, perhaps given her from Shakespeare by some forgotten lover—"Love sought is sweet," she had said so low only he could hear, "but given unsought is sweeter far. . . ."

And so it had been in dozens of nameless hotels and motor courts and furnished rooms and other unsavory places, she completely his, agreeing to any price he wished her to pay, to any terms, as long as she could be with him—all of her passion unreserved, unpretending, just for the short stolen hours, just for the smile he might flash her or the pat on the arm. And her humble joking remark in the mornings of their terrible hangovers: "A cup of coffee and a few kind words are all I want from you, sweet man—and just to be with you forever and ever. . . ."

So now the forever and ever was those few short years and they were gone and the kind words were over and done with and the coffee had grown cold, and she now had nothing for him at all but the cold stare and the hatred and that old fire for some other man. Well, he knew how it must have been for his friend now. And he knew how the dead must feel who have no mourners at the wake.

There was a soft knock on the door, then two little rings on the buzzer.

He left his jacket on the bed and walked into the drawing room. He had meant to leave the front door partly open. When he pulled it wide, there she stood in the soft light of the rich hall in all her glory, as dazzling as he had hoped.

Jacqueline had been a show girl, winner of several beauty contests and a model, and she knew how to wear clothes. She was a tall, full-figured girl, almost Junoesque in her proportions, with magnificent red hair and a dazzling white skin. Her eyes were gray, wide and guileless with luxurious long lashes and her lips full and perfectly shaped. She smiled the slow, practiced smile of a girl who is fully aware of the effect she has on men. She was no intellectual, but she was something far greater, Carlyle was thinking: she was beautiful.

"My dear," he said, "you leave me speechless. You're even more ravishing than when I saw you last."

Carlyle was able to toss off these compliments scarcely moving his lips.

"Oh Mr. Carlyle," she said, "you do say the nicest things!"

Her vocabulary appeared limited, Carlyle thought unkindly.

83

It was obvious she reserved that one phrase to deal with all compliments.

"Come in, my dear," Carlyle said. "I am just finishing dressing and I have ordered you a martini."

"Thank you, Mr. Carlyle," she said. "You look good to me yourself." She clicked regally into the suite like a queen entering the throne room.

Carlyle poured her a martini from the iced shaker on the low table.

They pretty well covered the circuit before it began to dawn on him. At Maynard's they had three drinks called Suffering Bastards which Tolly, the bartender, told them was British Egypt's favorite drink. They took a cab to Le Bel Coq and had pressed duck and marmalade and a bottle of sparkling wine. They watched the show at Toby's and sipped highballs, and Jacqueline told him her life story over again.

The man she had married, it seems, had implied that he was a big contractor, but it turned out that he was a construction foreman, and even that job fell through when he had trouble with the union. He was a louse, Jacqueline repeated. Carlyle was morose. God has forgotten us all, he thought sadly.

Wherever they went, Jacqueline's regal entrance caused a murmur in the crowd. She was spectacular and became more so the drunker she grew. Carlyle did his best to drown the slow terrifying realization growing on him. The world receded slightly in the fog of liquor, but he could not rid himself of it. It kept rising through the mists and he would try to turn his mind off. He struggled to wash it away again and again with the liquor and the talk.

"I can't see how men could deceive a girl like you, Jacqueline," he said, as they sat at another small, white-clothed table in another smoky, noisy club. "A man would have to have no heart at all to lie to you. But that's the way it is. The world's growing more like Celine's version of it. You may not know Celine, but he said: 'The greatest defeat is to forget and above all to forget what it is that has smashed you,' and he also said, 'We must tell the whole thing, without altering one word—everything we have seen of man's viciousness and then it will be over and time to go. . . .' "

"Mr. Carlyle," Jacqueline said, and she turned her large, now blurred, guileless eyes on him. Her voice was distant. "Mr. Carlyle," she said, "you do say the creamiest things."

"And you, Jacqueline, how I admire your barbed wit. But don't ever change. Stay as beautiful as you are—even to all eternity. Beauty is truth, truth beauty—this I know . . . the hell with it, Jacqueline. Do you ever read?"

"Of course, I read," she answered, turning to him with her lovely, vacant stare. "The chintzy thing is I can never remember what I read. . . ."

"Well, don't worry about it, Jacqueline. Fade my four, for the Lord's sake, as one of the boys used to say. Tell me about you and that Esther Tanninger again. She sounds to me like an A-Number-One, first-class bitch."

"Oh Mr. Carlyle," Jacqueline said. "I come into the apartment and on into the bedroom—she was my roommate then—and there she was lying in my bed with him—with Mr. Bagenolle, as bold as you please! And Mr. Bagenolle had come all the way from Pittsburgh just to see me and give me that bracelet he promised. And I'd kept him off purposely—not allowing him to get fresh or even so much as a kiss because I knew he'd want to marry me after a while and a girl has to think of the years ahead. So there was my girl friend, Esther Tanninger, that said there wasn't anything she wouldn't do for me and that I helped get into the Dell Club lying there—and in my bed too—maybe she was afraid she'd get her own dirty—with that fat, ugly Mr. Bagenolle. Well, you can bet that ended that. 'Excuse me,' I said very cold and I turned right around and marched right out."

"A nice .32-caliber Iver Johnson would have fixed that, don't you think, Jacqueline?" he said.

"Oh Mr. Carlyle, I don't believe in the use of firearms!"

85

"I'm glad to hear that," he murmured morosely.

As the evening wore on, Jacqueline became more regal, more dégagé and more blurred. Her feelings for Carlyle also assumed a warmer tone, an amorous warmth that he found strangely soothing. Leaning toward him, teetering on her high heels, she was like a tall, lovely, flowering tree. She was taller than he and only about twenty-odd years younger, so that he felt they presented a ludicrous and somewhat trite picture together of the polished middle-aged man and the tall gorgeous show girl. And this was the way he liked it. But he could not keep the slow terrifying sensation from rising and rising, washing up out of the depths of his consciousness, gnawing at him through the drink and the clamor of the long evening.

"Let's go back to your place, Mr. Carlyle," Jacqueline said finally in a hazy voice. "A girl could learn to love you, Mr. Carlyle, to feel a great affection for you," Jacqueline said distantly, pressing his arm against her bosom. He knew he could prolong it no longer.

In the cab, he tried to think of something to drown the knowledge that was now on him. Jacqueline took his hand and placed it inside her dress. The low-cut gown partially revealed that perfection which people had been staring at enviously during the long night. "Oh Mr. Carlyle," she said, "this has been such a wonderful evening! I've had such a marvelous time!"

In the suite, she walked straight through to the bedroom. She sat down regally on the bed and began to remove her earrings and pearls. Tell us where the long road ends? he thought. So I didn't make it, after all. So now I know and what can I do? It was like looking down a loaded barrel. He knew it was all over. He knew there was nothing more he could do. He knew it was still Stella after all. He realized now at last that he did not want anyone else or anything else. He did not want the tall sex goddess, the beautiful bosom, the Junoesque body—he did not want the soft words; he wanted no one, nothing except Stella. He could not disguise it from himself any longer. He could not pretend. There was no one else he could even touch. He could

not even try any more. And the old ache was with him again—
more terrible, more devastating than ever before. There was no
use searching, or pining or hoping again. He had reached the
end of the road. He had arrived at the place where there was no
farther to go.

"Jacqueline," he began softly, "I'm terribly sorry, but we came
back too late. My wife will be here any minute now and . . .
and . . ."

"What?" she said. Her large, beautiful, somewhat blurred eyes
widened. "Mr. Carlyle," she said, "you can't do this to me."

"Jacqueline," he said softly, "will this help a little?"

He searched through his pockets for the rest of the bills.
In the bureau drawer he drew out a small packet. "I'm not trying to . . . to pay you for anything, Jacqueline," he said slowly.
"I want you to have this because I think you are beautiful and
I want you to stay as beautiful as you are forever. Also I want
you to know I do care for you. I love you. Get yourself something nice to remember me by. It's just that . . ." He paused.
What more was there to say? What was the use? He was caught
in that old spell, and no one could do anything for him. No
one could help him. No one had anything he wanted except
Stella. There was nothing, nothing else.

As the cab approached the apartment building where he lived,
he told himself once more that it was particularly foolish to
return like this two days early and in the evening. It was something he had realized from the beginning, but he couldn't seem
to help himself. What had been the use of prolonging that week
on the town—the week that had taught him the sad and desolate
truth, the week that had begun so auspiciously and had turned to
ashes so suddenly at the end. He might as well come home again
to whatever debased and sullied shambles he could call home.
But he knew it was a mistake—this arriving early and particularly arriving in the evening. She would probably already have
gone out. But what did it matter? There was no percentage in his
worrying about anything she did any more, and there was no

use in trying to drown the terrible ache any further. He had tasted the dregs. There was nothing left to drink.

He noticed the startled look on the doorman's face as he paid off the cab and picked up the suitcase. The doorman and the elevator man exchanged glances. Good Christ! he thought, this place is as great a whispering gallery as the office. So she had not been discreet after all.

In the hall the music enveloped him. It was emanating from their apartment—the phonograph turned moderately loud, the melody a soft saccharine lilt he knew Stella loved. She had a dishearteningly trite taste in jazz and a persistence in playing her favorites over and over again, endlessly and continuously. At the door, he hesitated, listening. He knew what he would find— and somehow now even with his heart pounding and that dreadful ache there, he knew he would have to face it.

There is a night in everyone's life, he thought, and this was his. Yes, he had had enough. He would not flinch any more. It was odd that there was even now no curiosity left as to what the man looked like or how he would act or what Stella would do. Every-thing had been washed away. The fare had been paid. He knew that nothing worse could happen to him. And he knew what he had to do.

He inserted the key in the door and pushed in. In his memory, it seemed almost as if time had hung over them frozen. It was like the hush after an explosion. Afterwards, the man remained a blur in his recollection, but Stella had stood there, drunk, and the look on her face as she turned and saw him was with him still. It was a look of cold fury.

It was now eleven-thirty and she was gone—gone finally for good. And he had at last reached the end. Somehow, he did not feel as badly as he had thought he would. Somehow there was a sense almost of relief, of satisfaction, that it was finished. There would be no withdrawal symptoms for him anyhow. There would be no more of that terrifying and undissolvable ache. He knew what he would have to do at last, but it would be all right.

After all, he'd had it—as few men had had it in their whole lives. You can only do anything first once, and people always seemed to have this sordid hankering for repetition. Well, that was one weakness he was over and done with now. He'd had everything and he didn't want any more—no more at all. And perhaps after all, he would be able to take something of his manhood back with him.

It made him smile a little when he thought of her face—Stella's lovely drunken face—when she saw him as he came in—was it just three hours ago? That look of cold fury. And her lover—he could scarcely recall what the man had been like. He was young, he remembered, but immediately upon his entrance, the man had walked over, picked up his hat, sidled to the door and slunk out. That was the kind of man Stella had given her love to—the love that had belonged to him.

But that had been only the beginning. She had stood there, and then she had started to open her mouth, when he said it, and the words had had the old ring of his authority, of all the years that he had been a man.

"Get your clothes," he had said to her quietly, "and get out."

"Jeff," she had begun, "what do you mean by coming into . . ."

He broke in on the impending tirade coldly.

"Just do what I said, Stella." He spoke low. "Get your clothes and get out. You're through. You've reached the end of the line. This is where you get off."

"And what if I don't want to, Jeff?" she asked, her haughty mood changing slowly. It gave him pleasure now to remember the dawning surprise on her face.

"You have no choice, Stella," he answered softly. "You played it wrong and I'm calling in the chips."

"Jeff," she said, and now her voice had changed, become sultry and warm, as it had once been for him in the old days. He knew it was not that she had changed. It was that she wanted to regain her supremacy, to re-establish her dominion over him. There was something in her that needed it, that needed this final

89

victory, but there was also something she did not know, something that only comes to one when one has taken the last ride, when one has tasted the final defeat. After all the smoke and fury have passed away, after the completion of ruin, there is finally left in the ashes one nugget of truth, of revelation, of fulfillment.

"Jeff," she asked again, "can't we talk it over a little bit? Are you sure you want it this way now?"

"There's nothing to talk over, Stella. You said so yourself. It's all been said a thousand times before and I'm not going over it again."

"Jeff," she repeated, and now her tone was soft, pleading, "Jeff, what has come over you so suddenly? Tell me what it is has changed you?"

"You changed me, Stella. Now please, let's not stand here and talk. Just get your things and get out. It's all over, and I've had it. There's nothing more to say."

So she had turned, her lovely figure a bondage to him even then, the fragrance of her, even drunk as she was, even heartless and faithless as she was, still sweet and overpowering to him, so that he had had to go into the other room while she pulled together a few of her things into an overnight bag.

She had stood for a moment, tall, the full, jeweled jet-black hair aglint in the warm light, the lovely Madonna face, the superb body poised, looking at him searchingly, wonderingly.

"It was a long ride, wasn't it, Jeff?" she said softly.

"It was a long ride," he answered.

"You know I won't be back," she said. Her voice was very low.

"I know," he said.

She had closed the door softly, going out—the first time she had ever closed a door softly in all their years together.

He had stood there looking and looking at the place where she had been and hearing that soft goodbye. It was the last and the best, he was thinking, the last and the best of all. And with her going, it was really finished.

Now he walked to the easy chair beside the bed. He

placed the little bottle with the twenty white tablets on the side table and set down the highball glass of rye and water beside it. He was in his dressing robe and pajamas. Everything was ready. The big sleep, he thought, the big sleep. It didn't bother him at all. A man outlives everything in the end, he was thinking—the good, the bad, the indifferent. It was nice to have had a good life, and to remember one's past with pleasure was really to have lived twice, but once one has had everything, that was it, and he did not want to be around for the aftermath, for the anticlimax, for the loss of manhood again, for the constant, ceaseless Friday to Sunday evening aching, for the terrible long nights without Stella, for the wondering where she was now, with whom and how she was doing. He'd ended the play as it should be ended, and if he stayed around to try to live it all over again, he would only bring it all down anyhow, degrade everything he had possessed, and all the same lose everything in the end. No, this was the best way. This was the way a man would choose to do it. This is the way a man would like to complete it—the full life and then the big sleep.

He'd regret a little not being able to take over in the office, but then that had never been his major ambition. They'd given him almost everything, and he'd had a lot of good times on them. It was a good place, strange and vast as it was—a good place, and . . . well, they'd never pulled the card on him. Now they would have to in the end.

He sat down on the large bed.

He poured twelve of the tablets into the palm of his hand, and they lay there gleaming, white and beautiful—the little grains of crystallized sleep. He looked at them for a moment, thinking there they lie, ready to wash away a whole life and all that I knew and cared for. Will you bring me anything as good? Or only nothingness—where time has ceased and I can never care again? At least, it is an adventure. And that is the kind of fulfillment a man who has lived fully should face—whatever lies beyond. And if nothing lies beyond, then that is comforting also—nothingness can never harm.

91

Slowly, he placed the little tablets in his mouth, one by one, and washed them down. Then he lay back on the bed and closed his eyes. He began to think of the good days again, the great times, the laughter, the love. For a long time, he lay there quietly, thinking of them, thinking of them all, lost in the golden dream, and then slowly the darkness began to come creeping, creeping out of nowhere across the misty fields of the mind, and lingeringly, gradually, the world of consciousness, the world of ticking clocks and of love and of fear began to slip softly away, and the good times were at last over forever.

BOOK II   Somers

1

WHAT HAD HAPPENED to Jim Somers was something entirely different.

Now on a fine, sparkling morning in spring, the office was abuzz. The boys had been working overtime for some weeks. So much had changed. A new regime had taken over, and it was a typical Wednesday at the coffee break. Five of the men who occupied the outer office were at their desks. The others had gone down for coffee or were out chatting with associates. April stood in the general office area talking to the press manager, Mizner. Martin Brill and Carruthers were still away at the plants.

Saunders had entered somewhat late in his usual breezy fashion with the air of one who is ready to take over and set matters straight.

"All right, boys, relax, relax!" he had boomed jovially, "Old Sandy is here to save the fort. The Marines have landed!"

Philip Harwood turned at his desk, his handsome thin lips drawn back in a grimace. He had fine white teeth.

"The big chum," he said with ill-concealed distaste, "the big chum. Can't you enter a room without lifting that braying voice?"

"Thank you, Mr. Harwood, thank you," Saunders intoned dramatically. "You make us all feel so good. You lift our spirits."

"I hear voices crying in the night," Miland remarked plaintively. "Will you fellows love each other somewhere else? This office is for work."

The absurdity of that remark was apparent to them all. "You boys are maladjusted," Cy Travers commented, looking up ab-

95

sently. "What we need around here is more coffee drinkers and less drudges—a little more gracious living."

"That's all we have around here—" Harwood said—"coffee drinkers. Saunders even drinks coffee on overtime. This office is the sole support of Brazil. . . ."

"While the rest of us live out gray lives in this Nirvana, let's at least not give in to the degradation of work," Cy replied gloomily. "Let's listen to different drummers; let's have the broad margin to our existences. . . ."

McKenzie had been buried in the new syndicate material. He raised his head. "There's no time for broad margins now," he remarked. "We'll have to put our bleeding hearts on ice for a while." He sighed. "Things have speeded up."

"I am a horse for single harness," Cy continued, "not cut out for teamwork."

"Well, if you are, you certainly picked the wrong environment. This is not the place for single-harness horses—or for different drummers, either," McKenzie said. "From now on, we're going to proceed strictly along the furrow. We're going to mind the store or they'll start stunting our growth."

Harwood leaned back, his cool, piratic gaze on Travers.

"Mac's right," he said. "You boys are in a new field now, and it's smart to be on your toes. It's another set of assignments."

"Well, let's have a little gaiety in this anyway," Cy concluded.

"It's getting so now you syndicate boys want to live like people," Saunders commented cheerfully. His large, aspic eyes were gazing into the distance, contemplating April as she stood talking near the entrance to the outer office. Travers leaned over also.

"The way they package 'em nowadays," he murmured. "And all for nothing. What a darb!"

Saunders heaved his bulk back in the swivel chair. "You never know," he said. "You never know."

"You're cruising the wrong number," McKenzie sighed.

Jim Somers had been sitting apart from the others, sunk in that loneliness that was becoming more and more characteristic, and it was then for the first time that he had noticed April's eyes on him. . . .

Jim Somers was a gentleman.

He was also an extremely handsome man. Perhaps, as they said later, he was somewhat "hard of thinking," but the Empire could boast of relatively few men with brains and talent, whereas it abounded in personalities and just plain people whose intelligence was, to say the least, suspect and whose abilities were mediocre. It was founded on the mass of cipher heads, zero faces, whose cumulative efforts, feeble as they might be singly, were in the mass impressive and even awe-inspiring. And among them, Jim Somers possessed, not brains, but a keynote quality. He had loyalty.

Now as he sat there listening numbly to the aimless talk and wisecracking, he felt again that aloneness, that sense of disparity.

For to Jim, the Empire was a symbol. He had arrived at the job late and was considerably older than he looked, although his fine appearance and meticulous manner of dressing may have disguised some small symptoms of physical deterioration. He had been thirty-six when he was hired in the years before the war, and he had had a little trouble securing the job since the country was just emerging from a depression. His record was no worse than that of most men who had had to find work just after that vast social and economic hemorrhage.

Jim was a personable man, meticulously and beautifully dressed in high-quality clothes which fitted him well. His face was regular and quite composed. He was of medium height and moderate build, though slightly inclined to fullness in the hips and buttocks. His manner was reserved, often blank, and he was sometimes considered unresponsive. But he had a pleasing and unaffected personality which aroused in women a protective instinct. Everybody liked Jim and felt a warmth and sympathy for him.

It was thus perhaps his good looks and also that air of loneliness that on that fine spring morning attracted the gaze of the beautiful April. To understand what really happened, however,

97

one must go back a little. It all began before the end of hostilities during that period of maximum build-up for war. . . .

"No more brains than a decorticated cat," McKenzie was saying. "Absolutely crazy—a candidate for the laughing academy. . . ."

"You have to have brains to be crazy," Saunders replied.

The office routines were in full swing.

Jim was essentially a man's man, enjoyed the company of men, and felt at ease in their presence. While women were attracted to him, he found it difficult to respond. In fact, he could only entertain a romantic interest in extremely young girls—girls generally so young they were almost certainly virginal and could not, therefore, make any real demands on him.

Two years before, on vacation, he had met a girl of sixteen in Cincinnati—a slim, dreamy girl with wide, saucerlike hazel eyes and a sweet, helpless manner. She had a double-jointed given name, Betty Lou, and her family were nice people without other children. The leaves were turning brown, and it was time for Jim to depart. But he could not bring himself to leave behind this pretty white-faced child.

"Take good care of Betty Lou," her family had told him. "She's always been a delicate child and sometimes even a little odd. Be good to her."

"I will," Jim had replied, and he and Betty Lou as man and wife settled at last in the big town to begin their fitful, flickering and shadowy marriage.

They moved into a smart little apartment on one of the side streets in the Village and began to find themselves a part of all the "latest thing" type of activity of their neighborhood. They had friends in to musical evenings and drank gin and lemon. They became acquainted with the latest French cinema and they went to see the revivals of ancient movies which were then the rage— Buster Keaton in *The Saphead,* William S. Hart in *The Cradle of Courage* and Conway Tearle in *Marooned Hearts.* They attended the newest nonobjective exhibits, and they started to collect the

98

last cry in cute jokes—shaggy dog and sophisticated off-color—
and they liked enormously the songs the smart set in the cafés
were singing to the accompaniment of one piano. And they
picked up old songs too. "Is it possible you're possessible?" they
sang. And they would quote the latest down-to-earth remark:
"Happiness isn't everything," they would say; "money counts
too!" and "What do we need," they would say, "a cup of coffee
or a whole new life?"

And then it happened.

Betty Lou was going to have a baby.

Jim could remember clearly the morning they went to the
doctor's. The doctor was a tired middle-aged man. He shook his
head.

"Yes," he said quietly, "your wife is going to have a baby all
right, but she will have to be very careful—very careful. She is
much too thin and anemic now and the bone structure is . . .
well . . . well, we'll see. . . ."

So they went back to the apartment.

"I'm going to have that baby if it kills me," Betty Lou said.
The laughter was strained.

While there were periods of happiness that spring, the difficulties began to be foreshadowed almost immediately by Betty
Lou's severe attacks of morning sickness. These attacks soon
grew so violent that the doctor was worried. She could not keep
down food and even the injections she was finally given did not
quiet the nausea. Toward the end of spring, however, the nausea
began to abate somewhat, but Betty Lou was now so thin and
drawn and exhausted that it became evident something radical
would have to be done soon. She was stubborn and surprisingly
determined. Jim pleaded with her to listen to the doctor, but she
did not like the doctor and grew more and more exasperated with
everyone. She seemed to have developed the fear that he and the
doctor and others were trying to take her baby from her, that
somehow a conspiracy had been formed to remove the poor little
thing by some diabolical premature operation.

The doctor now told Jim that he was definitely alarmed at

99

her situation and that there was the possibility that her physical condition might deteriorate to the extent that it might become a matter of her own life or the baby's and that even then he was not sure that the baby could be saved if she would not permit a Caesarean.

Jim walked home slowly in the humid summer drizzle. Never a very articulate man, he felt now as if he were strangling with the terribleness of their misfortune. He felt if he did not have a drink he would die. The burden was almost more than he could bear. He stopped and had two quick ones at Callahan's and then he continued slowly on home, wondering what he could say to Betty Lou, how he could make her understand the seriousness of the situation.

In the living room, he sat down numbly. Betty Lou was moving around in the bedroom and she had not answered him when he called out to her. He sat there for some time. He did not know exactly where to turn, what to say, how he could work it out. The frightful and oppressive sadness of it weighed him down, robbed him of any volition. He felt completely defeated, done in.

Finally, he rose and walked toward the bedroom door. From the room, Betty Lou's voice—a voice that had become in the last few weeks cracked and strained—called out to him: "Don't you dare come in," she said suddenly. "Don't you dare come in." Her voice sounded strange. "I know what you two have been up to— you and that doctor. You think you can put something over on me because I'm not well. Well, you can't. I won't have it. . . . I'm going to have my baby the way I want it. Nobody is going to take him away from me—not you or that doctor or anybody else either. . . ."

For a moment, he stood where he was, stunned. Then he turned and went over and sat down. The misery within him welled up and up until he did not know how he could contain it any further. He rose slowly and approached the now closed bedroom door. He stood there quietly, numbed with misery. He did not know what he was going to say but suddenly the words poured out of him—anguished but in a low, almost guttural voice.

100

"Betty Lou," he said . . . and suddenly it all poured out, low, agonized, completely defeated, "Betty Lou," he said at last, "nobody's going to take your baby—our baby—nobody. You can have your baby just the way you want it. Nobody is ever going to touch you—not while I'm alive and here to see it. Nobody, Betty Lou, nobody! Have your baby, our baby, any way you want, honey—only don't shut yourself away. I'm on your side. It's my baby too. I'm always on your side." He could feel the choking, the surging in his throat. "Do you hear me, Betty Lou? I'm always on your side. I'm with you against them all, against the whole world. Trust me! Trust me! I told your folks I'd take care of you, I'd be good to you, and I'll never be anything but good to you—never, Betty Lou—never. Don't shut me out, Betty Lou. Don't shut me away. They'll never come near you while I'm around. They'll never take our baby, never. . . ."

Slowly, the bedroom door opened a crack, then a little wider. He stood there in his complete misery, the tears streaming down his cold, expressionless face. She was in the doorway now in her nightgown, her absurd, scrawny, childish face white and cadaverous, starved-looking, her big belly thrust out pitifully.

He walked stiffly to her like an automaton and took her in his arms. "Betty Lou," he said, "oh Betty Lou, why has God forsaken us . . . why . . . why?"

In October, the baby was born dead, and Betty Lou hovered on the edge of death for about a month. When she finally returned to the world of consciousness and travail, she lay quiet and depleted in the hospital bed, too far spent to care what had happened. It was days before Jim finally had to tell her the baby was gone. He stood there above her and she turned her head away from him and cried weakly like a kitten. She no longer seemed to care whether she lived or died.

Every evening he walked from the office to the hospital. He told nobody. He could not bring himself to say anything to them of the incredible events that had befallen him. What did they know of suffering? he thought dimly. What did those loud, clod-

101

dish, cheerful, senseless men who sat near him know of the death of a man's spirit? of the enveloping darkness and defeat that close down so hopelessly and senselessly on a man? Saunders with his vibrating, braying voice . . . Miland with his endless scribbling . . . Brill, the golden boy . . . thank God, they had sent him out and he wasn't there to add to the confusion and bustle of the office and to the staring eyes . . . And the others . . . only April Tremaine with her soft, warm glances, wondering, speculating . . . But he couldn't tell anybody. It was too deep a hurt, too secret, too terrible. Often he would go and sit in one of the beer halls near the apartment after visiting the hospital and drink a few beers and sometimes a rye or so to make himself sleepy, to ease the constant ache. It wasn't only Betty Lou—she finally appeared to be mending slowly after all—and he thanked God for that, although she was still very weak and cold and withdrawn. But it was also the baby. He could not forget that baby. It would have been—it was—his baby, the only one he had ever had, and it was gone. He could not shake off that feeling for it. He missed it so badly, so terribly. He sat there in the warm, dimly lit bar and ordered another drink. Mike, the bartender, spoke to him laconically at intervals, approaching with his wet rag. He had known Mike from the days of those "latest thing" perambulations when it had been smart to know Mike, when everything had been so new and golden and so much fun and they had had those wonderful little parties and entertainments and they had been happy. He had not liked Mike. Mike had not liked him, but he sat there now and ordered the drinks.

So it was at the height of the war assignments at the office that Betty Lou finally was allowed to return home from the hospital. She was still weak and drawn and spent most of the days in bed. And in the mornings Jim would arrive at work, feeling logy and shaken. It was not that he was drinking much; he just could not pull himself out of the depths. And it seemed to him that had it not been for the routine, the work and that deep feeling of security that belonging to a part of that vast kingdom bestowed on him, the feeling that they could never finally sink him while he was in the service of the Empire, and that somehow they would eventually take care of him, he would not have been able to survive at all. Carlyle had been the boss then, and for that entire autumn it seemed as if finally, except for the sadness over the loss of the baby, the rest of their distress would ease and perhaps eventually the world would be all right after all.

His work was not good, but no one appeared to notice it, and the pattern of life continued almost at a normal rate. At home, Betty Lou remained in bed during the mornings. She had grown silent and withdrawn in the last months, a contrast to her former childlike, chattering self. For she had been a magpie in the old days, able to fill quite easily the long silences he himself was prone to slip into. His contemplative moods, they called them, but sometimes even he did not know what he was thinking and sometimes it almost seemed as if he were not thinking at all, just sitting there in a mindless mood.

But Betty Lou had never noticed these silences or indeed paid them any attention. She had always kept up an almost uninterrupted flow of chitchat and even their friends often commented, Good Lord, how Betty Lou did go on! Now, however, she was frozen and silent. She did not appear to blame him or the doctor for the loss of the baby—something they had had a mortal fear she might do—and for this they thanked God, but she would not talk about it or permit any of them to approach the subject. He had already, long before she arrived home, disposed of the bassinet and the baby clothes so carefully prepared.

Then one evening—it was an evening in January—Jim arrived at the apartment. It was a crisp evening, cold and clear, a beautiful, bustling winter evening in town. Jim had stopped as usual on the way for his two drinks. When he climbed to the apartment— they had never minded the one-flight walk-up—he was surprised to hear no sound. He called. Then he looked into the bedroom. There was no one there. He entered the kitchen. There on a stool near the pantry, Betty Lou was sitting quietly. Her eyes were wide open and vacant and she was just sitting there staring.

"Why Betty Lou, honey," he said, "what's the matter?" He

could feel his pulses start to pound again. "What's the matter, honey?" he asked more loudly.

She turned her head slowly. Her eyes upon him showed no recognition whatever. The look was one she would have given a stranger, someone she had never seen before in her life. "Betty Lou," he said more firmly, "Betty Lou, it's me, Jim. What's the matter, honey?"

She looked at him steadily, those wide, vacant eyes, once the beautiful saucerlike eyes of a child, staring and staring, without expression, without consciousness, withdrawn from the world of their hopes and fears. "Betty Lou . . ." he began. She looked at him once more.

"I have put my baby in the oven," she said steadily.

2

THERE WERE two men in the office Jim had little use for. One was Saunders and the other Brill, whom he thought of as "Carlyle's golden boy" and who at the time had been sent out to cover the Chicago Works.

On the other hand, Jim particularly admired Harwood with his smooth face and fine teeth. Harwood struck him as the epitome of the rising young executive—bright, alert, smart, with a gift for wisecracking. Although Harwood possessed less experience than Jim and was younger, he seemed to be doing much better in every respect and on occasion at Jim's expense.

When Harwood had breezed into the office from his brief stay in one of the works earlier in the war before the assignment for Carlyle, Jim had occupied the desk near the back window, generally known as the preferred position. Somehow in the shuffle, as new people advanced and assignments were revised, one morning Jim found that Harwood was to occupy that position, and Jim had ended in the second place with Saunders, Brill, Miland and McKeller, a new man, at the other locations.

Actually, it had not bothered Jim particularly. Already his difficulties were making him less aware of what was going on. Harwood had returned before any of the others from the plant project and had maneuvered into being the collator of the material being collected. His own reports, despite a veneer of brightness, had not seemed adequate, and Randall had been requested by Carlyle to pull him back and set him to work formulating uses for the material.

But these assignments had—and on two occasions—given Harwood, and Brill too, something Jim did not have—something known as "plant experience," regarded in the Empire as a valuable part of the portable furniture of a career.

But now for Jim the darkness had begun to descend, and the flood of his misfortunes to drown the other interests and concerns of his life. The winter evening that he had arrived at the apartment to find Betty Lou in terrifying withdrawal had been almost the last crushing blow. He had somehow managed to lead her to bed and then he had walked the streets the rest of the night. In the morning, he struggled into the office, shaking and exhausted. Betty Lou had regained consciousness, although she remembered nothing of her seizure or what had happened the evening before. Jim was terrified. That night he drank himself to sleep, and every morning that week he entered the office stupefied with liquor. It was Saunders who had helped him through the third day, and Saunders who took him home that Friday.

But as in the case of the earlier blows, so in this devastating turn of events, he could not bring himself to confide in anyone. His enlistment with grief was complete. Everything was slipping, being swept away in the gathering darkness, and only one straw remained for him to clutch, one anchor in the flood—the Company and the job—and obscurely he felt the Company demanded that somehow he must save himself.

It was on a morning when he sat at his desk in the office, shaky and hungover, that he was approached by the kind and barbarously lovely April. "Buy me a drink," she had said, "and tell me your troubles."

And that was the evening of their first date.

They sat in a little cabaret uptown near Thirty-fourth Street in the neighborhood where April lived. It had soft lights and was smoky and music played incessantly. It was a Tuesday night and the place was not crowded. Jim had been drinking steadily, and even under April's aimless and dulcet chatter he could not seem to pull himself out of the depths. Across from him in the mists he could see that face, so sensuously beautiful, but it aroused in him no passion, no longing. He noticed only that two men at the bar were ogling her. It gave him a brief proprietary pleasure. Then something of what she was saying reached him:

". . . We none of us," she was saying softly, "can live to ourselves alone. If you have troubles, you must learn to share them with those who . . . who care for you. Otherwise they . . . they will not understand. Jim," she added softly, "tell me what's wrong. I know something terrible must have happened. You haven't been yourself and . . . and the eyes are always on you in that place. You can't escape it . . . you can't . . . can't hide. You know that. . . . Tell me, Jim. . . ."

"I suppose so," he answered coldly, bitterly, after a long pause. "Why should I say anything to them?" he added. "It . . . it has to do with Betty Lou, my wife, and . . . and it's none of anybody's business . . . it's nothing anybody can . . . can help with. And—and also we . . . we lost a baby. . . ."

Now that he had said it, abruptly the flood of his misery, too profound for words, broke, and he turned his head away. The cold, expressionless face with the wetness on the cheeks melted her heart, but she looked down at her drink and pretended not to see.

When he could speak again, she looked up at him and said softly: "I'm sorry, Jim. . . ."

"Just don't tell them," he said at last, low and feverishly.

106

"Don't tell anyone—not anyone. . . . It's not something for them to know. It's not something to be traded on the marketplace . . . it's not mass produced; it's my own. . . . Don't ever tell. And now . . . now Betty Lou is . . . is not well. She's never recovered from it and, and . . . well, what can a fellow do?"

He sat there silent so long she began to search for an answer. "People can help one another," she remarked. "People can . . . Can't I come in and help take care of your wife, help somehow?"

"No, no, no . . ." he answered even more emphatically. "I can't . . . I can't have anyone see her . . . see her now. . . . She . . . she . . . well she wouldn't understand and any-how . . ."

Dimly the thought of the ravishing April in all her splendor confronting poor, scrawny, miserable Betty Lou filled him with terror and grief. And what would Betty Lou in her sad, little, childlike suffering think of his bringing this soft, glittering girl, the swale of light about her, in on them now?

"No," he said again, "no, no . . . nobody can help. Nobody. It must be ours, ours alone."

She was silent for a long time. Finally, when she spoke, she sounded rebuffed, hurt, but she was not thinking of it.

"They'll know sometime at the office, Jim," she continued. "Everything comes out there eventually. Not that I shall tell them—ever—unless you allow me to. But your job, Jim . . . the work . . . they begin to notice."

That had aroused him. She had touched a sensitive spot.

"Are they beginning to talk about my work?" he asked at last in a low, sullen voice.

She was silent.

"I know things have been a little . . . confused lately," he said finally. "It's . . . it's just that I can't seem to get started in the mornings, and . . . and . . ."

"Please let me tell Mr. Carlyle, Jim?" she asked. "I under-stand your not wanting to do so yourself, but I could sometime do it for you, and he—he'd understand. He has the kindness . . .

107

They're only beginning to talk now, Jim, but you know how they are . . . you know them. Don't the boys talk about me?" she asked abruptly. "You know they do. . . ."

He felt embarrassed.

"It's written all over your face," she said. "What do they say about me? Please now. . . ."

"Oh April," he mumbled embarrassed, "you know. The boys like you."

"I suppose they'd like to sleep with me," she said, looking directly at him.

He squirmed. "Yes," he answered laconically.

She waited, but he added nothing.

"That's all men ever seem to think about," she said coldly. "Except you, Jim . . . you're different. I like you. I wish I could help you."

"You're nice too, April," he replied. "Thanks, thanks . . . you can tell Mr. Carlyle sometime, if you want. But not right away, April—not yet. Give me a little time."

"I understand," she answered.

So the first of their dates began.

"And Jim," she had told him later, "please, please, don't drink. It won't help."

Women, he had thought as they parted at the door that night. All they really want is to reform a man, to take away his little pleasures—that's all a woman really wants after all.

Then the water began to close over him.

He arrived home late one winter evening. Betty Lou had been all right since that evening some months ago when he had returned to find her in that dreadful seizure. True, she had never recovered her old gaiety or chatter. She remained a mere wraith —silent, pale and withdrawn, but she appeared to hear and see him and respond to his awkward attempts to show her how much he cared for her with something like normal warmth. That evening, however, again she was not in the living room and she

108

did not answer his call. Nor was she in the kitchen this time. But when he walked into the bedroom, there she was . . . sitting on the floor cradling an old pillow in her arms, rocking it back and forth, back and forth. When she looked up at him, standing there near the doorway, her eyes were wide and vacant as before, and he knew this time there was nothing—really nothing he could do. "Don't you come near!" she said to him. "Don't you come near my baby. . . ."

He turned and walked slowly into the living room. He sat down on the sofa and leaning forward, put his head in his hands. His misery was too great to bear. He had arrived at the end. So this was the way it is to finish, he thought. This is the way it is to be—this is how my little child-wife—the girl I said I'd make a home and a living for and protect—this is how she is to finish up. And our love, our marriage . . . Oh God, he thought, God, what have You done to us . . . ? Well, now it was over. He could cope with it alone no longer. He could protect her no longer. The disaster had passed beyond the boundaries and was out of his hands.

He rose and walked to the phone. Slowly, he began to dial the doctor's number. . . .

In the end April never had the chance to tell Carlyle after all. For while Jim commenced to sink into the depths of his misery, as Betty Lou was certified and her parents arrived from Cincinnati to take her back to a sanitarium, the big change took place in the office. The shock of Carlyle's death had struck them all and, scarcely noticed now by Jim Somers amid the turmoil and bitterness of his own pain, the new regime began.

Two months later, war ended. It happened without undue excitement and with little celebration. The mood was one of relief and also exhaustion. The production war had been won half a year ago; the military victory had been assured by spring and now in late autumn it was all over, and the problems of peace were at hand.

109

RANDALL SAT in his new office—the office Carlyle had occupied —and mulled over two decisions. They were his first major efforts as information manager and he wanted to show skill and firmness in handling them to impress their new director, a man named Mansard. Randall wanted to get off on the right foot.

The first problem was to secure the immediate retirement of old Tom Sullivan, the production supervisor, and the other and more important one was to select someone for the job formerly held by himself—that of information supervisor.

Randall had often in the past mused that, were he in Carlyle's shoes, there would certainly be some changes made. He prided himself that he had risen from the ranks, that he was of the old school, the school that believes that business is business and a man should be tossed in to sink or swim as best he could and none of this coddling of people.

"Anyone who sees power only in divisions or in bread and machines alone is not so much cynical as naive," Carlyle had once quoted, and he did not know what Carlyle meant. It did not make sense to him. Carlyle had been more brilliant, more loved, it is true. Still a manager's job was not a popularity contest. It was a rigorous task of handling people so as to secure the most work out of them. Randall was a responsible man. He was not a playboy. He was no hail-fellow-well-met like Mizner, and he had no aspiration to become the best-loved manager the department had ever had. It was time to take stock.

He rose and poured himself a drink of water from the silver decanter. He buzzed Miss Kelly.

Mizner had requested April Tremaine, since his former secretary, Miss Pendleton, was retiring, and of course it was well known over the office that Mizner had a weakness for the girl.

110

Randall had to admit he had not protested. He had become accustomed to Miss Kelly.

Miss Kelly's anxious maternal face appeared in the doorway.

"Would you send in Tom Sullivan—that is, if you can find him and he's in today?" Randall said.

"Yes sir," Miss Kelly answered.

Now why had he had to rub it in like that about Old Tom? It was true Sullivan was one of the most repressive, cantankerous and incompetent production supervisors the Company had ever had, but actually Randall rather liked him. The problem was to persuade the old man to retire now rather than to wait until his normal retirement age of sixty-five. He was sixty-three. It was one way to relieve the pressure on that overstaffed department.

Furthermore, Tom, as even Randall had agreed with Carlyle, had never been precisely an asset. He was vindictive and bullying by temperament, fawning to his superiors, a holy terror to those who worked for him. He masked his basic ignorance under a vast accumulation of insignificant, irrelevant and inconsequential detail and under a blustering manner that combined rudeness with unintelligibility. He was, in short, a gentleman of the old school.

The years of the war had made even Tom's indifferent efforts of some value, but now his usefulness was at an end. It was Phil Harwood who had made the remark that most succinctly characterized Tom. "Tom," Phil had commented, "is the kind of man who, if you ask him the time, will tell you how to make a watch." Essentially, he was afraid, that was true.

But in one respect, Randall felt a sympathy for Tom. They both shared a genuine distaste for things as they were now. They both had deplored the passing of the old virtues of self-reliance, independence and thrift, and the old feeling for the safe, conservative world the war had swept away. Until just toward the end, Randall had never really believed in the war. Nor had Tom Sullivan. Tom's ideas were sound although he expressed them crudely.

What had happened to the days when a man minded his own business and didn't go poking his nose into the affairs of those

111

miserable, greasy foreigners? They had been squabbling among themselves for as long as man could remember and would continue to do so, despite all we could do, until hell froze over. If they wished to kill each other, why, damn it, why not let them?

Not that Tom, or Randall for that matter, were bigoted or would countenance intolerance of any kind. Far from it. Randall did not believe in that sort of thing. You couldn't go pushing people around, even the way Tom sometimes had pushed around the people who worked for him. After all, this was a free country. But the place was getting to be governed by people with these goddamn foreign ideas and intellectuals . . .

Randall looked up.

Tom Sullivan stood in the door, his scrawny, turkey-gobbler's face red with choler or anxiety. He was gulping rapidly as he always did just before he was about to launch into a tirade.

"Come in, Tom. Come in a moment," Randall called cheerfully.

Tom's face worked in an agony of haste but he shuffled into the large office and sat down with a groan. The words finally poured out.

"Christalmighty, Mr. Randall," he said agitatedly, "what can we do? What can we do? It's all going to pieces out there! It's all coming apart at the seams. Nobody's got any grip on it at all. They're all crazy—a bunch of crazy incompetents I've got working for me. They can't understand anything. Now take those training booklets . . . What do you suppose it is, Mr. Randall? Are they against us? Do you think those crazy rundown bastards are deliberately against us? I don't know, Mr. Randall. I just don't know what to do any more! I do my best. I try to keep some sort of control. But Jesusgodinheaven, do you see what they're letting get by? Did you see what happened to the syndicate material that was going to press?"

Randall struggled in the flood. He knew that if he allowed it to continue he would be lost. Tom could keep this up for hours, incoherent, fantastic and unintelligible. He made a supreme effort and seized the situation in midair.

112

"Not now, Tom, please, not right now," he said. "I understand your difficulties and appreciate them, but right now I've something important at the moment. Now Tom," he said slowly, "now Tom, I'd like to talk to you about retirement. . . ."

Randall looked at his watch. It was almost noon. Tom Sullivan had finally left. He had not found it too difficult to persuade him to retire after all, even though it meant a slightly lower pension. Tom was fundamentally a yes man to his superiors. The office, Randall thought somewhat sardonically, would be glad to see him go, though he himself would miss him. There would be fewer of them left—fewer of the old-fashioned people, the little band of finalists like Tom and himself.

Randall looked at his watch again. He did not see why Mr. Mansard, the new director, never asked him to lunch. He had asked Mizner on two occasions, and Mizner was certainly one of the most unsound, off-beat people it had been his misfortune to team up with. Well, anyhow, it was just as well today. He would have to mull over that second problem—finding a man whose name he could place before Mansard tomorrow for the job of information supervisor.

He buzzed Miss Kelly again.

"Would you have something sent up for lunch, Miss Kelly?" he asked pleasantly when her anxious face appeared in the doorway. "I'm afraid I'll have no time to go out."

Miss Kelly registered concern.

When she had taken his order and departed, he swiveled in the chair, leaned back and looked out the window. It was a windy March day, but with the softness that gave promise of spring. This was the time to make the decision, he thought. This was the moment. There were very few men really eligible anyhow, he mused, very few, and certainly not the men Carlyle had favored.

For he and Carlyle, he was aware, had disagreed in their assessments of most of the men. He would admit some accomplishments for Brill and Carruthers. But, for instance, he had

113

considered Somers' work negligible. Carlyle and he had had a talk about it once.

"Dave, I don't think you're right about Somers," Carlyle had answered, fixing him with that cool, quizzical stare. "Somers is basically a sound and conscientious man—perhaps a little on the slow side, but loyal and hard-working. Right now I think he's having a difficult period, maybe something in his personal life. If we leave him alone, he'll pull out of it and eventually he may have more to give than many of the smarter ones, the wise boys. . . ."

And he had answered Carlyle bluntly, for after all was he not a plain, blunt man? It would be all right with him, he had replied, if Carlyle wished to indulge Somers, but it did seem that something should be done about the way Somers was arriving in the mornings and someone should speak to him. Furthermore, Harwood had on two occasions complained about Somers' not turning in the reports.

"What reports?" Carlyle had asked. "And what has Harwood to do with it?"

"The activity reports," Randall had reminded him. "I ask activity reports every week on all my men, and Harwood compiles them for me. Harwood has pointed out on more than one occasion that Somers' affairs are in a mess."

Carlyle had been silent. At last he remarked—and this was one of the conversations that remained most clearly in Randall's memory. "Dave," he had said, "watch that boy, Harwood. He's bright and he'll go far, but keep your eye on him. You need men you can trust in our business—someone who'll never turn you in when the going is rough. And Dave," Carlyle continued softly, "there's nobody on earth for whom the going won't be rough sometime."

Now Randall sat back and gazed out at the windy March sky. Clouds drifted high above the skyscrapers, and there were small squally mists of rain that appeared to evaporate as fast as they descended. He would have to make the decision now. And of

114

them all he could think of no one better qualified than the man he had in mind. Yes, he would have to give it to him. It was Harwood. It would have to be Harwood. Harwood was the best man —that was all.

The appointment would cause a stir—any such appointment would. But Randall doubted that it would arouse resentment.

He rose and walked to the window. Outside it had settled into a fine spring drizzle. Problems . . . problems, he thought. The good days would not be with them long. This was only the beginning. They had become swollen, bloated, and the time for retrenchment was at hand. A phrase quoted by one of the others touched his mind: When a small man casts a long shadow, it is a sign the sun is going down.

He wondered why the phrase haunted him.

4

MARTIN HAD ARRIVED back in the city to a new and rearranged world. In town, away from the sordid and exhausting five months of exile at the Works, he had been so tired that he had scarcely noticed any of the directions of work or new tensions at the Building. He had felt nothing except the relief of seeing once again the clean and shining office faces, hearing the familiar, educated voices and basking in the peace and privacy of their quiet, spacious and pleasant surroundings.

For the first few weeks, he still suffered from an overpowering residual fatigue which he could not seem to shake off, the shreds of that old night-shift exhaustion he could not seem to drown. Like a tired fighter, he figuratively hugged the ropes. He did nothing, went home early, took long baths, slept twelve and fourteen hours, and read and dozed and listened to music for whole weekends. And he made ready to get out as soon as his

115

strength returned sufficiently for him to find something else. Also, a new element had entered—the savage beauty, that telephone number.

It was surprising how he began to think of her again and to look for her. And in the office the old involvements slowly began to pierce the numbness. It was a new regime now—not one he would like much, he realized, nor one he intended to remain with long, but while he remained, he found he was caught again and he would have to serve it as best he could. It filled him with a vague apprehension, almost with a sense of dread. He had learned a thing or two at the Works. He had matured or, at least, hardened. There he had had the chance to see at first hand a small part of the Kingdom from afar, a part where the payoff was, where the work was being done.

That weekend he sat in the messy but comparatively luxurious room in town after those long months and tried to assess his situation. His main job now was to attempt to pull himself back into the old security of the world he knew and to leave the sound of machines behind. The world he had loved was entirely different—a world of books and music, of ideas and conversation, where the tides of his ambitions were of no consequence, but this old world now suddenly seemed to him remote and unreal.

The real world had regressed for him for so long into that sickening sound of machinery at night and later the murmur of voices in a large office in a strange and monstrous building that the soul-drain of these familiar routines was beginning to appear the most essential element in his life. He guessed he was a born wanter. He had become involved in a world of ambitions and strains and despite himself they began to seem important. It looked as if someday he might fall into that pattern, turn out to be a System Man, holding all the prescribed beliefs and slipping into all the myths that made up this odd and painfully sincere world. Here they were all in earnest. They took themselves and their labors seriously. The shadows were becoming the substance. But that was his trouble too. He was in earnest. He was a wanter. Actually, also, he was a plodder, a drudge—a good organizer. They could

116

use him, he guessed. Yes, he was afraid that somehow they could use him.

So the evening passed.

In the morning, he went to the office as usual.

It was at the retirement party for old Tom Sullivan at Guido's that he had first really noticed what was happening to Jim Somers.

There had been whispering from time to time—the kind of whispering that was like a sibilant undercurrent in their group, always sifting the movements, the reputations, the inner wants and disappointments of them all . . . a long murmuring that never ceased, that flowed beneath the surface of their lives and brought to one or another of them always some driftwood of information on one or another of the group itself, some flotsam and jetsam of secret lives. And now this debris was drifting up on Jim—"Seen Jim Somers lately? Three martinis at lunch. Corks in in the morning with a breath. Didn't get back from lunch at all yesterday. . . . Too bad . . . nice fellow"—broken lumber, driftwood from the shipwreck of a life.

It was always there—that whispering, like the current jokes that were always being run to death in those strange subterranean caverns of their world, whispering . . . whispering . . . whispering. Fortunately, the victims rarely heard it or realized that their names were on the rubble floating about in that secret sea. And in the depths of his own misery, Jim did not care what they were saying, did not in fact hear them at all. Even on the other levels he scarcely heard or noticed any of them any more. For now the days of agony were at hand.

That empty apartment first . . . that was the first of the nameless terrors. Somehow he would have to move out and find himself another place—one without memories, without residual whispers of a former existence. It was becoming increasingly difficult to return at night to that place, so silent and strange. He would enter and there he would be in the gloom of the unreal living room with its ghostly agonies and its shadows and he would

117

seem to hear a rustling in the bedroom or in the kitchen and he would stand there holding himself in to keep from looking, looking, peering. . . . And then there were the times when he came in, generally a little stupefied with drink, and before he realized it would call out automatically to her. . . . And the sound of his slow, drunken voice in the emptiness and silence would abruptly clutch at him, and the realization he kept trying to numb was with him again—the loneliness . . . the utter sense of failure and sadness . . . the sense of her having gone forever like a candle blown out in the darkness.

As the misery increased, there were the evenings he stopped longer and longer in the friendly, softly lighted, smoky air of Callahan's and on one or another occasion time had slipped by without his knowing it and it was two or three in the morning and they were shaking him and he did not know exactly where he was.

"Come on, old man," they would be saying to him gently. "Time to go home." Or perhaps a stranger's voice, kind and pleasant, a stranger's hand shaking him. "What are you celebrating, old chap? Don't you think you've had it for tonight? Come on now. . . ."

And during this period, he had found unexpected qualities in the strangers of this shadowy nocturnal neighborhood world —they were kind and friendly. They were willing to talk to you, to tell you their troubles or just to pass the time—and that helped. He would never be able to express his misery, but it helped to listen to the voices—different voices, friendly voices, voices of strangers—a tremendous blessing—changing perhaps from voice to voice as the evening grew later, from one sympathetic or sad face to another, each becoming progressively blurred until it was time to hit the trail, time for the last nightcap, the last roundup and the walk with dragging steps home in the spring nights. Sometimes it was getting so that he could not even remember what had happened to him that evening. Sometimes, it almost seemed as if one evening would blur into another.

But amid the shapeless days and nights, there was one tie

118

holding the disintegrating pieces together. Somehow he had to rise in the morning and get downtown to business. In the depths, he could scarcely remember exactly what he was supposed to be doing when he arrived, but no matter how dreadful the morning after seemed, there was that huge and sinister building downtown in the dawn hours, drawing him as if it were some giant magnet. And he would stumble out of the rumpled and damaged bed, his eyes gummed together with the rheum of sleep and the disaster of the last evening still clinging vaguely to him. And though his numbed and ruined mind would not awake, though his nerves cried out for mercy, some obscure compulsion, even though the death-drive was still deep within him, would force him to rise and dress, to try to shave, and with shaking hand and bloodshot eye to step out into the mornings toward that vast and hivelike magnet of a building.

Then at last in the office area at his desk, he could sit there quietly, the voices lapping around him like the sound of a distant sea, soothing to him, easing the wracking headache, the dry mouth, the dull throb of pain, the papers before him with words or figures on them blurring. . . .

And then one weekend, he had suddenly escaped from the apartment and its haunting silence. He had found himself another rented room. It was a Saturday afternoon—spring now—and he was walking from Callahan's to the little bar on the next block when he noticed a sign on an old apartment house advertising: ROOM FOR RENT. INQUIRE WITHIN. Numbed as he was, he had walked down the two steps of the doorway and peered into the gloom. It was a major effort now for him to do anything, and coping with people except under extreme necessity seemed to him the hardest of all. He had removed his dark glasses as he stepped into the doorway, but he still could scarcely make out the names on the name plates, and he was about to give up, as was his wont, when an enormous woman with a red Irish face opened the inner door and confronted him. "You want to see the room," she asked, more in the manner of a statement than a question. And so at last he had escaped. The old furniture in his former apartment

119

he had sold, and moved only his clothes, a few knickknacks and a pair of ivory figurines, one depicting Fertility, the other Ancient Darkness.

Another phase of his existence had begun.

In the office that afternoon of the impending party, April Tremaine was standing at his desk. He had scarcely noticed the stir among the men who were around as she entered, and it was a moment before he realized it was her voice speaking to him.

"You're going to Mr. Sullivan's retirement party, Jim, aren't you?" she asked.

He looked up vaguely. He had completely forgotten about it. "I . . . I guess so, April," he replied.

It was as if deep in the mists of his numbness, the remembrance of other, older office parties, lived through long ago, stirred faintly. Whether he had enjoyed them or not, he could not remember, but in those days one was always there, one never wanted to miss anything of the scandal and the entertainment and the people who made fools of themselves. He said again faintly: "Yes, I . . . I think so, April, if you'll be there. . . ."

Anyhow, he thought, there'd be something to drink. They could drain the cup.

"I'll be there," April replied in a low voice. "I'm glad you're coming. Will you pick me up at my place at six?"

"Yes," he answered numbly.

Guido's was an expensive restaurant and bar in the downtown section not far from the office. Its atmosphere was commercial underneath the soft glow of the lighting and the coral-colored high stools at the bar and the *intime* circular booths, but it provided a room upstairs for private parties.

As Martin lingered in the shadows near the entrance, he could see a number of the men standing at the bar, talking and drinking. There was Howard Turner—tall and angular and arrogant-looking—who had just returned from the army. He

120

looked, as someone had uncharitably described him, like an eagle with cataracts. He had been considered one of the division's outstanding men before he was called up, had become an officer and served in Europe and was now back to take up where he had left off. He worked for Kilgore in Mizner's department. He was tall, had a large curved nose and pale hooded blue eyes. He wore tweeds and wore them with elegance. Beside him on the left stood Kilgore, a little pale next to Turner's dazzle, but Kilgore with his light unforgetting eyes, the word had it, was the new power in the division. Jestingly, he had been called "The Brain." He was a quiet man, younger than he looked, but at the same time somewhat forbidding. On the other side of Turner stood Rutherford, quiet and dirty-spoken, another of Kilgore's men.

Martin moved out of the shadows, said hello to them and looked around for faces that were more familiar. He said hello to one or two others, then went upstairs. Saunders was standing in the upstairs room with Seymour and McKenzie. They were grouped around the cocktail bar at one side of the room. Long tables, forming a giant horseshoe with seats for the sixty-odd guests, gleamed with their white cloths and sparkled with the silver and the glasses. Bowls filled with black olives and celery added a festive touch. Saunders and McKenzie waved to him, Saunders holding a martini.

"Well, it's about time!" Saunders brayed. "Where've you been?"

"I didn't know you cared," Martin said.

McKenzie's glasses glinted in the indirect light. He had had a couple and his shining face had turned lobster red. Miland was standing in a corner talking earnestly with a thin girl who had rather stringy black hair and an intent, myopic expression. He was explaining the second act of one of his unfinished plays, and the girl was obviously impressed.

The other girls were milling about, the prettier ones having gathered one or another of the men in tow. No husbands or wives

121

were permitted at these parties with the exception of the guest of honor's wife, and Tom Sullivan was a widower. His wife had died with a sigh of relief many years before.

Martin stood with the three men and sipped a manhattan.

"What's with you?" McKenzie asked him.

Martin was looking for someone. It was odd—the intensity of his wanting, even just to set eyes on her again. She was not in the crowd. He did not wish to appear to be searching, but his glance, despite himself, kept sliding away from them at intervals.

"Same old sheaves," he said. "Bill here and I—" Seymour was helping him with the syndicate material—"Bill and I certainly have the garbage detail of the division now, the old pick-and-shovel corps."

"Yes," Seymour said, "but we don't worry about it. We'll never get out of this world alive." Seymour was fond of irrelevancies that appeared to have crept into his conversation from some alien train of thought. "We certainly won't be inundating the System with sparkling material if something isn't done about the present approval program. . . . Oh hello, Sherry," Seymour called.

Sherry Fields, tall and auburn-haired, one of the office beauties, was sweeping by on Cy Travers' arm. Seymour's eyes had slipped out of focus. She hardly gave the group a glance. She had never liked Martin since the day he missed their first date through having been called out on an assignment. It had inconvenienced her, and she did not like men who inconvenienced her. Her beauty had gained her privileges with men which she now felt only her due, and though secretly she did not really like men, she found one of her deepest satisfactions lay in making them perform for her against their own will and often even to their detriment. She was cool, aloof and splendidly proportioned, with a lovely, sulky face.

Now her thoughts fanned briefly over the men in the group and then evaporated, leaving her untouched. She had become aware earlier—at what instant she did not exactly know—that

122

most of the men there who were free could be made completely susceptible to her. Now, with the equally sure instinct some women have in these matters, she became aware that Martin, whom she had been almost sure of, was an exception.

"I could go for that stuff," Seymour said, rather obviously, Martin thought, as she disappeared with Cy amid the crowd at the bar.

"No heart," Martin said. "An iceberg, a five-for-three girl, a real iceberg."

"You break me up," Seymour said. "I'll still take her. You ever been out with her?"

"No, she wouldn't give me the time of day," Martin answered. He was glancing away again, searching, searching.

"Everybody wants to go to Heaven," Seymour said, "but nobody wants to die—that's a song."

Martin brought himself back with an effort wondering whether he had missed some part of the conversation. It seemed to him to be progressing in looping ellipses like this with gaps in the meaning. But that was always the way at parties. You couldn't always watch everything. Some of it slipped away from you, particularly after the second drink.

"A mistake is evidence that someone tried to do something," Saunders was saying in his loud, carrying voice.

"That in itself is a crime," McKenzie replied.

"Furthermore," a voice was saying in back of Martin, "there'll be blood on the tomahawk if the old man ever finds out we filed the papers where they belonged—in the wastebasket."

"Cute as a flute," another voice was saying, "phony as a coney. . . ."

Music was sudding softly from a small band downstairs, a piece called "The time is not propitious, Aloysius," and the voices were growing louder and less restrained. Soon it would be time for them to gather at the tables, and then the formal and generally more boring part of this typical retirement ceremony would begin. He went downstairs to the main bar. The crowd had grown thicker and moved with a turgid and amoebalike

123

animation from the bar itself to the clusters of people standing or at the tables in the main part of the room, then back to the bar again, following a slow and sinuous, almost dreamlike movement back and forth, back and forth, as if in some strange invertebrate samba.

It was then that he saw them. . . .

She was with Jim Somers, sitting at the bar and surrounded. Mizner was standing behind her, his chewed-over cigar dripping ashes on his sloppy coat, his humorous, dissipated eyes crinkled in the soundless laughter that was one of his characteristics. On the other side, standing next to Mizner, was Doyle, his red face slightly flushed, the look of intense haste which he could never shake off still clinging to his person.

She was beautiful, beautiful. . . .

Martin stood in the shadows for a moment looking at her. He had a terrible longing. He had left a lot of places behind in his life; he had forgotten a lot of people and put the memories of them away and he knew what it was like to desire, to want what had gone; and watching her now, that same longing, that same dark drifting away was with him again, almost a sense of losing something without which he could not survive.

"There's a terrible case of love," a voice spoke at his elbow. He started. Morton Casey was standing behind him. ". . . Somers for that April Tremaine," Casey was saying slowly. "You noticed what's been happening to Somers?" Casey asked. "He's been in awful shape lately. . . ."

"Yes . . ." Martin replied vaguely. He was trying to drag his gaze away from the girl. He could not pull himself out of the slough, from that indissoluble longing. "Yes . . ." he said.

Casey appeared to melt away. Martin was lost. The murmur was all around him like the surf from a vast Sargasso Sea. With anyone else, he thought, I could just go up and say something witty or flip and thus catch her attention and maybe her interest. Or I could just ask for a date. But with this terrible feeling inside, this paralysis—what is it holds one back? What is it keeps one rooted here, unable to make the crucial move? A man can't

124

just stand there and let it all slip away, let her escape amid the laughter and voices of those others who, no matter how much they cared, must care so much less than he did.

Slowly he made his way forward toward the bar. Doyle smiled at him. Mizner turned around. "Well, if it isn't old Brill," he said in his throaty, gravelly voice, "the golden boy. Have a drink on me, son!"

Martin suddenly liked Mizner very much.

"Thanks," he said, "thanks. Hi, Jim," he said. "Hello, April. . . ."

" 'Hello, April.' " Mizner mimicked him. "Listen to the change of tone. . . . I don't blame you a bit, my boy," Mizner said, his eyes crinkling, "I don't blame you a bit!"

April turned around and looked at Mizner. She put out her tongue at him. Then she smiled at Martin. "Hello, Martin," she said, "where have you been?"

"Looking for you," he replied, in what he hoped was a light tone. "I wanted to buy you a drink."

She turned her slow green eyes on him in faint surprise. "Why, thank you, Martin," she said. "A little later perhaps. Jim has been buying." She looked at Somers fondly. He had a smile on his numb face for the first time, it seemed to Martin, in months. "I think Jim and these other men are trying to ply me," she added, "and I can't think why."

Mizner leaned over and kissed her loudly on the back of the neck. She gave a squeal. Martin's heart contracted. "You beast, Andrew," she said.

Mizner's face always looked as if he had not shaved adequately, and it was obvious that he was not young, although no one knew exactly how old he was; but almost everyone liked and admired him, and, gray and grizzled as he was, he was probably the most popular press manager the Company had ever had.

Martin drifted away, feeling lost and rather lonely. The voices swirled around him, now more blurred, more dreamlike. "We all have our little hidden virtues . . ." someone was saying, and another soft-water voice was speaking low: "You have to start

125

at the bottom here and work everybody. . . ." "Unhampered by sanity . . ." someone else murmured, "completely unhampered by sanity. . . ." At the summit of the stairs, he ran into Mitzy Dale, an attractive little Irish girl who worked in one of the outer offices. She seized his arm. "Are you going to buy little me a drink, Martin?" she asked. Someone had apparently already bought little her a drink. At that moment across the room, Talbott, who was Sullivan's immediate supervisor, began to bang on a glass to round up the people and bring them to the tables for dinner. Someone went downstairs to find those in the main restaurant.

Martin maneuvered away and watched carefully but could not secure a seat anywhere near April. There were place cards, and he found himself placed between the glamorous Sherry and a small, pasty-faced, rabbitlike girl with glasses, whose lower lip twitched. Now, seated beside this girl, he wracked his brains for her name. Finally in desperation he leaned toward Sherry, who was listening coolly to an animated dissertation by Cy Travers on her right.

"What's the girl's name sitting next to me on the other side?" he whispered. Sherry turned her head slowly. She gave the rabbity girl a regal look. "Why, hello, Theresa," she said loudly.

The girl jumped as if she had been touched in a delicate spot by an acetylene torch. Sherry had never spoken to her before. "Why, hello Sherry," she answered in a low voice. "How are you?"

Sherry had performed her duty and now, feeling no need to continue the conversation, turned back to her other dinner companion. Martin searched desperately for something to say to Theresa. This was not one of his more social evenings.

"Would you care for my drink, Mr. Brill?" the girl finally asked in a low frightened voice. "I don't drink."

"Why, thank you, Theresa," he said. "I believe I could use it."

Far up the line *she* sat between Mizner and Somers.

The skits began.

126

Talbott was the master of ceremonies—a smooth, moon-faced man, who obviously enjoyed an audience. He had risen and stood at the main table next to the guest of honor, old Tom.

"Ladeez and gentlemen . . ." he commenced. The voices began to die away slowly into a low murmur and then a restless hush fell with only the faint clink of the silverware and glasses. "All of us are here tonight to say goodbye to an old friend." Talbott's voice was smooth, unctuous. "It has been the custom since time immemorial to bring testimony of the many fine things and secret kindnesses that a man like the man we hope to honor tonight has performed in his long, useful and splendid career. We have been witnesses ourselves to many of these—may I use the word?—precious moments of this career, and we are gathered now not only to honor him but also to bring back and to remember with him some of those great days he has spent with us and with the Company. We have them here like exhibits in a courtroom—a series of exhibits which we have labeled Exhibit A and Exhibit B and so on. You are the witnesses at this trial of one of our more beloved associates. You were there when some of these events of his career took place. You—many of you—were the beneficiaries of his unselfishness and enthusiasm, of his vast experience and his unfailing willingness to share that knowledge and enthusiasm with any and all who needed it. But enough of this preliminary. We shall return to a consideration of the man himself later. Now I shall ask you to shift around here in your seats so that you can see the first of this array of exhibits—Exhibit A. . . ."

The stertorous tones flowed impressively over the somewhat stunned diners, caught halfway through their soup, as the performances commenced. First there was a huge photograph of Tom Sullivan, blown up almost to life-size, depicting him as he had looked some thirty-five years ago when he had first arrived, young and green, in the Company as an eager and hopeful installer. In those days he had been wearing what looked like a handle-bar mustache—a fine broth of a boy. It appeared to one or two sitting there a rather desperate thing that time had

127

done to Tom—from that fresh-faced, eager, not unhandsome young man to the man who was sitting up there at the table of honor that evening. What had happened in the years? What mysterious alchemy had turned that boy into this . . . this miserable and mean old man? But their thoughts were quickly cut off, as the laughter and clapping rose to a crescendo.

Then came the next exhibit . . . and the next, various members of the department stepping up to act out a few mythical parts of old Tom's—as the master of ceremonies put it—"distinguished and enviable career." There was some good-natured attention paid to Tom's unreliable temper and one or two sly digs at a few of Tom's little foibles, and each skit was received with good-humored laughter and hearty applause. Indeed, as the skits continued, the laughter and applause increased, and in some quarters it increased in direct proportion to the number of drinks consumed.

Martin was enjoying every moment of it. He had scarcely known old Tom Sullivan, but as he toyed with his chicken and ate, now absently, now with abandon, the salad, green peas and mashed potatoes or chewed on a piece of celery, he punctuated his eating with laughter and clapped loudly, scarcely tasting the food, and he thought what a fine man old Tom must have been. The courses thus succeeded each other amid the noise and laughter, and then abruptly the exhibits were over, and it was time to be solemn.

"Friends," Talbott concluded softly after the last laugh had died away and the last murmur had subsided, "friends, and I use the word with no little emotion—" a tremor had now crept into his voice—"I—and many of you too—have known Tom Sullivan a long long time . . ." Heads turned and necks began to crane at the thin turkey-gobbler-like figure in his best suit, sitting in the guest of honor's place at the center table. Suddenly it seemed to them all as if the wizened and wrinkled figure seated there impassively munching on an olive had been one of their more delightful and wonderful personalities. Their hearts went out to him.

128

". . . and no one—no one, I say—who has ever worked with Tom, with this splendid man—" Talbott's voice was low and shaking with emotion; all the stops were out—"no one, I say, can have failed to appreciate his wide and recondite knowledge, his unfailing kindness, his resourcefulness in time of need, his amazing faculty for finding a way to do the job and to do it right, his flair for the exact moment, the right time, and last but by no means least, his unflagging willingness to help others.

"Many's the time," Talbott continued softly, "as all of you can bear witness, when we—the department, the whole division even—was in a jam. We had to get something out—something had to be gotten out—not tomorrow, not today, but, as it were, yesterday. And to whom did we turn?" Talbott asked softly. "Who was the one man we could find to perform the miracle? We all knew." Talbott's voice dropped an octave. He was steaming in at the finish now strongly. "There's an old story—some of you may have heard it. . . . It is put down in a great book—a book without which none of us would be able to travel very far in this world, and it goes something like this: 'And I heard the voice of the Lord saying: "Whom shall I send and who will go for us?" Then said I, "Here am I; send me. . . ." ' That," said Talbott softly and sonorously, "that was Tom Sullivan—our Tom Sullivan. And Tom—Tom always—and I repeat *always*—came through. . . ."

There was a hush as the sound of Talbott's mellow voice died away, and then a soft rustling. They were all deeply moved. They had all known Tom. They all knew Tom was incompetent. They all knew Tom was the last man anyone would turn to if he wanted a job done right. They were all aware that, if time were of the essence, if it were essential to procure something quickly, old Tom Sullivan could qualify as the one person not to call on—that his rank as the undisputed champion time-waster of the entire division was forever secure. And they were aware of considerations even more fundamental in any assessment of Tom's personality. A bully, a tyrant, a coward—rude, incoherent and ineffectual—Tom Sullivan had irritated more people, ground down more spirits and blighted the careers of more young men unfortunate enough to be placed in a position to report to him than any other single man in the recent annals of the group. But none of these things counted now. Good old Tom, they thought, under the influence of the mellowing atmosphere, the soft lights. They would never see him again, and it all seemed rather sad. Good old Tom. They would miss him, miss his gobbling high-pitched scream, miss his incompetence, his scrabbling gait across the office with sheaves of papers fluttering in his hand, his Adam's apple bobbing up and down. They would miss his insufferable meanness. . . .

"And so," Talbott concluded softly, "and so we say to this splendid man: 'Goodbye, old friend,' we will say, and 'Pleasant journey,' and 'May you enjoy many more years of the leisure and relaxation that you have so richly earned, that should be your reward for these thirty-seven years of service to the System.'"

The silence at the conclusion of this peroration was complete. A few of them had tears in their eyes, and they were all, men and girls alike, deeply affected. Then abruptly the applause burst forth, and the hurried murmur of favorable comment, and finally someone, possibly Sims, Martin thought—one of those who had reported to Sullivan—rose to present the "little gift and token of their affection and esteem." The little gift was an enormous suitcase of fine leather, suitably initialed in gold with old Tom's initials, and then it was time for old Tom to speak.

For a moment, there was an intense hush, as the old man struggled out of his chair, almost upsetting his highball glass on the table beside him. He stood rather unsteadily, peering out at the sea of expectant and glowing faces, his Adam's apple bobbing up and down in his effort to bring something out. Finally, with a burst of furious energy, he yelled in the silence:

"Fellow friends . . ." Then he choked up. He stood there swaying a little for what appeared an eternity, then, tears streaming down his face, he choked out: "I can only say, humbly, from the bottom of my heart: Thank you, thank you and thank you.

And God bless you all." And with that he sat down abruptly.

The applause was deafening. It seemed to them at the moment that they had never heard such an affecting speech or one that welled so deeply from the heart. Now the applause was dying down slowly, gradually, and now chairs began to scrape and in groups of twos and threes they rose from what all agreed had been a very satisfying and heart-warming retirement dinner.

Martin caught her almost immediately afterwards downstairs in the bar. She was still with Jim Somers, Mizner, Doyle and now Seymour. He blundered into it. He had no more tact or control now. "April," he said in a low voice, "can I speak with you?"

She looked up at him, completely nonplused. Slowly she turned around. "Be right back," she said, as Mizner threw her an arch look. Jim Somers sat stonily over his rye and ginger ale.

Martin had a feeling like that of a man who has just let go on a toboggan slide and is bucketing along unable to grasp anything to slow himself down or to break the dizzying descent. He knew he had done this all wrong. He had stumbled into it. He might as well keep right on sliding, he thought. There was nothing to do about it.

"April," he began desperately, "I'm sorry I broke in on you like this, but . . . well, would you go out one evening with me?"

She looked at him in almost complete surprise. Something about his face irritated her. Golden boy, they had called him —a good-looking, friendly, magnetic, man—a little too good-looking with that faint sense of strain. She had seen his kind before, and she had seen that longing in men's eyes; yet somehow now it angered her.

"Why?" she asked, gazing full at him.

He looked down. He knew he had given himself away, and what was the use?

"Because, I guess, I like you," he said slowly in a low voice.

She stood looking at him steadily. At last she spoke. He

131

watched those soft full lips, that deep bosom partially revealed in the low-cut dark cocktail dress.

"I don't know whether I like you enough, Martin," she answered thoughtfully. "Maybe sometime . . . sometime later. I'll have to think it over a little." She stood looking at him for a moment. Then she turned and walked slowly away.

He watched her leaving him, and that indissoluble longing was with him again. Somehow he felt she would not have said that to anybody else. She might have refused but she would not have done it so bluntly. She would have been kind. Well, the cup was empty. I might as well have another drink, he thought. The voice at his elbow stopped him. It had an amused drawl. "What's the matter, lover—no response?" He turned. It was Sherry, standing tall and composed, her lovely face twisted in a scornful smile. . . .

It seemed to be much later.

Saunders, rather the worse for wear, was telling them how he'd walk a mile over broken glass not to have to spend an evening with the spouse and kiddies. Someone in the background was singing:

> *"She was a butterfly's daughter*
> *And I was the son of a bee . . ."*

Carbury, one of the older members of Doyle's department, was saying rather sadly: "And after all, adultery is still better than celibacy . . ." and it was now about the hour when the saddest farewells have begun to take place, when old friendships start to disintegrate and old associates begin to say exactly what they think of each other, and the ranks of the great buddy-buddies are thinning. He had about reached the end of an evening.

A soft voice spoke his name.

He turned. It was, surprisingly, she—as beautiful as if she had just arrived, beautiful as his dreams, but her white forehead was wrinkled in a frown.

"Martin," she said. "It's Jim. Will you help me with him?"

132

Martin stepped away from the others and took her arm.

"What's the matter with him, April?" he asked.

"He's just had a little too much," she said softly. "I can't get him home by myself."

"I'll help you," he said.

She turned and he walked after her toward one of the small circular booths in the shadows. Jim Somers sat there with his head in his arms, deep in a sea of oblivion.

Martin leaned over him and shook him gently.

"All right, Jim," he said. "Let's go. Time to go home."

Jim stirred restlessly. "Go 'way," he mumbled.

Martin shook him again. He sat down beside him and placed an arm on his shoulder. "Come on, Jim," he said. "Make an effort. You've had it, old man. Let's go."

"Where's April?" Jim asked in a slurred voice.

"She's here, Jim," Martin replied softly. "Look, Jim, she wants you to go now. You've got to go. She wants you to go home. I'll help you up."

"Aw righ'," Somers said. He was very tired. Deep in the mists of his consciousness, the vague knowledge that April wanted him to rise and go forth sank slowly. He struggled. Martin slipped an arm around his waist and hoisted him to his feet.

In the fresh, exhilarating spring evening, the cool air revived him, and Martin had no difficulty pushing him into a cab. April sat on Somers' left and Martin climbed in and slammed the door.

"Do you know where he lives?" Martin asked, looking hard at her.

She returned his regard steadily. "Yes," she said. She gave the driver the block, and the cab started. In the taxi, Jim sank once more into the depths. He placed his hand trustingly in April's, and his lips moved faintly, soundlessly forming her name. She looked at him, Martin noticed, with a maternal tenderness. His heart contracted savagely.

At the door of the rooming house, Martin eased him out. "I'll take care of him," he said. He held her gaze again. "You

133

might as well take the cab back to your place. He'll be all right. I'll look after him."

"No," she answered. She climbed out. He paid the cab and they watched it drive off.

They walked down the two steps of the old building into the darkness of the small entrance. Somers appeared to come back to life. He fumbled through his pockets and with difficulty finally produced some keys. Martin tried them. One of them opened the front door. Up the stairs they stumbled. At the door of Somers' room, April turned to him. "All right," she said, "I'll go now. You take care of him, will you, Martin?"

"I told you I would," he replied angrily; "you should have kept the cab." She stood there a moment quietly. He looked up. She was gazing at him full in the face.

"Martin," she said softly, "it won't do you much good, but I'll go out with you, if you want."

"I want," he said.

She turned and walked slowly down the stairs, her high heels clicking loudly. He heard the front door shut. Then he turned to help Somers.

It was not until a Friday evening two weeks later that he had managed to secure their first date. Since the night of the party she appeared to have been eluding him very effectively, but one evening he took his courage in his hands and called her up. He knew he had been acting like a schoolboy. He knew that he should have learned the lesson each must learn sooner or later: that there will always be some who want you and some who do not, and it is vain to cry for those who do not or to waste one's time in futile struggling. It was not entirely that he was lonely. He had been lonely before and he had not really minded it too much. And there were the books and the music and, if necessary, there were the other girls—but the fact remained, none of them made any sense now or meant anything to him. Some lines from Gide returned to his mind vaguely . . . "He seeks to distinguish in the darkness—for night is falling—where the winding path has chosen to lead him . . ." and that was how he felt—like a man walking down a dark and winding path, following it along despite himself into the unknown. Why, when there might have been so many, did it have to be this one? he had asked himself. Why—when he had seen beauty before; he had glimpsed it often —did it have to be just that particular hair and green eyes and that particular voice and face? He had walked away from others, even from those who had cared for him and might have given him much, and he had let the doors close and had ignored the weeping —and he had had one or two since, but now it was all as nothing and it had become his turn to do the wondering and the dreaming and perhaps in the end the weeping.

Well, there was no use deceiving oneself. He was a simple fellow and he knew what he wanted. I am what I am, he had said to himself in his rooms the evening he had decided to make the call, and why should I try to pretend differently? There are values I should like to possess, qualities I should like to have—above and beyond what I am and what I have, but here it is impossible to deceive oneself. Here one must be always the man he is, even if it means remaining lonely all your life. For some men, there are many girls and all of them are good. For others, it is passion, pure and simple, and any substitute for love will do. But there are a few who cannot make the substitution, who cannot be content with the many, and he was one of them. And now he had found the one. . . .

On the telephone, she had said to him: "You never give up, do you?"

"I know what I want," he answered.

"But what about what I want?" she asked softly.

"I will give up when I have to," he said.

"All right," she answered at last, "make it seven o'clock Friday evening."

So the week before the date passed for him in a mist of pleasure. He was completely bemused. For the moment the old world had returned. In the evenings he played his recordings— the Brahms No. 2 in D major and the Tschaikovsky of which he was so fond. And he searched for an essence in himself, an enterprise that would be different and new and would take him out of the ruck of their existence, out of that mire of those worldly ambitions that they were all so hopelessly sunk in.

And then it was Friday.

"What makes you so dissatisfied?" she asked. They were sitting in a bar and restaurant a few blocks from her place. At the quiet corner table, she was looking at him with that faintly veiled hostility. She felt at ease in the situation, as does one who knows she has the upper hand in love, and yet an essence about him disturbed her, half aroused her slumbering senses.

"Everybody wants to get on in the world," he said. "I'm one of those who don't want to sleep before evening."

"Yes, but they know what they want to do," she answered thoughtfully.

"I can't help it, April," he replied. "I know this isn't it, and that there must be something else waiting somewhere for me. Otherwise, I shall end up, my whole existence no-purposed away. I wanted something else, and not to have set the world on fire is something no man, if he is honest, can forgive himself. . . ."

"And you're smarter than the rest of us?" she asked provocatively.

"Don't tease me, April," he said

"I'm not teasing," she replied. The vague hostility was stronger in her. Who did he think he was?—the reflection brushed her mind.

"Waiting appears to be one of your specialties, though," she said. "If you have something, you have to take it out and show it in the marketplace. . . ."

"You're unbearably practical, April," he said. "Can't I tell you my life story? I'm sensitive. Tea and sympathy, you know. That's what beautiful blondes are for."

"You kill me," she said.

"But seriously, April, is it worth a man's life to spend his

136

years on trivialities like this? Pretty soon these little projects come to seem important—and then you're caught . . . you're hooked. . . ."

"I don't know, Martin," she said. "These longings aren't my dish. Mine are different. But you're not the only one who has wanted something else. There have been a lot of them—a lot of live wires from nowhere who felt they were wasting themselves here, who felt they had too much to give to be spending it like this on the routines. Most of them had nothing to give, really. They didn't have it. They just wanted something for nothing, and they never had had it. Perhaps you're different. I don't know, Martin. Perhaps, some opportunity will open up, as you believe it will, and you'll go out and leave us flat, and we'll be saying that we knew you when. . . .

"Don't misunderstand me, Martin," she added after a pause. "I don't mean there haven't been people here and in other places who found something better, more satisfying than anything the Empire could offer them. There've been people like that. . . .

"But there are a lot of men, a great many more, really—men like . . . like Jim Somers—who have found in the Empire exactly what they want, who have been happy here and have understood its . . . its essential values and received—I guess you'd call it—a certain fulfillment. . . ."

He looked down.

"You like Jim, don't you?" he said.

She paused. "Yes," she answered shortly.

"Do you think you could ever like me?" he asked. "And please don't tell me that you do like me, because that isn't the way I mean it, and I'm aware that you really don't like me anyhow. . . ."

She bit her lip slightly.

"You exasperate me," she said. "If I ever do really, I'll tell you," she answered finally.

"You'll give me a chance?" he asked again.

"Perhaps," she replied.

"Well," he said slowly, "after that passionate response, where would you like to go now? Would you care to hear some good music up at my place?"

"As a matter of fact, I would," she said.

She liked the apartment. She liked the books on the floor and the books lying every which way on the shelves. She liked the soft light, the warmth. She liked the color of the rug and curtains, and she had two highballs and listened to Brahms and Hadyn. But the faint hostility toward him remained.

There was a picture of his mother on the table but none of anyone else—no girls, she noted briefly.

"A flute is all things young
Beginnings without an end . . ."

he quoted. She wanted to hear the rest. "That's all I know," he said. "My mind is a hodgepodge of odds and ends. I've tried to read them all, hear them all, love them all. . . . That's why I've never gone anywhere."

"You don't know where you want to go," she answered.

"But I know what I want," he said, looking at her directly.

She glanced down. "I wish I did," she murmured. "I think I know what I want sometimes, but then again I find it's something else—something else keeps intruding. . . . Maybe I'm cold—or too practical—or maybe it isn't there for me to really care. . . ."

"You're not exactly an idealist," he commented softly.

"You can make a lot of mistakes in just one lifetime," she said. "I've made them."

He gazed down at her. She was sitting on the floor beside a pile of recordings. Her full red lips, creamy skin, long curved lashes veiling green eyes, the great piled blond hair—all ravished him. Why did she not care for him? Why did he not have it for her, as he had had it for others? She was everything he wanted —everything. . . .

In the end, as it was about time for her to leave, she said:

138

"This has been a lovely evening, Martin. I didn't think it would be. I was afraid."

He stooped down as she was about to rise and slipped his arms around her from behind. She rose and twisted, her face was turned toward him and he held her tight and pressed his lips hard against her soft lips. For an instant, she seemed to respond. Then she pushed him away. "Don't," she said. "Don't do that again. Don't ever do that again," she added, "unless I tell you, if you want to go out with me."

He stood back, still in the glow of holding her. "It was only a kiss," he said. "I didn't rape you."

"I didn't come to kiss," she said.

"I did," he replied angrily.

They walked slowly in the warm summer night. He was at ease and happy, yet he felt her latent hostility still there. As they passed the corner drugstore, he asked: "Do you want a drink or a soda?"

"A soda," she said.

It was after midnight, yet the town was lit up and sparkling. The summer exodus to the country was just beginning, but the city still appeared to have a lot of people in it and a lot of them were out late. At the counter, they sipped sodas through straws and talked.

"You don't like to talk about your work, do you?" she remarked.

"No, I don't," he replied. "I'm sensitive. I'm trying to forget. Tomorrow will be here soon enough." She looked at her watch.

"It is here," she said. "Come on, you can walk me home."

"If you think for one minute I intend to walk twenty blocks back even with you," he replied, "you have the wrong boy. We are going in a cab and then I can stand outside near your place and talk to you some more."

"Is it that far?" she asked. "So it is. Well, let's take the bus then."

"A cab for you, April—nothing but the best." He whistled at one parked on the corner.

In the cab, he held her hand. She allowed him to hold it with his own hand resting lightly on her knees but seemed passive and unaware. They descended two blocks from her door, so that she could have a last short walk.

There were trees on the street, well-cared-for lindens throwing shadows, and they stood together under the glow of the street lamp and near one of the trees outside her apartment house.

"Did you enjoy yourself?" he asked.

"I enjoyed myself," she said. "You know it."

"Then you will go out with me again?"

She stood quiet a moment as if lost in thought.

"You have to do me a favor," she said at last.

"What is it?" he asked.

"You know Jim Somers has had some trouble at home. I . . . I can't tell you about it. It's something to do with his wife. She is not well. But he's . . . as you saw, he's having a little trouble in the office too—trouble with his work. I want you to . . . to try to help him out a bit. You know what Randall's like, if a man has a low streak. It . . . it isn't like when Mr. Carlyle was there —he would have understood—and . . . and I don't think Harwood understands either. . . . Well, what I'm asking you is . . . is to see if you can't somehow help Jim out. . . ." She faltered to a stop.

He stood there for a long time, furious and depressed. So that was what she had wanted of him. So that was why she had consented to spend the evening with him. That was the reason for this sudden sweet symphony of friendship. He could feel the blood drain from his face. Her large sea-green eyes were fixed on him. So that was the way she was going to play it, he thought. Not that he cared. She should know what a woman who bestowed her company for a consideration was called. Well, if that was the way she wanted to play it, that was the way it would be. She could have her gentleman Somers, her handsome Somers, but eventually he would win out. He would have her at her own

140

price; he'd pipe her tune now and she would have to pay for it later. He would have her in the end. All that savage beauty, he thought bitterly, and the heart of a whore.

He swallowed hard.

"All right, April," he answered softly. "Have it your own way. I'll do my best for Somers. I'll take care of it. I'll do my best."

Something of what was in his mind must have reached her, for she said: "Are you angry with me, Martin? I . . . I'm just trying to help someone who's nice and whom I'm fond of and who is down and out."

He shook his head. "Does my assistance rate a goodnight kiss?" he asked coldly.

"Oh Martin, please," she said. "Don't take it like that."

He seized her suddenly again and pulled her to him in the shadows. "You are absolutely heartless," he said in a low voice, "but I shall have my kiss anyhow. You can't raise a fuss over a little thing like a kiss. It's a small consideration for all I am to do for you."

He pressed once more to her soft full lips and held her close. She remained passive. Her lips were cold and there was no response. He let her go roughly. He started to say something, then turning abruptly, began to walk away without looking back. He walked down the dark street, his footfalls sounding loud in the silence of the spring night and of what suddenly seemed to him like a deserted town.

I shall dance to her tune now, he thought again savagely, but someday she will dance to mine—someday.

5

IT WAS a period of tremendous expansion.

The emergency calls were out: three shifts and the modernizing of machinery and processes and the blueprinting of new and vaster networks. The boys were up late burning incense to the new god: Reconversion. And with it all an enormous financing program had been launched that meant reinvestment, the floating of great stock issues and the making of vast loans.

It was now in the force of engineers, specialists and scientists that the shortages began to appear. But the Empire still held a great reservoir of skill, and it turned this force to the building of new resources, to the stretching of its towers and lines into new areas, to the making of greater networks. . . .

And in this mounting avalanche of activity, Jim Somers and his small operation were completely buried. The effect of being let alone and of the movement around him were beneficial, and for the first time in months, faint glimmers of light began to dawn in his personal life. For reasons that escaped him, the misery that had been with him night and day now began, intermittently, to lift. His visits to the little bars grew less frequent. And he started to notice what was taking place around him. He seemed to note also that others were expressing an interest in his efforts. On several occasions, Brill, surprisingly, had stayed after work with him during an evening or so, when he decided to catch up, and had helped him finish.

Actually at this time, Jim had no personal life, no existence outside the one that drew him downtown regularly every morning —and he had no wish for any other life. If out-of-hours activities could be said to exist for him, they were the occasional evenings he spent with April at little restaurants or bars around town. He liked April. Theirs was not, he congratulated himself, the crude and sordid relationship in which others in these circumstances might indulge. Theirs was a relationship somewhat like that close and pure one he had experienced with Betty Lou. There could be no possibility of his marrying now under the present circumstances at least for the time being, but perhaps someday when this nightmare was completely ended . . .

So the slow bloom of the expansion continued, as Jim gradually emerged from the darkness, and the fever of activity began to rise. And all might have been well with them, had it not been for

142

a sudden, odd, and because it was so unexpected, frightening turn of events in the late summer and fall of that year.

For no apparent reason, in the midst of all this activity and amid the feverishness of a vast expansion, like a bolt from the blue, business abruptly began to fall off. It was not a gradual drift downward. It was a sudden sharp drop everywhere. They had been sailing along, and suddenly instruments began reading zero all over the country. Steel had become scarce and prices everywhere uncertain. Stormy weather had set in, and the prophets of doom began their pilgrimages in the new deserts, proclaiming another depression.

All of this hit headquarters like a hurricane, and as management began to take in sail, and in all quarters the accountants and comptrollers—those harbingers of disaster—commenced to pore over their figures, the news like a series of ugly rumors, of poisonous gossip sifted down to public relations. The day of the locust, just as predicted, had arrived again. . . .

Martin had been sent out earlier on an assignment to report on the establishment of one of the new small plants springing up everywhere in the wake of the earlier renaissance.

He had left on a Tuesday early in August. It was late at night when the plane landed at the airport, and he took the limousine into town to the main hotel. He climbed into bed completely exhausted and wondering where he would be able to find the System men who had been sent out for the job.

In the morning about ten o'clock, he rose, dressed and went down to the coffee shop for breakfast. As he was drinking his coffee, it occurred to him that perhaps System men from Chicago might be registered at the hotel. If so, they were his. If not, he would call up Cassidy long-distance and ask for instructions on how to find them.

"Yes," the clerk said, "there are three Chicago men in town registered here. Take your choice."

Martin used the house phone and picked one of the men at random.

A hard voice answered.

143

He explained his mission.

"Yeah, New York told us to expect you," the voice said. "Come on up. Suite 820."

Martin knocked. In the rather elegant suite, three men were sitting in various positions of relaxation with their coats off. One of them was a tall sandy-haired angular man in sloppy businessman's clothes. The second man had light hard eyes and looked like a thug masquerading as a respectable commuter, and the third man was slight and willowy with the face of a cashiered British officer.

"Take your coat off and sit down," the sandy-haired man said. "So you're public relations, eh?" he continued with his tight-lipped smile. "Can't even get away from you boys up here in the wilderness, can we?"

Martin unbuttoned the bottom button of his jacket and slowly took it off. "That's our job," he replied mildly, smiling. He knew how to get along with these men. He'd seen their type before. "They figured you boys were having it too easy up here, so they sent me out to complicate matters."

"So you'd like to see how a plant is started?" the tall man remarked carefully. "Well, you come to the right people. . . . That's our specialty nowadays."

Martin relaxed. Yes, he'd seen these types before. They were no phonies. They were hard men with a lot of soft, sloppy talk to cover it all up with. They were born organizers. These were the men down on the trudge-shoot-and-burn level, the kind the Empire sent out when it wanted someone to get a project started in a hurry. They were the Company's workers.

The tired man spoke with an ill-concealed yawn. "You want a good story," he said with a sigh. "Well, we just leased a building downtown that has a stuffed buffalo in front of it. God knows what the Company is going to do with it—either the building or the stuffed buffalo—but that's what we've done so far. . . ."

The tall angular man broke in.

"Yep," he said, "Trevor's right, and that's not all we're doing for the good ol' System. We're hiring this morning, and you know

144

what the first girls we hire are going to sit on? I'll tell you. They're going to sit on wooden boxes, because we just haven't been able to round up any chairs so far in this town. They just don't seem to sell chairs here. Yes sir, you angle right along down with us, son, and we'll show you how to get a good ol' plant started with plain nothin' to start with. . . ."

And that was Martin's first day. He was back on the circuit again.

Martin was still out on the assignment when the storm warnings began to fly in late summer. At dead center, in the office, the atmosphere had grown grim. The economic blow was in full force. The figures on economic paralysis were starting to flow in, and medium management—those in the operational fields who had control of the valves—as they had so often in the past, began to panic. The boys were beginning to throw themselves head-first over a wall. It appeared to them as if the old days that no one could seem to forget had come again. And once more, the terrors of life were with them, the ancient fears—loss of position, degradation, defeat. . . .

On the third Tuesday in August, Mr. Mansard called a meeting of his managers in his office for ten-thirty.

Randall had been working on a revised budget for his department to take into account the recession. Doyle, always a hard man with a nickel, had already cut the advertising program to the bone. Mizner alone, whose attitude could only be described as cynical, had decided to ask for the whole program and, in fact, suggest an increase in his department's funds. He did not expect the increase but he had a point to make. Now he was sitting in his large, rather messy office, riffling through unanswered correspondence. He had a luncheon engagement with two newspaper friends and he hoped Mansard would not be keeping them into the lunch period. He buzzed.

The green-eyed blonde appeared.

"April," he said, "give these letters to Bob Kilgore to have answered for me. And also ask him to get out our budget for last year and make up something for this year from it that he thinks has a chance of getting through. Tell him I want every project we have on the fire provided for, and if it's too much, tell him to give out with some of that persuasive palaver of his in a memo, so that the Old Man can't say no. . . .

"And April—" he stopped her as she turned to go—"if I'm not back from the meeting by noon, call Avery, will you please, and tell him I can't make it today. Make it for . . . let me see . . . Thursday. And wish me luck."

"I'll cross my fingers for you," she answered. She held up her crossed fingers and smiled at him. Then she turned and walked out.

Mizner slowly lit another cigar, threw the chewed stub of the old one in the wastebasket and leaned back. He had all of fifteen minutes. Mizner was that rarity in the Empire—particularly in lower management at headquarters—he was an outsider. That is, he had been there some thirty years but he had transferred in from an outside job in which he had been successful—a newspaperman. The real System men—the insiders—had on the other hand started with the Company, as the saying was, young, slim and single, and had learned all they knew as they moved up from the ranks.

Now Mizner sat there, a sloppy, middle-aged man, chewing on his cigar and wondering vaguely what damnfool thing management was about to perpetrate. All this because of a small recession. He would bet his bottom dollar it would be over within the year. But a little setback here was like a little pregnancy— you couldn't just outwait it; you had to have the whole baby. They reacted like a bunch of old women, a bunch of gutless summer soldiers—which most of them were. It was difficult to see how, with every indicator flaunting the need for expansion, the need for exploration of new fields—and even those up the line able to visualize this—that this so-called recession could be anything but temporary. Of course, they'd been burned before, but for the love of Mary, were they going to set the place on fire every time the stock market lost a few points? Did every condition of life

146

have to have a Dow-Jones index to these godforsaken babies? He knew how much of the future was not listed on the Big Board.

Oh well, he thought a little wearily, it won't be long now. I'll be getting out of here and back on the old town again where I belong. And this time with a pension. It'll be thirty years—thirty blessed years—a year from next May, and will I love it! It'll be one big relief not to have to drag in and sit around here all day, not to have to listen to the old bellyaching the first little feather-dust out of the routine occurs or to see the fat, contented faces, hear the soft-living voices—and all of them looking exactly alike. He could spot an Empire man anywhere. Some of it may have rubbed off on him, for all he knew: it was so catching. That was their trouble—this world put a stamp on them, and the stamp he saw was not a pretty one . . . it made them look all exactly alike.

Well, what the hell . . . he thought. I suppose I'd better be moseying along up to see what lovely little horror they've cooked up for us now. If Mansard had already received the word from on high, he knew what that would mean. They'd be ramming it up all right. He could hear the screams now.

He rose slowly. As he was about to pour himself a paper cup of water from the silver decanter before leaving, Doyle poked his head into the office.

"You ready for the execution?" he asked.

"Ready," Mizner said.

"Bringing your budget figures along?" Doyle asked. "I have mine with me just in case."

"You know I never have my budget on time," Mizner said dryly. "When the day dawns he wants to put us over the hurdles on that, I'll be unprepared as usual. I don't think that's what he wants to see us about. Where's Randall?"

"He's up adding the finishing touches on a project that he thinks will impress the Old Man," Doyle said. "You know Dave: as if you could impress the Old Man with anything. He said he'll meet us there. I doubt that he'll get a chance to present his big program anyhow."

147

"You are so right," Mizner agreed.

In the elevator, Mizner was aware of an odd feeling of apprehension. It was reasonless and despite himself. I'll be out of here soon, he thought again, and what will it matter anyhow. But somehow it did matter to him. And the fact that it did irritated him. That's the way they get to you in the end, he thought. You just reach the stage where you stop worrying about yourself—you know you're safe; they can't do anything to you, and then you find you've started worrying about them—about all those mean stupid sonsabitches that can be hurt. Well, he'd be glad when he made it, when he was finally out and back on the town.

In the anteroom, they found Randall bending over Miss Kerrigan's desk, putting the last-minute touches on his great project. He greeted them with absent portentousness. Miss Kerrigan emerged from the inner sanctum. "Please step right in, gentlemen," she said. They filed in slowly.

Mansard sat in the gloom of his huge office like a small sparkling toad in a vast cave. As had been his predecessor, he was almost lost behind the large mahogany desk. His face was a thunderstorm, and he kept his eyes glued doggedly on a paper before him. "Good morning, gentlemen," he muttered, "please be seated."

The three men found chairs across from the big desk and sat down nervously. The room seemed very quiet. The louvers of the venetian blinds on the large windows were almost closed to keep out the morning sun. The Old Man continued to sit there silently, staring stonily at the paper.

Mansard was a small grumpy man, elegantly dressed in an expensive double-breasted suit and a fine blue silk bow tie. He wore a cornflower in his buttonhole. As the Company's executives went, he was a rather off-beat man with a desperately commercial mind. His training had been as a district commercial manager, and though he was generally liked and respected by higher management, it was felt that his talents for perusing expense accounts uniquely suited him, in some inexplicable fashion, for public relations. He had been a severe shock to the three managers, but Randall and Doyle, at least, admired his realistic and down-to-earth mind and his ham-handed approach to his administrative duties. Mansard had all the subtlety of a steamroller. Although he liked Mansard personally, Mizner's opinion of his abilities in the public relations field was unprintable. He wished that Carlyle were there. Oddly enough, Mansard himself, for reasons that escaped them, obviously preferred Mizner to his other managers.

On the occasion of their first meeting with Mansard when he assumed his new administrative duties, Randall in his customary earnest fashion had made the mistake of asking an earnest question: "Mr. Mansard," he said, "exactly what, sir, would you say was your philosophy in this job? Or may I put it another way, what would you say is your conception of your functions as the new director of public relations?"

Mansard had peered at Randall as if he suspected him of burning the orphanage down. There was a measured silence while Doyle and Mizner both cringed for their unfortunate colleague. Mizner had once remarked that Randall had the seven deadly virtues; he was always doing something like this, and always with the best of intentions.

Finally, Mansard had replied in his peculiarly dry and penetrating voice: "Mr. . . . er . . . Randall, I don't know whether I understand your question aright," he said slowly. "And I am not so sure that the question has any bearing on our present problems, but I am . . . er . . . flattered that you care. If I do understand you, let me express my philosophy to you . . ." and he turned to the others . . . "and to you all as succinctly as I can. Let me say this: my conception of my functions in this office, as it has been in others, is to do whatever higher management tells me to do, and to do it promptly and efficiently. A corollary of this may be added: I feel it is also my duty to find out what it is higher management wants me to do and to see that

149

as far as public relations is concerned, it is done. That, sir, I think, is what I was hired for. And now, gentlemen, shall we get down to business?"

The silence after this somewhat less than heart-warming show of idealism was deafening. It was evident that Mr. Mansard was not dedicated to the higher sentiments. It was further evident, as they settled to business, that Mr. Mansard was not what was called an idea man. He could take ideas or let them alone—and he preferred to let them alone. He was a shrewd and forthright administrator, and no appeals in the realms of the Beautiful and the True were apt to get anywhere with him. He was all for laying it on the line every time, and no nonsense.

Mizner's feeling about his new boss on this initial occasion could be summed up in his abbreviated thought after the session had been ended: Well, higher management has done it again!

Now Mr. Mansard sat there before them, as he had on that first occasion and on many occasions since, like a small grim Buddha, hunched over his desk, contemplating his navel and brooding. It seemed to be some time before he finally looked up. His penetrating dry voice stabbed the silence.

"This meeting will be brief, gentlemen," he began. "I intend to come to the point immediately. There will be no crying towels passed around, so please bear with me. The ax has fallen. . . ."

He peered at each of the three men as if he suspected one or another of them would attempt an escape. They returned his gaze, each after his own fashion.

"This division," he continued at last, "has been ordered to make a force reduction of ten people—six men and four girls. The girls' names will be placed on a list for circulation to other divisions. The men there is no help for. That means each of you will reduce your groups by two men. You have two weeks in which to make your final selections of those to be laid off temporarily, and to inform them of the fact. You will naturally pay attention to the usual bases of selection of individuals. But I should like to have you place particular emphasis on ability

150

rating in your final choices. This division—and indeed we are not the only division erring in this respect—has been too lenient on nonproducers. Now is the time, it seems to me, to make the adjustments necessary." Mansard paused briefly. "I know this is a burden none of us likes to face," he said mildly, "but we have our orders, and they must be carried out."

"Oh, for the love of Heaven, boss!" Mizner broke in. "They'll be hiring 'em all back in another two or three months anyhow. What has got into 'em? They act like a bunch of old women. It's just a temporary setback. They never used to do this sort of thing!"

Mansard peered at the sloppy, middle-aged man with the fall of ashes on the front of his coat. "What do you want me to do?" he replied angrily. "March into Mr. Wygand's office and tell him it is our considered opinion that they are a bunch of dolts upstairs, and we have decided not to carry out these instructions? Mr. Wygand gives me my orders. I carry them out. You, Andrew —and the rest of you—will do likewise!"

The meeting was over.

In the marble hall, the three men stood together uneasily. "Well, I had a lunch date," Mizner said, "but the hell with it. Let's go downstairs to the dining room and eat."

Randall lowered his head. "I can't eat now, Andrew," he said. "You two go ahead."

"Oh, come on, Dave," Mizner said. "Not eating is not going to change it."

Randall shook his head.

"Well, we better get together and do this job in conference," Mizner said finally. "I'll see you later this afternoon, if you agree."

"All right," Randall replied. And to Doyle: "See you later, Harry."

They watched him walk along down the marble corridor, his head lowered. They both felt the same way.

151

6

I⊤ ᴡᴀs a sparkling Thursday morning in September that Randall finally called in Jim Somers. He had been sitting in his office restlessly for some time, trying to put it off.

The palms of his hands were damp with perspiration and he kept rising from his seat and gazing out of the window at the summits of the buildings limned distantly in the bright blue late summer sky. What is the use of it all? he thought. Why can't a miracle happen, some reprieve from this piece of stupidity. If it is to be temporary, what is the sense to it? But he knew what they meant by temporary. Temporary, in that corporate eternity in which they lived, meant temporary forever, and no miracles occurred in their world. The weight of their inertia was against everything that happened, and any decision trickling down from on high was like a snowballing force, gathering weight as it rolled, until by the time it reached them it was inexorable.

Some of them might try to amend or wriggle out from under or fail to carry out the intent of the orders. Randall could not bring himself to this. He had always been a man to go by the book. In the end, he thought, it worked out better. It might be painful, but the Company knew what would be best in the long run. You had to face that. He would execute his orders as they had been given. A man has a responsibility to things as they are, as well as to things as one would have them.

There had been that last meeting of the three of them, when the final list was presented. He remembered it with a shudder. Randall had had a particularly difficult time making the list up. The new man, Bellamy, was obviously marked, but the other victim—that had been the rub.

In the end he had had to send for Harwood. That session returned to him also. It was a late afternoon and warm even for early autumn. He had been sad and depressed. Miss Kelly had found Harwood and Harwood had entered, his handsome, smooth face composed in the serious lines that were now habitual with him.

"Yes sir?" Harwood said.

"Phil," Randall had begun slowly, "we have been ordered to make a force reduction. Perhaps you've already heard."

"There have been rumors," Harwood replied quietly. He pulled a chair nearer the desk and sat down in that easy, relaxed way which increased the confidence people felt in him. "What's the bad news, boss?" he asked pleasantly, then added with faint humor, "I'm not the first to go, am I?"

Randall ignored the remark. Levity of any sort frightened him, and this was no time to indulge one's sense of humor.

"Phil, I need your help in this," he continued. "We have to let Bellamy go though I hate to lose the boy, but the other of the two who must be dropped—well I can't decide. It narrows down to three possibilities. You're the supervisor and I want you to review for me their qualifications. . . ."

He paused and rubbed his heavy face.

"First, Casey . . . he's low on service, married, no children. Ability, according to his card rating: fair. It's hard to tell really —he's on the syndicate with Brill and Brill is the star of that show. What do you think?"

Harwood leaned back and furrowed his brow. He paused, then he said: "I'd rather reserve judgment for a moment, sir, until we have discussed them all."

"All right," Randall answered. "Now next is Somers. He has service—eight years. Married. No children. Rather old—forty. You'd never think it, would you, but . . . well, I had to pull his card because of his work. Frankly, Phil, I've never honestly known what that man does to justify the position. He's a nice enough fellow. But what would you say?"

Harwood sat quietly, relaxed in his chair. Slowly he lit a cigarette. He drew a deep puff and let the smoke flow out of his mouth and nostrils.

153

"Well, boss," he answered at last, "you're putting me on a spot. These boys are all old friends of mine and it's a little hard to walk in here and presume to sit in judgment on them. But I guess if you want me to, I have to. It's particularly difficult in the case of old Jim Somers. Jim was here when I was brought up from the Works, and—well, he was one of my first friends, so it really goes against the grain to consider him. But I'll be honest with you. Jim simply hasn't been himself. He hasn't been the same. And there have been rumors about his drinking. I don't know what it is. They say he might have had a little trouble at home, but the fact is—well, the work simply doesn't justify it. The performance simply is not there."

"What do you mean: there are rumors he's had trouble at home?" Randall interposed. "Is it anything the Benefit people should know about? Does he need help?"

"It's only a rumor. I actually know nothing about it."

Randall remained silent for a long time. He was looking at Somers' card.

"How about Seymour?" he continued wearily at last. "He's short on service. Married but separated from his wife. One child. Rating in job: fair to moderate. . . ." Randall paused for a moment, rereading the card. "Rating: fair to moderate. Oh hell," he said, "that lets Seymour out. So now, Phil, it's between Somers and Casey. . . ."

Harwood lounged, smoking.

"Boss—" he broke the silence at last—"I wouldn't want to help you make up your mind on an important matter like this, but here are my thoughts. This Casey is still pretty young, and I don't believe he's been given quite a fair shake in his rating. It appeared to me that perhaps a few of the achievements Brill receives credit for may be partly his also. But don't let me influence you," he added hastily. He fell silent once more. "Of course," he concluded thoughtfully, "that drinking with Somers is growing to be a problem. I may just have to find someone to help finish that work sometime soon. . . ."

Harwood looked at Randall with level, thoughtful eyes. He

154

knew now that that had done it. Yes, it was all over. Somehow he felt both glad and in a way sorry. Somers had been a good man and he had hated to have to do it to him.

Now Randall turned from the window and sat down again. He did not see how it could have turned out any other way. Well, now he had to face it. No use sitting around trying to find excuses. He might as well get it over with as quickly as possible. He buzzed Miss Kelly.

"Send Jim Somers in, will you please?" he said.

"Yes sir," she answered.

He stood near the window a moment longer. The sparkling blue of the sky was like a judgment on him, a reproach, belying that sense of frustration and wrong he could not shake off. Over the towers of the city shone the flawless radiance of the winy day. Oh hell, he thought. Then he walked to his desk and sat down.

Somers' handsome, impassive face appeared in the doorway. "You want to see me, sir?" he asked.

"Come in, Jim," Randall began kindly. "Sit down a moment. I'd like to talk something over with you."

Somers walked toward the desk slowly and took a chair. His face was rather pale and his eyes had dark smudges under them, but otherwise he appeared his usual self—well dressed and composed. It seemed to Randall indeed that he looked much better now than he had lately, and Randall was gratified. Somers was a good-looking man—there was no doubt about it. One would never believe he was forty years old. He certainly did not show his age.

"Will you have a smoke?" Randall asked, offering a cigarette from the silver box on his desk.

"Thanks," Somers said. Randall noticed that the man's hand trembled as he held the cigarette.

"Jim," Randall began slowly, "I'm afraid I have some bad news for you." He paused, marshaling his thoughts for a way to soften it. "You see, as matters stand, every firm, every organiza-

155

tion—even the Empire—has been caught in a squeeze, and the fact is it is now necessary for us to make a substantial force reduction. Some of the jobs are for the time being in the process of being eliminated or curtailed. And it gives me no pleasure to say that the motion picture section is one of those areas where economies have to be made.

"So—and I want to emphasize again, Jim, that this is just temporary—I am afraid we are going to have to eliminate your job. At the moment there is nothing else for you, but meanwhile we shall be looking around for something in the near future. You will, of course, receive—having your length of service—a very substantial severance pay, and I can assure you . . ." Randall hesitated, then continued in a firm voice. It was about over. "I can assure you, Jim, that at the first break, the first moment the fog begins to lift, I will see that you are called back. I don't anticipate that that will be too long either. . . .

"Meanwhile," Randall concluded quietly, "why don't you use your desk for the next two weeks to explore the possibility of other contacts, temporary though they may be? It will not be too difficult for a man like you to pick up another job, and you can be assured that I shall note on any reference your loyalty and conscientiousness. . . ."

Randall paused. Somers' rather tired, impassive face had grown paler but otherwise exhibited no other particular signs of shock. When he spoke, his voice had the slow, slightly hesitant tone of a man who finds it difficult to express himself.

"Well . . ." he said, "well, thank you, Mr. Randall."

"I'm sorry, Jim," Randall said again quietly. "I wish it could be otherwise. . . . A man of your . . . your personality will not be without work long. And if there is anything we can do, please don't hesitate to ask us. As I mentioned—and again I repeat it—this is only temporary, and we shall undoubtedly be getting in touch with you shortly to invite you back to the old job."

"Thank you, Mr. Randall," Somers replied again haltingly. It

156

had been almost too easy, Randall thought. Somers rose slowly and stood a moment, apparently bemused.

"I expect I'll be seeing you before you leave," Randall offered. "Please stop in, will you, Jim?"

"Yes sir," Somers said slowly. His face was impassive. He turned and walked woodenly to the door and out. The day was still blue and sparkling—one of those halcyon mornings in the fullness of autumn.

Martin came back from his assignment two weeks after the layoffs. The office had already simmered down. There was little talk on the subject. It was easy to forget. The waters had closed almost without a ripple over those who had departed, and the old routines, scarcely varying, were rubbing away the last traces of the lost personalities.

Now it confronted each of them: the terrible dispensability of them all. It was more than just here today and gone tomorrow. It was that really, basically, you were of no consequence to the firm as an individual. They might pretend otherwise, but the Empire had seen a thousand like you, and it would see other thousands like you in the future. You were nothing here— nothing. And if you went out tomorrow, the waters would close over you immediately; there would be no remembrance, no recourse, no sign. A saying returned to him from Emerson, one he had learned long ago and with which he had once comforted himself: Every man is wanted but not much. Well, here they weren't really wanted at all.

He shook off these contemplations and began to muse about April again. She had been his first concern when he had returned. Flushed and anxious, he had walked down to see her at her new desk near Mizner's office. She had greeted him without great warmth, though pleasantly enough. And she had put him off. Now in the days since Somers had left, she appeared scarcely to notice him or, in fact, to notice anyone else. It angered and worried him at the same time. That evening he had de-

157

cided to call her up again at her apartment. He dropped the nickel into the pay phone at the drugstore and let it ring and ring—five . . . six times. There was no answer. So she was out. And probably with Somers, he thought. His heart contracted. Somers, of course, would appeal to her more than ever now—losing his job, needing consolation. Not that he hadn't received, it was rumored, eight months' pay—a month for each year of his service. And already in the city, the crisis was receding . . . jobs were opening up. In the checkering glimmer of reassessment, confidence was once more rising. Bellamy, one of his friends in the office had heard, had already landed a place at an agency at half again as much salary as he had been drawing in the Empire. Consolation, Martin thought again. I wish it had been I instead of Somers.

He walked out in the cool autumn night. He was in an agony of jealousy. Should he give it all up? What then was the use? It was obvious where her heart lay. He drifted along down the street to the corner. If he only knew where she was—where they were, rather, he thought bitterly, perhaps it would be more bearable. This was going to be, he realized, a lost evening for him. Tomorrow, he would put in an application for another job. He had to break away. Since he could not have her, he would be far better off not being compelled to see her every day. It was too bitter a sweetness.

He glanced up—the night was fresh and damp. The high, far sparkle of the city lay all about him. This was the saddest time of the year, he thought. This was the trough of the wave. It seemed to him momentarily that he would never live through this season.

The next morning Harwood called a conference. Lorraine Lewis, Harwood's secretary, required a few minutes to round them all up.

"Well, gentlemen," Harwood began in his smooth, earnest voice, as they sat restlessly in the moderately large office, "we've just about crawled out from under. For some of us, the wings of the vultures sailed awfully close. . . ." Harwood allowed his

158

handsome eyes to settle on each face around the room. What was the purpose of this session anyway? Martin thought again. "It has happened before," Harwood continued softly, that cool gaze still on them. "It happened just now, and it could happen again. Now I don't want to put into any of you boys the fear of the suspended option or anything of that sort, but it appeared to me that it was time we got together—all of us—for a little soul-searching. Yes," he said again slowly, "a little soul-searching. I scarcely need remind you or even review for you the events of the past few months. But the fact was that it was on our record, and our record alone—in other words, on how well we were doing our jobs—that the judgments were made.

"Let me say this—just between us, gentlemen, and in strictest confidence. I happened to be in at the time this unfortunate reduction was finally discussed—several of us, in fact, were invited. And we were asked to express our opinions, and naturally—no one wants his group reduced and we are all friends— so naturally I did my best for everyone . . . but let me tell you, men, it was a sobering experience. You all know Dave Randall —you know what kind of a boss he is—and there's none better, let me tell you. But let's face it: he is sometimes a little exacting, and I received the impression—and this is the reason I feel we should get together once in a while for an assessment—I received the impression that in the case of many of us, all was not well. There was just a small amount of dissatisfaction about the kind of job we are doing, a little feeling that perhaps we don't have the grip we used to have on our affairs. So now our problem is: what shall we do about it?"

Martin was puzzled and so were the others. He could feel his stomach tightening despite himself. What was the purpose? Was it possible Harwood was trying to substitute Randall as the new bogeyman, the grim reaper of the department? Was he attempting to place at Randall's door his own feelings, or was he merely trying to throw a good scare into them? And if so, why? What was the angle?

There would be no wrists silently slashed in the night over the

159

kind of job they had been doing—of that Martin felt confident. And yet . . . and yet . . . That was the trouble. Whatever Harwood was driving at, he was getting to them. Martin noted the faces around him. Most were depressed. One or two were worried.

"In what way, Phil?" Carruthers began slowly. His voice seemed rather lost after Harwood's confident tones. "In what way, Phil," he said more loudly, "have we been falling down?"

"Well now, Sam," Harwood was tolerantly friendly, "don't misunderstand. This isn't my judgment. Matter of fact, men, I think we've been performing pretty well in many respects. This little get-together is just to let you boys know what is going on— what judgments some of the higher-ups who are not aware of our problems appear to be making on our efforts. Now frankly, I don't know exactly what to do. I'm in there pitching for you all the time. But let's take the warning. Let's start thinking of how to reorganize and integrate our work more carefully. Re-examination is the watchword. They're out for us now. They're going to keep us barefoot and pregnant. Let's not deceive ourselves. Let's put it out and put it out in quantity—quantity production as well as quality. Let's not slacken in any quarter."

Later Casey remarked to him worriedly: "Martin, what was the object of that conference? Are we really on the skids? Phil's a nice guy and all that, but he's scared the living bejesus out of me. The atmosphere of this place has become downright gruesome."

"He gives me the creeps too," Martin answered thoughtfully. "Maybe," he added slowly, "that's what he wanted to do—scare hell out of us. A good scare, they say, is worth more than good advice. I don't know. There's no use letting it get you. They don't give you points for worrying."

But now for the first time, the subtle and oddly terrifying rule of Harwood commenced to exert its power over them, and a few of them began to realize that it was not Randall, nominal head of the group, conservative and unimaginative as some of them considered him, who was running the department; it was some-

160

how Harwood, a new, a more modern, a subtler ruler, the agent of a bland tyranny they did not know how to combat and one whose sway they found they had gravely underestimated.

None of these matters seriously concerned Martin, however, except in minor flurries. They were shadows flickering in the background of his inner life. He was ready and willing to leave, and somehow, for one could easily sense such nuances of feeling there, he understood that somewhere along the way he had earned Harwood's enmity—in what obscure manner he would probably never know—and he was almost certain that he would be out soon, face down—his card would be pulled. The anger welled up in him.

April Tremaine sat across the little table from Somers in the softly lighted restaurant. She was worried. Jim appeared to have been drinking again, and frankly she did not think he looked well.

"But Jim," she was saying, "why don't you accept one of the positions uptown that are beginning to open now? You know Bellamy found a job right away. You could just take it temporarily while you are waiting for them to call you down here."

Jim focused with some difficulty.

"Oh, Mr. Randall said it wouldn't be long, April," he replied quietly. "I've plenty of time. No need to rush into anything yet. I'm not anxious for just any kind of job. And I'm pretty well fixed—the Company was more generous than I had any right to expect—and I wouldn't want not to be available in case Mr. Randall or someone should call."

"Oh Jim," she burst out, and suddenly her voice was hard, "Jim why don't you face reality? The Company hasn't been good to you. That wasn't generosity—to fire you after eight long years! A man like you! What's so generous about that? And now you trust their soft talk after what they've done. Why should you believe them? Why should you think they'll ever call you back? You worked for them for eight long years. . . ."

Somers raised his hand. "Please, April . . ." His face had

161

tightened. "I'm surprised at you," he said slowly. "The Company's never pursued any policy to my knowledge that it need be ashamed of. It's always been extremely . . . well, extremely kind to me in all the years I was there."

"Jim," she continued, exasperated, "try to see it the way it really is. They kept men who had a lot less service than you. They kept men whose jobs were no more important and some a lot less important. They . . ."

"Well," he broke in wearily, as if to end the distasteful conversation, "anyhow it's . . . it's only temporary, April. I know they had good reasons whatever they were, and they'll be calling me back again soon. Mr. Randall as much as said so himself and so did Phil Harwood. They wouldn't let me down."

She saw the look in his tired, sodden eyes, and then she knew it was hopeless. "Oh Jim . . ." she began. Suddenly, she burst into tears. She rose and, turning, walked quickly through the restaurant foyer and out into the cold October evening. She felt rage, pity and tenderness. He was a gentleman. He was something special. She could never let him escape like this—never. She would call him the next morning at his boardinghouse. Then she remembered that he had no telephone. Would he ever call her again? she wondered. Well, she could never let him go like that. She would somehow see him again.

That was not the last evening they had together, as it happened. He did call her the next week, and they spent a pleasant if rather drunken evening at the Champon. But he found it somehow more and more of an effort to see her. First of all, she objected too often to his appearing drunk. And after all, he only had had a few to start off with. He found it also easier, while he was waiting for them to summon him back, to spend his time in one or another of the friendly little bars in the neighborhood —the very ones, in fact, that he used to frequent during that long and desperate period of his misery and loss. Now it was different. He knew this was just temporary, and soon, either in a week or a month, there would be that phone call, and it would be

Mr. Randall telling him to come on in—the old job was waiting. That would be a great day! He savored the thought as he sat there in Laidlaw's on his third drink of the morning.

He did admit that once in a while he found himself putting away more than he should have done, and nowadays at times, in fact, those blackouts were commencing to recur again— the kind voices, the changing from voice to voice and face to face as the evening wore on, and suddenly it was morning and he was lying fully dressed on his own bed or on one or two occasions, as it happened, flat on the floor in his room, and heaven only knew how he had gotten there.

But Mrs. Flaherty, the fat Irish landlady—why, she must weigh over two hundred and fifty pounds—she took splendid care of him. She was very kind, in fact, after she found that he really wasn't a deadbeat. He really did have money in the bank and those checks he gave her for the rent or to buy him a couple of bottles were good and did not bounce.

Indeed, it was sometimes easier just to ask Mrs. Flaherty if she wouldn't be obliging enough to order him a bottle over her phone—the one in her apartment—since he had none, and to bring it up to him. And she was invariably kind enough to do so. It was even better than going out with April, and he didn't have to watch himself so carefully.

The trouble with people you knew—even nice and understanding people like April—was that you had to watch yourself. You couldn't allow matters to get away from you. Like the time April had invited him to her apartment—so pretty and appealing—and had made such a nice supper for him. But he had had a few afterwards and he'd felt dizzy and fallen into her bathtub. She had laughed but he could see the worry, the anxiety, in her eyes. And—well, maybe he didn't really look so well any more. But wait till that job opened up again. Wait until they called him; he'd be all right then.

"Jim, are you sure you are eating properly?" she had asked him on another occasion. And that maternal tenderness was beginning to wear him down, to grate on his nerves. Of course

163

he was eating properly. Did she imagine he was a child to be treated with this exasperating sweetness?

It was, finally, her trying to water his drinks that capped his irritation. One night at her place, he had wandered into the kitchen, and there she was pouring plain water into the bottle of good bourbon he had brought along. He was becoming, he would admit, sensitive about his drinking, but he felt with, as he told himself, ample justification that watering good liquor was in all conscience going too far. An old expression returned to him—a lot of branch water has flowed into the bourbon since the days when he was young, and that was the way he felt now.

And soon it would be winter. The other seasons had their beauty, each with its promise and its loveliness, but winter had never appealed to him, and for some reason this year the thought of it with its sleet, slush and snow, its overflowing gutters, its overwhelming dreariness and dirt, dismayed him more completely than it ever had. With each onset of cold weather, and now and then a snowy day, his spirits declined, and as the holiday season approached, he could not say why, but he felt more depressed. He tried to tell himself that it was no use worrying. The good days would dawn again. It was not that he doubted that the call would be forthcoming or that they would be asking him to return. It was another kind of depression, the mornings especially, waking up in that rumpled and damaged room, unable to pull himself together or to function properly. And then, though he had strictly warned Mrs. Flaherty to let him know when the summons arrived, there remained the nagging suspicion that she might forget. Or even worse, perhaps he might be out when the call came and not available.

One late afternoon just before Christmas, he rose from the bed. Once an extremely meticulous dresser, he now tried to dress as carefully as he could, indeed more carefully than usual. He stood in front of the fly-specked mirror and tried to tie his tie. The room seemed to him to be in more of a shambles than he had at first realized. It had not been cleaned in some time and the scuffed and ancient furniture had never been the best and

164

now appeared more run-down and dirty than ever. But then, he had been spending more and more of the days in the room. It was becoming increasingly an effort to go out. The streets would call to him but he would not heed them or answer. He was afraid of what would happen if the streets ever caught him. He had not gotten around to having his clothes cleaned either, he realized, and it was difficult to find a shirt or a pair of trousers that were not worn or soiled. He'd have to buy himself new clothes soon, he told himself again, and send these shirts and shorts out to the laundry. Well, what he had on hand would have to do, and anyhow the old overcoat would hide it all.

It was a bright, cold and pleasant winter afternoon. The skies were blue, the streets crowded and gay with people carrying Christmas packages. Jim's head was throbbing slightly and he had a moderate hangover, but the fresh, exhilarating air and cheerful, bustling passers-by with their shining faces a little bit nipped with the cold made him feel a great deal better.

The last time they were together, he had promised April that he would have Christmas dinner at her place, and she had told him that in that case she would not have her usual friends— the girls—over. She would prepare dinner just for him, she had said. The prospects pleased him even though he hoped she would not expect so much of him as she had at the Thanksgiving dinner they had had together. He had done too much celebrating that day, it is true, and had disappeared from the party about five o'clock in the evening and he could scarcely remember exactly what had happened to him until he had found himself, a little the worse for wear, on the floor of his own room.

Someone must have struck him or he must have become embroiled in a fight, for he found he had had severe bruises on his face, and of course—it had happened to him before— he had lost his wallet. That had been happening to him with increasing frequency. Money was always slipping through his fingers, and he could never account for any of it, and now it was beginning to worry him. The early experiences with jack-rollers had shocked him profoundly. Not that he remembered clearly what had occurred, but he would wake up and feel as if he had been beaten—his clothes torn and sometimes his face scratched or bruised. The first time his wallet, with eighteen dollars, was missing; another time a new wallet with forty-seven dollars in it had vanished. He began to feel almost philosophical about it.

But today this seemed to be all in the past. Everything appeared bright and cheerful, and the shadows, the increasing shadows in his life, were in abeyance. He had not had a drink for a few hours, and the brisk afternoon air fresh from the mint of time raised his spirits and, as if after a long long period in darkness, made him feel once more on top of the world. It would be all right after all. Those difficulties vague and unformed but increasingly ominous appeared now like shadows from a bad night full of unpleasant dreams. He had been upset; he had grown depressed—he would admit it. He had had his moments. . . . Thou art in the gall of bitterness and in the bond of iniquity—the words returned to him; and from somewhere the old saying like a tired expiration: Heaven is far away and the world is nigh. . . .

Well, they would call him soon now. . . . They would not forget him. Heaven is far away, the old words went . . . well, the world was certainly with him, but they would not always leave him here. They would be calling him very shortly now, and he would be hurrying back, and the old routines would save him. For the Kingdom of Heaven, the old parables ran, was likened unto—what was it? What was it? He was becoming confused. Perhaps it was like the rich man and the eye of the needle, and then again many were called but few were chosen. . . . Well, they would summon him back right after the holidays. He had a feeling about it. And he would answer; he would be there waiting when they called.

At Fourteenth Street he took the downtown express. It was surprisingly crowded for that hour—people standing in the aisles poking each other cheerfully though tiredly with their armfuls of bundles. The red and silver wrappings predominated. The

166

faces here were more tired, a little more worn and harassed, yet even here was the faint undercurrent of impending festivity.

There were two stops before reaching the station in the downtown section where the great Building stood. That station was located in the basement of the Building itself, in fact, and he now faced the problem of getting off and slipping out of the station without running into anyone who might know him. He particularly did not wish to see any of the old associates or friends who still worked there. His only purpose in making the trip was to see the Building again. It seemed to him that he had missed it, as if it were a symbol of a quality big and important in his life that he had somehow lost. It would in an important way perhaps renew his flagging spirits to glimpse it again after so long a time.

How long had it been? He was not entirely sure now. Time had slipped away from him—whole days at a stretch; the movement of the hours from day to night, from night to day, had somehow developed the habit of telescoping, of being swallowed up in the lostness that was becoming an increasing part of his world. Was it months ago that he had left? He could scarcely tell. The gray stretches were now so much a part of that period.

But in that great Building it would all be the same—of that he was confident. They would arrive and go, but the routines there were as unvarying as the seasons, as steady as the rhythm of the equinoxes. Nothing there ever really changed—that was part of the beauty of it. Out of the maelstrom, out of the endless stream of the world, the rock of their low and steadfast labors would remain. The faces will change, the people will change—we shall depart, but not the Building and all it stands for—that will endure with all its routines and its patterns. . . . *For a thousand years in thy sight* . . . the beautiful words murmured through his confused mind like wind through a field of grain. . . . Yes, he was thinking, we pass away. . . .

He emerged from the subway and into the jostling crowd in the late afternoon glow. Across the street from him now were the massive granite pillars, becoming slightly empurpled in

167

shadow. He walked slowly down the street in the direction of the river, away from them and away from the Building. There was a particular spot he knew, a spot a little way toward the lower part of the island from which the Building could be clearly seen against the sky, and he shuffled along down the shabby cluttered streets in the cooling air.

At the vantage point—a street near a long, low warehouse—he turned and leaned against a rusting iron fire-escape ladder. Then he walked over and sat down tiredly on an embankment near the warehouse loading platform. In this backwater part of town, everything was quiet and abandoned. Little businesses had crawled away here to die and old wrecks of larger businesses —medium-size wholesale houses, once busy importing firms with the scents of coffee and spices from the days when ancient ships put in from far places—were quietly rotting away. Yes, he thought, old wrecks—perhaps like himself—had dragged down here to decay. No business was now transacted. No trucks lumbered through the narrow streets at this hour. He suddenly felt very tired and old, almost beaten.

He looked up.

There in the lavender dusk rose the Building—vast, heavy and solid against the evening light. At its very top was a beacon, but this could not be discerned in the glow of the late winter afternoon. It must be almost the shortest day in the year now, he thought. Then his mind began to haze over and he was looking at it and looking at it there in the distance—beautiful and eternal—the great Building, the symbol of all security, of solidity, of those qualities in life that can never pass away. . . .

It increased abruptly the sense of impermanence within him. We pass away, he thought again, we do not last, we are fleeting things, we spend our years as a tale that is told—a little breathing out and in, a long sleep, but you—you will last forever, you will endure. They cannot break you as they have broken me. You have given me a quality out of life that nothing else has. . . .

For a long time he sat there on the cold embankment, until

168

it began to grow dusky and the chill had seeped through his old coat. Yes, he said with a sigh, looking up once more at the great Building—now a huge shadow on the horizon in the still and confusing air, a giant bulk rising out of the canyon of other lesser shadows in the late afternoon—yes, he said to himself again with a sigh, man goeth forth unto his work and to his labor until evening, but you, you will stand there long after those that went forth and came home are gone and new ones to take our place have come and gone also. You will still be there. You are eternal.

He rose stiffly. The works of mercy irrelevantly began to sift into his mind again: to feed the hungry, to give drink to the thirsty, to clothe the naked, to harbor the harborless. . . . It was really chilly now and he needed a drink. Slowly he lowered his head and shuffled up the mean dirty street in the gathering gloom—a shabby, once handsome man in an old coat. The glow was gone; he was tired and he needed that drink badly.

BOOK III   Harwood

1

HARWOOD SAT at his desk and weighed the prospects. He didn't want to make a mistake.

He was not what you would call a nice fellow. But there are a million of those. He was something far better than that: he was smart. He knew what it was all about. He knew where the duck would fall. He had traveled a long way from Laurel Park, Illinois, and he didn't fool himself about it, for, as the old song had it, he still had a long way to go. Harwood was a college man—that was the term used in the Empire to describe a man who had graduated from an acceptable college but not from one of the three Eastern universities, Yale, Harvard or Princeton. They were called Yale men or Harvard men or Princeton boys. It was better in the Empire to have attended an acceptable college as had Harwood than, except under unusual circumstances, one of the others. The others smacked of pretentiousness or of being arty or effete, unless, of course, the graduate was a specialist or an engineer.

Harwood could have wished to have had an engineering or a business administration degree, but he was not the man to pine for them. He would make out all right with this middle-of-the-road background—a nice little town in Illinois and a good Midwestern college and the family life to match it farther back. He'd make out fine, as he always had, even though sometimes one had to tie oneself to inferior people to do so.

But there was no getting around it. Almost everything he had had to offer for the record looked good—looked, in fact, just right.

There was the high school. He had been president of his class in his freshman year, although, oddly enough, not in succeeding years. He had always been a handsome boy, and too bright for his parents and the people around him. His father had taught in the elementary school and although he possessed a modicum of social standing in the town by reason of his being a teacher had failed to take any advantage of his position. As if a nerveless love of teaching in that intellectual Gobi in which they lived were a sufficient end in life in itself. His mother, a quiet, rabbitlike woman, was the kind of person about whom one would never have anything derogatory to say, a simple and also, now that he thought of it, rather plain woman who adored him and who had the great defect of liking to do favors for others and wasting an enormous amount of time doing them.

Philip they both regarded as the child of morning, the light of their life, and as he grew older they accepted the fact that he was their superior in almost every respect. Harwood had learned early too—at exactly what age or under exactly what circumstances he could scarcely remember—that there were two kinds of people: those like his parents, rather ineffectual and well-meaning, who were born to be dupes and servants, and those like himself who were born to be superior, to have power—to rule.

It was not a completely conscious conception on his part. It had evolved from hundreds of little experiences and observations of the ways of the world in the quiet, deadly streets of the sleepy little town, on the boyhood playgrounds where the bullies, big and stupid, dominated until he became too clever for them, in the classrooms where he found older people, teachers, adults liked him instinctively and furthered his interests. He realized that they found his fresh boyish beauty, the wide blue eyes, the handsome even teeth, the well-scrubbed look of his fine healthy skin irresistible. Here indeed was a boy born to be a hero, even if gradually some of the children of his own age did not take to him any more as they once had.

174

For Philip as a boy, step by step, came to realize through many experiences, including the example of his parents' weaknesses and insipidity, what Harwood as a man now knew—that nobody gives you anything, that you must learn to take what you want as you learned to take by force or by guile what you needed to maintain your standing in the little world in which you moved.

The little world had become a big world here, but the basic principles had not much changed. As the leader of a gang in school which was remarkable for the fact that it was not rowdy or particularly ill-behaved, he had shown his ability to understand and handle people. His gang had not fanned out to pick fights or push other smaller boys around; it had had more basic, more fundamentally useful ends. True, there had been all the trappings of boys' clubs—the secret, sometimes nauseating initiation rites, the secluded meetinghouse, all the paraphernalia. But the club did more than merely serve as an outlet for childish clannishness and infantile hostilities. School lessons were completed almost on a communal basis, and small sums of money were earned or stolen by various members and put in a communal fund so that ice cream parties could be held from time to time and candy could be secured almost at will, and the members could provide themselves with various insignia to indicate their status and importance in the community.

Actually, it appeared as if Philip were a good influence on his associates. He urged them not to irritate their parents or get them "down on you," as the saying was. The members were admonished to be cheerful, eat supper, not to leave food on the plate, and pretend to obey even if they had no intention of doing so.

The world of adults was, as always, an alien and hostile world, and they were in league to outwit this world with its large, ham-handed people and to do so by guile, if possible. Philip did not care for the crude and stupid devices of petty thievery—entering a five and ten cent store and stealing small objects—that was too dangerous and obvious. There were so

175

many easier ways to secure what was needed: drives, for instance, to help the Boy Scout troop or to make a community center for boys. He could send a few of them around, and in no time they would have collected enough to do anything they wished—to go to the movies, to buy special articles of clothing or to drink cokes.

But Philip soon tired even of the gang and its operations. Where was it leading him? What possibilities did it really suggest in the expanding world? As the boys were growing older, their ties were beginning to snap. Altercations increased, and it was increasingly difficult to keep them in line. A few of them were outgrowing the group, and the personal power and profit he derived from the organization had diminished to the point where the effort did not appear to him worth the results. He abandoned them in plenty of time, and as a gang they began to disintegrate quickly.

In college Philip lay low. He could have been manager of the baseball team. He could have secured some measure of control in the social clubs. He could have studied. But he was already bored with these playthings. They did not seem to him to lead anywhere. What he needed, he felt, was a larger field, a greater scope for his talents. The swale of brightness was about him and he needed a field where the kinds of social ability he possessed would have a free play, where he could build a reputation and a social status and thus indirectly the position of power that was his due. For the world was a jungle, and you had to watch where you were going. There was no percentage in the little town where he lived, in the quiet college where he was securing his education—in the whole of the Midwest itself, with its provincialisms and its imitations of the big time. The minute he had his degree and could put aside his white flannels and blue coat, secure the introductions and references that might be useful from all those doting adults and friends, he shook the dust of the sticks, as he thought of them, from his shoes. He said goodbye graciously—no telling when

176

one would need their help again—and turned his face, as if in sorrow, to the big town where the big rewards lay.

But he had not been deceived by the big city either, nor overly impressed. He knew what he was doing. Underneath, they were all the same. They were easy. The world was a racket and he knew it. With a letter from one of the high school teachers to an old friend in the city, he had quickly secured a job as a contact man in a large advertising agency. He had none of the false pride of immaturity. He was willing to take anything at first. His purpose was not the job itself but the ingredients to compose a frame of reference. He had also met through an old friend of his father's a young lady from a good family in Long Island.

Philip was not easily influenced by girls, although his unusual charm made him extremely popular. This young lady, Jo-Anne Collins, was captivated. She expressed a wish to see more of him. She was a girl of refined appearance but anemic and easily swayed. Her father was a gruff, dominating executive of a large insurance company, where his considerable talents had placed him in a position of authority. Philip knew a good thing when he saw it.

After their marriage, Philip settled with his bride in a house on Long Island which Jo-Anne's parents had helped them purchase. And Philip now looked around for the main chance. The agency, he quickly realized, was not the answer. The insurance company of which his father-in-law was an executive did not seem to provide the opportunities for a swift enough rise for his purposes, and it appeared to him to be extremely dangerous to till the same field as his father-in-law, at least until he had acquired more experience in business. Yet a big corporation in his opinion promised to be the best area for his singular abilities, and he decided that the company he chose might just as well be the largest and the most powerful.

With references carefully manufactured by a close friend in the agency, he presented himself during the brief upswing before the war to Harold Doyle in the advertising department.

177

Doyle was impressed with his experience, properly composed and not overelaborated, and with Philip's personality. Here was the kind of young man so rarely met with nowadays who understood the problems in the field in which they worked, and who yet had the disarming eagerness and strength of character needed in the System. It did not take Doyle long to hire him.

Philip remained in Doyle's department long enough to find out the lay of the land, and to search where the promise and the glamour of the division might reside. It appeared to him that the group which received the most attention from higher management and was most favored was Carlyle's, and he proceeded to set in motion the machinery to have himself transferred there. He did it simply. He went to Doyle and had a heart-to-heart talk with him, informing him that he would like to broaden his experience and would appreciate working for a while—even on a temporary basis—in the information group. Doyle was not the man to stand in an eager, earnest young man's way, and, under those circumstances, he prevailed upon Carlyle to take Harwood temporarily.

It was about then that the first calls for draft registrations were launched. This brought to Harwood one of the most delicate situations in his entire career. Actually Philip was not afraid of being drafted. Neither army life nor the possibility of having eventually to go to war particularly disturbed him in themselves. He felt he could survive under almost any circumstances, and he did not feel that by any remote stretch of the laws of possibility— although he was aware such events did occur in war—would it happen that he could be killed or wounded. That was for other and lesser men. But nevertheless he did believe that, given his talents and the exigencies of the situation, it was not his particular duty to place himself in such a position that he would be drafted, if it were possible to avoid doing so without any disagreeable consequences.

He presented himself, therefore, to Carlyle one morning. Carlyle had fixed him with his cool, quizzical stare. "So you think a

178

stretch in the Works would help you along, is that it?" he asked after Philip had concluded his engaging story.

"That's what they say, Mr. Carlyle," and Philip assumed his disarming smile. "I'll be honest with you, sir. I want to do this thing right. I've found in the time I've been here that if you don't have plant or operating experience, you're generally not considered for the jobs that mean a real career."

Later Carlyle spoke to Mizner about it.

"I'll wager that bright boy is up before the draft board again."

"Why d'you say that, Jeff?" Mizner asked.

"They're taking married men without children now even in essential industries—except in plants. Now I may be doing the boy an injustice but it seems to me he both escapes the draft board and secures the plant experience he feels he needs in one fell swoop here. You better keep your eye on that boy, Andrew: we'll both be working for him before very long!"

Carlyle smiled. Mizner laughed. "You going to give it to him, Jeff?" Mizner asked.

"Why not?" Carlyle replied. "There's no law against it. The Works can use him. You can't keep a good man down, you know."

Industrial relations at the Works was a shambles. There was little union activity, since it was war, and the problem was manpower. They spent a great deal of time compiling a work on manpower needs in a war plant, and received great credit for it. Harwood put in a few weeks of intense concentration to establish the fact that he was a worker. He found them childishly easy to understand and manipulate in the plant. Those tough babies were always the easiest in the end. And if there was anyone dumber than an engineer or a production man, he didn't know who it might be. They gave those babies sawdust for brains, and their knowledge of human nature about equaled their knowledge of the facts of life. The old wheels may turn in the plant itself, he thought, but they didn't turn in the heads of those boys.

It took him five months to pick up all he needed in the Works.

179

Then, his status with the board carefully established and the contingency past, it was time to return to the Building. He had mastered the production man's argot. He had created his impression. He had given the boys over there one or two nasty turns when he happened to mention casually his intimacy with certain of the nabobs at headquarters and had transmitted rather subtly their present dissatisfaction with the way operations were going in the plant in general and in industrial relations, as a matter of fact, in particular.

Now it was time to get back. . . .

Well, all that had been over long ago and was on the record. His card must measure up pretty well, actually. He could about imagine how it would look. But at present he had other, more pressing problems.

He leaned back in the swivel chair and allowed his cool gaze to drift over the office and its appurtenances. He wouldn't be surveying precisely this kind of place or outfit forever now. It wouldn't be long before the decanter from which he poured his water would be silver and the rug would be green. The desk would be larger. . . . He had Randall's number now. And it wouldn't be long either before Randall found himself on the skids. Not the way some of them had smashed up—old Jim, for example. It was really too bad about old Jim. Jim Somers had been a gentleman and not worthy of Philip's efforts—and then too he'd been harmless—Harwood could see that now. It irked him that he should have pangs of conscience for a mental blank, an intellectual vacuum like Somers. But after all, Jim had been pretty far along when he had had to give him that final shove, and in the end it would only have been a matter of time. He had not really wanted to do it, but you start trying to protect weaklings and you wind up floating face downward in the stagnant water.

Randall, on the other hand, was another sort of fish. No one would actually have to do much to him. He would pick himself apart in his own way. He was a bleeder. And he could easily be

180

driven from here to Thursday and back with the application of a little pressure in the right places—the kind of pressure perhaps that the position he occupied would almost normally place upon him. Then, of course, it might be that the men could be stirred up a little. In a large organization like this, Randall would certainly not be budged from his entrenched position by ordinary methods, but he would grow more and more to need a man like Harwood to help him face the problems flooding in. And then again, Mizner would be retiring within two years or so and there was that splendid opportunity opening up.

But the main problem remained: how to break through the crust, how to crash the magic barriers, the Chinese Wall that separated them all on that level from the really important men, the men who could do something for you—the men upstairs. The opportunity rarely presented itself to a young man in his position, but it seemed to him there must be a way in which he could help such an opportunity along.

This was a jungle all right, he mused, and a man must look out for himself. Well, there was always a way to cut down people who needed it and right now he could profitably try to shape up his own group into a more useful unit—an organization that could show these old fuddy-duddies how an organization ought to function. There was no need for some of them. There was no demand for stars or prima donnas—he didn't like people like that, this golden boy Brill, Carlyle's man, and McKenzie, he was dangerous, with his utterly literal, tactless mind. He was the kind who always, even though accidentally, fouled things up. They would have to go.

He'd committed only two real errors since he had been here, and he did not like to make mistakes. The essence of intelligence was never to make the same mistake twice, and he could not afford the luxury of errors if he were to go on up. Fortunately one of these miscalculations had been erased by death, and the other—well, perhaps it was still not too late to rectify it, and it would certainly only cause him a temporary discomfort.

But he had had his triumphs also. That compilation, for ex-

181

ample, *War Diaries of a Defense Plant*, composed principally from the stuff Brill and one or two of the others had sent in during Carlyle's assignment to them, had been an unexpected success, far beyond anything he had imagined it would be. His own name was the only one which had been listed on the title page and it had been modestly listed as editor.

The work had received unusually pleasant notices from outside the Company, but better still, from his own viewpoint, it had apparently been commented favorably upon by such people as Mr. Stenson and Mr. Wygand and others of the higher-ups. So that had been an achievement worth the participation. It wasn't as if he had not praised Brill—and far more than he deserved—since the material Brill contributed was really almost raw material, and only the most skillful work on it had made it sparkle. It was not that Brill had complained at not receiving credit—Brill with his purple-heart routine, his earnestness and his silly posturings after other values, was not the kind who would understand, much less care about, such implications.

He had most of them taped right, and he certainly had Brill pegged. A good organizer, and a worker with a certain imagination and flair. He showed evidence of being, like Carlyle, the type of man the Empire favored, but he was not the kind of person he, Harwood, wanted around. His cravings for something better, for a larger sphere, perhaps for something he was even less suited for, might in the end provide the weaknesses that would be his downfall. Yes, these weaknesses would tag them in the end. And whether there were profounder talents or larger possibilities in Brill would not concern him, for they would do Brill no good here. Well, so much for these people. He couldn't worry about them now.

There were many more important problems. He needed Mizner's support, since Mizner, despite the fact that he remained odd and off-beat, appeared to possess influence upstairs, and there was one piece of great luck. He had had the chance through his father-in-law of joining the same country club as Mr. Keesling, the System's vice president of finance—a very

182

swank place, much more expensive than they could afford, but it would be well worth it in the end, he felt, and Jo-Anne had enough money in her own right to swing it.

One of his shrewdest moves, he new felt, had been in his insisting that Jo-Anne keep her own money intact. This gesture had not only deeply impressed her family, but it had also fostered the illusion that he was poor and struggling, a nice young fellow who could use all the help they could give him. Furthermore, when her money was needed, it was no trick at all to secure it. The trouble with Jo-Anne, like most women, was that she was not very smart and she was almost completely ruled by her emotions, and her emotions were wrapped up in him. He had managed, through this attachment to him, to teach her a little how to bend her moderate social graces to more useful ends and to understand more clearly how the delicate debits and credits of social entertaining might be converted to practical means. She was learning. Not too rapidly and, since she was not bright, not too skillfully, but she was doing her best. It was a fact that as a man had to learn to sell himself, so a woman also had to learn to be a prostitute one way or another, and she might as well learn to do it not in the crass physical manner but in a way that was refined and that brought desirable results.

Many of the men, he knew from experience, had traveled far through the considerable social graces of their wives. He doubted that Jo-Anne, nice-looking though she was in a dull way, would ever present him the advantages some of the most talented wives were able to give their husbands, but whatever she had—and that was a pleasing quality in her, he thought—she would do her best for him with it. The two little girls—for there were two little daughters now—might well prove more effective later on. They were certainly pretty little things, if he did say so himself, and they created a wonderful impression when he brought them in during a party at the house, everyone exclaiming over their lovely blond curls.

Well, tomorrow night would be one of the big opportunities— perhaps one of the major opportunities of his life. They were

183

having a country-club dance, and he was aware that Mr. Keesling would be there: the Keeslings were on the committee spon-
soring the event. That would offer him his big chance.

Meanwhile, he had better get to work on that weekly report
for Randall. He was sorry he had ever dreamed up this device,
although it still possessed considerable usefulness. But it was a
bore. He would have to contrive sometime to mention to both
Randall and Doyle that he had run into old H. F. Keesling at
the country club the other night—did they happen to know him?
A nice fellow and very pleasant to meet socially. . . .

2

MARTIN PREPARED for an interview. The winter had about
ended, and the economic storm had blown over. Boomtime was
with them again. Once more they were in the midst of the vast,
seething construction program, and the scientists, the specialists
and the engineers were now bearing the main burdens.

"There are three kinds of people," Mizner had often remarked: "men, women and engineers," and many of them found
it distressingly true. The problem was that the slip-stick boys,
the slide-rule geniuses, were in the saddle and by nature found
themselves more concerned with a narrow accuracy and a dreadful fear of what "those fellows in publicity," as they liked to call
them, would do to them, than they were in securing for the
Company an audience for their achievements or in promoting
a cross-fertilization of advances in their profession by publication in technical journals. An engineer, Martin soon came to
realize, fears exaggeration in the same way a motion picture
magnate might have a horror of understatement. An engineer
also had an even deeper terror of the intrusion of any human
element into the narration of his accomplishments or the accomplishments of others. The human element was the big lie, and

they fought it with all the cold fury that their carefully nurtured scientific attitudes could summon. Their values of life had been formed in fields where the human equation was a distressing nuisance, and nothing that they had subsequently seen of human nature had caused them to revise their assessments.

Furthermore, there existed an old and natural antipathy between public relations and the engineering force, nursed on both sides by a concatenation of misunderstandings down the years. On the one hand, public relations regarded the engineers as zombielike individuals that some unkind Frankenstein-creator had summoned up to grub about amid the whirring machinery of the whole inferno, and on the other hand, engineers were convinced that PR had for years been the receptacle of the dregs of the Empire—a place of refuge for engineers who had been found hopelessly incompetent or Bohemians with berets who, having had to vacate the bars through lack of funds, had wandered into this oasis of dedicated and useful men. This had remained the situation almost up to their own time, and many overtones of this feeling still lingered on both sides, despite the fact that public relations had had the chance to deal with human engineers and that public relations as a part of the industrial scene was not only respectable but also fashionable in the outside world.

It was thus not difficult to understand that securing approvals, now that the engineering boys were riding high, was an ordeal that the new members of the division found both exasperating and bewildering. Harwood had always had singular success in this field. It seemed to him now that it would be well if certain of his men could have a taste of it, since he had had all the contacts there he needed.

"Why don't you go up yourself, Martin," he said one morning to Brill, "and try to push these releases on the new plant situation through Hooker. You have to see Scott first. Hooker—well if you even manage to see him, we'll come and get you in a basket."

185

Martin dialed Scott's number. It was a cold and dismal spring morning outside.

Scott's secretary thought Mr. Scott could see him about two-thirty that afternoon. Martin had lunch with Casey and McKenzie. At two-thirty, he took the elevator to the fourteenth floor and entered the imposing portals of the Engineer of Plant's organization. The outer offices were vast expanses of desks at which young engineers and draftsmen sat busily at work. There was an air of terrible urgency about the whole place, a tenseness, a feeling of nervous crisis. Scott's private office was at the south end of the floor; beyond were the offices of various other E. of P. supervisors and at the corner the plush anteroom of the E. of P. himself—the terrible-tempered E. R. Hooker.

The secretary, an efficient middle-aged woman, immediately ushered Martin with his sheaf of releases into Scott's presence.

Scott was a handsome, leisurely man in his early fifties—ruddy-complexioned, with gray hair and a waxed snow-white mustache. He was sitting at a desk piled high with papers, and smoking his pipe in a relaxed and unhurried manner.

"Come in, Brill. Come in," he called pleasantly. "Have a seat. So you want to have Mr. Hooker go over your story, do you?"

"You and Mr. Hooker, sir," Martin answered. "I'd like your opinion as to our chances of securing the E. of P. approval on this story. And, if possible, we'd like to have it approved within two weeks."

"Well, let's have a look at it, Brill," Scott said slowly. "If it's urgent publicity, we'll give it a whirl, and I'll get the Old Man to read it."

"It isn't urgent," Martin replied. "It's what we call a mood feature for the syndicate that goes to our people and those of the Associated Companies. Its purpose is simply to tell the story of our plant expansion and it includes a detailed piece on how a new plant was born."

Scott glanced through the sheaf of releases. He read here and

186

there, humming softly to himself. He appeared perfectly at ease, relaxed, serene. The telephone rang. He picked it up.

"Is this a short one or a serial?" he said into the mouthpiece. The voice on the other end uttered sounds unintelligible to Martin.

"Well, let's put it off then," Scott remarked. "I've got a bunch of people in my office now. I'll call you back on it."

He hung up. He jotted a number on his calendar and went on reading. He buzzed twice on his buzzer. The middle-aged secretary appeared.

"Take my calls, please, Miss Letty," he said, "and let me know when it's three o'clock. I have a meeting."

He read for a few minutes longer. At last, he swiveled in his seat toward Martin. He sighed.

"Very well written," he commented pleasantly, "a very nice story. I doubt seriously that you'll ever in a coon's age get this through Hooker. Now don't misunderstand me," Scott continued in his quiet, pleasant voice, "Mr. Hooker is God's gift to the Company as an E. of P., but he's a holy terror on feature men and writing. I think it only fair to warn you. Should there be any commas missing or semicolons out of place, Mr. Hooker will spot these errors and you will hear about them. Mr. Hooker is a connoisseur of writing. He believes no adjectives should be used—only verbs, and very short ones at that—and it is his conviction that young men today do not discipline themselves the way their fathers used to."

Martin looked rather bewildered. Scott smiled.

"I like your piece from what I've read of it, and I am going to try to put it through for you. Unfortunately, Mr. Hooker and I do not see eye to eye on all matters having to do with public relations or with writing. I am aware that I know nothing about writing and am a very average reader. Mr. Hooker was once an editor of his high school yearbook and has never recovered from it. I am just preparing you for the interview that may result from this. Mr. Hooker is a man of decided opinions and

187

there is nothing in his make-up to prevent him from expressing them. He has never, I may say without fear of exaggeration, been successfully contradicted."

At that moment Miss Letty opened the door.

"Mr. Hooker is on the telephone," she said, rather nervously, Martin thought. "He would like to know where you are. He would like to see you immediately."

"Tell him I have gone to the men's room for a few minutes, Miss Letty," Scott answered serenely. He smiled. "I know you can put that tactfully," he said. "I shall be in to see him in a few minutes."

"Well," Scott concluded when she had exited, "I guess I shall have to tear myself away, Brill. The master's voice, you know. I shall try to process your story as fast as our procedures allow. I shall arrange any final interview necessary with Mr. Hooker and if you can weather his suggestions I think you have a fair chance of getting your story out."

Martin stood in the outer office. He felt stunned. From a distance, he heard a loud and stertorous voice, raised as if in anguish.

"Mr. Hooker wishes to see Mr. Birn immediately," someone was saying as he raced by. Martin turned and walked slowly out, feeling like Alice in Wonderland.

"Yes," Mizner was saying to Martin and Casey, as they stood in the corridor on the ninth floor near Mizner's large office, "that Scott is a terrific man. I've known Norman for years. No one except him could have survived that job. Meetings . . . conferences . . . those big boys—they live in conferences. Scott was just saying the other day that they're like a herd of mating elephants—all that stamping and trumpeting, and then it takes two years before anything comes of it."

Casey laughed. Martin was nervous.

Two weeks later, he received the summons to the great Hooker's lair. After a short wait, he was shown into the vast mahogany office. Behind a glass-topped mahogany desk sat the great man. He was enormous, perhaps six feet five inches tall, and built proportionately. Rimless glasses glinted on his beak-like nose, his sparse hair was awry above a weathered, sun-tanned face, and a hearing aid protruded from his left ear. His desk was clean except for one large ashtray in the form of a ship's wheel. Mr. Hooker rose abruptly and, leaning over, unexpectedly seized Martin's limp hand and shook it with a bone-crushing grip.

"Glad to see you, Grill," he boomed. His voice carried nicely into the nearby offices.

"Brill, sir," Martin said. "The name is Martin Brill."

"Well, glad to see you, Grill. Like to see you fellas down in public relations once in a while. Used to do a little writing myself, you know—nothing much really. School yearbook, you know." Hooker's voice shook the building.

"Miss Kennen," Hooker yelled, "bring me Grill's papers."

"Brill, sir," Martin repeated faintly.

Miss Kennen delivered the sheaf of releases, now somewhat the worse for wear. Martin's name and extension number were typed on the top of them.

"Why didn't you tell me your name was Brill?" Hooker boomed. "I've been calling you Grill!"

"I know, sir."

"Speak up, man," Hooker said.

"I know, sir," Martin repeated more loudly.

"That's the way, Grill! I like a man talks nice and loud. Sometimes have a little trouble with this danged contraption. Made it myself. Doesn't work.

"Well, Grill . . ." Hooker began riffling through the releases, which were now covered with a tiny meticulous network of handwriting. "I've made a few minor revisions in wording here. Cut out a few adjectives. Don't believe in adjectives.

"Furthermore," he went on, and his deafening voice assumed an accusing note, "furthermore, there are fourteen instances here of errors in the use or omission of commas, and an instance,

189

Grill, of a sentence in which no period was visible at the end. You realize, Grill, that a sentence ends with a period, do you not?"

Martin shuddered. "Yes sir," he said, "I do."

"What?" Hooker shouted. "Speak up, Grill! Do you or do you not realize that a sentence ends with a period!"

"Yes sir," Martin enunciated more loudly. "Yes sir, I do."

"I am glad to hear it," Hooker replied coldly.

"Now I'm sorry to say that the story is all very well, but I cannot permit it to be released. You see it talks about how we constructed a temporary plant here for quick production, and while we did put one together that way in this instance, that is no way to put together a plant. You understand me?"

"Yes sir."

"So the story is killed. Good try, Grill. Show me some more sometime. Oh, Miss Kennen!" Hooker yelled. This time the building trembled on its foundations.

Martin found himself out in the marble corridor at the elevators. He felt somehow in a state of shock. His hand clutching the releases was trembling. He caught himself about to yell "Grill" and choked back the impulse. He felt he had had it. This had been, he could honestly say, one of his less successful afternoons.

The winter was almost over, and Jim Somers lay on the dirty unmade bed in his room on the side street. He had the low, nagging headache that was almost always with him now. The bottle on the bedside table was about empty. There had been only one or two interruptions during the winter's long, troubled semi-slumber. For now he found it difficult to rise in the morning. Mrs. Flaherty would leave the bottle, and each week he would leave the check, though sometimes the days would slip away from him and it would be two or even three weeks in that grayness.

Once Mrs. Flaherty had come up and said to him: "That blond doll was here again, askin' for you, Jim. I told her you

190

was gone, you'd moved away. She wanted to know if I knew where you was. I tol' her no. No use you gettin' mixed up with a gal like that. Them pretty blondes ain't no good—suck the very bejesus out of a man."

"Thank you, Mrs. Flaherty," he said. He was in a stupor, and he was glad she had given April the long goodbye. Not that he didn't love her, but he didn't want to see her any more. The effort was too great. It had all passed for him, all slipped down the drain. Even when he was feeling well—and that was not very often now—he did not want anyone around except strangers . . . the vinous reek of some little bar . . . the slab faces of strange bartenders on the dirtier, meaner streets.

Once in a rare while, he struggled out. One night he found himself—not knowing how he had gotten there—in one of the squalid little night spots that catered to the more advanced musicians. All around him was the hot acid blare of jazz: *Meet me in no special place,* the slurred words ran, *I'll be there at no special time. . . .* He sat there, sodden, unshaven, his clothes dirty and torn, and fingered the glass of liquid balm. *Who has enough,* the rhythm went on, *of that necessary stuff . . . ?* There were people like him now out in the slushy streets, in dirty doorways, but they were the men who had let the streets get them. The golden days were gone. He must not go out into the streets. He knew that. He must stay inside as much as possible, because when the streets began to get you, you were lost.

So the winter was over.

Martin returned from a tough assignment. April had finally, after he had almost despaired, called him up shortly after Christmas. "Come over," she had said. She had sounded worried. He knew immediately what it was.

"I'm so upset about it, Martin," she began, after they had had supper. "Don't be angry with me. It's . . . it's the drinking . . . You know Jim . . . Jim Somers. I had invited him to dinner Christmas, and . . . and he never appeared. I don't mind because of . . . of false pride, Martin, but it's . . . it's

191

as if he were a baby, a child that I was responsible for. Do you understand?"

Martin sat relaxed on the sofa and gazed at her, her lovely face so soft and ravishing in the mild glow of the lamps.

"No one likes to be used," he remarked quietly. "You've been using me."

"And I suppose your . . . your motives toward me have been so high," she said. "I know what you want with me. I'm not stupid. . . . You think because I'm . . . I'm unattached and . . . and I look the way I do that . . . that it would be easy. Jim did not treat me that way. He was a gentleman. There was nothing like that between us."

"All right," he broke in savagely, "so I want you. You make me sick with that high-flown talk. I want you—yes. I want you for yourself because I'm crazy about you. Is that so terrible? Of course, I want you the only way that a man should want a woman—the low carnal way that's so repellent to you." Oh, what's the use? he thought.

She was quiet a moment. "Martin," she said at last, "I won't quarrel with you any more. If you . . . if you want to take me out, to see me maybe once or twice a week, I'll go with you. But don't ask me to forget Jim Somers. Something dreadful has happened to him. I know it. I just know it. I . . . I told you once what it was drove him down at first—the baby and then the . . . the terrible thing with his wife. . . . And now it's . . . it's the Company. I'll never forgive them, Martin! He loved the job—you wouldn't understand. It was his life. He still thinks they'll call him back. Do you think so, Martin?"

He was silent a moment.

"Not in a million years, April," he replied at last. "Not in a million years. The waters closed over him as they will over all of us eventually, as far as the Empire is concerned. You know maybe I'm leaving the System too next fall. Don't tell anyone yet . . . I'm not sure of it."

She was silent for a long time. "Well," she said finally, "I'm

192

. . . I guess I will be sorry to see you go, even if . . . **if** sometimes I am mad at you. . . ."

"You're mad at me?" he said in surprise. "Whatever for?"

She looked down. "I don't really know," she answered.

There was a silence between them.

"Well," he continued, "you only have until fall to put up with me, April. Then you won't have to worry any more. It's second best, I know," he added quietly. "I guess I don't mind. . . ."

That was the first of a series of regular meetings that ended farther down the misty road than either of them had ever dreamed.

Standing in the foyer of her pretty apartment, he tried to kiss her again. She did not struggle this time, but he could feel her heart pounding and she turned her lips away after a moment. Then she said, "Hold still," and taking her handkerchief, she wiped the smudge of lipstick from his chin.

"You like that sort of thing, don't you?" she said. He saw that she was breathing hard, her bosom rising and falling. Her green eyes were shadowed.

"I like it," he said, "with you. I'll always like it that way."

3

THE COUNTRY CLUB was a blaze of lights when Harwood and Jo-Anne drove up the spacious, graveled circular drive. It had turned out to be a fine early-spring evening after all—much milder than they had anticipated.

From within sifted the faint throb of music, and as the tires of the car crunched slowly to a stop in the parking area, now already crowded with magnificent automobiles, the sounds of mingled voices and laughter assailed them, forming a smooth background of well-bred gaiety. He sat a moment quietly with Jo-Anne. He lit a cigarette, while she fussed with her hair.

"I'm scared," she murmured in her low flat voice. He looked at her. She was a nice-looking girl, sensible and well-bred. Her coloring was in the medium shades—sand-hued hair, soft, almost regular face, matter-of-fact hazel eyes—a nice girl, one could see at a glance. She had tried to dress fashionably in an off-the-shoulder evening gown and had succeeded in looking only slightly ill-at-ease. That was the way she should look, he thought. They would say Jo-Anne was a nice girl. No nonsense about her. She was no flibbertyjibbet or sinuous flirt. She would neither convulse them with envy nor irritate them with lack of breeding. She was a plain, slightly above average suburban wife.

"Don't worry about it, honey," he said. "We'll make out all right. Just remember not to waste your time on the young things. Try to be pleasant to the old wives. Let them do the talking. They may be old and fat and complete bores, but they are the ones who are important here. Do the best you can to make them like you."

"All right, Philip," she answered submissively, "I'll try."

"Good girl," he said.

Despite his experience at social gatherings, Harwood had not been to one of precisely this type before with the combination of the country-club atmosphere and the formality. But he sized the situation up quickly and he felt they had worked it out just right. He was dressed carefully in a dark suit, black tie and button-down shirt—a studied casualness fashionable for such an occasion. He was handsome and he knew it and kept his fine teeth flashing as he was introduced to one or another of the overstuffed members.

The interior of the plush and rambling club was a symphony of casual wealth, with a fine deep-carpeted hall and to the right rear as one entered, a lovely winding staircase, leading upstairs to the card rooms. Lights were blazing and decorations of fresh cut flowers gave an added touch of color to the swirl and sparkle

194

of the spacious main room and lounge. The usual crowd of wealthy suburbanites were there—the horsy group, the rich businessmen, a few of the impecunious but dissipated members of old families, the heavy drinkers and the social climbers, the incorrigible golfers and the sportsmen. They were all there . . . and Harwood found himself in his element. He was not overly impressed, but these were the kind of people he understood, and this was the sort of place where his talents would have their widest scope.

It did not take Harwood long to orient himself amid the voices and laughter, but it was not until toward the end of the evening that the big moment arrived for him.

"Mr. Keesling," he was saying with his disarming smile, "my name is Harwood—Philip Harwood. I work in the System also. . . ."

Keesling was a large bearlike man with a genial heavy face until one noticed his eyes. They were hard, cold. He wore his sloppy evening clothes, however, with an air, like a man who cares nothing for clothes and is graciously acceding to some minor fetish to please his inferiors. He exuded the habit of authority and stood towering with his six-foot-three frame over the other groups of guests in the noisy and luxurious main hall. Harwood's handsome face and clean-cut appearance immediately created a good impression on him, and the crinkle lines around his eyes deepened.

"Well, well, well . . ." he boomed, "another System man in the crowd. Glad to see you! Glad to see you! Harwood—is that your name? Harwood? Well, glad to have another Empire man in this crowd of bores and wine-bibbers!"

"Yes sir," Harwood said, smiling, "I work in Mr. Wygand's group under Mr. Mansard in public relations."

"Well, well, well," Keesling boomed again, "so you know old Percy Wygand! Fine! Fine! Percy is a real sport, I can tell you. Known old Percy for years! See him every Tuesday in the meetings—a great man, old Percy is! A great man!"

"Well, sir—" Harwood broke in. His smile flashed on like a

row of lights—"well sir, I can't claim that I know Mr. Wygand. I don't move in that rarefied atmosphere. I just work for him, sir. I'm a supervisor in the information group."

"Oh, then you must know old Mizner," Mr. Keesling said jovially. "There's a sport for you—old Mizner! One of the rarest—that's what he is! Absolutely, one of the rarest! Do you ever see old Mizner?"

"Oh yes, sir," Harwood replied, "Andy Mizner and I are old friends. Andy's a remarkable man, Mr. Keesling, a remarkable man! Some of the more conservative in the place may think him perhaps a little off-beat, but on him it looks good! For my money he's tops—absolutely tops."

"Right, right, old fellow—what did you say your name was? Harwood? Well, Harwood, you hit the nail on the head that time. That Mizner's a personality—a real personality!"

Then the inevitable question. Keesling might occupy a lofty position, a position of power and authority. He might be socially elite and director in many other firms. He might possess wide and unrelated interests, but this question tagged him in the end as an Empire man.

"How long have you been here, Harwood?" he asked.

Harwood knew exactly what he meant. He did not mean how long had he been at the party. He meant how long had he served the Empire.

"About eleven years," Harwood answered quietly. Then he had what he knew was an inspiration. "I came here just before the war. I was one of Carlyle's men," he said in a low voice.

The effect was exactly what he had imagined it would be and all he had hoped for. It seemed as if since his death Carlyle had assumed the status of a legend in the System, one of those quiet influences that grow with the years. The name did not crop up often but somehow it was generally known everywhere, and it almost appeared as if there were many of "Carlyle's men," as they called themselves, among the younger executives now in key positions. Keesling placed his large hand on Harwood's shoulder, and his voice when he spoke exhibited

196

genuine affection. Perhaps, Harwood thought, as he listened, he had made his first big mistake in underestimating Carlyle, but he had certainly compensated for it since. Of course, he was not really one of Carlyle's men in the sense in which that was meant. He had, first of all, been hired by Doyle, and his transfer to the information division while Carlyle was in charge of it was an engineered move, but there was no reason to be picayune.

"Well, my boy," Keesling was saying, "I knew Jeff Carlyle well, and it has always been my opinion that the Empire lost one of its most brilliant men with him. Yes sir, my boy, I hope you will stop up and see me at the office sometime. I am not as aware of what is going on in public relations as I used to be, but I'm always interested in finding out about our activities in this field. Perhaps we could find something to talk over."

It was not until midnight—at almost exactly the proper time —that Harwood and his wife prepared to leave. The couples and individuals who had sampled the punch most avidly, the marauders of other men's wives who would be most talked about the next morning, had begun to get out of hand, and the respectable element was looking for its coats.

Jo-Anne had waltzed over to bid her adieux to Mrs. Keesling, a fat, red-faced old lady from the Middle West, whose rambling "just folks" conversation had flowed ceaselessly like maple syrup over them all, and had almost stunned Jo-Anne with boredom. Mrs. Keesling had been interminable about her collection of spode, but she had let fall one valuable bit of information when she had mentioned her husband's collection of firearms as those "nasty deadly things" in the game room. "They must be so decorative, though," Jo-Anne had commented sweetly. And Harwood had made a mental note that his knowledge of old firearms would abruptly increase perhaps a thousandfold.

Now they drove in silence in the mild night. About them were the beautifully landscaped lawns of large estates and the carefully manicured topiary-cut evergreens. Someday, Harwood thought, we shall live in a place like these—not that that was

197

simply his aim in life by any means, but a twenty-room mansion would be part of the trappings of his position, and position—the strategic position—was what he primarily desired and needed for his larger vision.

He wondered whether poor Jo-Anne would be able to live up to what was in store for them. Not that it really mattered too much. Look at Mrs. Keesling. If he had ever seen a commonplace old bore, she was it. He wondered why it was invariably necessary for people who possessed business acumen and talents, wealth and power, to be so stupefyingly dull. Mr. Keesling was undoubtedly one of the System's great princes—a financial genius, a man who ruled over perhaps fifty thousand or so people in accounting and finance divisions all over the country, and whose abilities to organize and integrate great aggregates of capital had made him an invaluable asset in the gigantic financial operations necessary. His group was riding high at the present time, since one of the Empire's major problems was the securing of more capital and this involved, in part, new drives to raise the rates for its services.

All of this Harwood was vaguely aware of, but the fact remained, as he was beginning more and more to realize, that Keesling, impressive as he was, was probably, like most of them, a crashing bore. It irked him that in the field in which he had decided to exert his talents, there should be so many of the people of importance who were not only in most respects dreadfully stupid and ignorant but also dull.

"Why are you so quiet, Philip?" Jo-Anne asked sleepily. "Didn't things go off all right?"

Harwood pulled himself from his revery.

"They went off splendidly," he said with pleasant emphasis, "splendidly! You did very well, my dear," he added. "That Mrs. Keesling's an appealing old thing, isn't she?"

Jo-Anne moved nearer her husband and placed her head against his driving arm. Yes, Harwood thought, it had been a good evening.

* * *

198

Mizner sat comfortably in one of the leather seats in Mr. Mansard's large office.

"Why is it, Andrew," Mansard was asking testily, "that while the others can work out their budgets promptly and stay within the permissible limits, your budget is not only always late but you are now running over the ten per cent leeway allowed?"

Mizner looked depressed.

"The impression I receive from the expense accounts in your department," the old gentleman went on, "is one bordering on sybaritic self-indulgence. Your people apparently deny themselves nothing in pursuing their mad rounds of pleasure—obviously for the benefit of the Company. I should like to draw your attention, Andrew, to the fact that a certain amount of restraint in the items listed as dinner and entertainment would not be construed as a dereliction of duty in the eyes of higher management. If we are a little more careful we may yet aspire to the status of being thought of as a business organization. Our superiors do not have that impression at the present time."

Mizner sighed. He had grown accustomed to this sort of conversation, the finger shaken in his face.

"Every silver lining has its cloud," he said wearily. "There are some of us who would be glad to give up the mild pleasures of dinner and entertainment with newspaper and magazine people for a quiet evening with the wife and kiddies. But the fact is, boss, last year was, as you may be aware, one of the most active in the history of the department. We had more work on a less liberal budget—due, you may remember, to the recession—than we had had in the three previous years together.

"You may remember also," Mizner went on slowly, "the memorandum so masterfully put together by Kilgore on our budget needs for this year. It was presented unfortunately at the time of the recession talk and received scant consideration. Its main points have been amply borne out by the events of the last few months. We are being besieged by national publications for data to fill out their stories on the new boom, since the Empire is one of their economic bellweathers. We have

199

further been asked by the boys in the new plants for material that will help local 'em to death, as the saying is, with our good-citizenship act."

"We are good citizens, aren't we?" Mansard asked with some asperity.

"We most certainly are, boss," Mizner answered. "But we carry our self-consciousness about it a little too far." Mizner sighed. This had been a difficult conference all around. He sat there, feeling like a man with a team of mean mules.

Mansard abruptly looked up.

"I have something further to discuss here with you," he continued in a more friendly voice. "It's something quite important for all of us. The Finance Division has notified us that they are looking for a man to work up a good presentation on the necessity for rate increases. This work will be compiled from data they supply, but they want it to be a top job. It's for presentation before rate commissions and in rate hearings and for release to the press in a more informal newspaper style. They are of the opinion we can take the material they have and produce a dossier anyone could understand—both persuasive and impressive. They would like to detach a man who could do this kind of a job from us temporarily and use him as a consultant and organizer of all the presentations they are required to make on rate cases. The rate cases are scheduled for this fall, and since the System has got to secure more revenue, this is classed as of prime importance—in fact, as of A-Number-One concern. Now I want to offer them a good man, and I mean *good*. Is there anyone whom you would suggest?"

Mizner sat quietly, thinking it over. There was no question in his mind, but he was wondering how best to present his recommendation.

"We do have someone who would well fit those qualifications," he answered at last. "In fact, in my opinion, he is the only man in the division who fits all of the qualifications. The job is a real stinker and it will take not only talent but brains

200

to get the most out of it. The only one, in my opinion, boss, who could possibly do it, is Kilgore."

Mansard gave a snort. "That cold fish," he exclaimed.

Mizner leaned back. He seemed serious for once. "You asked me," he said.

"Your assessment of the kind of job it is and what is involved in it," Mansard went on, "appears essentially correct. But it strikes me there are several men in the division who could in one way or another handle it adequately. I can scarcely see sending a man with the dull personality Kilgore exhibits out to represent us in higher management, when we have so many sparklers in the division. I am not, I hasten to add, basing this job upon personality alone, but you know as well as I do that personality is a factor. . . ."

"You seriously underrate Kilgore's personality, boss," Mizner replied quietly. "If you require a job of real distinction, he is the man to send, personality or no personality. A real beryllium brain. He makes the rest of us look like sawdust. There are one or two of his kind a corporation picks up by accident once in a decade."

Mansard looked startled. "Why, Andrew, I hadn't realized you felt that way about him, and I certainly had not noticed all this in the work we do," he observed dryly.

"He's that good," Mizner replied softly.

Mansard shrugged. "I don't see how I can refuse to consider him after what you've said," he stated. "I hope he is as good as you say he is. I am, however, sending up Harwood's card also as my own nomination. We shall let the big boys decide for themselves which one they would like to have. I suspect Harwood will perform much better in many respects than your boy—and particularly in the impression he makes on our superiors. I scarcely need emphasize the importance of this assignment in the impression we create as a division. The mark these men make—or whichever man they choose makes—will reflect in the eyes of management our own capacities as a division, and will thus result in a reputation for us for good or ill. And of course," Mansard concluded wryly, "this is the opportunity of a lifetime for the man who is chosen. The cards will be sent up in the morning. We may hear from the people in Finance as to their selection by fall. They need the man soon."

Mizner slumped silent a moment longer.

"I have one more request, boss," he said. "I need another man—a pretty good man for securing material and organizing it the way Brill did on that *War Diaries* piece. The magazines, as I said before, are clamoring for material on the big economic expansion, and there is no reason why we can't take advantage of their interest to present the Empire's growth in a favorable light—particularly in view of these impending requests for rate increases."

Mansard leaned back in his large chair and brooded.

"It was my impression that it was Harwood who composed that *War Diaries* booklet," he said. "Where does Brill come in? I know very little about Brill except that he seems to be considered the fair-haired boy."

"Brill did the work. He's now one of Randall's boys on the syndicate with Casey and McKenzie."

"Why does Randall need three men on that syndicate?" Mansard growled querulously.

"Oh now, boss," Mizner said. He wondered briefly why simple murder had not become more popular. "You're putting me in the position of, at least figuratively, cutting poor Dave's throat while he's not here to defend himself. For all I know, the syndicate may need five men instead of three. But I'll be frank with you. I would like Brill. I think he could do the job."

Mansard sat there for a moment, like a glittering toad, his head lowered. He seemed to be almost in pain.

"I must say, Andrew," he observed finally, "that I deplore this sort of extravagant empire building on your part. Your group is about as large as it should be, and it seems to me you should be able to get along with the men you have. However, in this one instance, I'll consider the matter."

202

"Thanks, boss," Mizner replied.

Mansard looked up suddenly, his sinister face twisted in a grimace.

"I should be derelict in my duty, Andrew," he concluded dryly, "if I did not point out that if the division were run the way you run your department, we should all be bankrupt, and furthermore higher management would most certainly find other fields for our efforts, such as they are."

Mizner sighed. He rose. The conference was ended.

Martin turned as the icy, soft voice behind him spoke:

"Where have you been lately, Martin?" she was saying. It was Sherry Lewis, aloof and beautiful, with the faint smile. They were standing in the green-carpeted reception room near the main area.

"Why hello, Sherry," he replied. "I've been around."

"Whatever happened to that date we were going to have?" she asked. She allowed her cool, long-lashed eyes to rest on him.

"How would you manage to fit me in with all your other dates?" he said.

"Oh, never mind." She walked away a few steps, then stopped. "The invitation is still open," she murmured. "I'll see you some other time."

Martin stood a moment after she had gone, puzzled. She was a beautiful girl, all right, but calculating and hard. A knife-in-the-sleeve personality. She aroused nothing in him now but a faint distaste.

It was after a session of records that he mentioned her to April that evening—one of the two nights a week he saw April. She had been particularly difficult and sad. "Why do you think Sherry spoke to me?" he asked her. "We have never been exactly close."

"I'm sure I don't know," April replied nastily. "She wants all the men on the string. Maybe she likes you, Martin, but I can't say I like her. She has the reputation of trying to make

203

every man mad about her. She once worked on Jim Somers, but he would have no part of her."

"Meow," Martin said.

"I don't care," April replied angrily. "I usually like girls and I have a lot of girl friends, but Sherry's not a nice person."

"You are the original nice-Nelly yourself, aren't you, April?" he said.

"I didn't mean it that way, Martin," she replied, irritated. "I certainly wasn't referring to her morals. She may be as pure as the driven snow, for all I know. I mean as a person. Very few people like Sherry."

"That is, none of the girls," he baited her.

"You make me sick," she answered.

She was sitting on the sofa. He walked to her and leaning forward kissed her on the lips.

"A girl like you," he said, "is apt to drive any man to Sherry. I'm sure even Sherry wouldn't be so cold. . . ."

He kissed her again, and the beautiful, sullen face turned up toward him, her eyes ablaze—savage and warm. Slowly she pulled him down toward her, and he could feel her teeth bite at his lips.

"This is what you want, isn't it, Martin," she murmured. "This is all you've been dying for," she whispered, her breath sweet and hot against his nostrils. And suddenly he was against her on the sofa, tearing at her clothes.

"All right, Martin," she was murmuring softly, "take it, if you want. Take it. Take it. Take it. I don't care. . . ." Her breath was coming fast. Her dress ripped at the bosom, and he snapped the strap of her brassiere, tearing it away. "All right, Martin. . . ." Her voice was a soft singsong of passion. Her eyes were closed, and she began to tremble and clutch at him. The surge of his passion was like a return to adolescence, mindless and intolerable.

When it was over, she lay there quietly amid the ruin of her clothes. "No more," she murmured. "Please, no more. . . ."

He was kissing her gently, her white lovely arms and her

neck. "Oh April," he said softly, "I love you so. You're everything I've wanted, everything. . . ."

"You had what you wanted," she said. She turned her face
away to the sofa. "Now let me go . . . I . . . I hate you, but
I . . . I guess I wanted you in that way. It's . . . it's not the
right kind of love, Martin. It can never be the right kind of love.
We could never make out together—this . . . this gutter
love . . ." and she began to weep. "Not the way it was with
Jim and me . . . Oh God . . ."

Slowly her voice subsided into a whisper, and as he held her
close, gradually she fell asleep.

For the first time in what seemed to Martin eons, he felt really
happy—really happy and content.

4

THE BIG SUMMONS arrived on an afternoon in late May.

Harwood was lounging at his desk looking over copy, when
the telephone rang. Two weeks earlier, he had sent up a note to
Keesling's office concerning a rare and ancient derringer.

The voice on the telephone displayed one of those cultivated,
Bryn Mawr accents affected by executive secretaries.

"This is Miss Enno, Mr. Keesling's secretary," she said. "Mr.
Keesling would be delighted to have you stop up a moment, if
you are free."

"I shall be right up, Miss Enno," he replied.

Now he sat there quivering, trying to quiet himself before
making the big journey to the fortieth floor. The fortieth floor,
generally referred to as Heaven, was the aerie of the lords of the
Empire. From here, the vast multibillion dollar enterprise
stretching over the land and part way over the world was ruled
with an iron hand.

Harwood felt a surge of pleasure. He had at last made it. He had at last broken through the crust. It appeared to him now as if it had been too easy. He had not believed that it would ever have fallen to him so soon. But now he must be careful. He must take no chances. He must calm down. There must be no mistakes. If he worked it right, this could mean the first of many such visits, and eventually who knew what might come of them? But he must start off slow and easy. He must not push too hard the first time.

He rose and took a deep breath. He walked into the main area, then through the reception room into the marble hall to the elevators. Everything suddenly appeared to be in slow motion—the faces of the men passing, the distant sounds of voices. He found it difficult to concentrate.

"Forty," he said to the elevator operator. There were three men in the elevator. Two of them glanced at him from the corners of their eyes. They got out several floors lower. Forty was the top floor, the last stop. No one else was left with them. He stepped out into a large marble replica of the other floors, but much quieter, much more hushed. And the doors leading to the anterooms of individual offices appeared more ominous, more imposing. He walked slowly across the wide hall toward the reception room entrances. As he approached, he noted the names, strange, sonorous and awe-inspiring—*Office of the Vice President—Manufacturing* . . . *Office of the Vice President—Traffic*—and here it was—the one he was looking for—*Office of the Vice President—Finance*—and below, the name *H. F. Keesling.* He wondered briefly what the *H.F.* stood for. There were other titles and names farther along. He pushed open the door.

The anteroom was luxuriously furnished with sofas, easy chairs, maroon carpet and soft ceiling lights. On the right stood the broad desk of the executive secretary; on the far left, a smaller kidney-shaped receptionist's desk where an attractive girl was sorting mail. She looked up and walked toward him inquiringly.

"Mr. Keesling asked me to stop up a minute," he said to the

206

pretty girl. "My name's Harwood." At that moment, Miss Enno emerged from the main office.

"Oh, Mr. Harwood?" she asked, ending on a note of rising inflection.

"Yes," Harwood said.

"Won't you go right in? Mr. Keesling is expecting you."

She walked back with him to the door and opened it. He smiled mechanically and entered.

The vast office was in a state of undersea gloom—the Venetian blinds so drawn that the diffused light afforded an air of being in a great twilit cave. At the far end behind a streamlined desk sat Mr. Keesling, his large hulk in a relaxed position in the armchair.

"Come in, Harwood," he called pleasantly. "Glad to see you again, my boy. Sit down." He waved at a comfortable armchair on the other side of the desk, and Harwood sat down.

He noticed now the handsome fireplace and over the mantel two breechloaders crossed.

"Nice of you to send me that note on the derringer," he said. "A very fine specimen."

He turned in his great chair.

"Harwood," he began conversationally, "I know very little about public relations, my boy, and I am not consulting you now in any sense in an official capacity. I should turn to my good friend, Percy Wygand, if I were asking your division for assistance. But as a personal matter, I have a little problem here in finance and I should like your private opinion as to the possibility of public relations being of help in solving it. The problem has to do with presenting the Company's case before rate hearings and acquainting the public with our needs in a wholly persuasive and acceptable manner. I can't go into the matter further than that. But it seemed to me you might be able to give me an opinion on whether this is best handled by Finance people or by Public Relations people?"

Harwood sat for a moment quietly, as if deep in thought. When he had been young, he remembered, the corner store used to offer a kind of hard candy called wining balls at two for a penny, and he could recall the problem that faced him every time he appeared there—should it be two wining balls or four gumdrops? That was the choice now. He would have to play it carefully, however. He would have to watch out how he expressed himself. He knew he was being tested.

"That's really a problem, Mr. Keesling," he began at last. "I think actually the answer lies in a collaboration of some sort between the Finance and Public Relations groups—or perhaps even better using a Public Relations man as a consultant. . . ."

Harwood paused. Keesling was nodding gravely.

"Finance knows what it wants to do," Harwood went on. He was aware now that he had struck the right note. This man might not be too difficult to handle, after all, he thought. In fact, he might be easy—like all the rest. "Finance knows its own problems intimately, and it could perhaps benefit from the counsel of those downstairs who know how to formulate effective presentations. Of course," Harwood added gravely, "Public Relations cannot make something out of nothing. But when we have a good case, as ours undoubtedly is, then its techniques can be very useful."

Keesling leaned back in his chair and took out a cigar. He had not offered Harwood a cigarette, but now he leaned forward and pushed toward him a silver box with his initials elaborately inscribed on it.

"Have a cigarette, Harwood," he said thoughtfully. Harwood took one and slowly lit it.

"Your analysis of the situation is very good," Keesling said at last, almost as if to himself, "very good. Some arrangement like the one you mentioned has occurred to me."

Harwood held himself in with difficulty. He waited while he drew smoke into his lungs and exhaled slowly. "I should imagine, sir," he concluded, "that you could find a number of men in Public Relations with the experience and . . . and skill to help in handling the assignment—a man with . . . with an all-around grasp of the situation."

208

Keesling puffed on his cigar for a moment. He seemed deep' in thought. A little of the tenseness began to ease out of Harwood.

"Harwood, you put out that piece called *War Diaries,* didn't you?" Keesling asked quietly.

"Yes sir, I did."

"It was good," Keesling commented softly, "good. It must have required much research and careful organization."

"Yes sir," Harwood said in a low voice, "it did require considerable digging and the pulling together of a number of elements. It represented months of work."

Keesling turned away and looked out of the windows nearest his desk. The Venetian blinds had cut down the glare but through the half-opened louvers the faint distant towers of lofty buildings could be glimpsed in the blue haze of late afternoon.

"Tell me something, Philip," he asked softly, "do you happen to know a man named Kilgore in your group?"

"Bob Kilgore?" Harwood repeated in surprise. Instantly all his faculties leaped to the alert. This was a turn he had not expected. He wondered where the Old Man had heard of Kilgore. And even more, what was behind the question. "Why yes, sir, I know Bob Kilgore well," he replied quietly. "A good man—a very good man. He seems perhaps a little on the intellectual side, but that's neither here nor there, and it does give us something to make mild fun of in the office at times. But these doubledomes do keep us on our toes after all, don't they . . . ?"

"An intellectual," Keesling echoed softly. A look at the Old Man's cold eyes told the story. Harwood found it difficult to prevent himself from feeling a sense of satisfaction. He must be very careful now. He must watch himself.

"Well, of course, it's certain elements in his background," Harwood added hastily, as if trying to retrieve a slip his own honesty had inadvertently forced from him. "You see Bob was a Ph.D. at Harvard, and I suppose you would call him a liberal. . . . He's lived in somewhat of a rarefied atmosphere, and it seems to me he should be forgiven perhaps if he looks down on the lot of us corn-fed Middlewesterners."

Harwood now realized that he had struck the right note. He had uncovered one of Keesling's major distastes—a *bête noire* not uncommon with many of these big, experienced and well-trained but partly self-made men. Also the note of liberalism was a shrewd stroke in the climate of opinion in which these large men lived. Very little further prodding would be required to crystallize the estimate the Old Man was forming of Kilgore, and Kilgore himself, Harwood surmised, would, more than less, tend to bear out the impression.

"One of those boys," Keesling repeated softly. His voice when it was quiet, soft like that, had a ring so ominous that it made the blood run cold. Keesling would never raise his voice, would never pound or swear. He would be quiet, almost gentle.

"A doubledome . . . a Ph.D. . . . a liberal . . . What would you say were his interests?" Keesling asked again in that soft low voice. "He does sound a little on the ethereal side to me, Philip, if I may say so. Is he a good friend of yours?"

"Well, he's a friend," Harwood answered with careful intonation, "but perhaps not a close friend. You see our interests differ somewhat. He plays a game like chess. I'm a little more of a golf and hunting type."

"Chess . . ." Keesling remarked, and it was obvious that a knowledge of this game was not one of the Old Man's basic forms of entertainment and added nothing to his estimation of Kilgore. "Don't believe I understand the game myself," Keesling added. "Well . . . well . . . very interesting. Well, Philip, thank you very much for coming up. I believe we shall have more to talk over in the near future. Remember me to your charming wife, will you, my boy? And again, thank you."

Keesling had risen, and Harwood was out of his chair, smiling and debonair again. "Thank you, sir," he said quietly. "Any time I can be of assistance. A great pleasure. . . ."

Harwood could scarcely remember how he had made his way

back to the ninth floor and did not return to earth until he found himself walking along the marble corridor toward the Public Relations offices.

Randall sat quietly in his office opposite Harwood and tried to relax.

"I don't know what it is, Dave," Harwood was saying, "but I don't like it—this criticism. We've been receiving a lot of that kind of underhand comment from the field lately. It makes me nervous."

Randall himself had been feeling somehow more and more isolated and uncertain of late. It was a haunting sensation—one he could not put his finger on. Vaguely he had the impression that he was being done in, and he did not know exactly in what way. Mistakes were being made. A number of minor problems were closing in on him. The men appeared to misunderstand his instructions or in all sincerity to produce the kind of work that most irritated him. This was one of those days.

"Actually," Harwood was saying, "our work has not changed substantially nor our manner of presenting it. The demands have piled up—there's no getting around that—and we have a great deal more to do than is reasonable for the size of our group. But it's something more than that."

Yes, Randall thought briefly, that was only a small part of it. It was the atmosphere, the feeling of pressure and haste. It was not like that in the old days. There had been an entirely different aura about the place then. In those days, one felt oneself a part of a larger, more important operation that could survive any strain or any mishap placed upon it—a project that time could not damage. Today, everything was hurry and forget.

Now as he watched Harwood, sitting opposite him and drumming with his fingers on the desk, he had the sense of haste, a sense of tension which even Harwood—of late grown so serious and overtaxed—could not dispel. Harwood had been a great blessing, though. There was no question about that. He didn't know how he could have survived without that boy. Harwood

211

had been acting as a sort of spy for him, a disinterested outrider among the men, dipping up for him from the rumor factories whatever had been brewing—and many of these rumors had been, to say the least, disquieting.

"It appears to me," Randall broke in as Harwood paused, "that we are letting these misunderstandings undermine our confidence. If our work is good, we have nothing to worry about. We must just take the rumors for what they are—baseless and the usual undercurrent of restless carping that always crops up during times of exceptional activity and expansion."

"I hope you are right, Dave," Harwood replied in a low voice. "I hope you are right, but I don't mind telling you that our position has me worried. It seems to me that there may be those upstairs who are not happy about us."

"I think you're imagining, Phil," Randall replied at last. "Well, the only thing we can do is try a little harder. . . ."

"You got the rent?" the big red-faced woman asked.

Jim Somers sat up slowly in the soiled and disordered bed. He was unshaven and his eyes were bloodshot. He began to cry soundlessly.

"Never mind that," Mrs. Flaherty said. She had seen a lot of them. Mr. Flaherty had been one. It never did any good to try to put up with them.

The man on the bed looked around vaguely. The face seemed to waver before him—a mist from the night-colored bend of nowhere. "My checkbook," he said. "I can't find my checkbook."

"Them checks ain't no good and you know it," Mrs. Flaherty said. "Last two come back. You got nothin' in the bank."

Jim looked about the room. It had all been so awful lately. He had been all right a long time ago, it seemed, a long, long time ago. Then he'd had a wife, a job, a necktie. Now they were all gone, all vanished. Everything sold or lost—they'd all washed down the drain. Now there was nothing, nothing. . . .

"Look, mister," she said—the old days of friendship had

212

evaporated too, it appeared—"you see what you can do getting up the rent. You got one more week here for the furniture and stuff you brought, then out you go . . . I got my own troubles."

It seemed no sooner had the voice—that rasping coarse voice —died away than she had been gone for hours and there he was still lying on that rumpled bed, the smell of soiled clothes and gin and urine haunting him. The heat was dreadful and he lay there perspiring. There was nothing left in the bottle, so he'd have to go out pretty soon anyhow. Everything was getting away from him, slipping into the night and the grayness, and that street was an old tar baby. It kept beckoning, saying "Come on out. . . ."

He sat up slowly. His head ached so badly he felt it might drop off. Slowly he began to search the room. It was a shambles and his progress with that splitting head was painstaking. In the bathroom was one gin bottle with almost a finger of the stuff left in it. He drank it off thirstily. Then he sat quiet a moment until it helped him feel better.

He'd have to get out anyhow, and what was the use returning to that harsh complaining voice . . . ? Yes, he'd vacate this time for good. The streets wanted him; the streets could have him. He wasn't afraid of them any more. He sat still a moment longer—a dirty, unshaven man in ragged trousers and sweat-shirt.

No use saying goodbye. He'd said goodbyes before—goodbye to them all: to the baby, the little baby that never lived, to Betty Lou, to April, to the men, to them all. Goodbye, goodbye on every clock, at every place. I'm no good, he thought dully. I was never any good. This is where I belong. They did right to let me go. At least, I have that to remember. Then his thoughts veered and began to mist, as they had so often of late. The Empire, he thought again dully in that strange mystic trance. We are fleeting things, but you will endure. Farewell . . . goodbye . . . goodbye . . . You need never call for me now. I can never help you. You can never help me. . . . Goodbye . . . goodbye.

213

Slowly, he opened the door of the room and peered blindly down the dark hot well of the narrow stairway. He could hear no sound. Mrs. Flaherty would be out shopping—that all-pervading smell of boiled cabbage . . . He shuffled slowly down the stairs, being very careful. He did not want to fall again. Through the dirty glass door and out into the hot air.

It was evening of a beautiful August day. The heat dazzles were fading, and the smell of asphalt and tar was pungent. He blinked in the lavender and coral light. "Goodbye . . . good-bye . . . " he kept saying. Laughter of a young couple walking up the street arm in arm reached him.

He turned slowly—a ragged man, unshaven, dirty, greasy-looking—one of the vagrants and derelicts he had himself seen many times in the old days in that run-down section of the Village. He stood a moment numbly, then he shuffled slowly down the street.

5

KEESLING SAT in the monstrous private office and leaned back in his armchair. He had about made his decision. It would be Harwood. There was no doubt about it: that boy could do the job. Before him on the big desk were two envelopes containing the cards. He had not had the time to look at them yet. One was the card of a man named Kilgore. The other was Harwood's. Looking at them would be just a formality now, but he felt that he ought to go through it, if only to be businesslike about this whole matter.

Keesling was, in cold fact, a brilliant man, and his bumbling bearlike body, his anti-intellectual organizer's mind concealed a cold, hard personality that was alive with instinct. He could feel when something was right, but even more important, he could

214

sense when something was not right, and he had always had brains enough to follow his instincts.

Now, there was everything right about Harwood. Of this he was at present convinced, although he had not had the opportunity to bring himself to bear upon the situation too fully. It seemed to him, in fact, so much a foregone conclusion that Harwood was completely sound that he had not given himself the trouble even of interviewing Kilgore. Harwood had handled himself in what he could only say was a masterful fashion and had displayed a quick mind and a sure grasp of the situation. He would be easy for the men to work with.

Yes, the job involved required real brilliance—something conspicuously lacking in the System. All over the land, once the program had lumbered into action, expert financial and operating men would be presenting themselves and their briefs at rate commission hearings, and at the same time a vast program to educate the public to the need for higher rates for the System's essential services would have to be launched. This was not an easy task. Rate commissioners might be underpaid and in some respects stupid, but they had the feel for the false and tricky, and they would never approve an increase unless they were thoroughly and completely convinced of its necessity. The public also must be persuaded that these rates were necessary. And the boys from Possum Glory would certainly not be persuaded easily—nor by surface tricks, either. The rural rates were especially hard to handle.

Keesling turned in his big chair and gazed once more toward the windows. It was a warm early-autumn morning and he wondered whether he could snatch a few days off for hunting later on this fall. The big job would be underway by winter and he would be so busy he would hardly have time to breathe. So perhaps . . . Well, this was no time for daydreaming. He might as well look at the cards and get that over with. Then he could call Wygand and tell him they would be needing Harwood in about a month.

215

He bent forward and picked up the large envelopes containing the cards. With his big paws, he slipped out Kilgore's card first. The photograph in the corner was not very prepossessing, but then it struck him that these photographs the Company contracted to have taken for the personnel files were an outrage against human dignity—his own did not exactly flatter him, either, he was aware.

His trained eye skimmed down the card over the entries and the background. He missed nothing. It was somewhat as Harwood had said it would be, but it was, nevertheless, an amazing card. Born: Walthingham, Connecticut. Father: school building superintendent at a girl's college. Mother: a Master of Fine Arts from Bryn Mawr. Kilgore: A.B. Harvard; M.A. Harvard; Ph.D. Harvard. Thesis published. Comments were made—one was by Lattimore—that was the fellow in personnel relations; Carlyle . . . hmmm . . . let's see what Carlyle had said. *Unusual man—brains and integrity. Does outstanding job on general releases. Rigid taste. Too good for the jobs we give him.* And down farther, Randall with a simple comment: *Very good man—not necessarily executive material.* And then . . . let's see . . . oh yes, promotion here to press supervisor—four men reporting to him. Now, let's see . . . Mizner's comments at the end: *Absolutely top quality man. Loyal. Rigid in taste. Tends to be uncompromising.*

Keesling leaned back. He was impressed despite himself. Not exactly the sort of man one would want to work with perhaps, he mused, but a very good card. He guessed Kilgore was a man to watch. He sighed. It did not, however, change his mind in the least. Harwood was the man—there was no doubt about that. It struck him more than ever what a splendid personality Harwood possessed—a very sound man, and he would be easy to work with. His men would have no trouble with Harwood. There was no rigidity or temperament in that young man's make-up.

Keesling was pleased with himself. He liked to see a young man forge ahead—or so he often had told himself—and Harwood was the type of young man he felt he could advance with-

216

out qualms. Well, it was as good as settled, and he was glad to have this minor flurry off his hands. Let's see—he guessed he might as well take a look at Harwood's card also for good measure. It was a superfluous gesture, but it never hurt to be thorough about these investigations. He knew what he would find and actually the matter was not all that vital, but Keesling was a man who did not let little things slip through his fingers, who did not leave stones unturned. He liked to do a job right.

He picked up the other envelope in his large, clumsy hands and dumped the card out on the big desk. He turned it over and right side up. He began to read it. Slowly he skimmed down. Then he lifted his head and shook it slightly. He gazed for a moment out of the windows. What was the matter with him? he wondered. He picked up the card. He began skimming again. This time he did not look up until he had finished reading it carefully. Then he put the card down on the desk slowly. There must be something the matter with me today, he thought again. There's absolutely nothing wrong with this card.

He began reading it again. It was almost eery. The whole effect was out of kilter. He had read it carefully three times. There was absolutely nothing in there that anyone could take exception to. It was a good card—an absolutely straight card. It had just what he had expected to find in it. There was no comment by Carlyle on the card, however, and it did seem to him that Harwood had mentioned being Carlyle's man, but that was of no consequence, and he may just have misunderstood. Let's see . . . well he didn't really remember Harwood's actually saying that. It was just an impression. But even so, there was nothing to balk at in the card. Let's see . . . everybody appeared to have spoken well of Harwood. His schooling was right . . . his background good . . . he had had plant experience in industrial relations during wartime. His progress was above average. What was it then? What in the name of heaven could it be?

He twisted in his big chair. Try as he would, he could not see what it was, but the fact remained that, taken as a whole and

Harwood's career, though he did not know it, was over. As the ink dried, Keesling finished it off by scribbling his initials just below and blotting them. He looked at the card once more before turning it face down. He felt no compunction whatever. He was a man without sensibilities or pity. He was a man who always obeyed his instincts, a hard man who knew when he was right. The scrawled words had closed one set of books. He did not really care. Harwood—he could scarcely remember the name now—had had his day. The show was over.

The Old Man picked up Kilgore's card again. Might as well have this processed right away. He wondered vaguely how Kilgore would work out in the long grind. There was no more time to be wasted, however. He might as well tell Wygand right now it would be Kilgore. He rang for Miss Enno.

The words buried forever in Harwood's file were simple. The three words read: *Not suitable material. HFK.* They were little enough to end a career.

BOOK IV   Kilgore

1

"THERE'S NOTHING like the recital of others' misfortunes to cheer a man up," Mizner was saying in his cracked, growling voice. "It seems to me, Bob, that Randall's taking an awful beating on this syndicate—lateness, the wrong items. . . . It looks as if some smooth bastard is trying to slit his throat. Randall's all right, but he's too sincere. He doesn't know what time it is. Somebody has got to him. Wait till he tries to turn his neck and his head rolls off. . . ."

Mizner was sitting in Kilgore's office. Kilgore—a thin, pale, sandy-haired man with cool, intelligent gray eyes—lounged back, relaxed, exuding that aura of extreme quietness which was almost his hallmark. He looked thoughtful. He leaned forward and began to knock out his pipe on the ashtray.

"So now we have Brill," he said. "It must have been hard on Randall to lose him."

"Yes," Mizner said, "so now we have Brill, the best there is. Put him on the new job."

Kilgore watched Mizner shuffle to the door and out, and thought of him with a quick flash of affection. He was not interested primarily in people but in ideas and situations, and his mind—a mind of extraordinary acuity—was involved at the moment with another problem.

In the "practical" world in which he moved as an obscure and unimportant cog, Kilgore was gaining an insight into the imperfect workings of the kind of organization on which he had lavished such a mountain of study and research when he was in

223

college. Strangely enough, the practical life suited him. The routines and drudgeries were entirely to his tastes.

He was sedentary by nature, inclined to procrastination, and the demands of the work on him were slight. It seemed almost, as several who had known him well had commented, a dreadful waste of a remarkable brain. In the evenings when he went home—he lived with his two elderly sisters—he had leisure to read, study, smoke his pipe and play the cello, his one vice. He had never married. "There are enough women in my life now," he once said, referring to the two sisters.

To have brains is to be lonely, and Kilgore was by nature a lonely sort of man, despite the warm affection, first of his parents and now of his two sisters with their fussy love. As a boy he had lived apart from those of his own age. At eight he had been able to read and digest the classics, including Gibbon, Voltaire and Taine; at ten he had finished the equivalent of high school, although his father—a kindly and understanding man who worked as the janitor at the girls' college in town—deliberately held him back so that he could for a brief period have the chance to play with those of his own age.

At sixteen, he entered Harvard, emerging at twenty-four with his Ph.D. So of necessity his had been an isolated and disjointed existence, and now the patterns and routines of the world in which he found himself and, after hours, the life of the mind were all the pleasures and satisfactions he desired.

There had been times when he had thought he would have liked to marry or perhaps to have lived the sort of existence that warmer-blooded men had lived, to have escaped into that murky, twilit world of women or drink that seemed somehow to bring them, if only momentarily, so close to the essentials of life. But in the end he knew he could not find that world nor could he ever bring himself to it. "Live all you can," Henry James had said. "It is a mistake not to. If when you come to the end you have not had your life, what have you had?" Yes, with this he agreed. His mind agreed wholly and completely. But he would never have been able to live fully in that way—just through

224

the body or the senses, whatever they might say. The Lord had blessed him with a mind of great power and sensitivity, and it was through his mind and what it could accomplish in the world in which he had chosen to live that he would drink to the dregs, that he would empty the cup. He had chosen the Empire, and in its service, with all its defects and trivialities, its routines and its degradations, he would live.

For he could see it with a broader vision than these others. Even insignificant and of little use to it as he felt himself to be, he could view it with more perspective and scope. It was the old argument over again that he had had many a time with Mizner. "I am where I want to be," he had replied in his gentle voice when Mizner in his throaty croak accused him of wasting his talents there. "I deliberately chose to work here. I expect the Empire will eventually find a use for me, as in my own small plan of life I have found a use for it."

"I must say, Bob," Mizner had replied in his tired drawl, "people can find the damndest excuses for selling out to the enemy."

"Why do you think I'm in the enemy's camp?" Kilgore asked.

"The System is by its very nature," Mizner replied angrily, "hostile to brains. A man with drive, ambition and ruthlessness might perhaps get on here. A man with a pleasant personality and not too bright but a real sparkler is bound to get on. But a man with brains—God forbid, Bob—that is anathema—the conspiracy of the dull-eyed against the mind. Why, the Empire is founded on mediocrity—on the man with a low sort of skill, on the minor expert and the petty plodder, and most of all on the vast, faceless masses of people. Brains are a commodity they can do without. And in our field especially, to have intelligence is an insult, something in very poor taste that can only exasperate and antagonize everybody. There must be a G.I.—that is, General Instruction—on the subject, though I can't put my finger on it at the moment—something that says: No brains allowed on the premises. People with intelligence are troublemakers."

225

"And you, Andy?" Kilgore asked in his low voice. "How about you?"

"And I—a mountebank like me, a clown—why I'm almost perfect for my job. The only thing I lack is sincerity, and the Empire has enough of that to pave the streets to hell and back. Sincerity comes in carload lots here. We get it by the ton, every minute, every hour on the hour. The Empire is founded on sincerity."

"You kill me," Kilgore said softly.

The afternoon was gone. Tomorrow Kilgore would have a meeting with the men.

Martin turned and looked at the beautiful face, the blond hair falling in profusion over her eyes, the covers on the wide day bed disarranged. She was in one of her moods.

"You liked it?" she asked. "You like?"

"I love you," he said slowly. "Please don't treat me like this."

"I treated you nicely, I thought," she said nastily. "Look at what you've done to me. You want to do it again?"

"Please, April . . ." he said.

"I thought you were such a man," she answered, pushing her lower lip forward. "You were the one would never get tired. . . . You started something. Now you can finish it."

He leaned forward and kissed her on the neck. Her beautiful bosom gleamed in the soft light.

"It's almost midnight," he said. "When will you stop baiting me and just let me love you as I want to—the way I really love you, everything about you?"

"If you want it again, stop talking and take it," she said slowly, sullenly. "You've made it; now take it. It's all yours. It's what you wanted—now stop giving it all that pretty talk. I feel like it. Go ahead. . . ."

He placed his hand on her breast and turned against her, brushing his lips across her soft, perfumed skin. She would be like that until the drowning ecstasy exhausted her; then it would

226

be the old plea: "No more . . . no more. . . . Go away. . . ."

Suddenly he was angry, exasperated.

He turned away from her and put his head down among the scattered pillows.

"So it's nothing to you but that," he said, his voice muffled. "You give me the body but not you. Thanks for the use of the body—is that it? You keep telling me that's all I want. It's not true. I do want that. I want it, you know. I want it as much as and more than you do, but not that way—not that alone—not the way you're giving it to me. . . . Don't you like me just one little bit, April? Don't you want anything else from me—not one other thing?"

"Oh, stop the talking," she said, and her voice was low and sultry. "We've been all over it before. Let's not kid ourselves. . . . You have what you wanted. I'm your gutter love and that's what I'll always be. That's enough—that's all I can give you, and let's forget the rest. Now will you please turn around? I want some more. . . ."

"It's still Jim Somers, isn't it?" he began again, his voice muffled. And suddenly in the midst of his great happiness, the misery crept in once more, the ebb tide of that old longing from which only for those golden drowning moments of immediate passion could he be wholly free. Her words to him from the beginning returned as in the fullness of their passion—whispers returning again and again, the shaken voice: "I'll never really love you . . ." the words reverberating through all their moments of passion . . . "I'll never really love you as I loved Jim. . . . You forced me and the kind of love you'll get from me is the kind you wanted—a gutter love. . . . It'll always be a gutter love. There're only three things you can do for me now. Take me to a hotel and get me drunk and take your dirty love out on me. . . . That's all I want any more. I've never been to a hotel with a man before. I'm not really a woman any more. I'm just your gutter love and that's all." And so it had been from the beginning. Now these words sifted back to him in his anguish,

227

And he said again: "It's still Jim Somers, isn't it? That's who it will always be."

He turned back and gazed at her.

"I went out and looked for him, April," he continued in a low voice. "I walked the streets looking for him for your sake. . . . I've let myself be used by you—for any purpose your fancy dictated. I've even told you I was willing to be second best, but still you won't give me anything but this . . . this contempt, this gutter passion, as you call it. With anyone else, it would be enough. It isn't with you, April. If it's all you have for me, I'll take it now, and I'll treat you the way you want to be treated, until you wear out this love. You'll wear it out somehow, sometime, April. And I'll be glad. Then maybe you'll see how it was —after it's too late. I hope so, April," he said, "I hope so. I hope you will be as sad and hurt as I am, as full of longing. . . . Now let's have our gutter passion—just the way I'd do it with any tramp I picked up in some cheap bar around town. Come on," he said.

He pulled her over toward him, digging his fingers into her shoulders.

"You're hurting me," she said.

"Isn't that too bad!" he said bitterly. And suddenly in an access of his frustration and longing, he struck at her again and again. She cried out and crossed her arms to protect her breasts; then abruptly she was fighting him, savage and flushed, her barbarous, disheveled beauty overwhelming him with passion and despair.

When it was over, she sat up slowly against the pillows. With the edge of the coverlet, he dabbed at the blood on the corner of his mouth where she had bitten him.

"I'm sorry," she said, "but it was your fault. You started it. Anyhow," she smiled her slow, ravishing, sleepy smile, "anyhow I liked it," she added softly.

He turned away. It had not made any difference, any difference at all. Nothing made any difference to her. It was still the gutter love. That was all she wanted of him—everything she

228

would ever want. Well, he would play it her way until the passion wore out. He could not help it. That was all he could do. That was all, he guessed, he would ever have.

Kilgore let his gray eyes rest on each of the five men in turn.

"So now," he was concluding quietly, "with the addition of you, Martin, there will be six of us in this group handling all general news services, and there should be plenty of opportunity to cover our expansion activities, both completely and in detail, for the outside press."

Turner remained after the others had left. "The main stories now," he said easily, as he stretched his long legs, "are the new television relay towers going up across the mountains, and the rate cases. Can we put Brill on them?"

Kilgore nodded thoughtfully.

Turner sighed. "Brill is a good man. He could do all right, if we can pry him away from his girl friend."

"His girl friend?" Kilgore asked in surprise.

"I suppose everyone in the office must know of Brill's attachment to Mrs. Tremaine," Turner remarked in his clipped, cultivated voice. "That is—everybody but you. Gossip is the life-blood of this place."

Kilgore looked bewildered.

"I realized the boss used to have a weakness for her," he said in an injured voice, "but Brill is a new one on me. He has a career here if he wants it," Kilgore added. "I hope he doesn't ruin it."

When Turner had departed, Kilgore leaned back and sighed. He was thinking of Brill. Another able man, he supposed, lost to the Empire. Women, he thought again.

Then he began to muse on his own defects.

Sometimes he wished he were able to make a better showing in this world which he had chosen for himself. Not that he was particularly ambitious. He was, if anything, conspicuously lacking in the drive that an Empire man should possess. His deepest pleasures were to be found in that inner perfection of things as

229

they were and as the mind could conceive them. But these were not the interests or concerns of the people around him. And it did appear to him that he was remarkably unfitted, that indeed he was singularly lacking in the qualities most valued by the Empire. For instance, in that quality called personality, the ability to make quick and easy friends, to sparkle, to display suavity and heartiness, always to be able to find the right word, not necessarily the truth. "Human relations" was what they liked to call it. He had about as much human relations as the black puma in the Central Park Zoo.

But Brill had what he lacked. He had drive, intensity. He had great organizing ability and that inner self-confidence and poise that made people notice him. Brill would go up. One could scarcely blame the Empire for seeking a type different from himself for its more responsible efforts. The Empire was, after all, a vast human reservoir—a network of people with conflicting emotions and motives, and the ability to organize, to assess and deal with people rather than with concepts would be the most desirable of assets. He was fine at concepts. His cold personality and his inability to compromise did not, however, suit him to their needs. Sometimes it disheartened him.

2

"TELL ME," Martin asked again, "will you still see me between trips now that I'm on an expense account?"

They were in Martin's room. April was in lounging pajamas sitting on the floor with the piles of recordings beside her. She let her long-lashed green eyes rest on his intent face.

"What do you think?" she said. "I'm the original passion flower—remember?"

Martin looked at her abruptly. "Now, Martin . . ." she said.

"I can't help it," he replied softly. "I'm so crazy about you."

230

He walked over and leaned down, and she turned her face up to him. His kiss smeared her lipstick. "All right," she said. "I know."

He walked back to the sofa and flung himself on it. He was tired.

"April," he continued, "my instinct says I should ask to stay where I am. I shouldn't try this expense-account life. The trouble is you can't refuse a transfer. Not if you want to remain here and make a career."

"It will always be that way now, Martin," she answered matter-of-factly. "You have to face it. It'll keep getting harder and harder to break away. Actually, I don't see why you're worried about the new job. It's a lot better than many I've seen."

"It isn't the job, April," he replied slowly. "Maybe it's just myself. I don't mind the work and this new assignment sounds pretty good, really. But it's that nagging feeling I have that there must be something better I should be doing, there must be something more significant. . . ."

"If you knew what you really wanted to do, Martin . . ." she answered. She was silent a moment. Then she spoke without looking at him. "I'll tell you what's in my heart, Martin. I don't honestly think you have any secret gift to bestow on the world. I think you belong here. They think you're outstanding. Why not accept that much and be satisfied?"

"As long as you'll still be there when I get back," he concluded quietly.

"You're sometimes very sweet," she said to him. Then she smiled at his serious face. "Martin," she murmured, "don't take it so hard. It isn't that bad."

On Monday morning, the news was all over the office. Martin had no sooner settled at his desk than the buzz-buzzing began. It was not about him. The boys were talking about Kilgore, and it was spreading, the tides of rumor flowing, the driftwood beginning to seep in.

No official announcement had been made, but it was just as if a warm wind had blown through the office, and anything new was good in the way of rumor. Kilgore had been selected to go to Finance on a special assignment—a deal that had infinite possibilities and it was rumored he would be moving up within the next two months.

Mansard was sitting in his large office, bogged down in one of his fits of ill humor as he told the news to his three managers. Randall sat in the armchair on the left of Mansard's desk. He was pale and run-down looking. His nervous habits of pulling at his lip and opening and closing his fist had become accentuated in the last few months and it was evident that he was under strain.

"I must say," Mansard was remarking, "the Finance people's selection surprises me. You are to be congratulated, Andrew," he said to Mizner acidly, "on your understanding of the tastes of higher management."

Randall, who found it difficult not to make vocal his agreements with the boss, leaned forward and remarked: "I'm surprised too. It still seems to me my own candidate would have made a better impression."

The observation only increased Mansard's irritation. To his tough administrator's mind, a *fait accompli* was something to be respected, and the very fact that Management had spoken had, despite his own grumbling, set the seal on the merits of the respective candidates. It was unfortunate that Randall possessed the habit of nettling Mansard, particularly during recent months. It now struck Mansard that Randall's observation was ill-timed.

"Experience has not shown," he remarked coldly, "that initial impressions are always the soundest, and I don't think at the moment when our own house is not in order that we are in a position to criticize the judgments of others."

Doyle winced, but Randall was too crushed to be further wounded by Mansard's unreasonable irritation.

On the way down, Mizner put his hand on Randall's shoulder.

232

"Dave," he offered quietly, "I was almost certain your boy would get it, but I can't say I'm not pleased about my own boy."

Harwood was sitting in his office when he first heard the rumor, and he could scarcely believe his ears. It was Randall who had the misfortune inadvertently to let him know. The actual announcement was not to be made until the next Tuesday. Randall mentioned it offhandedly and in the obscure and bumbling manner most calculated to outrage his assistant. "It should have been you, Phil," he ended quietly, after floundering in a final explanation.

Harwood's face was a mask as he listened. His lips felt stiff, but he said mildly: "I'm sure they knew what they were doing, Dave, if your information is correct."

Randall shook his head. He stood in front of Harwood's desk, his shoulders bowed like those of a whipped man, so that it appeared almost as if Harwood were the supervisor and Randall the bumbling middle-aged retainer who had somehow mishandled an important assignment. Harwood's voice was very quiet when he spoke again.

"Perhaps your information is not completely reliable," he said in a low voice. "You know how these rumors get started. I would not repeat it, Dave, until you were quite sure it's true."

Randall paused. "It's true all right," he offered sadly. "I wish it weren't, for your sake, Philip, but it's true. The announcement will be made Tuesday, but perhaps you had better not mention it anyhow. It was meant to be confidential."

As Randall turned to walk out—for he had stopped only to talk to Harwood and had had no intention whatever of letting slip this piece of news—he did not see the glare of utter hatred that the younger man directed toward him. It was as if, to Harwood, the whole blame, the whole sense of frustration for this almost intolerable and utterly unexpected disappointment somehow lay at the door of this tired, aging man who had never done him an iota of harm, who indeed liked and trusted him implicitly.

233

As Harwood pondered there alone in the office, he could not prevent the welling up of his fury and bitterness at the enormity of this blow. What, he wondered, could possibly have occurred?

The answer must be that someone had knifed him. In the world of dupes and knaves, in the tough street on which he lived, there could be only one answer to the miscarriage of such carefully laid plans—some subtle treachery had been overlooked. At the moment he could not think how it had been accomplished. Nor could he imagine who it might be. Could it have been Mizner? he wondered. He doubted it. Mizner possessed neither the subtlety nor the presence to reach Keesling. And, more than that, Mizner was, like most wise guys, disarmed by his own tolerance and sense of humor. Cynical people tended to become ineffective. He felt he had little to fear from Mizner.

Could it have been Kilgore himself? He considered that possibility. No—he was sure it was not Kilgore. He had been watching his moves. He had never let up on Kilgore for a moment. He was sure that Kilgore had never even been aware of the existence of this project. Certainly, he had never been called for an interview.

What enemies then could he have made? It had been his policy not to make enemies at all, if he could prevent it, even where he could see no possible harm in doing so. His hand might be heavy on those who worked for him, but the responsibility would lie elsewhere—for example, with Randall. He knew that enemies rise up in the night, that they creep out from unexpected, from unremembered, places and are there when one least anticipated, when one was weak or disarmed.

It must have been, he surmised, some dreadful, if unintentional, blunder on the part of a man who had been trying to befriend him. A saying returned: God protect me from my friends; my enemies I can contend with. That must have been what had happened. Someone who had meant well had put the quietus on him. It was the sort of dreadful bumbling stupidity that Randall would be the most likely to commit. And though he could not see how anyone could actually take anything Ran-

234

dall said or did seriously, it struck him that Randall would be the only one in a position to make such a blunder.

The thought of this was almost more than he could bear. All his inner rage and frustration churned up. I shall get that imbecile if it is the last thing I do, he thought. Then his rage became general. All of them, he thought savagely, all of them—fools, dupes and blunderers—they will regret their stupidity, their complacency.

It seemed to him, in this brief paroxysm, that the superior man was always trapped like this, always hemmed in or snared by bunglers and fools. One could build ever so carefully, plan stone by stone ever so perfect an edifice—a life, a career—for the time of triumph, for the time of power, and then some dreadful cipher-head, some common stumblebum slams into it and without realizing what he is doing brings down the whole house.

He had always had a bone to pick with life. An unachieved objective was to him like a lost love, painful and sad, and he had been gnawed more than once by the rats of midnight disappointments. They had blocked him here now, but let them beware. . . .

So the paroxysm passed, and he turned his attention coldly, rationally to his situation. It was a desperate one. It seemed to him now that it was almost as if he had been subjected to some obscure disgrace in not being selected for the assignment, whether people knew it or not, and he must somehow recover. Nothing of these reflections appeared outwardly on his smooth, handsome face. Looking at him, as he lounged there quietly in his well-appointed office, the glow of that beautiful October morning suffusing the air, one would have thought him to be the kind of young, competent man in whose hands one could trust the work of this age. This is the kind of man on whom the Empire should confer its honors.

The news reached Kilgore one afternoon a week later. Mizner sat in the younger man's office.

"Well," Mizner concluded in his growling voice, "I guess you've made it, Bob. It's a miracle too, considering the criteria

235

by which they select their people around here. Finance—" he added—"God help you. You'll really be among the cold-eyed boys. But it's one of the key places, and you'll certainly learn something up there. I hope you won't be crucified."

Kilgore smiled. "It isn't that bad," he said, "is it? You make it sound like the road to the pagan sacrifices. I doubt that I'll ever be valuable enough to sacrifice. Anyhow, Andrew, I can tell you one thing: the afternoon I go up there will not have been my life. It's only one step."

"The journey of a thousand miles begins with one step," Mizner quoted gruffly. "I know my Confucius as well as the next one. At any rate, Bob, you have two months before the ascension or the slaughter, whichever it is to be. Meanwhile, Brill will have to start out right away. The assignments are tough."

"He's ready to leave," Kilgore replied.

"Good," Mizner said.

Kilgore leaned back. The expense-account life, he thought. I'm probably the only one who doesn't envy him. . . .

The evening before he was to leave Martin spent with April, as usual.

"What is his name?" he asked. They were sitting in her apartment, the lights soft, and she was sewing a tear in a blouse.

"Horace Deering," she replied in a low voice. "I met him at Marlene Sawyer's party a couple of weeks ago. He was very nice to me. He thought I was the most beautiful thing he had ever set eyes on. He was very polished and handsome."

"I suppose he wasn't married," Martin continued, his voice unemotional.

"A widower, Martin," she said. "His wife died last year. He's in his early forties, very cultivated, and Anne Dolan is mad at me. He brought her and spent all his time with me. He is apparently the head of some kind of advertising agency."

Martin was silent for a moment.

236

"I was afraid this would happen, April," he began at length. "You've always been dazzling . . . and since I don't have it for you, I knew someone would come along. Maybe this is the one."

"Don't be silly, Martin," she replied. "I have no feeling for him that way, and how can I ever take someone seriously when I . . . I'm . . . when you and I are like this?"

"All right," he said slowly, "but I'll be away a lot of the time now, April. It's . . . can't you promise me anything else?"

She sat sewing in silence for a moment. "No, Martin . . . I can't," she said at last. "Let's go along like this for a while longer. Maybe—well, maybe something will happen to change it all, but right now . . ."

It was late when he left. Outside, the autumn night was cool and fresh, and the leaves of the trees along the walk near her apartment building rustled softly and dryly in the mild wind. Well, that was over . . . and he was alone once more. And this time, he knew, it was permanent.

His self-absorption, as he walked slowly along the wind-swept street, closed in more tightly upon him, imprisoning the misery deep inside. He would never ask her nor humble himself for her again. He was through, through for good. Loneliness was something one can learn to live with, and so is unrequited love, and neither of them were so earth-shaking after all. He was a man now, not a boy, and his mother had left long ago. Love was at a discount and there was no market for passion, and it was time he acted the part of a man.

He turned east and crosstown. It was after midnight and no cabs appeared. Well, it would do him good to walk. Twenty blocks is not too much, and he would sleep. For that's what he needed—sleep. And for one night at least—perhaps for many nights and then for all nights afterwards—he would not think of her or dream of her again. It was almost like a weight off his heart. You will come back, his pulses seemed to say. You

237

will return. But his rhythmic footfalls on the silent streets seemed to answer: Maybe. Maybe not. Maybe. Probably not. I am taking you away. . . .

You will return. Maybe. Maybe not. At least, if he did come back, he would do so having lived. He would return exhausted, having squeezed the lemon, having tasted the whole of it down to the dregs, and he would not care.

And he would thus, if only through exhaustion, escape from her at last, for even love cannot survive exhaustion. What lasts too short a time? the old song ran. The answer: Love. And he would in this way perhaps escape from the Empire also. He had stayed because of her and he had been trapped. Now, however, it was giving him the chance to live the whole of his sadness away, and he would take that opportunity. Somewhere along the line there might even be a bonus: he might even discover what he was really good for and learn what road to take for his belated fulfillment. But discovering or no, he would be ready to break the strands when he was through with this assignment. Of that he was certain. Of that he was sure. Now and tomorrow, however, the party was just beginning. . . .

As he crossed Park and turned down the side street toward his own building, dark in the shadows away from the street lamp, he experienced a sense of relief, of assuagement, and also that vague inner excitement that a man feels just before the big race or before the promise of a Saturday night in a big town.

3

KILGORE MOVED UPSTAIRS on the second Monday in December. And that was the way he met Bartholomew.

It was to the Office of the Chief Statistician—General Research that he was assigned, and the chief statistician himself was Herbert J. Bartholomew. His group had been given the preliminary co-ordination of the project—preparing material and outlining the general information that would be used in presenting the requests for higher rates in each area.

If the first few cases before the commissions proved successful, management reasoned, the rest would find the going easier, and the Empire spokesmen could cite precedents. So all the ingenuity and the vast resources of the network were to be thrown into this project, and higher management wanted no blundering on a matter so vital to the Empire's financial health.

Kilgore arrived on the seventeenth floor on his first morning, a clear cold day in early winter, and was shown to his new office, a far more elaborate one than the one he had had on the ninth floor. He was greeted by a pleasant, hard-eyed man named Cummings who introduced himself as one of the staff who would work on the project.

"Mr. Bartholomew is not in yet," Cummings said pleasantly. "Won't you make yourself comfortable in your office, and as soon as he arrives, Miss Hayes, his secretary, will inform you. Mr. Bartholomew is anxious to see you and have a talk before we start."

"Thank you," Kilgore said.

It was ten-thirty before Bartholomew was ready to see him. He walked along the marble area to the anteroom, and Miss Hayes, a tall statuesque brunette, smiled at him as he entered the big office.

Bartholomew was obviously an important man from the size and richness of his office. He had the green rug and mahogany, furniture of a division chief—just below an assistant vice president, and of course the silver decanter, smoke stand and the fine low bookcases. Bartholomew was ensconced quietly like an ancient idol behind his large mahogany desk.

The first impression one gained of him was of a jolly fat man. But it was a superficial impression. On more careful scrutiny, one could not be so sure. He was squat and thick-set, with powerful shoulders. He had a round face with high color, small porcine features and little eyes with crinkle lines around them.

239

It was only when Kilgore had drawn closer that he noticed how hard and cold they were.

"Come in, come in, Kilgore," Bartholomew said genially. He had a pleasant baritone voice and a beautiful, almost angelic smile. His manner was both friendly and easygoing.

"Glad to have you with us, Kilgore," he said disarmingly. "Sit down, and let's kick it around a bit."

Kilgore had never found it easy to evince the warmth and cordiality necessary to bridge a first acquaintance, but in this instance he did his best.

"Glad to know you, Mr. Bartholomew," he said. "I'm looking forward to the job."

Bartholomew's initial impression of this cold stick of a man was not reassuring. Doesn't look too bright, he thought. But perhaps he's a technician and can do a neat, satisfactory job on the more routine aspects of the presentation. These public relations boys were apt to be phonies anyhow, but there must be no nonsense in this project.

"Well, sit down, Kilgore," Bartholomew said again. "I'd like to have Cummings and Link in on this too. You remember the old routine: if you don't know anything, get three people together and spread it around."

Bartholomew's laughter was deep and throaty. He was completely relaxed.

Cummings was polite, good-looking and adept. Link was disheveled, his hair on end, and abstracted. He wore horn-rimmed glasses. They took the chairs at the right of Bartholomew's desk.

"The purpose of this meeting," Bartholomew began genially, "is to outline the elements that are to be provided for our rate-case master plan. These elements, as you probably know, may be grouped in three categories: information that relates to the kind and complexity of our business, information that relates to the economics of our business, including all the usual statistics and balance sheets, and information that relates to the material used previously and the results of former rate cases. Out of

240

this data, which it will be the job of you boys and your departments to provide, Kilgore here is to assist in putting together a master presentation that can be employed by any of the operating units, as they desire, in the hearings. A part of our job will be, also, to make recommendations on the timing in launching rate cases, perhaps even to suggest in which area or areas it would be wise to launch the first request.

"Now our objective is to have this material ready for higher management's approval as soon as possible, but in any case no later than March. The first hearings are scheduled to be held by spring. . . ."

In his new office, Kilgore settled behind the desk and mused.

It seemed to him that the job would be easy, and if it took him three months he would be greatly surprised. What did it amount to? Gathering the material and organizing it, and he could do that almost in his sleep.

He buzzed.

"Miss Clinton," he said to the secretary assigned to him, "would you collect for me the records of the last rate hearings. If we need to send out, as I believe we will, to one or another of the operating companies for material not on file here, I shall give you a letter for them. Let me have everything here, however, first."

"Yes sir," she replied.

It was clear to Kilgore, as he sat there turning the matter over in his mind, that in this project, as in any other in business, the final test was whether it worked in practice, and he did not intend to conceive the whole of it until he had sifted the Company's experience in former cases and winnowed out what had been effective and what ineffective. It was as simple as that.

But he felt in a way that there was a great deal more to it than its immediate use as a tool, an instrument. The realities of the situation, the mere facts of the Company's reasonable financial needs, would not necessarily be effective as arguments unless they fitted properly into the atmosphere under which the hearings were conducted. These hearings, like so many industrial trappings, were ceremonies, necessary ceremonies though they might be—a part of the mythology of ordinary business enterprise—and if the ceremonies were not properly enacted, the ends for which they were performed might well not be achieved. All business, he was aware, was full of these ceremonies, and it was as important for the practitioner to understand them and to carry them out properly as it was for the witch doctor to perform his tribal dance to appease the angry gods. They—like these corporate ceremonies—had the further effect of enabling people to carry out useful practical measures.

So his job would be not to secure just the superficial facts of the cases but to understand how properly to approach the commissions. Each operating company would understand its own rate commissioners and their practices—would be aware of their likes and dislikes, and would be able to send in rundowns on them and their probable procedures that would be useful in organizing this master presentation. The problem here was completeness. There must be no question unanswered, no development unprepared for, no objection unexpected.

He leaned back. He was already beginning to miss his old friends and the former routines. It would be time to go to lunch soon, and he wished he were going with the old gang. It was foolish. It was ridiculous. He must be growing old prematurely and set in his ways. He was thirty-eight, but then he had always been like this—old for his age, old and set in his ways. Now he must try to pull himself together, make an effort to be pleasant and sociable with this new group of hard-eyed men with whom he was to be associated for some time. These men were not his kind of people, but there was much he could learn from them. They were men who could tell the difference between the net and the gross. They lived in a world where all the myriad exertions of men—the sweat and the thinking and the doing— were reduced to balance sheets that told at a glance the story of success or failure. There were no spiritual survivors in this hard world. The profit-makers alone endured. You operated at

242

a loss, and you were through. Everybody's price was somebody else's cost, and there had better be something left over on the black side of the ledgers when you got through paying the bills. *Debt* was an ugly word.

He was to learn later, however, that their world was no more rigid than any of the others, that there were many ways to look at balance sheets and that economics was as idealistic and myth-ridden and as divorced from reality as any other of men's philosophies and preoccupations. And these people also, he found, knew as little of any ways of existence but their own, were just as little aware that there are variant arrangements of human life.

But the main force in this new world was Bartholomew. And he was to come to know Bartholomew in a way he would never have suspected and to learn more from Bartholomew of the practical necessities of their cosmos than he had learned from a mountain of cloistered research over the days of his apprenticeship and even from his experience thus far in the practical world.

Bartholomew ate with the executives at a club and spent his days in the mysterious upper regions of conferences and off-hour discussions, but every week or so, there was a meeting of the four of them to assess their progress, and more and more the crude hard bulk of Bartholomew's personality began to weigh on him.

It was not that Bartholomew was not satisfied with their work. He seemed to be. It was that Kilgore's pale, anemic personality, his diffidence and gentleness, violated every code of Bartholomew's concepts of a good man. Yet Bartholomew found he could not explain away the sharp incisive mind, the real organizing talents the younger man displayed. So, unconsciously, he took it out in a sort of brutal attempt at bullying and a use of the coarsest language. He rightly understood that crudity was physically repellent to Kilgore, that while Kilgore could perceive its relative harmlessness, even its desirability, in some personalities and under certain circumstances, yet it irritated

243

him, and he found he could not prevent himself from wincing inwardly, although he maintained outwardly an expression of indifference.

The third meeting was typical. They sat around the mahogany conference table in Bartholomew's large office. With the four of them were Danvers, an area executive, and Rich, one of the attorneys. They were discussing a method of comparing the return on investment of each area company with the return on investment of other similar companies in the nation.

Danvers was a personable man in his late forties who had been detached from his area to contribute his experience in rate-case procedure to the group. He was under no illusions about the way the System would have to handle the job.

"We have to start out right," he had commented during one of the pauses. "With one or two successes under our belt, the pill isn't so hard for the other commissions to swallow. But you start out wrong with a couple of kicks in the teeth, and suddenly the public feels they're being gouged and a big rich corporation is trying to milk them of their last nickel. The commissioners generally feel the way the public feels, and you squeeze very little blood out of hard hearts."

"What you're trying to say," Bartholomew remarked with his genial, sunny smile, "is once you can get the end in, you can get the whole thing in—right?"

Danvers smiled and Cummings looked up from his notes. Link was seated a little way back from the table. He seemed not to have heard.

"My impression is," Kilgore spoke quietly from his place at the end of the table, "that we're not trying to screw the public; we're only trying to get a decent return on our investment."

Bartholomew smiled, his fat Buddha face relaxed.

"You are absolutely right, Robert," he said. "That's exactly what we're trying to do. I withdraw my remark," he continued pleasantly. "It was not well put. By the way, gentlemen," he added to the newcomers, "this is Mr. Kilgore, detached from Public Relations to help us put together the presentations."

244

The two gentlemen nodded politely. Kilgore murmured an appropriate word or so. He had not been introduced prior to the meeting.

"I am not adept at expressing myself," Bartholomew continued with exaggerated politeness, "and I hope you gentlemen will bear with me when I put my concepts in the language of the streets. I'm just a plain, down-to-earth comic-book reader, and I shall have to depend on you for the adequate expressions to clothe our efforts. But let there be no mistake about our goal. Our motives may be ever so high—and I hope they are—but we have a job to do here and I am not so much concerned with receiving points for noble sentiments as I am in getting us more money."

He gazed around the table from face to face, his genial warm smile still playing at his lips but his small porcine eyes hard and cold.

Kilgore felt his flesh crawl despite himself.

"Now, Robert," Bartholomew continued in a soft voice, turning his gaze on Kilgore, "since you are the custodian of the System's sentiments, I should like to bring to your attention once more two points we wish made before the commissions. First, revenue is used only for operating expenses and does not cover our need for expansion. Secondly, expansion and increased labor and materials costs have advanced our over-all operating expenses by roughly twenty per cent. . . . Those are our clinchers."

Bartholomew paused.

"I believe we have covered those points completely," Kilgore answered. "We made a great deal of the fact that, as demands for our service increase and we connect more subscribers, the cost of operating the new plant advances geometrically, outstripping any increased revenue at present received. We have a pretty clear illustration of this, indicating the added cost of each new central office and related equipment for each ten thousand new subscribers."

245

"Yes, yes," Bartholomew said slowly, "the presentations so far appear clear and comprehensive."

Kilgore had the impression, however, as Bartholomew's pleasant, coarse voice drawled along, that he was listening to other secret voices he, Kilgore, could not hear and that as far as Bartholomew was concerned, he had been relegated to a minor role. The younger man did not fancy himself as a dreamer. He was aware that men were not moved by appeals to reason, so beloved of the philosopher and scholar, that attempts to reach men this way were largely a waste of time, and that it was the burly sinners like Bartholomew who would know what really persuaded these men to see the light.

On the other hand, he had been secured to produce a presentation, and he would play the part and finish it the way it should be completed.

So one of the typical meetings ended.

He took to having lunch with Cummings and Link and to gossiping with them insofar as he could. But it was almost by chance, one day, that he stumbled upon the crux of the plan, and he was often to wonder afterwards whether he might not have been better off had he not attempted to concern himself with something in which he had no real interest and with which he was, after all, not really entitled to concern himself.

It was Link, the economist, a woolly-minded man, who first inadvertently revealed this phase of the plan. One morning he and Link were sitting in his office, poring over paragraphs on the subject of the net profits in each area and marking the figures on a map.

"The first request is going to be made in this particular area," Link said, pointing to one of the Eastern areas.

Kilgore let his gaze fall on the section indicated on the System map. Then abruptly he sat up. He looked again.

"Why that area, Ron?" he asked mildly. "Our net profit and return on investment there is one of the highest in the System. It would seem that that would be one of the last in which to make a rate-increase request. We have little justification for a

246

request there, and in some of the other areas we are really desperate."

Link hesitated, his owlish face with the horn-rimmed glasses displaying a faint discomfort.

"Well," he said, "strictly speaking, you're quite right, Robert, but . . . but . . ." He paused again, not certain how to continue. Finally, he spoke in a rapid voice, as if to be finished with the distasteful subject quickly.

"This is only a rumor, Bob," he said, "but the word is that the boys in that area have somehow, someway, that is, gotten to one or another of the commissioners. . . . Well, you know how it is in that city—the corruption and all, and with elections approaching in the spring. You have to fight fire with fire. The crowd that's in now is no good, and apparently in that place that's the thing to do, if we want to survive, but . . . well, somehow—I wouldn't vouch for this—but the word is that one of our boys has possibly greased the right palms or made certain arrangements, and the whole thing is all set. It would be only a formality. . . . Now, Bob," Link ended in a monotone, "please don't take this as gospel. It's just a rumor. I don't really know a thing about it."

Kilgore sat there quietly, holding himself in. He knew he must show nothing of the turmoil he felt at this inadvertent slip. It was foolish, he told himself. It was absurd to allow himself to react like this, but the stupidity of the whole procedure appalled him.

"Is . . . is Bartholomew going ahead with it there first then?" he asked at last in a low voice.

"Yes," Link replied slowly. "That's the final word, I guess."

"Do you think he really knows what he's doing?" Kilgore asked softly.

Link looked up, surprised, his owlish eyes somewhat bewildered.

"Bartholomew?" he said. "Why Bartholomew always knows what he's doing," he answered with quiet finality. "I've worked for Bartholomew for six years now and I can tell you without

247

any question or shadow of a doubt that Bartholomew knows exactly what he's doing. He is not the kind of man who makes mistakes."

"I see," Kilgore replied in a low voice.

There was no use saying anything more. Apparently the die was cast, and they were, incredible as it seemed to him, willing to take the chance and make the plunge.

When Link had gone, he sat for a moment, thinking about it. He had been astonished at the agitation this discovery had aroused in him, surprised and dismayed. It was not that he was unaware that this sort of chicanery existed, that that was the way the world went, and one should not expect everything to be exactly as one wanted it. Those were the hard facts of life, and it was too late for him to go into a state of shock over it. Furthermore, he realized that it was really not his affair and any attempt at interference would only bring down on his head the wrath of those responsible, those who had had the hard lot of making this delicate decision. Such unjustified interference would mean, in all probability, the end of his own career, and he would view this prospect with apprehension and sadness. He liked it here.

Yet every fiber of his being recoiled at the thought of what he considered a dreadful, an egregious blunder. It was not only the moral aspects, it was everything about it that seemed wrong and stupid. He leaned forward. He must put it aside now, he told himself. He must wait for the agitation to pass. It was almost as if he had been caught in a personal dilemma, tangled emotionally in a piece of nonsense that was, after all, none of his business.

Yes, that was the crux of it. It was none of his business, and his emotional reaction was merely evidence of his own childishness and inability to accept situations that did not conform to his idea of how things should be. He swung around in his chair and looked at the map. Even so, he thought, even so . . . Putting aside all moral scruples, he could not seem to find one iota of merit in the plan. The gamble was too great for the stakes.

248

He sat back once more turning it over in his mind, trying to see what could have possessed them. The agitation was gone now, and the old rhythms of his thinking were returning. Let us look at it dispassionately, he thought. It had probably been done in that area successfully before. Long practice had perhaps made it almost respectable under that municipal government. Small items, not traceable, maybe a little money, would change hands—nothing that would be really embarrassing. These boys were not stupid. They would protect the area company completely. They would know how to take care of their own. They were doing it in the only effective way they knew under the circumstances, and that was what they were paid for—not high moral sentiments. It was at least a short cut.

Now he came along—a nobody, a pipsqueak whose experience lay in alien fields—and got up on his high horse and started to supply them with moral judgments in place of practical alternatives, to impeach their taste and understanding. He was suddenly in the position of a defender of the faith amid the infidel hordes who were nevertheless doing something that needed to be done in the only way they knew how to do it. They would have a fair case against him, he realized, a pretty fair case.

One of the things one learned—as one learned it in life—was that there are variant ways of performing, and one method is not to be condemned, if it is effective and serves the need, simply because it is sordid. Whom was it harming? The moral fiber of the recipients? The System itself? The Empire had a history of a gigantic and unbroken integrity of which it was justly proud. It had never in any dealing in all the years been guilty of the faintest breath or hint of malpractice, and its moral power as the foremost of the big organizations, the bluest of the blue, was massive and unquestioned. Now, could a little dereliction like this touch it? Could a small breach hurt it? And who, after all, was he to tell these tired, hard-working citizens what was moral and what was not? On moral grounds alone, it appeared, he would have only the most shaky of justifications.

249

Then was he to criticize them on practical grounds? Here, it seemed to him, he had a clearer case. But the fact remained it was not his business. He had not been hired to make that kind of judgment. Yes—he sighed—yes, he would have to drop it after all. It was none of his affair.

On Tuesday afternoon, after the meeting, Kilgore stayed behind in Bartholomew's office. The palms of his hands were damp with perspiration, and although his voice remained low and firm as usual, he felt, as he spoke, as if he were going over the falls in a barrel. This was it, and it seemed to him that the thud of his heartbeats could almost be heard above the sound of his voice.

Bartholomew's expression did not change while he listened. When the last sound of the tones had died away, a silence fell. He had spoken his piece. It was all over now. Bartholomew leaned back in the big chair and gazed at him quizzically. He was in no hurry. He had all the time in the world. In his fat pagan face, there had not been a sign of his reaction as he listened, not a flicker of expression. The silence was prolonged. Then at last, Bartholomew, still leaning back, relaxed, spoke. His voice was quiet and pleasant.

"Robert," he said, "you're a smart boy and I like you. I am going to offer you a piece of advice. It's good advice, Robert, and I know you'll take it in the spirit in which it is given. There's an old saying that begins, 'We are in this earthly world . . .' and that saying fits the circumstances here. Now I could tell you that this matter you have brought up, even were the story substantially true—and I am not saying that it is— does not concern you. I could tell you that we—most of us here entrusted with this project—have had a lot more experience in this sort of work than you have, that we are older—even if perhaps we are not as smart—and have a deeper understanding of the ways of the world. All of these facts I could point out. But I will not do so. I will not say any of them.

"You are a young man, Robert. I don't know exactly what
250

your experience has been, but I imagine it has been very thorough in the fields in which you have been working. But this is an entirely different field, an entirely different sort of work—less glamorous perhaps than the ones you have been used to—more grubby, and in some ways it has its squalid aspects. We cannot—much as we should prefer to—operate on sentiment here. This is one of the Empire's bread-and-butter jobs and it has to be done, and done in any way it can be done. It is right now one of our pressing problems. The System has to make ends meet. We need money and we need it badly and we need it right now. We must somehow induce the commissions to raise our rates to secure that needed revenue, and in many cases we will not get them to do so just by singing a sad song. This case you are talking about is one of them. The beauty of our story, the eloquence of our presentation will squeeze no tears from these commissioners. They are just plain, slightly battered citizens like you and me, taxpayers who get in a cold sweat when the bills fall due at the end of the month and who worry if they have to put a dime into the pay phone rather than a nickel. They won't be thinking of us, and they don't care; they—like the public—will only curse the greedy interests that have brought this upon them.

"But there are ways of reaching them. Their interests are of concern to them. If you wish to use ugly words, they can be bought—just like you, Robert, and like me. We have been bought. We are bought every day by that little pay check that is presented at the end of the month, and in return we give of our best. That's the way it is. The Empire, we say to ourselves, has reached us in a just cause. Well, the Empire has reached these men also, and in a just cause—assuming the conditions are as you say, and I am not so sure that they are.

"Now, Robert—" and Bartholomew's smile was as warm and genial as it had been when he had first begun speaking—"now, Robert," he concluded, "you come to me, full of your forebodings and fears—you come yelping like a turpentined dog and ask us to call the whole project off, to reconsider our timing,

our choice of venue—the where and the when of our strategy—
and all because someone has been feeding you rumors that may
or may not have any substance to them—rumors that induce in
you a moral reaction. As I said, I won't tell you that it's none
of your business. I'll ask you only that you try to trust us, that
you leave these matters in our hands, that you allow us to do
our work for the Empire and believe that we shall not let you
or it down."

When the warm tones of Bartholomew's voice had faded,
Kilgore sat there opposite the big man in silence. He felt lost
and depressed. He felt broken.

"Are you telling me, sir," he asked tiredly, "that the rumors
I heard are without foundation? If so," he added in a low voice,
"I should like to apologize."

"I am telling you nothing, Robert," Bartholomew replied
softly. "I have told you all I intend to on this subject."

The younger man sat there a moment longer in silence. He
gazed up at the big man in the big chair. Above the warm and
genial smile were those eyes—machine-gunner's eyes—cold and
hard. He knew in that moment that he had had it. It was all
over. It was as if his throat had been cut, and when he turned
the blood would flow gently. Yes, he had known this would be
the end result. It would soon be all over for him.

That evening he sat at the music stand in the study at home
and sawed on the cello. He worked on one of Saint-Saëns
"Encores" and the results were not promising, but the music
soothed him and made him feel better. Later he listened to
recordings of Casals. His sister Angeline, feeling very cranky,
brought him Sanka and crackers and he read late. The aware-
ness returned to him again that his career downtown was about
over, and this reflection saddened him. Curiously enough, however, it did not dismay him as much as the thought of what
those idiots were about to do.

It seemed strange to him—and once more he sat there
reflecting on it—that even a man like Bartholomew, powerful,

252

shrewd and impressive as he was, would fall for a sucker's gamble like that. People like him had their virtues, their strength, but they had their weakness also, and a foolish deal that looked good was the kind of weakness such a man would have. A man like Bartholomew would be governed, as the sages would say, by maxims of low prudence, and by and large, he supposed, that was the way a business should be conducted, but not when it came to this kind of deal.

In all probability, the rate readjustment would be made in that area without a hitch, and there would be no repercussions. The new elections in the spring would sweep out, at least temporarily, the corrupt element, and since the rate raise would already have been approved, no more would be heard of it. On the other hand, everything might not go so well. And the fact was the Empire did not need to enter into any arrangement of that sort, even indirectly. It did not need to start with that area at all, and actually would be on firmer ground if it left that and the other wealthy areas until the last. It had, he knew, perfectly good cases for readjustment in at least a dozen other areas, areas where the return on investment was so low as to be unbusinesslike and unsound. With careful planning and proper presentation—all of which naturally involved far more effort than the plan proposed in the corrupt Eastern section— the Empire would almost inevitably receive what it was asking for, and the cases were bound to go its way in the long run.

To accept an easy fix with all its appalling dangers was, in his opinion, a move of the wildest folly, a risk that even the millions of dollars per year increase in revenue could not possibly justify. It appeared to him also that anyone merely glancing at the figures on net profit and return on investment would wonder, as he had, why that area company was launching this drive. Somehow, it seemed to him, the newspapers might get hold of the possibility of corruption, and then the area company and the Empire itself would spend years living down the stigma, and all those decades in which it had built up a reputation for impregnable honesty would have gone for nothing.

253

It was curious that he should care so greatly—he whose career there had substantially ended the moment he had stuck his finger in the pie. Bartholomew had been right in a way. The Empire had bought and paid for him, as it had bought them all, but even so, he could not induce himself, though he was aware of the impending disgrace and perhaps the loss of the job after all these years, not to give them his loyalty and the best he had to give.

The only question that remained was how to prevent this egregious blunder, how to smother the deal, how to stop them from launching the first rate request there. It was the only problem that he had left to work on, and as he sat in the quiet of the study, drinking his caffeinless coffee, the first outlines of a possible solution were forming.

It was not really a way of solving it, but it had some vague chance of bringing the matter to the attention of those higher up who could see at a glance the danger and who would never have countenanced such a measure. His plan was at the cost of his own personal disgrace, but then he was about done for anyway, as far as this job was concerned, so what would it matter? He sat for a few minutes longer in the study—a quiet, pale man in conservative clothes, his thin, nondescript hair beginning to turn gray.

The contemplation of his situation discouraged and saddened him. Mizner had known what he was talking about when he said it would be a slaughter. He should have realized himself that he didn't have what it took for this kind of job or even this kind of world. There would be those, he supposed, who would rejoice over his downfall, not through mere malevolence but because it would bear out their sense of the fitness of things, and those who would mourn. Mizner, for one, he knew, would be sad: he had expected much of him. Yet, if the Empire needed the best buyable minds, he imagined it could have found a better use for his somehow than it had found, but now it was too late, and he guessed he would have to work it out this way.

Well, he was tired and tomorrow would be another day. He

could make the gesture tomorrow just as well. Might as well get a good night's sleep. Perhaps some better move would occur to him during the night. If not, although he shrank from it since it violated his deeply ingrained sense of the way things should be done, he would have to carry out the plan. For his plan was simple. It was nothing more nor less than a formal request for transfer—a sort of resignation—a memorandum addressed to Keesling, who had brought him over, with a copy of this memorandum to Bartholomew, asking release from the work on the presentation and a transfer back to Public Relations, and presenting in some detail his reasons, with particular emphasis on his objections to the course being pursued. The memorandum would conclude with the statement that should the rate review request be launched in the area under discussion, his opinion was so strong that the company involved was making a serious mistake that he felt his own usefulness in the project would be at an end and that his continued presence there could only hinder the plans already made.

He went to bed trying to think of some other way of preventing the measure, since he was convinced even this unpleasant and certainly affected gesture would not do the trick. For a long time he lay awake, gnawing at it and worrying. Then he drifted off. Around midnight, he woke up again. Nothing had come to him. He rose and turned on the light. At the small night table, he wrote out the memorandum in his scrawling, almost illegible handwriting, substantially as he had conceived it. Then he crept back into bed. In the morning, it would be typed and the original would be sent by messenger to Keesling, while the first copy would go to Bartholomew. That was all he could do. He knew it was only a gesture and probably a futile one at that, but it was all he could think of. Now, he felt, he had done everything he could, and he would have to take the consequences. He lay awake for a few minutes longer. The feeling of sadness, of having spent himself, gradually died away. Drowsiness finally enveloped him, and he slipped off into the sound sleep of exhaustion.

4

IF HE EXPECTED ANYTHING to happen in the morning, he was doomed to disappointment. The memoranda went off, and he sat back to wait for the sky to fall in. He had a feeling almost of relief—an impression that he had at least done all he could, but now the lack of response was almost as if he had been cast into limbo, cast adrift on an uncharted sea with no land anywhere in sight and no compass. Absolutely nothing happened. Two weeks went by and no word seeped down to him, no request to appear before the tribunal, no nothing. The Tuesday meetings were canceled on some vague pretext, and an air of restraint appeared to have crept into his association with the men, although they remained polite and pleasant, and it was nothing he could put his finger on. Yet he had the feeling, almost as if he were becoming invisible.

One morning, in the midst of this long hiatus, he decided to call Mizner for lunch. They were to meet at one of the more obscure restaurants downtown on a side street. He arrived early and secured a table in the rear. He was thinking that he must pull himself together and forget the superficial concerns that had been absorbing his time and attention of late, that there must be more inwardness to his life, when Mizner arrived. A surge of pleasure and a renewal of hopefulness swept over him as he saw Mizner's stocky, shuffling figure enter the restaurant, the chewed cigar in his mouth and the ashes all over his vest. He watched him as the middle-aged man approached the table.

"Well, how is the boy executive?" Mizner greeted him heartily in his throaty voice. "You meeting me here so you won't be seen in the company of us serfs? You boys must dine on caviar and milk toast every day now!"

256

He smiled faintly at Mizner's sally. He was too depressed to share the old man's usual cynical good spirits.

"I'm really glad to see you again, Andy," he said in his low voice. "How have you been?" Mizner noticed that the younger man looked paler than usual and drawn.

"Are they working you too hard, boy?" he asked, when they were seated and had given the orders. "You look run-down."

"The work is easy enough," he began slowly. "It isn't that. But as you predicted would happen, I did it up brown, I ruined myself. I just wanted to warn you that you may have me back on your hands again sooner than you think. I . . . well, I've failed on the job and I've asked for a transfer back."

"You've what!" Mizner said, laying down his knife and fork carefully.

"I've asked for a transfer back," he repeated softly. "Well, the truth is I made a mess of it all."

"Of what?" Mizner asked. "The work? I don't believe it."

"No . . . no . . . not the work. That was easy, but it's just my . . . well, my judgment of a move one of the area companies intended to make and which appeared to me a serious blunder. I . . . well, I expressed myself on it."

Mizner sat and looked at him. "Bob," he said quietly, "if I know you and indeed if I know anything at all, you were right, dead right, in your opinion, but you know as well as I do that you should not have expressed yourself. That, my boy, as you must be aware by now, is a major crime! Any opinions to be offered will be made by constituted authority and not loosely thrown around by the newcomer to the seats of the mighty! You have just cut your own throat . . . I can see that. . . ." Mizner paused.

"I was aware of that, Andy," he replied. "It just seemed important at the time that something be done. I was quite prepared to take the consequences."

"Well—" Mizner picked up his knife and fork slowly—"well, a man can't help the way he is. He must do what he feels he has

257

to do, Bob, and you were undoubtedly right. Anyhow, I'll be glad to have you back under any circumstances. One thing you must realize, however: it will be rough. The vultures will be there in full wing. You may find it more than you bargained for—a real hell on earth."

"That doesn't bother me, Andy," he replied very quietly. "I will expect it. But I'm sorry I . . . well, that I failed you—I let you down, and all those who hoped I might amount to something. I'm really sorry."

"As far as I am concerned," Mizner replied angrily, his heavy face dark, "you already do amount to something. But, Bob, I'm letting out no secret when I tell you that Mansard will not be pleased. . . ."

"Well, I don't know," he said to Mizner finally, as they sat drinking their coffee. The lunch hour was almost over; the crowds were thinning out. "It's been weeks now since I sent in the request for transfer back, and the silence has been deafening. I don't know. I just wanted to warn you, Andy, that there's a price on my head and the boys can pick up their money. I'm sorry."

That was the way in which the days passed, when all at once, three weeks before the hearings were scheduled in that Eastern area, the cork blew off, the bottom dropped out.

It all began as a preliminary skirmish in that town before the spring municipal elections. The opposition—a reform group— had apparently been collecting evidence of corruption that previous fall and winter. They lit the fuse and waited two months before the primaries. The explosion went off on schedule. Three of the city aldermen, the public works commissioner and the mayor were indicted for malfeasance and accepting bribes on a street-widening project. It was the opening of the cesspool, and the details of this and other forms of corruption poured out—details of such a nature that even the hardened citizenry were shocked.

The job of the reform element had been well done. The town had always been notorious for its gambling and prostitution, but the "outs" had avoided earlier mistakes and the time had been ripe for a change. The political scandals, coupled with the disclosure of gangsterism at the nearby race track, were too much. The people swung solidly behind the reformers and a hue and cry was raised with a will.

The newspapers devoted their headlines and most of their front pages to the succulent revelations of iniquity, particularly to prostitution, which was apparently discovered for the first time to be one of the staple enterprises. One would have thought that not another city or state government in the land had ever harbored such a collection of vile and unregenerate politicians, such a sickening procession of confidence men, swindlers and petty criminals. The words "one with Sodom and Gomorrah" were used tirelessly in describing what would happen to the community, and civic virtue, never conspicuous for its popularity, suddenly came into fashion.

The impact of this explosion on those about to initiate the first rate-review request in that particular area was demoralizing, although the details were never fully known to Kilgore. But as he sat there reading the morning papers with their first black headlines, the beads of perspiration stood out on his forehead.

Careful perusal, however, had not revealed any public service commissioners mentioned in the scandals, and the area company had apparently not had the chance even to file preliminary papers. No word had yet sifted to him from upstairs, and it had now been a month since he had sent up the memorandum, asking for a transfer. Nor had he heard from, or even seen, Bartholomew. It was definitely limbo.

As he lounged there, worrying over the papers, it occurred to him that, had he only waited a few weeks or even minded his own business, there would have been no need to send up that memorandum. The scandals would have removed the danger of initiating the rate hearings there anyway, and he

259

might have saved his own career. It had seemed at the moment so important, and now . . . well, now at least, they were spared taking that unnecessary and foolish risk, and perhaps the true enormity of the danger in launching the program in the manner contemplated was made clear even to the most practical and down-to-earth realist. Not that that would do him any good. Being wrong was well enough and one could forgive that, but being right, particularly under circumstances like these would, it seemed to him, be more than flesh and blood could bear and would certainly not have increased his popularity upstairs.

Actually, one final element was involved. His suspicions had not been well founded, although he did not know it until much later. There had never been the slightest question of bribery or subornation in the whole proceedings. The "influence" referred to in the rumor had consisted in nothing except the fact that area company officials had two relatives on the commission, and through these sources had been given to understand that a rate-review request in the light of the facts would not be unsympathetically received and might secure immediate attention. It was no more and no less than that. They had passed on that information in good faith. No promises had been given or asked. No palms had been greased. No presents had been offered.

How the ugly rumor had risen from these meager soundings of ultimate possibilities on the part of two friendly commissioners, no one would ever know.

On March 3, six weeks later, a meeting took place on the fortieth floor between two of the Empire's demigods, H. F. Keesling and Percy Wygand, in Keesling's enormous mahogany office. Keesling's big, bumbling hulk sat in a relaxed position on the leather sofa near the windows. Percy Wygand leaned elegantly against the marble mantel of the large fireplace, his rocking-horse nostrils flaring and his mournful eyes gazing into the distance. It was misty outside, but the faintest tinge of spring softened the damp air. Keesling was irritated.

260

". . . So we're going to take your man permanently, Percy," he was saying, "although I'll confess there are some aspects of his personality that seem hard to bear. The trouble is he called the shots one hundred per cent, though how he guessed that town would blow up is beyond me. He was right the whole way. He's bright and he's intuitive, and his record is, to put it bluntly, outstanding. He's just too damn good not to get the job and there's no use trying to ignore it.

"Bartholomew has admitted that he was caught off base, though how he ever brought himself even to contemplate going in there first is quite beyond me. I've been in this business more than thirty years and in that time have seen some real boners, some real beauties, but the one old Bartholomew and those boys cooked up was one of the all-time classics for my money. Bartholomew's a good man and there's nothing to be done about it now; he's learned his lesson, I think—never to pay attention to anything but the facts—and he's useful, but you couldn't entrust an entire division on the rate-case problems to him— and these problems will be boiling now for another five years. You'd never be sure with a man like that—he might jump off the deep end again sometime. . . .

"That man of yours, though, Percy—well, I don't know as I'd want to attend a party with him. He's a ramrod, but you'd never stay awake nights wondering whether the place would burn down if he were on the job. Did you see the presentation? Bartholomew himself admitted it was put together almost entirely by Kilgore; and then the man's background—did you look at that card?"

"I don't have time to look at all the cards in my divisions," Wygand answered mournfully. He had a cold, and he found Keesling dreadfully overpowering. He was glad they had discovered someone for the strategic rate-case job, but he did wish they could finish bumbling around and have the transfer settled so he could return to his own office and find his nose spray. His sinuses were beginning to give him trouble in this weather.

Keesling slumped even farther on the sofa and stretched his long legs.

"So you have no objections?" he asked.

"Of course, I have no objections," Wygand answered petulantly. "I'm glad you found him in my group. I like to see my boys move ahead."

Keesling thought once more what a stupid ass Wygand was with all his airs and foppishness. Granted he had once been a skillful and effective corporate representative in Washington, yet now, it appeared to Keesling, Percy was becoming more old-womanish and hypochondriac than he had ever been and less able to concentrate. Well, that wasn't his affair, and if the Old Man liked him, he supposed he could put up with him also.

"I think we'll have no trouble securing the Old Man's approval with this boy," Keesling concluded slowly. "I intend to hand him a couple of really tough ones and try him out for a year or two. Then if he makes it, I'll let him have the hot seat. And I'll give him the title to go with it. He'll be about the youngest assistant vice president in the business. He's only thirty-eight now. . . ."

"I suppose so," Percy Wygand echoed disinterestedly.

"Is it all settled then?" Keesling asked.

"Yes, yes," Wygand answered shortly. "It's up to your boys to fix up the transfer papers and . . . well, to get the Old Man's signature."

"I'll do the work," Keesling said quietly. "The transfer should be effective by the beginning of June. I want him ready to take over by then. Most of the rate-case hearings will be in full swing at that time."

So the meeting ended.

Thus it was that on a day several months later Kilgore was officially attached to the Finance Division on rate-case work and disappeared from the Public Relations organization and his familiar haunts into the mists—into the lofty places where higher management dwells.

To at least six people, this fantastic and unexpected success was a source of satisfaction; to many more it was a source of wonder and even dismay. And to them all, it appeared as if nothing like it had ever happened before.

BOOK V Brill

1

No, it had not seemed that long.

Where had the years gone? Where had they flown?

That morning—was it only a few hours ago?—there had been four of them eligible for the big step upward, and only one for whom the lightning would strike. And that morning also, there had been one dream that had ended forever, one last discard of what once had been a deep devotion. It had not been his.

He sat there now in the large office contemplating the fragments of his life, the debris of his own years. Somehow the events of the years were mingled with the events of that morning. And the question again: "Were the years wasted, Martin? Did you win after all?"

What could have happened there along the way? And where had he become what he now was—committed, professional and hard or—as he suddenly realized—a man bought and paid for? The seeds had all been there from the early times—from all of them who had drawn him into the whirlpools. The secret inner struggles of the other men—of men like Carlyle . . . Somers . . . Harwood . . . Kilgore—they had provided the paths but he had been sucked into the patterns himself.

The years when he went out . . . the years of love . . . the years of struggle . . . and finally the expense-account years.

He rose and walked slowly to the far window and stood gazing out over the city. There in the rose cobwebs of dusk, in the net of oncoming lights over the city lay the wastage of those years—sad, squalid, but even so, beautiful and pregnant with all he had hoped for and lost. The expense-account years . . . the years in bondage, in service—how relevant they seemed now to all that had passed before and to all that had come after. The lights of how many cities had he gazed upon during those restless, sordid, hard-worked days. . . . Surely, this morning's ending must stem partly from them.

And now as he stood there, they were with him again. . . .

2

THE MANY EVENINGS of those years . . . yes, they were with him again. The thoughts on Harwood and Kilgore, on Carlyle and Somers, had all faded now. It was the expense-account years . . . the later evenings that were with him. He could remember certain of them now with a nostalgic vividness no subsequent regret could diminish. There was that evening he had been driving along the ocean highway near San Francisco after a business conference. It was ebb tide and the air smelled of kelp, and the fog was rolling in over the old town. There were the sounds of bells somewhere and mingled with them the low, insistent moan of the foghorns. Beside him sat one of the girls of those days—prettier than most, with blond hair and full petulant lips. They were driving to a cabin down the peninsula.

He had had a difficult week. It had been one of those tough co-ordinating jobs, and the traveling had become a delirium of fragmented days in cities and towns all over the land—the beginning of the expense-account years.

Now he was motoring down for a rest with one of the good-time girls in a beautiful town and even in his weariness he was happy. Besides, he had had a couple of drinks and felt better.

It was these parties with the boys that really dragged you. The big wheels and the good-time Joes—they could really break you up. Middle-aged men away from their wives, executives of one or another of the area companies, on the town on an expense account, either his or their own. One would think they had never seen a girl before or would never have another drink. They drank as if this were the last time ever.

Or there were the hard-bitten professional newspapermen, or the swank editors—the martini circuit boys who discussed the great stinking abomination of the world with a bland and tired smile—and the only thing they had against sin was that it was so boring. But they would be willing to try it again perhaps. "Let's sit here and pretend we're not missing," they said.

Another scene returned to him of a rainy night in St. Louis.

He had arrived to cover a convention of communications engineers, among them hundreds of Empire men. The main talk was to be delivered by a Laboratories scientist—one of the real hot-shots of the field—a young-looking man with horn-rimmed glasses and a crew cut, one of the ex-atomic boys, who lived a deracinated life in some atomic city under the cloak of security.

He saw them all later in a smoky joint watching the cold-eyed stripteasers give them the business to the measure of a twelve-bar blues. Having a little fun on the town, it was called. Even these boys were far from home. And it occurred to him as he picked up the check that—thank God!—they still liked the same old things, even though hell was so far behind the times.

The trouble was he had reached the point where he did not like it any more, and some other obscure element had drained all the fun out of it. He had certainly lost the inwardness of his life, even the banalities of his Marcus Aurelius or his Seneca. Everything is but for a day, both that which remembers and that which is remembered, and now it was the rootlessness that began to irk and to nag at him. There had been a lot of little deaths with the bottle, and it was progressively easier to live in the rich slums in which he moved for the Empire. One could

269

cry for madder Muzac and for stronger martinis, and one began to hear the same sad stories all over again.

It had not been what one would call a hard life, though, and hotel beds are generally a lot more comfortable than one's own. The food at Antoine's or Sweet's was even better than that mother used to make, and the way you were taken care of—the shoes shined, the laundry laundered—could make home life hard to bear. But after a while, you get tired of hangover heaven and are willing to settle for the disordered apartment, even though the life has a big hold on you and you find it hard to let go.

At first, however, it had all been fun.

There was the night before he left on the first assignment that he had been walking home from April's apartment. He recalled it as the night that was to mark the end of his bondage to April, and memory would always return it to him thus.

Not that the tie had been completely severed. No tie could be fully broken where so deep a part of one's life was touched, where the need had been so great—all the aching and the wanting and the not having. But the trips had intervened and the pleasures of the new life and the other girls and the nights on glittering streets in strange and glittering towns, and pretty soon the image of the one blurs into the images of the many, and the blond hair is like a sea of blond hair—he has lain in so much of it and the green eyes shimmer into other eyes that were warm and soft for him and the white skin is lost in the perfume of other white flesh—anonymous now but just as lovely and just as transitory. He could not say that that had not been fun.

There had been the interval in town after he had returned from that first trip. In his own apartment, he had reached for the phone to call up April, and suddenly he had stopped, thinking: "Why should I? I'm tired. I'll give her a rest for a few days, and let her call me for a change."

His pulses had said earlier: You'll be back, but his footfalls that night before the trip had answered: Maybe. Maybe not. Maybe. Probably not. His pulses had said: You will return, but his footfalls had answered: I am taking you away, and that was what they seemed to be doing.

At the office, she looked surprised when she happened on him.

"When did you get back?" she asked.

"Night before last," he said.

"Why didn't you call me?" she said.

"I was tired, April," he answered softly.

She watched him walk away, and suddenly she was angry. That soft, half-suffocating feeling rose inside of her. Well, Horace was taking her out again that night anyhow. She couldn't have seen him even if he had asked, and she would be busy the next few days also. She had begun to receive quite a rush in the last few months. There were Charley Burns and the boy who sailed all the time, calling her up every week or so. She would let Golden Boy have a rest for a while and see how he liked it.

On Thursday of the next week, it was his voice on the phone.

"How are you, April?" he said. "Long time no see."

"I've been busy," she said, "and you've been tired."

"May I come over this evening?" he asked.

"I don't know," she said. "Horace is to call if his business engagement ends early, and we were going to the theater."

"I'm leaving on assignment Saturday," he said. "I'll be away a week or so."

She was silent for a long time.

"All right," she answered at last.

She had no sooner put the phone down when it rang again. It was Horace.

"I'm terribly sorry, dear," she said. "I promised this friend I'd see him off. Can't we make it tomorrow?"

She could tell from his voice that Horace was upset. The trouble was she did not care.

"Well, may I make it Saturday evening as usual?" he concluded stiffly.

"Yes," she answered. Horace was a lamb, but they all be-

271

came that way after a while, as if they owned her. Only one man had ever meant anything different and . . . and there would never be another. "Oh Jim . . . Jim," she said to herself, "oh Jim, where are you? Oh, if you would only come back. If you would only remember a little . . . a little. It would all be so different!"

Well, Martin would be arriving. She might as well dress, and dress to slay him—low-cut bodice and the fitted skirt. It would teach him a lesson. Let him try any of his tricks tonight. He would see how far he would get. That part was over.

He arrived twenty minutes late.

She swallowed her irritation and greeted him pleasantly, although with a hint of restraint.

"We haven't seen much of you since you've been back, Martin," she said. "How was the trip?"

"It was fine," he replied. "You look wonderful, April," he added. "I've missed you. I hear you've been chasing all over with this new tycoon."

"Horace finds time to take me out once in a while," she answered. Her voice was cool. "Tell me about the trip," she said. "Did you meet any new girls? I understand you and Sherry are going around together."

He was surprised. "I bought Sherry one drink last week," he said, "when we were both stranded at the bar across the street the night of the sleet storm—if that's what you call going around together."

"I'm not complaining, Martin," she remarked slowly. "In fact, I think it would be good for you to meet a nice girl at last —a nice girl, I said, though. I don't particularly like Sherry."

"I know that, April," he replied quietly. "Thanks for your solicitude."

He felt subdued and sad. This was all instead-of talk and that old choked-up feeling was with him again, the insoluble longing for her. He had not been away long enough.

They ate at the little, softly lighted place near her apartment building. The food was only moderately good, but the at-

272

mosphere was intimate and they had eaten there many times together. There was an air of restraint over them. He was miserable, but he felt somehow he should try. He was doing the right thing, attempting to break away from her, he knew. One should always act from one's inner sense of rhythm and one's inner sense of self-preservation.

He watched her eating, the magnificent blond hair caught in the misty light, the full, sensuous and vulnerable mouth. He knew that none of it was for him, that he must burn himself out to forget them. He must outgrow them somehow.

She was cool and quiet. She talked calmly about nothing. She mentioned new recordings she loved and once or twice the name Horace dropped in inadvertently in the minor recital of some play she had seen, some restaurant at which she had dined. He could have matched it with his own restaurants, but the heart was not in him. Somehow he was aware that the dismissal had been made. They were on another footing altogether. Even passion had not held in the end, he thought.

At her apartment later, he turned to say goodnight. Instinctively, he reached to kiss her, and for a moment her own instinctual reaction was to embrace him. Then she paused and drew away.

"What's the matter?" he asked softly. "Not even a kiss for an old love?"

"What's the use?" she murmured.

"I thought you were the passion flower," he said.

"It's different now, Martin. You see . . . well, Horace has asked me to marry him. I . . . I can't go back to the basis of our old . . . well, our old relationship under those circumstances."

"Well, you can kiss me goodnight," he said. "Are you going to marry him?"

"I don't know, Martin. Please, I don't know. Don't ask me these questions."

He swung around and walked without a word into the foyer.

"Martin," she said.

273

He paused.

"You can kiss me goodnight—or is it goodbye?" she added softly.

He turned and came back. He put his arms around her and almost instinctively she pressed her mouth to his. The sweep was too much. He could feel the throb of her against him, the old passion welling back and welling back.

"No, Martin," she said, "no, no, please . . ." She tore her lips from his and tried to push him. He picked her up and scarcely noticing her struggling carried her kicking and moaning into the pretty feminine bedroom.

He held her a moment. Then he flung her on the bed. She lay there, passive, as if exhausted, the sullen look of hatred and passion on her face.

"All right," she said, "take me if you want to again, but I won't love you, I won't even like you any more."

He approached the bed and leaned over to kiss her goodbye. As he bent over, suddenly her arms were about his neck and she had pulled him down on her in a frenzied embrace, and the old pattern was with them once more.

"Yes," she said later, "I wanted you, Martin, but I am angry with myself now. I will never do that again with you—never. That part of it is over. It's all over."

"I know," he answered quietly. "I'm glad it ended that way, though."

"You will come and see me again sometimes anyhow?"

"Yes, of course," he replied. "I'm leaving town day after tomorrow. I will call you when I get back again. Perhaps we can have supper together."

"Yes," she said, "perhaps. Good luck, Martin. Take care of yourself."

"You too," he said.

So the first soft slide of separation began. And he was away for some time on the next trip.

*   *   *

274

There was a place in Chicago, and a throaty singer was singing, "Every little movement has a meaning all its own. . . ."
He had had a few drinks, and the girl with him was informing
him that they did not appreciate her sufficiently at the studio.
What she said was: "The way I am miscast is crazy, completely
crazy. There's absolutely nothing wrong with that show," she
added, "that a miracle couldn't cure." She was on TV and she
was a model, and she was known as a good kid. They all called
each other good kids, he was thinking, but Margo—for that was
her name—wasn't a good kid. She was venomous and spiteful,
but she was young and beautiful in a particularly well-upholstered
fashion. She was one of the staple products in the field. They
would never be able to do without her, without thousands of
her. But she was not a nice girl and everything bored her.

"Let's get out of this creep joint," she said as they sat there
in the third swank Gold Coast club they had visited that evening. She wanted to see somebody famous—celebrities—and
this appeared to be the night celebrities were staying away in
droves. Martin was not hip. He did not know one celebrity
from another, and he was ignorant of the television producers'
and actors' world, the one in which for her celebrities lived and
moved and had their being. And he was dragged.

"Let's knock it off for tonight, Margo," he said. "I have to
take some of the boys out on this new construction job tomorrow, and I have to have a little sleep."

"Why darling," Margo replied, her voice suddenly liquid
with concern, "it's so early. It's hardly one-thirty and you can
sleep at my place and go straight to your appointment from
there."

"I have to have a clean shirt, Margo, and I look like a bum,"
he said. "So please . . . we'll do it again another night. Besides, you have to be up for the show at ten, you know."

Margo had not been happy. It had not been a reet finale, a
real gone occasion. It was winter, and the snow was falling
softly, and the big town lay in its massive squalor under a haze

275

of electricity and neon tubing. For once the wind was not blowing in from the lake, and he could walk the five blocks to his fashionable hotel without being cut to ribbons by the cold.

Why did he go out with girls like Margo anyway—with all the Margos? he asked himself, when there were so many really nice girls who were equally pretty and sweet too? Furthermore, he had suddenly realized women liked him, that, for reasons that escaped him, as he had grown older and harder all kinds of women appeared to have become unusually attached to him. But he guessed he had learned to like the hard type—there was no nonsense about them, and with the money and the smart places, he had found himself more and more in the company of models, stray wives, bit-part actresses and the good-time girls who had just shed a husband or a lover.

They were everywhere. Like the evening before. He had been standing in the lobby of the hotel for a moment lighting a cigarette, and over near one of the big pillars was a glittering girl with a distinguished older man. As he snatched a glance at her, she gave him abruptly a brief smile. He had never seen her before, but he knew the meaning of it instantly. It happened to him all the time. There must be some mark on him, he thought, that told them he liked them. He could not get away from it. There she was—a beautiful piece of tall work, a dazzle job—probably married to someone who was twice the man he would ever be, but if he sauntered into the softly lighted cocktail lounge and sat on one of the stools at the bar, it would not be long before there she was—like a butterfly in an alfalfa patch, just happened to stroll in without her escort, and she would just happen to find herself sitting there next to him looking through her glittering, expensive pocketbook with that pretty helplessness women reserve for the moments when they know exactly what they are doing. She would be rummaging for a bill with which to pay for her drink, and he would say, "Allow me . . ." and that would be how it would start.

And that was what had happened the night before. There had been others like her everywhere he went—wealthy, heartless

276

and big-timey. He needed them as he needed a hole in the head. Brilliant Brill, he had thought afterwards tiredly, a refuge for wandering wives, chalk up one for the wonder boy—one goose egg. The time was approaching when he would have had all the beautiful jobs he would ever want—all of them from the big town to San Francisco, from here in Chicago to New Orleans, with all the stop-offs in Dallas or Kansas City.

There was the redhead in Kansas City who lived in a dreamy women's magazine world. Facts had no authority over her behavior, and she had wanted him to take her away from it all— away from two Cadillacs, a house on the Heights, a round of gaiety and a hard-working, heavy-gambling husband who seldom came home. The secret of a successful marriage, she had been told long before, was learning to run a one-man whorehouse, but she had found the wrong man. She was a gay girl but dreamy, completely dreamy, and her intentions were no longer good. "Cookies taste sweet or they don't get stolen," she had told him, when she appeared at his room in the hotel at eleven at night in a magnificent sable coat with nothing underneath.

It was too much sugar for a penny. There were more of them than he could ever use or than he would ever want for that matter. But he had liked them. It had been the fun he had thought it would be, even though it was exhausting. For there was the job too and the newsmen and Company officials he had to take out or bring together and the great Empire whose servant he now was, whose advance man he had become in the marts of the land.

In the morning after those rounds with Margo, however, he felt terrible. He had an appointment, but it went off all right. By four in the afternoon, he was much better. He could see large permanent objects quite clearly. By evening with a girl named Estelle, another beauty with a lovely voice, he was content and began to enjoy himself.

He could not recollect exactly when it had begun to pall, neither the exact day nor the week nor the occasion, but it must

277

have been sometime during the second year of traveling. Already the towns had begun to blur, the succession of hotel rooms to have a depressing sameness, the men's faces in conferences to wear the same expression. Subtly also there was a gradual change in his responses and moods. There was no question he had become harder, more pleasure-loving. The evenings at home even in town with the music and books were no more. Now he found he was out almost every night, and the bars in town—like the swank night clubs in glittering cities—had grown familiar to him. And the breech between him and April had widened. The third or fourth time he had returned from one or another of the trips he had even forgotten to call her. The sound of her name, ringing now more faintly in his subconscious, stirred only a sadness. All was beginning to mingle and drown in the increasingly restless and empty night of his existence.

Several times now, during those early intervals when he was in town, there were messages from April awaiting him—notes that she had called or a scrawl saying: "Whatever became of you?" but some incident had arisen, there was always a party somewhere, and the only time he had seen her, they had had supper together, and all through the dinner, she had been unnaturally silent.

When he was saying goodnight, she asked softly in the dim light of the little bar they had ended up in: "Have you really forgotten me after all, Martin?" Then: "It seems to me I miss you, Martin. I don't know what's wrong with me."

"What about Horace?" he asked pleasantly. "Aren't you and he getting married?"

She was silent for a long time, holding his hand.

"I . . . I can't, Martin," she said at last. "I don't know why, Martin. But I can't."

"Well—" he was cool, although he knew it was unkind—"it'll come to you what you ought to do, April. Don't worry about it."

As he walked home in the early spring night afterwards, it was clear to him that something had happened to him, some inner strength had slipped over the widening months, over the spread

278

of time, out of his life. It was perhaps some essence of the capacity to love, the capacity to feel strongly, and it was haunting as well as sad. April did not stir his pulses as she once had. Somewhere along the way, in the months of work and uninterrupted indulgence, in the miles and miles of cities, the millions and millions of lights, the smoky night clubs, the incessant voices—deep, rasping, incisive and soft, clear and sultry—the bondage that had once been cherished had snapped, and he was everybody's boy now—and nobody's.

It was not a situation to feel strongly about. That was the trouble. That had been the way he had wanted it at first, but now he didn't know. He didn't really know. Perhaps he had been rash. Perhaps he had not foreseen the eroding process, the wearing away of that freshness, that inner responsiveness, the wastage of life. He had meant only to forget a little, but somehow every flow of sentiment, of love, had drained from him. Now as he walked in the mild dampness of the spring night, there above him in the twinkle of lights was the city's Gorgon face that turned the heart to stone, and he felt nothing . . . nothing but the sadness.

Yes, it must have been about this period that the change had grown noticeable, that he had become conscious that all was not well with him. The evenings began to be a little harder to take, the hangovers a little more prolonged. It was not that he was in poor physical condition. Quite the contrary. The fact was, as many of them commented, he had never looked better, more poised, handsomer. And he became aware with surprise that he was considered a good-looking man. He was also aware now that he was considered experienced and capable, a professional.

He had been witness to, and in fact taken part in, enough of the seamy side of empire building to have discovered this ability to get along with people, to understand their motives and to organize material for the purposes for which the Empire had sent him out. But now within himself, he noted those telltale signs: the periods of depression . . . the difficulties in getting up in the morning . . . the diminution of enthusiasm . . . the

279

boredom at the gatherings . . . the waning of any pleasure in making the milk runs to Chicago or San Francisco or Burlington or Baltimore or even the little side trips to odd places for odd ceremonies or for detail work on new construction of one type or another—all month after month and season after season. He was like a tired commuter who wakes up one morning and decides that he would rather die than catch the 7:58 ever again in this world. They had worn him down.

But he felt also that perhaps it might lie even deeper than the exhaustion from merely traveling. He had found the life of good food and the girls had made him too restless to stay alone in the evenings, even when he wished to relax and knew it would be good for his soul. He was aware that these were the signs of a sort of spiritual disintegration. And it was at this time that a new and sordid love entered his life.

The affair began quite suddenly.

On a Monday in April, Sherry Fields announced that she was being married in two weeks. The fortunate man was Stillwell K. Carson, a gentleman of sixty-eight, wealthy and in the Social Register. The rumors as to where she had met this desirable gentleman and how she had managed to present her beauty to his dimming eyes were many and varied.

On Wednesday evening of that week, as Martin walked into the poorly lighted hall of his apartment building, a glamorous apparition with auburn hair rose from the steps where she had been sitting on her mink stole and moved forward into the light. "Hi," she said.

It was Sherry.

"Sherry!" he said, surprised. "What are you doing here?"

"Waiting for you," she answered.

He stood a moment at a loss.

"Well," he began, "you surprise me. I suppose I should wish you happiness in your impending marriage."

"Never mind that," she said. "I don't wish to be congratulated. Aren't you going to ask me in?"

He sensed that she had been drinking, although he could not be sure. The hall reeked of her expensive perfume.

"Come in," he said.

He inserted the key into the outer door and stood back for her to enter. At his apartment, he produced the key again and pushed in to turn on the lights.

She walked in behind him and stood surveying the room coolly, noting the disarranged books and the phonograph records piled on chairs.

"Uh-huh," she said, "very nice. I like your place."

"Thank you," he answered. "Make yourself at home and I'll get you a drink. What will you have?"

"It doesn't matter," she said. "Why did you never claim that date you once asked for, Martin? I'm curious. You like girls. I know that."

"The competition was too strong," he replied politely. "I get discouraged easily."

"The competition wasn't any stronger than for April, sweet boy." The voice was cool, slightly amused. "You didn't become too discouraged there."

"Perhaps you've answered your own question, Sherry," he replied softly. He turned to face her. "Will Scotch do?" he asked.

She nodded.

"And now, since you won't sit down, perhaps you'll tell me to what I owe this great though unexpected pleasure?"

She stood there looking at him steadily, her beautiful gray eyes unblinking, the smell of her perfume like a sea around him. She let the stole fall from her shoulders, from the strapless gown which revealed cunningly the superb curve of her figure. "Can't you guess?" she said.

He remained standing with the glass in his hand, looking at her, looking into those beautiful gray eyes. He had seen it all before. It was not new to him. It was familiar and he was more mature now, but even so, it sent a faint shiver through him. Her voice was soft.

281

"A week from tomorrow, I'm marrying an old man—a rich old man," she said quietly. "He will give me much that I want in the world: wealth, social position. But there's one thing he can't give me. He's sixty-eight years old. He can't give me love —and I want that too. Martin," she said softly, and her silky voice had a quality of coldness he had never believed possible in one with such a warm, flamelike beauty. "Martin, you and I have . . . have much in common. We are the same type, the same kind of people—direct and realistic and without hypocrisy. I came because I wanted to. I'm here. . . ."

He remained there before her, feeling a mingling of anger and something else.

"Why . . . why, Sherry," he began. His voice was hard. He was trying to think of how to say it, how to express his turmoiled emotions. He was confused.

"You may just say no, Martin, and I will leave quietly, but I don't think you will." Her voice was velvety. "No man from my experience ever throws it away, Martin," she continued softly. "Not when it is presented to him like this on a silver platter."

She let the stole slide to the floor and stood there in the lamplight, lovely and depraved, like a model displaying an expensive evening gown. Her eyes were half closed and she was not smiling. She looked as evil as he suddenly felt she was, and as unscrupulous. He started to say something again, then he stopped. He knew suddenly that it was true. She had him dead to rights. No man ever throws it away. She knew them all too well— Circe and the swine, and he was just like the rest.

"All right," he said quietly. His tone was muted but he tried to make it as brutal as possible. "You can unwrap it, Sherry. It isn't what I had in mind, but I'll buy it."

That was the beginning of the affair.

Sherry's marriage was brilliant. All the papers covered it. He did not see her afterwards for a month. Then on a Thursday evening before he was to begin one of the trips again, she was waiting for him in the doorway.

"Will you please have a key made for me," she greeted him. "I don't enjoy sitting here on the stairs cooling my heels for you. The chauffeur is to pick me up in front of the theater in three hours."

"You kill me," he said. "How is married life?"

"Someday I will slap your face," she said.

"I'll be away for two weeks," he remarked later. "You can take the key and have one made. Leave this in the apartment when you have yours. I'll have the landlord let me in when I return."

"Please try not to stay away too long," she said. "Your trips are very annoying. Do you have other girls?"

"For the love of heaven, Sherry," he said. "Of course I have other girls. You and I know where we stand."

"I can make it up to you, if you won't," she said.

"You don't mean it," he answered quietly.

He was beginning to feel like someone who has come up to the line once too often. The trip this time involved a great deal of entertaining, and when he returned, he was exhausted. Moreover, he could feel that the breakup within himself was approaching. His nerves were on edge and the periods of despondency were longer and more devastating.

On a Saturday in July in town, he went early to the museum to look at some Rodin sculpture. He was nervous and he had a dreadful hangover. The morning began pleasantly cool, but by ten o'clock it was already hot. He spent half an hour looking at the magnificent marble groups, then walked out from the gloom of the huge edifice into the early glare of summer.

He walked along a path in the park. He felt miserable. He sat down on a bench in the shade of some tired maples and held his head.

"The dump truck," a voice said.

He looked up. A little boy perhaps three years old stood before him, regarding him with enormous saucerlike blue eyes.

283

"I lost it," he said. "My daddy gave it to me." It seemed as if he were about to cry.

"I wish I had a dump truck," Martin replied quietly.

The little boy's face cleared. That appeared to please him.

"If I find it," he said intently, his face deep in concentration, "I will lend it to you. You're my pal."

Martin gazed at the little flowerlike face, serious and intent. The baby put his hand on Martin's knee.

"Oh, there you are!" The voice was exasperated. He looked up. A wilted, scrawny woman was standing near them. She was young but tired and there were blue circles under her eyes, almost like bruises. She looked worn out.

"I'm sorry he bothered you," she said. "It's that dump truck. We can't find it anywhere."

Martin stood up, his left hand holding the baby's hand.

"Madam," he said, "will you do me a great favor?"

The woman looked at him startled.

With his right hand, he fumbled in his pocket and drew out two moderately large bills. He thrust them into her limp hand.

"Will you please get my pal here a new dump truck," he said, "as a favor to me?"

He smiled at the little boy. Then he turned and walked away along the path. They were still staring after him when he rounded the corner and disappeared from their view.

His headache felt worse, but the picture of that little flowerlike face remained with him. He could not get it out of his mind. He walked rapidly along, the heat pressing down over him. They were probably tired people, he was thinking, and the man probably returned home at night peevish and disgruntled. If they only knew how lucky they were, he thought—or perhaps they did. That little serious face—there wasn't anything a man wouldn't do for a face like that—not anything. Farther along the path, he found a bench and sat down and held his head in his hands again. I can't stand it, he thought. I shall have to pull myself out of this somehow.

*   *   *

It was in the fall in the midst of a nightmare of traveling that the summons came: this time to return to the office. There had been a shake-up.

3

"You have a new boss," Turner had said quietly. "Some changes have been made."

He was tired. He rubbed his brow and swiveled back toward the window. "I hope you'll be happy, Martin. It means a promotion. The new man taking Mizner's position was transferred from Personnel. He was a manager there. They say he's pretty high-powered. You're to be the supervisor reporting to him. I'm going over to Doyle as advertising supervisor. It'll be tough now that Mizner's retired," he added. He sighed. "Mizner was the best. The new manager . . . well . . ."

Turner paused and his strong, saturnine face darkened slightly.

"You've missed a few tricks while you've been out there, Martin," he continued in a low voice. "The political weather has not improved. I believe our friend Harwood thought they were going to tap him for this job also, and now that they've brought this new man in on a transfer, we're going to feel more of his displeasure. He never really recovered from Kilgore and he's pretty well torn up his own organization. The Old Man, Randall . . . well, Randall's the last of the former group. The new bunch are like Harwood—politicians—your new boss, for instance—a very smooth operator. But Harwood still throws plenty of weight around. You know what the boys call him?" Turner concluded softly: "the MVD, Ninth Section—Terror and Diversion . . . and that's about it. Anyhow, I hope you'll like your new boss. When do you meet?"

"Any minute now," Martin replied in what he hoped was a

285

casual tone. "He's sent word he'll see me as soon as he gets out of a conference. I understand he brought one of his own boys with him too."

"So you've heard already. Well, there's another of the new outfit. You'll note changes around here since the old days. Perhaps you'll like them better than I do."

When he had left Turner's office, he walked slowly down the corridor to the large area. There had been changes all right. He noticed the new faces. Somehow, they looked younger—and smarter. At the anteroom where April had once sat, a new secretary, a crisp, antiseptic girl, was typing. The gorgeous April had been promoted. She was an assistant vice president's secretary. She was going to be married.

He turned to walk back to his own office. "Oh, Mr. Brill," the girl said sweetly, "Mr. Fellowes would like to see you now."

He sat in the large handsome office and looked at the new manager. This was the beginning of the end.

"I know you and I will get along famously, Martin," Ray Selwyn Fellowes said in his quietly steady voice.

It was the smile that got him—that handsome, flashing smile. It cut like a knife.

"You're the boss," Martin replied in what he hoped was a genial tone. "I'll make it my business to get along."

"I like that," Ray Selwyn Fellowes remarked testingly. "Yes—" his smile abruptly flashed out—"yes, I like that remark. Well, Martin, we have things to do. Let's get down to cases."

Martin sat forward. His heart was like lead. For a reason that he could not put his finger on, he knew that it was about over. He knew that his goose was cooked.

It was toward the end that it came.

"Before you go, Martin, there's a favor I'd like to ask you. I've brought over from Personnel with me a young fellow who seems to me to show a great deal of promise. He's to be one of your boys and I would appreciate your sort of taking him in hand—you know, show him the ropes, help him get into the

286

swing of things. He's been very useful to me in other ways. I believe he has a lot on the ball. I think he'll go far. He's sitting right outside your door. I've asked him to stop in and see you when you get time."

"I'll do my best for him, sir," Martin answered. "Have you had time to meet the rest of the boys?"

"I'll get around to each of them, Martin. I've been going over their cards. I'll call you when we're ready and we can talk the work over some more."

As he left, the crisp young thing smiled at him sweetly. He walked slowly toward his office. The old nervousness and depression were with him again. The agency knife. He wondered vaguely whether he would survive.

He sat in the office a moment before going out to see the boys. He would need all the experience he had gained in this new job, and he had learned a thing or two. Not all of those expense-account years, despite the mists of memory, were wasted in an aimless indulgence or a fog of travel. Not only had his own organizing ability, his skills and knowledge of people increased, but also his understanding and power, during those years in the service of the Empire. And he had made powerful friends. His work had lain mostly in the fields of ritual and lore but the tasks had been none the less exacting and varied.

"Great organizations," Mizner had once commented, "must follow rituals and ideals that are emotionally necessary to them in order to do the practical jobs that were their original reasons for being. If these ideals are violated, the institution loses its power to hold people and the organization falls apart. Yes," Mizner had continued in his growling, cigar-strained voice, "people are incurable idealists. To be sensible with them is useless. I know. I've tried. Unless you realize that, you're naive. Men will only fight and die for shadows, circuses. They'll only work for high-sounding dreams. To get them to do anything, you have to propose for them blood, privation, desperate acts, misery and destruction. You have to offer them terror and dissolution in the name of justice, war in the name of peace, death

287

in the name of life. Then they'll listen to you. Then you'll have a following. And the Empire is like that too. Those outworn symbols that Turner speaks about are the Empire's stupid, fumbling ideals—the qualities that bestow on it some kind of moral existence in the world. That's all these crazy rituals are—its shadows and circuses—and it's got to have them or it won't survive. Men won't work for just a collection of buildings and machines, no matter how efficient, no matter how carefully engineered. That's the element that used to defeat us all—all the smart babies, all the efficiency experts, all the wise apples. . . ."

Martin looked up abruptly. Why had he been thinking of Mizner? Mizner had retired. You couldn't bring him back just thinking of him. Well, it was time for lunch with the boys. They were "his" boys now. It would be fun to eat in town again.

The young man standing in the doorway was tall and exceptionally good-looking with a face faintly scarred by arrogance and petulance. He had football player's shoulders and glossy, wavy dark hair.

"May I come in?" he asked pleasantly in a virile baritone. "I think Ray Fellowes told you about me. I'm Ted Newcomb—T. Everett Newcomb."

"Come in," Martin answered softly. "I'm glad you stopped by. Yes, Mr. Fellowes spoke of you. Sit down, Ted."

T. Everett Newcomb gave him a long look, man to man. When he spoke his voice had just the right volume and control.

"You know, Martin," the young man began confidentially, "I'm glad to find another fellow who went to the right school, who has the right background."

"What do you mean, Ted?" Martin asked.

"Well, I went there too, you know—Class of '50. You get awfully tired—and I'm speaking very confidentially now, Martin—of these boys from these Midwestern places nobody ever heard of. They really don't have the right background for this kind of work, do you think?"

288

"Most of them are very good men," Martin replied slowly, "better than the Corporation deserves."

T. Everett Newcomb frowned slightly as if shaking off a fly. It had been the wrong answer.

"That isn't exactly what I meant," the young man said pleasantly. "I think you know what I mean, though, Martin. You're really one of us, so to speak—one of those who, shall we say, have had advantages."

"I don't really know what you mean, Ted," he replied coldly. "And I don't agree with you. But I'm sure you didn't drop in just to chat about the boys."

"Well, all right, Martin," the young man said. "We understand each other, I think, anyhow. No, I stopped in because Ray Fellowes suggested you could give me something to do, sort of show me the ropes and get me started."

Martin shifted in his chair. T. Everett Newcomb was getting to him.

"Why, I believe I can get you started, Ted, if you're ready. . . . I thought I'd assign you to Jim Parr on the syndicate to get your feet wet first. . . ."

"But I thought I was supposed to be working with you, Martin?" the young man said in some surprise. His voice was still virile and controlled but a little hurt.

"You will be working with me, Ted," he answered quietly. "I think, however, you'd better start where you're in the stream of the System's news business."

"I am not completely suited to that type of work, Martin," T. Everett Newcomb replied. "I think Mr. Fellowes can tell you you would find me valuable in contact work. Perhaps a few months just becoming acquainted with people, being present possibly at one or two of the big conventions that are taking place this year . . ."

"I see what you mean, Ted," Martin answered. His voice was dry. "Mr. Fellowes suggested that I show you the ropes here. Suppose for the time being you start learning the ropes."

"I am not sure Mr. Fellowes will be happy with the way in which, shall we say, you intend to use my services. I shall, of course, have occasion to see him and he may ask me what I am doing. I shall be compelled to tell him."

"Ted," Martin's voice was low. "I should be very concerned to have Mr. Fellowes unhappy over any task he has set me. But while I'm running this show, suppose you let me worry about my living. You worry about yours."

The young man turned in the doorway again. His figure was magnificent, huge. His handsome face had become bland, closed.

"Perhaps you will hear more about this, Martin. Please don't feel that I hold anything against you personally. I am sure we could get along fine. However, perhaps you will wish to reconsider later on."

Then he had disappeared.

Martin sat at the desk staring at the blotter. His heart was pounding and his hands trembled. It was the blatancy that appalled him, the utter naivete of the approach. This kind of thing went on all the time and he knew how to handle it, but it seemed to him it had never been done so crudely. I know I shouldn't let it hit me, he thought. No use blowing one's top. The man is young, stupid. So he was sure we could get along fine, was he? So he doesn't hold anything against me personally? Well, if Mr. Fellowes were going to be unhappy about it, perhaps Mr. Fellowes had better be prepared to be very unhappy, because there were going to be no special privileges.

He took a deep breath.

So those were the new babies. He sighed. They almost made the old guard look good. Well, if he were to be considered one of the new ones, he would certainly try to be one of them with a difference.

4

THAT WAS when he hit rock bottom. It was the period just before the big blow that sent him out again, and it was a period of vicious underground struggle. He knew he was tough and able to take care of himself, but he found he was fighting against trying to smash the young kid, as he now thought of T. Everett Newcomb.

Parr had entered a month later and sat down, puffing.

"I don't know, Martin—that new boy . . ." He threw up his hands. "I can't do anything with him. He's an arrogant bastard, if there ever was one. As much as told me to go peddle my own papers. . . . You want me to get that material out, take this guy off my neck, will you? Give me back McKenzie. Give me a break."

Martin sat silent a moment, fighting the impulse to murder.

"Does he know how to organize the material, to write it up?"

"How the hell would I know?" Parr answered gloomily. "The sonuvabitch hasn't lifted a finger since I got him. What's the matter, boss—you mad at me?"

Martin sighed. "Well, Jim, give it another try. You're the best man to handle that kid I can think of. Let him have it. You won't suffer for it. It'll be my responsibility. See if you can't get something out of him, anything. . . ."

He sat silent at his desk a moment after Parr had gone. The boys knew that Fellowes had the ax out for him. They knew also that T. Everett Newcomb was Fellowes' man. It made it tough for them. But they were good men. They had shown themselves willing to take it with him. The trouble was some of them might get hurt with him. He didn't know precisely how Fellowes worked but he had a pretty clear idea. He didn't mind himself too much. But he was damned if he were going to let

291

them be railroaded because of him. He would have to protect them every way he could before the blow fell.

He rose and walked into the outer offices. At the far end toward the reception room he caught a glimpse of Randall, his thickset, clumsy body stooped, and once again there was the sense of shock. Randall looked so old, so done in. He had had very little contact with anyone in that department since his return. But he had not been able to dismiss Randall from his mind after the ugly surprise at first seeing him. Randall was in many ways stupid and regressed, but he was an honest, conscientious man, and he could not help liking him and feeling concern for him. For he looked so beaten.

He had run into Harwood once or twice also, the mask slipping a little on the smooth, controlled, satanic face. Harwood had been bustling past on those occasions as if in a great and portentous hurry. When they had first met after his return, Harwood had called: "Well . . . well . . . golden boy—the expense-account kid is finally back—the gifted suckling on the corporate teat."

"You kill me, Phil," he had replied.

Now the sight of Randall stirred again that sadness, that anger. It had been like the incident one summer evening years earlier when he and Sandy Saunders had been dining out together. He had been younger then and it had hit him harder.

They had been to a place called Moriarty's for dinner and were strolling along Third Avenue just above the Bowery amid the noise and squalor of midsummer when the mumbling interrupted them.

It was one of the many vagrants who drifted like refuse along those sodden side streets. The mumbling was typical, something about a cup of coffee or hadn't eaten for a week.

The face was before them for an instant—a total disaster: the usual empty sodden eyes, the gray unshaven jowls, the loose, liver-colored lips. Neither of them paid attention to the mumbled thanks or blessings when they had paid their toll. They walked along, Sandy resuming the train of his argument. They had

292

walked almost two blocks before he stopped. Saunders turned at almost the same moment. They looked at each other.

"No, it couldn't have been!" Saunders said. "It couldn't have been!"

He started to say something. Then they both swung about. The shambling figure—if it were the same one—was just shuffling around the corner of a side street two blocks back.

"It couldn't have been," Saunders murmured again.

"How should I know?" he had replied. He had felt as if he were suffocating. "How the hell should I know?"

Of course, they never did know. They would never know even if they had wanted to find out, but the face had been the face of Somers, and it had remained with him—remained with him all the years. . . .

He stood a moment longer looking at Randall, then walked down the corridor.

The counterblow arrived on schedule.

"Sit down, Martin," Ray Selwyn Fellowes said, quietly controlled. His flashing smile was abated.

He looked at Martin long and steadily, man to man.

"I confess, Martin," he began, "that I'm just a little bit disappointed in your handling of the new young man. Perhaps you found him just a little too spirited or possibly not as wholeheartedly responsive to routine as he could be."

"Those are the understatements of the century, Mr. Fellowes," Martin answered in a low voice.

The brows of the smooth virile face faintly shadowed. He spoke very gently, very quietly.

"I suggested, Martin, that perhaps you ought to give him special handling in this instance. It seemed to me his talents lie somewhat out of the ordinary routines."

"Mr. Fellowes," Martin answered after a pause, "let us put our cards on the table. You have other men in your group— forty of them—and many of them are very good men. They are hard workers. They came up the hard way. They did what

293

they were asked to do. They required no special handling. Ted Newcomb is not a good man. He will not take orders. He will not work. I have done my best for him."

The silence gathered slowly over the large office, a troubled, ominous silence, seeping into every corner. It seemed to hang over him. The regular tanned features of that smooth countenance were dark, faintly sad.

"Martin," the voice emerged at last, soft, a little regretful, "Martin, you are considered one of the toughest and most brilliant men in the field. That is the way your work and you are known, and I have no doubt that it is true. But perhaps your talents do not entirely fit you to deal with people in the offices. Perhaps you are a little hard on them. You expect too much. I have no doubt you are completely fair, and the men have an unusual devotion to you, I must say. But it appears to me . . ."

Now he knew what it was. He knew now how they would dispose of him. Exile. It was as simple as that. They would merely send him into limbo—out on the road again. It was common knowledge that if you were in the field long enough, they would forget you, you would grow out of touch with what was happening at the vortex . . . you would eventually get lost. A lot of them had been sent out like that, had lost touch, had eventually been forgotten. And that's how it would be with him. That was how it had been planned. He struggled dispiritedly.

"Don't you think, sir, I've been on the road enough these last few years?" he asked.

"Of course, Martin, you have done your part," Ray Selwyn Fellowes continued quietly, reasonably. "But this year there are these very important conventions—the one coming up in March is considered by the Empire important enough to send out the highest brass. And I'm afraid we shall be needing not just an experienced man but a brilliant man to handle our contacts and reporting there. Naturally, you may call upon any of your men to assist and I should deem it a favor if in the

294

case of the March convention you permit young Newcomb to participate—as an assistant, of course. But you see how it is? After all, you were the one to point out to me that a good man knew how to take orders, were you not, Martin?"

Mr. Fellowes smiled wanly—a quick flash.

He could feel himself smoldering inside, the sadness, the sense of defeat. That big boy was a smooth operator, all right. He had him. There was no getting around it. He knew just how to do it. Even to the wintry, flashing smile, the elaborate gesture of necessity and regret. He had him completely.

"Yes, sir," Martin replied heavily, "I know how to take orders."

He rose slowly. It seemed to him that he could not bear even the thought of that old grind again. Somehow, he reflected, he should have known he couldn't win, he couldn't outplay that baby. Yes, he'd been had. They'd really closed him out this time.

"As soon as I've made the arrangements to leave," he remarked tiredly, "I'll let you know, sir."

"Thank you, Martin." The voice was very soft, a little regretful.

5

It was eight long months, eight months of the old grind, the move from city to city . . . the rain-drenched conventions . . . the crowds . . . the businessmen's lunches . . . the scribbled releases . . . the travel-weary, frazzled hangers-on . . . eight long months before it finally arrived—the break he had been anticipating. The summons was given: he was requested once more and for the last time to return home.

He knew what it was immediately. Actually, he had been expecting it for some time. It meant nothing special to him,

295

nothing but a brief interlude, he knew, but any respite would be welcome. They had called him in on Randall's disability retirement. Harwood had won.

He sat in the hotel room that rainy late afternoon. His tickets were in order. He would be catching the plane back in the morning. Around him were the depressing evidences of his long drudgery—the half-packed suitcases full of soiled clothes . . . the cigarette burns in the bedspread . . . the crumpled remains of programs and releases . . . the used match folders and highball glasses from the gathering of newsmen and businessmen after the convention last night. Well, for the moment, he was through with all that.

Actually, he was not sure exactly on what grounds they were calling him back. Whether it might be to help temporarily in the large shake-up that would naturally result, or as a courtesy, since ordinarily he would have been one of the four men of the division eligible for the position. There would, of course, be other men eligible outside the division, since this was a major job, of vice presidential concern, a position that ordinarily marked the entry into higher management, since the incumbent would thereafter be under the constant scrutiny of the top echelon. He realized now that he had no chance—that in cold fact they would not even consider him. The job was basically the biggest, most important manager's position in their division —at least it had been under others. And in the normal course of events it would be again under whoever succeeded to it. Randall had been a single exception and the circumstances had been extenuating. It angered him every time he thought of what they had done to Randall. He looked down and sighed.

Well, he hoped Turner would get the job. Turner was difficult, but he would be fair. But it would most likely be Harwood this time. They couldn't keep Harwood down forever. Well, he might as well face it. There was no question—when Harwood went in, they would—all of them—be in for a rough ride. He supposed he could weather it. He'd learned enough, he had enough in him to know how to take care of himself. He supposed he was fairly hard . . . he could handle the toughest of them. . . .

He paused suddenly. Why was he thinking this way now? What had happened to him? Why did he care after all? So it would be Harwood? Why should he care so much whether it were Harwood or Turner? He was doing his job and after all it was just a job. It wasn't his whole life.

He looked around at the disordered, littered room—the symbol of the existence to which they had condemned him. No, this was not his life. But the fact was: he did care. And he cared not so much because of his own situation but because of them—the men for whose careers he had become at least in part responsible. Some of these men he had no particular brief for, some he did not even particularly like, but stupid as it was, he could not throw off a concern for them, for their chances and their welfare.

The new babies, the new operators, would be moving in— they already were moving in, and some of the old crowd, the best indeed—how would they survive? Particularly those who had done the work, those who had served the Empire most conscientiously. The operators would dupe them or subvert them or simply use them for their own purposes. It might not be fair, but after all, where did he come in on it? It was really no concern of his. The Empire might lose by it and some of the boys would certainly lose heavily, but his situation would scarcely be affected—it could hardly be worse anyhow. Nevertheless, stupid or not, he did care.

Well, now, at any rate, this was a brief respite and he'd be going back to see the old town once more. It had been a rough ticket—he'd have to admit it. But there had been some good things. There had been that rainy afternoon at the big March convention. T. Everett Newcomb had been sent out to "help" him. A lot of the brass would be there. He had also had a couple of his own men. He had been sitting unobtrusively in the lobby of the big convention hotel, resting between rounds, and this slight, ordinary-looking, quiet man, well dressed but appear-

297

ing bewildered, had let himself down wearily next to him on the long upholstered seat in that secluded area. The man wore a crumpled Homburg and his umbrella was wet from the drizzle outside. He was carrying a worn brief case, only a portion of which Martin could glimpse on the other side of the expensive raincoat.

"Nice weather for the ducks," the older man said.

"You can say that again," Martin replied. "I suppose if you have to suffer at a convention, this is the kind of weather to have it in.

"I was sitting here thinking," Martin began again after a pause, "of all the good men in service here to one little kingdom or another, of all the lives that are spent in such devotion to company and corporate interests and I was wondering whether these kingdoms were worth it."

"That thought occurs to us all at one time or another," the older man responded. "You are, I take it, in the service of one of the big ones?"

"The biggest."

"You like the work?"

"Like?" Martin answered. He felt a sort of kinship with this older, tired man. There was a certain warmth between them. "Like isn't exactly the word, sir," he said. "I am a supervisor of the System and in exile and . . ."

At that moment, one of the young men who had been ordered out to assist him rushed up. "Oh, there you are, Martin!" It was Dick Ellsworth and he appeared flustered and excited. "I've been looking all over for you. They can't find Mr. Holman—the special-projects vice president . . . he's to be on in half an hour. Ted Newcomb said to find you and find out where he is and he'd take care of him. Nobody seems to know where he is."

"All right, all right, Dick. Take it easy. Don't worry about it. Why in God's name they send out a poor overworked vice president to these conventions is beyond me. If he took a powder, it would be a good thing. We'll look up Scott and see

298

whether he may have someone who can go on in Mr. Holman's place, if we can't locate him. . . . Take it easy. I suppose Ted Newcomb is handling the big shots now. Tell that horse's ass to play it slow. They have enough to worry about without being ragged all over the place in the name of the press."

When Dick had vanished as if shot from a cannon's mouth, he turned to the man beside him. It struck him immediately.

"You're Mr. Holman," he said softly.

"Yes," the old man answered. "And you, I take it, are Martin Brill. Glad to know you, Brill. I'll be there. Don't worry about me."

That had been one of the pleasant moments. There had been others also. For actually throughout these long months and those of exile during the years before, he had been present at and himself played a role in too many of these conferences.

He leaned back and sighed.

The significance of those years, it now seemed, had largely escaped him. And when he turned in retrospect, as he sometimes did, amid the tumult and furor, the emptiness of his existence appalled him. For now it was clear how far behind he had left that other world—the world of youthful dreams, of music and books and perhaps a year in Paris. They had slipped away. They were no longer real. Reality had become for him the assignments, the tensions and the daily crises on which the power of the Empire was built—the necessities of meeting its hundred little deadlines, of shoring up its intentions, of giving it personality and force in the world of men in which it must do business.

For they had begun to use him on basic and important assignments. There had been the time he was appointed press representative at one of the vital bargaining sessions in Chicago. It was typical of the tougher jobs they had been giving him. He could remember the little room off the conference room in the hotel—filled with smoke . . . the low growling voices . . . the air of exhaustion and frayed nerves.

It was one time the union had gone out on a limb. They were tired of the Empire's glacial slowness, its ponderous considerations, and they had been rash. Their demands were unreasonable and in the exchanges, this union—already in a poor bargaining position—had made intemperate threats and released them in the public press. It was all part of the ritual, but it had gone too far. The extreme position had angered one of the Company's powerful engineering vice presidents. This was merely one of many unions the Empire dealt with, and its record, though largely favorable, had of recent years been somewhat erratic and often extreme. Now the Industrial Relations people were putting on the pressure. And it appeared to Martin that what Harrison, the vice president, really wanted was to smash the union once and for all.

Martin's assignment as press representative at the sessions was a key one. He was to make the Company's statements for the papers and to see that the Company's position remained strong before the public in the battle of words which was growing progressively hotter with each session. They had been at it now for six weeks, and it looked as if a strike were inevitable. The trouble was, Martin was aware, as was the union itself now, that a strike might well wreck the union. Its position was difficult, even untenable. The area in which its people worked was highly mechanized, and the System could operate almost indefinitely while new people were trained or supervisors took over. Furthermore, the men themselves were growing short of temper and exasperated with their own union officials. The union head, not one of the brainiest in the profession, had nevertheless been a friend of the Empire's over years of amicable negotiations and was a man of integrity, but somehow of late he had pushed himself into this serious tactical error and his reputation, his very career, were at stake. It was either he save face or in the coming union elections he would be discredited.

All of them were aware of this, Martin included. The negotiators understood quite clearly that the Company held all the cards, but it appeared to Martin they were under instructions to force the issue and it also seemed to Martin that in the long run this would be a grave, indeed an almost irremediable, mistake. A long and harrowing strike, even though it eventually crippled the union, would solve nothing. It would lead to rankling bitterness against the Empire and even acts of sabotage on the part of the men who had lost their jobs, and whatever the public might feel about the merits of the case, the Empire, which had cherished a remarkable record of fair and peaceful labor negotiations with half a hundred unions over the years, would now have this stain of violence spreading.

Martin could remember that evening just two days before the strike was to be called. The white-faced union men and the Company negotiators, exhausted and trembling, coming out of the room. There seemed to be no further chance. Martin had the statement for the press which began: *Tonight negotiations between the Company and the Union were broken off.* . . . It was to be strongly worded and left no doubt of the Company's attitude. They were calling the union's bluff. It was Armageddon.

He had adjourned to the smoky hotel room with the two Company negotiators afterwards. It was about one in the morning. They had had little sleep for the last ten days.

"I hate to turn this in," Martin had said quietly to Gilpin, the chief negotiator.

Gilpin was a horse-faced, mournful-looking man, wearing sloppy clothes and an air of earnest intensity. He exuded honesty. There was no phoniness about him, no flair, no swagger. He was one of the Company's ablest labor-relations managers.

"I hate to see you turn it in, Martin," he replied, "but what the hell can we do? Our explicit orders were to warn them, then let them have it. No more compromise. I can understand them, but they were just asking for it."

Gilpin's face was gray with fatigue. Cosgrove, the other negotiator, a snappier, more conventional Empire man in a neat serge suit, nodded agreement.

"They were just asking for it," he repeated. "That Sweeney —I don't know what's got into him. He's in a real squeeze this time. He'll never slip out of it now."

Martin shook his head.

"All the same," he said, "we're making a serious mistake in letting him hang himself."

"We gave him a chance," Cosgrove answered. "He wouldn't take it."

Gilpin was silent. Martin looked from one to the other of them. The assistants had departed to their various rooms to sleep the sleep of the exhausted. The night light in the hotel corridor threw an eerie, lonely glow—the aura of desertion. Martin knew Sweeney, the union head, must be tossing and turning somewhere on that floor in an agony of defeat. It was Gilpin's voice that broke the silence.

"No, we didn't give him a chance," he said quietly. "We got our orders from the top—from Harrison—and the way we were to handle it, he couldn't have agreed without being discredited. Sweeney didn't have a chance." Gilpin's voice was low.

Martin could feel the perspiration in the palms of his hands. He stood silent a moment. Then he turned. "Wait for me," he said. He went into the room and sat down at the table. He sat still, thinking. Then he took out a piece of hotel letterhead and began to scribble on it. He remained in thought a moment longer. Then he rose.

The two men still stood in the corridor.

He handed Gilpin the paper.

"What if we go to Sweeney now," Martin said, "and show him this. Tell him we have orders to turn in the release I have here or to turn in the one I've just scribbled. We want to turn in the one I've just written. All he has to do is meet the Company's reasonable offer."

Gilpin held the paper in a hand shaking with fatigue. He read it silently. When he had finished, he looked up slowly. For a long time he said nothing.

"We are under orders to do it the other way," he replied at

302

last. "Those are Harrison's suggestions. We know how Harrison feels. We know what he wants. His suggestions are orders. He would never sit still for something like this."

"Harrison is wrong," Martin persisted in a low voice. "You know it and I know it. He'll get what he wants all right—smash the union . . . Sweeney's scalp. But he'll buy us all a lot of trouble too, a lot of trouble. . . . It won't end there."

"Harrison may not be very smart," Gilpin replied slowly, "but he's something much better—he's vice president."

Martin was silent. He and Gilpin stood looking at each other.

It seemed to Martin, as he remained there gazing into Gilpin's harried, exhausted face, that what he was demanding was a risk only a fool would take—a risk not just for himself, though because the publication of the release was in his province, the main burden of the blame would fall on him, but also for a good, sound man whose usefulness in an important field might possibly be impaired by this move. Yet somehow he could not even hesitate. The consequences of their intransigence were clear. There was a time to be adamant and a time to show regard for human error. It would always pay off in the end. And what he was concerned with was not the feelings of regressed vice presidents but the pay-off. He held Gilpin's eyes.

"All right," Gilpin said at last. "I'll go along with you. You're right, of course, but . . . Well, it's only our scalps."

And Martin realized, on looking back, that he had not shown much smartness, either. But he had possessed something much better than smartness—he had possessed luck. Sweeney's gray, relieved face was with him still—and the moment at three in the morning that they had knocked glasses together and felt the tepid rye pour down their throats in that last toast to the agreement. The next morning's papers had run a story beginning: *At midnight last night, the Company agreed substantially to the Union's demands for* . . . and so it had gone.

They had felt the weight of disapproval later even though in cold fact it was the Company's terms that had been met and the union had received nothing the Company had not originally

303

offered it. But the union's face had been saved. And so had Sweeney, and that was the important thing. The Empire never had trouble with that union again. Martin had received his reprimands, strongly presented, but he had made a name for himself and he had made one powerful friend.

So in these struggles and triumphs, Martin became gradually aware he possessed a basic capacity for work itself. He had the intensity. He was able to give a problem the instant perception it demanded and to formulate the patterns that would solve it. And he was able to move people. Somehow along the way, without really noting it, his ability to organize had developed and his power to manage. And with it had increased that poise, that air of authority and self-confidence, which had now become so characteristic.

Yet with this increasing absorption, with the drive of these new assignments, he had left behind something fundamental. He had left behind love. But even here life comes full circle, and it was in the last years of that first exile that some of the old dreams and desires he had thought would never return— the bread cast upon the waters, as he had grown to think of it—surged back once more. . . .

6

IT HAPPENED on a rainy night in late fall. The music ends. . . .

Sherry had been waiting for him when he arrived at the apartment. "Where have you been?" she asked angrily. The rain was still dripping from his hatbrim. "I've been here twenty-five solid minutes," she said.

"How was I to know you were coming?" he asked mildly. "You must be in one of your moods."

She was sitting on the day bed in her slip. The face, provocative and divinely beautiful, had grown more petulant under the make-up. He thought, as he had found himself thinking so often now when he saw her: Why do I do this? There is absolutely nothing here for me, and someday she will harm me or I will learn to make a fool of myself.

"Come on," she said, leaning back against the cushions, "we don't have all night, you know."

"I've often wondered why you picked me," he commented as he was escorting her down to the street to find a taxi much later. They stood for a moment in the doorway watching the rain.

"Why do you suppose?" she replied. "What a foolish question! I . . . I always wanted you—you know that. And more than that, I knew you could be trusted. Anybody can see at a glance that you're the kind of fellow anyone can trust."

He was puzzled. "We'd better dash to the corner," he said. "We'll never find a cab here."

She made a face, but they ran out into the wetness. On the corner, he whistled a wheeling cab and it screeched to a stop beside them. He kissed her wetly and turned away as she slammed the door. This would be the end. He walked slowly back toward the apartment building through the rain, his trench-coat collar turned up. This was during that most aimless and distraught period of his life. And Sherry somehow symbolized it. He always felt better when Sherry had departed.

Yet as he walked, the soft slur of the rain around him, the dreadful depression began to close in again. The entire emptiness of his life, the heart hunger enveloped him like a cloud, like the very wetness of the rain itself. The words of a banal old song returned to him:

> *Love, you played the music,*
> *And I had the dancing feet,*
> *So happily together*
> *We marched on up the street . . .*
>
> *But now I hear, not distantly*
> *The years, long echoed, go,*

And now where is your music, Love?
Or are my feet too slow? . . .

It lilted briefly just beneath his consciousness, but it did nothing to lighten his oppression.

When he entered the dim glow of the lobby, the figure walked toward him.

"April!" he said. "Why April!"

Her blond hair was wet and so was the thin raincoat she was wearing. Little drops trickled down her cheeks. Her long lashes were stuck together in small horns.

"April," he repeated. "April, what are you doing here?"

"I was waiting for you across the street in the doorway," she said. "I've been standing there for hours."

"But . . . but . . ."

"I know," she said. "I saw Sherry go in as I was waiting for you, so I stood in the shelter there. I . . . I . . . Oh Martin, I . . . I've missed you so. I just had to see you. It's been so long . . . so long."

He stood with her in the dim lobby, exhausted, spent. She was looking into his eyes seriously, intently. He could not pull himself together.

"Martin," she said again, "don't I have anything you want any more?"

He stood huddled there, trying to collect himself. He did not know what to say. So many of those bright nights and so many of those other faces and voices, sweet and soft, had drifted between them, so much had happened to him since the days when he had longed for her, when he would have given anything for her. Now the longing had all vanished, all drained away as if it had never been, and only that sickness was in him—that restlessness and that tiredness.

He could remember a night in a hotel room after one of the many girls had left and the heaviness of the liquor was still in him and the mood of heartsickness was there. He had reached across on the night table, knocking over the empty glass with

306

the lipsticked rim onto the floor with a crash, and there was that Gideon Bible. He felt like weeping, and he pulled it toward him and opened it. In Luke, the words blurred up at him: *Abide with me, for it is evening and the day is far spent . . .* He had closed the book and put his head in his hands. He needed something and he needed it badly, but he did not know what it was.

All of those years were between them now like the flashes of a many-colored kaleidoscope, and what was the answer, what was the answer? Was there an answer any more? Was there any at all? These years had all been wasted, wasted.

"April," he replied gently, "April, you shouldn't have come. It's all gone between us, all slipped away long ago, long ago. You were the big love of my life, April. You know that. But even the big ones wear out, even love. I'm sorry, April. I'm sorry. There isn't anything left."

She began to cry.

"Martin," she said, "oh please, Martin," she said again. "I stood there waiting for you so long. Oh Martin, please, please . . . don't humiliate me . . . please. I love you. I've always loved you, but I didn't know. It's always been you, even if I've fought against it. I thought I'd always have you and I could look around at the others, but I'm nothing without you, Martin—nothing. Please, I'm just nothing unless you're around. . . .

"Oh Martin," she said, and she began to shake with her crying, "I know I've treated you badly but I'm sorry and I've tried the last few months, the last year . . . I've tried so hard to get you back, to make it up . . . I wrote and called and you never answered, you never paid attention . . . Please don't humiliate me. I'm not anything without you. It's never been anybody but you—never. If you don't want to marry me now, you don't have to, but I . . . I can't . . ." She stopped, the sobs shaking her as she covered her face. "You must stay with me. . . . You must. . . ."

307

He reached out in a gesture toward her, then let his arm fall. What was the use? What could he say?

Gradually, her crying diminished and ceased. "Martin," she said again softly, when she had quieted somewhat, "Martin, isn't there anything left between us—anything?"

Again there flooded on him, into his mind all the places where he had been—the alien cities, the strange rooms, the lost girls —all of these ghosts that lay between them, between him and her now. And there swept over him also the times that he had thought he would like to have a home to go to, a place in which to be able to forget all the turmoil and the emptiness. That also was perhaps an illusion, a trap, but it would be nice to have some focus other than himself or the next assignment. All I want is to get my money and to get home to dinner, he had once told himself. But now even that thought seemed without substance. Then suddenly, there appeared in his mind's eye, as he stood there in that dimly lighted lobby, the cool rain steaming down outside in a steady sizzle-sozzle and the beautiful blond girl there—now almost a stranger to him, crying—there appeared fleetingly the image of that little flowerlike face—the little boy, glimpsed so briefly during a passing summer afternoon at the time he had had that dreadful hangover—that little intent face, so moving, so complete, so enchanting. A man would do anything, anything at all for a face like that.

She was looking at him, he realized abruptly, the lovely green eyes with that infinite sadness and longing. He had seen the other kinds of glances before—the sultry glances, the warm glances, the sweet glances—but no one had looked at him like that, and almost without realizing it, his voice was soft in the shadowy hall.

"Oh April," he said, "I wish it had been a few years ago or even a year ago . . . I wish you had told me that. Oh April," he said, "oh April . . . I'm sorry . . . I'm sorry. . . ."

Evening . . .

Now he was alone in the strange office years later and it was evening. Before him the new low bookcases . . . the silver decanter . . . the green rug and the events of that morning still to face. And the years slipped away, vanished. Yes, the events of that morning. There had been four of the men, each in turn, who had descended at the summons, and he had been the last. He had not believed that he'd had a chance. It wasn't that, though; it was what had happened. He sighed. He would have to think of it; he would have to face it again.

But first, there had been the interview with Mansard.

As he walked to the elevators, he had realized they were all looking strangely at him. The others had just come up. Then there he was again sitting in one of the mahogany leather chairs in front of Mansard's enormous desk. It was certainly a rare occasion. Mansard was in his usual good form, his head bent, his eyes glued to the gleaming desk top. Well, might as well get it over, he had thought, one of them must have reached him after all. He couldn't imagine what horrors they had in store for him now. He smiled a little grimly.

"Yes, Mr. Mansard," he said.

Mansard looked up, his hard, enigmatic little face composed yet puzzled, as if there were still within him some interior secret conversation and he had been aroused out of it. He was impressed again by the odd glitter of Mansard's hard, limited personality. The man had something. There was no question about it.

"I don't know whether you are aware of the reason for this summons, Martin," the older man began suddenly. "Probably you are. Many elements of this complex career that has been thrust on us escape me and I had not realized fully how suddenly we are getting on—we of the old guard, so to speak—and now the new lights, the new powers are ready to sweep in. . . ."

He paused a moment. Martin regarded him curiously. It was so unlike Mansard. Something of what he was thinking must have reached the older man, for he smiled briefly.

"I know that I am generally regarded as simply an office boy, a highly paid messenger of the gods," he continued in a low voice. "And that's the way I choose it to be. That has been my career, and I am satisfied with it. Let the idea boys sit around in the brain rooms and drum it up. They still need us—people like me—to carry it out. Yes, Martin, it's strange that the next man here, when I retire two years hence, will probably be so different. I used the power conferred on me to carry out orders. The next man may use it to originate and influence policy. That is his concern. I am satisfied with the part I have played. It could have been larger. It was not given me to make it so. It can only be as large as the person. I did not play it to the hilt, but I could have done worse. . . . Well . . ." he sighed.

"Well," he said again, "now the new ones are beginning to sweep in. You, Martin . . . Yes, I had not fully realized how near you were and now you are here. I had not fully noticed what powerful friends you have, and I cannot say honestly that I understood completely how formidable your power was until recently, until today. Yes, you are the man of the future in this organization. I don't know whether I am happy about it or sad. I really know you very little. But I carry out orders—even orders that are mere suggestions. I do not stand in the way of the future. I bow to it. You are—as you must now be aware—

310

the new manager of Randall's department. Mr. Harwood has asked for a transfer and will receive it. You will be free to recommend another supervisor to report to you and I shall ask you to help recommend someone to take your place under Fellowes. . . ."

Mansard leaned back suddenly, as if tired.

Martin had sat there numb, completely surprised and shocked. It did not seem possible that it was he Mansard had been talking about.

Then Mansard's hard, yet muted voice again.

"Yes, Martin, I knew you had done brilliantly in the field and were considered a tough and experienced organizer and administrator, but I did not realize your influence had reached into such high places . . . Kilgore . . . even Mr. Wygand . . . Mr. Holman . . . where would you ever have met Mr. Holman?—he is the Old Man's favorite. Well . . . as you know, I shall be retiring in a couple of years, and then, I suppose, it will be your turn. . . . You will have the chance to see what you can do in my place. But I guess you were always one of the elect. I've seen them before—once in a rare while. I was never one myself though I served their purposes. You will go up there . . . you will be one of them someday. The mark is on you. Of them all here now, you will perhaps . . . well . . . you are the new power. . . . And now, enough of this. Let's go to Mr. Wygand's office and get it over with. There's a lot of work to be done. . . ."

That had been the morning cataclysm. When he came down, he was still numb, but there had been the other. It was the other that had really mattered.

The office manager, Pritchett, had met him as he was returning. Pritchett was a pompous ass. It all must have been prepared long before.

"Your new office is ready for you, Mr. Brill, if you'd like to move in now."

It was no longer "Martin." It was "Mr. Brill."

311

Martin stopped.

"There's one more thing, Mr. Brill," Pritchett murmured confidentially. "Mr. Randall stopped in to pick up a few papers he'd left and he's in the office and wonders whether he might be able to see you for a minute. Shall I just say you haven't returned and let you know when he leaves?"

Martin's voice was level. "Mr. Randall does not have to ask whether he may see me, Mr. Pritchett. Mr. Randall is my superior. He sees me whenever he wants. I'll go over right now."

As he walked down the corridor toward the big new office, his heart was in his shoes. It felt like rock. He had a premonition, a nameless dread of what would come, but he knew he had to see Randall if Randall wanted to see him.

He stood in the doorway a moment.

An old man was fumbling with some papers near the bookcase in the dim light.

It was Randall.

"Why, Dave," Martin greeted him softly, "it was kind of you to let me see you before you left. I didn't have the chance to say goodbye before."

The old man walked toward him brokenly to take the chair in front of the desk.

"No, no," Martin said, "I'll sit there. You sit in your own chair. This is still your office, you know. I wouldn't feel right without your being in that big chair."

He was aware that this rule-book approach would appeal to the old man. He could not bear to look at that ravaged face. It seemed incredible that this could have happened to Randall within the last few months since he had seen him.

Martin sat down and the old man let himself gingerly into the big chair he had once occupied by right.

"You remember when I first came, Dave," Martin said, "and I was sitting in your office while you gave me my assignment . . . I feel almost like that now."

The old man raised his head slowly.

312

"Yes, I always said you would make a good Empire man, Martin," he began quietly. "You were always a bright boy, a very bright boy . . ." The voice trailed off. Then abruptly the voice began again. "What happened to me, Martin? What did I do wrong?" The voice was low, but there was that puzzled anguish in it. "Where did I go wrong, Martin? Tell me—you are a man who knows these things. I tried. I believe I was conscientious. I played the game. I went by the book. What happened to me? Why do I have to leave? Where did everything turn sour? Why did they all turn against me?"

He sat there as if he had been stoned. He did not know what to say.

"Maybe you can tell me, Martin, why I failed. What is it that you, for instance, have, that I don't have? I've seen it once before. Jeff Carlyle had it, and now you have it. What is it that you need, that they want of a man? I always did my best. I always tried. I was as honest as I knew how. I worked hard. I had the right attitude. Martin, what is it? I cared for them. I do care for them. I played the game the best I could for them. They . . . well, the whole thing was my life. . . ."

The voice trailed off again. Martin could not bear it. The little muscle was twitching in the old man's ravaged face. His hands were clutching and unclutching. He looked down.

"You did nothing wrong, Dave," he answered softly. "Nothing. There were a lot of wrong ones, but you weren't one of them. You should not feel that way. Perhaps it was that you cared too much. One must remember not to care . . . not to give one's heart to something unworthy of it. Perhaps, it is like the . . . the love of idols. . . . We all do it, but it is not that important. It is only a job. And now Dave," he ended, "and now you are free. You have the pension and the security and you owe the Empire nothing. You squandered on them your best. You gave them far more than they will ever be able to repay. Now you are free."

The old man raised his head slowly. His lips, wrinkled and ashen, were trembling.

313

"I'm not free, Martin," he said in a strained voice. "I'm not free. You don't understand. This was my life. There's nothing without it. There's nothing for me except this. I didn't want to leave. I don't know what happened. Maybe if Phil Harwood had stuck with me, it would have turned out all right. I don't know. He shouldn't have abandoned me. He tried to protect me. He was the best man I had. Now I have nothing . . . nothing. . . ."

The voice ended in a whisper. Martin sat there, feeling shaken and sick. What could he say? A man's life. To have sold one's whole existence—for this . . . to have bestowed one's whole self, one's heart and soul on a bunch of buildings and machines, on a bunch of people who didn't care . . . to have ended like this. It was only a job . . .

He sat there, sick and numb. What could he say? What could he tell this man who had thrown away a life? For a moment, he sat silent, unable to move. Then he rose slowly.

"Dave," he said, and his voice was almost a whisper, "Dave, if . . . if there's anything I can do, if there's anything . . ." He could not articulate the rest. He stood a moment in the doorway. "If there's anything I can ever do for you," he repeated softly, "please let me know. I'm sorry, Dave . . . I'm truly sorry. It . . . it wasn't worth it."

He was about to turn when it happened. The old man uttered a groan and appeared to slump forward over the large desk. He had swung around and was at his side in an instant.

"Dave," he said, "Dave, are you all right?"

The lips were blue and the breath was coming in gasps from the sagging body. "Dave . . ." he said.

The blue lips moved faintly. "Pain . . ." they whispered. "Pain . . ." Then:

"Miss Kelly," he had called, his voice imperative. "Miss Kelly, dial medical! Get a doctor! Mr. Randall . . ."

The rest blurred about him. Two of the men had rushed in to help and then others. He supported the straining figure. Again

314

the blue lips moved slowly forming the words: ". . . whole life . . ." they whispered. ". . . whole life . . . here . . ."

The old man's bulk slumped against him as Miss Kelly and the doctor entered.

It had all been over before they could roll up his sleeve.

"Coronary thrombosis," the doctor had said quietly. "A businessman's death. It gets them all. . . ."

That had been the moment. . . .

Now he was sitting here, after hours, in the big, freshly decorated office, the debris of his own life about him, and around him the trappings of his new power, and it was with him again: that moment during the morning and all the years and what he had become. This was what the Empire had done to Randall. This was his reward for the years of devotion. And now *he* was to be the wave of the future. Had they not used that phrase for another, even more sordid crowd? It had an ugly sound. But he was one of the new ones who would not fall for it. There was more to life than that. He would not be deluded by the blandishments of the Empire. He'd seen the way they went—many a good man who had sold his soul to the corporation. Randall . . . Somers . . . they had not been able to take it. But he would. He had learned not to care. That was what he had become—tough, smooth, knowledgeable—the new man, the new corporation executive, the new power of the modern world.

And what had he lost? What had he surrendered for it all? Everything he had fought against and hated he had now become—the lackey, the agent, the rising ruler of a modern power. No heart but brains and guts. He had started to be something else, something entirely different: the whole man. And he had ended in the old formula. He had fulfilled the pattern.

They say new needs require new men. Well, if the world required that kind of tough and heartless instrument, why had

315

it selected him? He had meant to be different. What had happened to the dream? And then he thought once more of Randall. The good men would fall by the wayside. How many of them had the Empire taken? But they would not take him. He was too tough and the drive was in him. No, they would not take him. He would push on, and—the thought brushed over him with a sigh—no, he would not be the whole man he had dreamed of being, but he would in the end, as they had said, reach the top.

He swung back slowly. It was time to leave. April would wonder. She had turned out to be an exacting wife. Yet the marriage had been good, essential. Yes, he would admit it: it had somehow saved him. And there were the children, the flowerlike faces he had dreamed of.

Now he would be watching younger men making these gay journeys he had once made. He would be watching their lives forming the same patterns under the strange swirl of lights and hotel rooms and restaurants and towns, amid the thousand nebulous and forgotten places of his old pleasures and lonelinesses. All I want, he had once told himself, is to get my money and get home to dinner. Now it was too late. The Empire had bought and paid for him, and he would have to keep going up. . . .

He remained a moment longer, a handsome man in his forties, the hair gray at the temples, wearing the dark, expensive suit. There is the gray Homburg; there the brief case. The question had been answered. He turned and walked out.

Outside, the evening was cool and fresh, and the faint glow of a departed sunset still hung in the misty air. He walked across the street and down toward the bay. Two blocks from the ferry, he turned and stood looking back for a moment.

There in the misty afterglow of the fading light, it towered like a huge and shadowy fortress, heavy and sinister, rising out of the sea. It was the Building—the great, shadowy Building. It seemed to him, as he stood there gazing at it from the distance,

316

as if it were a symbol of the whole vast Empire—the granite stronghold of the mysterious powers of the age—fabulous, immense and strange.

He stood a moment gazing at its heavy, shadowy bulk looming there in the confusing evening glow. Then slowly he turned and walked, head lowered, into the gathering dusk.